About the Author

S. E. Ney was a teacher for c
writing for a lot longer (since ....
became fascinated with the concept of time travel after
watching the 1960 film of The Time Machine when she
was somewhere between knee high to a grasshopper and
shin high to a small rodent. As a result, after completing
her BA in Philosophy at the University of Durham, she
stayed on and did her PhD on *The Logical Possibility of Time
Travel.* Her conclusion (that time travel within one possible
world was logically impossible) put her off time travel in
film and television for ten years.

She has since recovered.

In her spare time, she has been a hospital radio show
host, ghost writer, barmaid, magazine editor, secretary and
trainer.

Read more at https://oslacs-odyssey.co.uk/

To Blair,

Eternity Beckons

Book VIII of Oslac's Odyssey

S. E. Ney

Please stay in touch!

∞0-0 Publishing∞

S. E. Ney

This is a work of fiction. Names, characters, places, and incidents either are the product of the author's imagination or are used fictitiously, and any resemblance to any persons, living or dead, business establishments, events, or locales is entirely coincidental.

First published in Great Britain by
0-0 Publishing

This paperback edition 2023
1

ISBN: 9798391369479

Cover design by T-Jay.

When Fortan trapped Alex within the program at the end of Powershift, I had no idea what was going to happen next. I knew Almega was angry, Alex was in trouble, and Daniel was frightened, but beyond that? Not a clue! As usual, my characters took me on a roller-coaster from which I'm still recovering! This one is a lot darker in places than my usual fare. Reader discretion is advised. While I don't go into undue detail, there's quite enough for the imagination to run riot and I don't want to be the cause of nightmares!

If anyone reads a couple of the chapters and thinks I've suddenly forgotten some rather large books, please remember that this is the original Oestragar, which we haven't visited since Ystrian Dreams. For all the other adventures, we've been taking trainings elsewhere. Also, a reminder that everything was reset at the end of Ystrian Dreams, which is why they don't remember their experiences in The Anquerian Alternative.

As usual, my thanks to my army of editors: Diana, Elise, Louise, Lis, Adam, and Shaun. I'd be lost without you! Sorry, Dellas didn't make it into this one, but I'm sure I'll manage to salt it in to one in the future!

Introductory Note

This is the eighth book in the Oslac's Odyssey series. It returns you to Oestragar where these books started, and there are subtle references to events in the first three books, but you can read it independently. All you need to know is that there are a hundred Eternals in Oestragar, but only ten in Anqueria. If you want to find out what's going on with levels upon levels, *now* you'll have to read those first three!

Chapter 1

Alex and Daniel made their way with Almega to the couches they'd use for their next trip.

"We'll be together for most of it?" Alex confirmed as she lay down.

Almega checked his readouts. "Daniel will come back first, but you won't have to wait too long. Even so, it's probably better to keep in separate rooms for this one. That way, he won't disturb you when he wakes up."

Daniel was standing in the doorway, watching as Alex prepared.

"You'd better have tea ready for me when I come out," she warned.

"Of course!" he smiled. "When do I not?"

Alex closed her eyes and Almega placed his fingers on her forehead to initiate the training. Suddenly, he jerked backwards.

"What the...? What in blazes is that lunatic doing?!" Almega cried.

"What? What is it?" Daniel asked, rushing forward. Alex was already calm and composed, her mind elsewhere, while Almega was furious.

"Fortan! That idiot is trying to re-write Omskep to do a training I told him couldn't be done!"

"While Alex is in the program?!" Daniel cried. "Can you bring her out?"

Almega tried, but it was fruitless.

"I've got to get to Omskep. Daniel, I might need your help!"

"To get him out of Omskep?" Daniel asked, preparing to jump.

"No! To stop me from trying to destroy that blasted troublemaker once and for all!"

***

Almega and Daniel appeared within the Omskep building to see Fortan sitting at the main console, feverishly inputting instructions. In a show of power that left Daniel stunned, Almega surrounded the errant Eternal in a shimmering ball of energy, effectively blocking his access to Omskep's controls. Fortan spun on his stool, staring in horror at his captor. He surged to his feet, flung the stool aside (which dropped harmlessly outside the barrier), and transformed into his energy state, trying to escape Almega's trap.

It didn't work.

While the ball of coruscating, fizzing energy around him warped and stretched to accommodate its prisoner's efforts to escape, it held firm. Furiously, Almega flung the Eternal against the wall. Pinned in place like a bug in a display case, he was left to morph from form to form, desperately trying to free himself, while Almega stormed over to the console and began working.

Daniel went to examine Fortan's prison and, tentatively, reached out to touch it.

"Don't!" Almega said, not even bothering to turn around.

Daniel snatched his hand back. "What did you... *How* did you do that?!" he gasped, his gaze shifting between Almega and the struggling Fortan.

"I'm the Guardian of Omskep. I have a few extra powers. Never, in all the millennia we've been here, did I think I would be forced to use them!" Almega snarled, still working at the console.

Fortan morphed back into the usual form he expressed when walking around Oestragar, his face contorted in agony.

"What are you doing to him?" Daniel demanded.

"Nothing he doesn't deserve!" Almega returned, merging with the massive, blue, flashing mass that was the Omskep computer to get at the programming more efficiently. The ball of power around Fortan remained in place. Just as Daniel again reached out to see if he could somehow free the fellow Eternal from his captivity, there was a power drain in Omskep that caused the glow that filled the area to dim. Again, Daniel snatched his hand back, looking around in confusion until the power returned and Almega reappeared. His face incandescent with rage, he bore down on Fortan.

"You have trapped an Eternal within the system!" he roared.

"No!" Fortan cried, his voice attenuated, as though being shouted over a chasm. "They were all out!"

"I'd just put Alex *in*!" Almega returned. The energy around Fortan tightened and the Eternal's eyes widened in horror.

"Almega!" Daniel cried. "Don't do this! Fortan's an idiot, and he's done something terrible, I'm sure, but we can fix it!"

Almega's eyes snapped to Daniel and the Guardian seemed to grow, as though filling the building while not changing dimension. Daniel felt as insignificant as a speck of dust. He cowered, fear he never thought possible as an Eternal washing over him.

"Almega, please! We'll find a way!" He pointed to Fortan who was writhing and screaming within his cocoon. "I don't know what you're doing to him, but if you destroy him, it'll screw up the system even more!" Summoning every ounce of courage he'd ever needed on the battlefield, he held his ground and tried reason. "We're outside time. His experiences in the program are *in*side time. If you destroy him, he'll be erased and the program will end up with a logical impossibility. He'll have been a part of it and not ever have existed at the same time!"

Almega seemed to shrink slightly, then the oppressive atmosphere in Omskep dissipated. With a contemptuous glance at the trapped Eternal, Almega flicked a hand and Fortan disappeared.

"Almega!"

"He's all right," Almega assured him, returning to the console. "I sent him back to his home. He'll be trapped there until I decide to release him."

"He was in pain!"

"Only so long as he tries to escape. If he stops trying, he'll be fine and he'll survive."

"And if he doesn't?"

"Then it'll hurt and maybe he'll learn his lesson."

Looking over his shoulder at where Fortan had been trapped, Daniel edged towards the other Eternal. "How did you –?"

"Daniel, the Guardian of Omskep has a duty to protect the Eternals who use it. Given our power, that would be impossible if I didn't have the ability to control those who would cause harm."

"But we're all the same!"

"Evidently not," Almega returned. He went back to the console and beckoned Daniel to join him. Daniel held his position, looking at the Guardian nervously.

"And this is why I don't let anyone know," Almega sighed. "It's all right, Daniel. *You* are not the focus of my ire, and I will release Fortan when he's learned his lesson."

"It's Fortan," Daniel returned, the tension leaving his form at Almega's calm voice. "In an eternity he will never learn."

"Then at least until he's prepared to admit that he was in the wrong. His access to Omskep will be blocked either way. Now, come and look."

The relaxed tone in Almega's voice reassured Daniel and, while still uncomfortable, he stepped forward to see the problem. He stared at the readout.

"What did he *do*?!"

"He learned that there were other possible universes in addition to the one we run for training purposes," Almega explained.

"Anything's possible," Daniel admitted.

"Yes, but he discovered that an infinite range of alternatives are within Omskep, they're simply not running."

"So?"

"He wanted to visit one of them. I told him that the option wasn't within our program, so he couldn't. What he's done is opened several of the other programs, and now he's running them concurrently."

"What?!"

Almega nodded and waved at the console. "We have a large number of universes open simultaneously, and I'm afraid the programs will start interfering with each other."

"I'm amazed Omskep permitted that," Daniel admitted.

"Omskep is... not like any other computer," Almega sighed. "It's capable of doing things that would blow the most potent mortal-made machine. Even so, that leaves us with a huge problem. First, characters from universes that don't belong together due to different physical laws or chemical combinations are now metaphorically knocking on each other's door..." He paused.

"And?" Daniel pushed.

"And I've absolutely no idea where Alex is, which means I can't pull her out." He turned in his seat. "Until we find her and get her out, we can't shut it down and reset it because we could shut down the universe that she's presently in. On the other hand, if I don't shut it down soon, the barriers will start to break down and, as the humans would say, 'all hell will be let loose'."

Daniel paled. "What would happen to her if you shut it down without finding her?"

"Her external form – her shell, if you like – would remain here," Almega replied carefully, "but her mind and

5

the energy that drives it would be trapped or lost forever. In time, even her shell may simply fade away."

***

The thought of losing Alex had Daniel eager to finish what Almega had started with Fortan but, knowing the errant Eternal was stuck in the energy vortex that Almega had conjured and getting hurt every time he tried to escape, helped to cool his anger. He now appreciated why Almega had exploded and was impressed that he'd managed to restrain himself. Daniel wasn't certain he could have been so forgiving.

"We have to get her out of there!" he cried.

"I know that," Almega assured him. "However, first I have to find her, amongst trillions upon trillions of possible subjects. Even if she went into the life she was supposed to be in – and there's no guarantee of that – I'm no longer certain she went in at birth."

"She has to be!"

"No, she doesn't." Almega took a deep breath and turned to look fully at Daniel. "Fortan switched on the other universes at the same instant I was inserting Alex into the training. That's what alerted me that there was a problem. One moment I had her, the next she'd been whisked away."

"So, she's in a baby something, somewhere," Daniel said, grasping at straws.

"She could be in anything," Almega replied, searching for a way to explain the problem in terms Daniel would understand. "There are lots of... oh, what's the term the humans used for gaming? Oh yes! Non-player characters. There are millions, billions of NPCs in the worlds you visit. Trillions if you include all the animals you could also occupy. Until an Eternal inhabits them, they fill out those worlds, else there wouldn't be anyone for you to interact with. Such characters are empty vessels. One of my jobs is to make certain that you are inserted into the right character at the very start of their existence but, theoretically, you could be inserted into anyone at any time in their existence, provided they're not already occupied."

"This is impossible!" Daniel cried. "How are we going to track her down in all that!?" and he waved at the glowing form of Omskep.

"Well, that's going to be the trick, isn't it?" Almega agreed, turning back to his console. "On the upside, because there was a foul up at insertion, she's still Alex, which means that, whatever age she is or species, she still thinks like the Alex we know. That means she'll realise something has gone wrong and try to alert us to her location."

"How? It's not like she can pick up a telephone."

"Telephone?"

"Comm, net connection, whatever!"

"Actually, if they have computers, a private record might be the best way," Almega muttered to himself. "If she can leave a written report that tells us where she is, we can find her." He bent over his console and started typing. "I'm running a search for references to Oslac, Eridar, Omskep, Almega, Oestragar, and the other Eternals."

"What if she's turned up before writing was invented, or she's a species that doesn't have a written language?"

"She'll leave marks that correspond to ours. No one on any of the planets would recognise them for what they are, but Omskep will. I'm searching for those, too." He turned. "This may take a while. I can contact you when I find her."

"And if you don't?" It was the nightmare scenario, but it had to be addressed.

"Sooner or later, she'll make herself known. The problem will be that every life or part of a life she lives before that will have already been filled, so I need to trace them all. Can't have an Eternal popping into an NPC that gets temporarily occupied in the future, unless that NPC is her in a future training."

"Wait. She can't move around."

"She's a free-floating Eternal. She's not constrained because she wasn't properly inserted to begin with. That means she can move between NPCs – once she realises how."

"And if she doesn't figure it out?"

"She'll be stuck in life after life, randomly being inserted into any NPC that happens to be nearby at the moment of her character's death until we find her. Could be a human, alien, insect, bird, mammal, or anything. I suppose," he added, gazing thoughtfully at Omskep, "she could even be a free-floating energy form. But, in that case, she won't be able to do anything at all. She won't have power if she's not inside something with a brain to control."

"Almega, you're describing hell! For one of us, that's hell. No planning, no choice, just random insertions without the possibility of prep, or floating around without the ability to affect her surroundings? Absolutely torture!"

"Then given Alex doesn't care for prep, it's as well she was the one who got caught and not you, wasn't it?" Almega replied, turning back to the console.

Daniel paced for a bit, then shot over to Almega's chair.

"Is there any way I can get in there and help her? Any way..." He paused, his eyes darting around the cavernous room, looking for answers. "If she doesn't realise that she can move of her own volition, is there any way I can get down there and act as a guide?"

"You want me to insert you into wherever I find her, and somehow make it so that she can see you and no one else can? And this when I don't know where she is or even what she is?"

"Can you do it?" Daniel pressed.

Almega stared at his console, then released a heavy sigh.

"Let me find her first, then we'll see if she's figured it out on her own. If not, I'll see if there's any way to make your idea possible, but I wouldn't bet your next training on it."

***

While there was no entropy in Oestragar, there was something akin to the passage of time. In terms of someone on Earth, it took Almega three days to track Alex. Rather than tell Daniel immediately, Almega then put a tracker on her energy signature in case she figured out how to move on her own and he lost her again, then tried to figure out a way to bring her back and then, when that proved a sticking point, how to put Daniel in. He was still mired in this investigation when Daniel reappeared in the Omskep building. He'd taken a break from pacing the room (much to Almega's relief), but he couldn't stay away for long.

"Have you found her?"

"Yes," Almega admitted warily.

"So? Get her out!" Daniel cried.

"I'm trying, Daniel," the Guardian replied in a long-suffering tone. "Unfortunately, she doesn't appear willing or able to be retrieved." When Daniel looked at him, confused, he continued, "She's trying to make a positive difference and isn't paying attention to my calls. I'm not even sure she can hear them. Even if she can and was willing to leave, I don't think what I'm attempting will work, but until I can figure out the interactions with her help, I can't find a solution."

"Have you found a way to put me in there? I'll talk her around."

"That's what I'm working on now," Almega replied. "To be honest, it would have been easier if Alex was here and you'd been trapped. She always has a more intuitive connection with Omskep." A light flashed and Almega scrambled to capture the moment, then fumed. "Missed her!"

"What happened?"

"She's figured out how to relocate, but she's relocated to another NPC and it's not in the original universe. That's odd," he mused. "How did she manage to…?" He paused, checking his readouts. Wait!" he added when Daniel opened his mouth to ask the inevitable question. "I put a tracker on her energy signature so I could find her if something like this happened. Wasn't expecting another universe, I admit, but the principle works the same regardless." A few more super-speed scans and then, "Got her!"

Daniel was pacing the room again.

"If…" he began, an idea forming.

"What?" Almega snapped when the pause went on too long.

"If you can track her, her energy is obviously different to those of the NPCs and even the other Eternals around her."

"Yes?"

"How different is it to my energy signature?"

"Every signature is different," he replied.

"Yes, I know that, but Alex and I… we seem to be different to the other Eternals. We never take erasure, we always find each other even if we're on opposite sides of the planet. Might there be something we share that we could use?"

"Hmm." Almega bent over his console and started interacting with it in his unique way. The console in Omskep was unlike anything normally associated with a computer. There was a series of floating projections into which Almega inserted his energy to push, twist, swipe and manipulate. It was tapping in the crudest sense, but it was much more than that. "Put your energy here," he instructed. Daniel did as requested, and an energy signature appeared in the display. Almega pulled up what Daniel assumed to be Alex's signature to correlate the two. "Yes," Almega muttered, performing more of his wizardry. "YES!" he crowed. "I can do it. If I put communications on that wavelength..." He did some checking. "You're right. There's a unique signature that only you and Alex share. I can send you to her."

"Excellent! Do it!"

"Woah! What are you going to say to her?"

"That she needs to return to Oestragar so that we can fix this mess and get everything back the way it was," Daniel replied, as though it were blindingly obvious.

"And if she says no?"

"For the sake of all the Eternals, we have to get the training back on track," Daniel replied. "If they have nothing to do, there'll be chaos!"

"Not initially, and there are no other Eternals trapped in there, so you can't argue that point either. Fortan was waiting for the moment when everyone was out before he started his stupid reprogramming."

"Where is he?" It occurred to Daniel that he hadn't seen Fortan since Almega had so precipitously removed him from Omskep.

"Still trapped in his house."

"He's still in your energy field?" Daniel said, horrified. Over the intervening days, Daniel's temper had cooled. He was still furious with Fortan, but the power had dwindled to the simmering frustration that usually marked his interactions with that particular Eternal.

"And he'll stay there until this is resolved." Almega confirmed. "I will not have that lout putting any other Eternals in danger."

"Almega, it's been quite a while. I imagine he's learned his lesson by now."

"You have more faith in him than I," he replied, his tone depressed.

"No. No, I agree with you but, once he's out, barred from entering Omskep, and everyone knows why they can't do trainings, he'll be so ashamed that he won't dare show his face. And," he continued, warming to the task, "when he does, you can put him in the worst trainings imaginable for a while. A thousand or so Earth years of not being anything but the poorest and least cared-for as penance?"

"Oh, I intend to do that anyway. In the meantime, he's staying where he is. He will not come to any harm. He doesn't need food or water and, provided he doesn't try to escape, he will find his cocoon quite accommodating. He can walk around inside his house, he merely cannot leave – the cocoon or the house." He turned and levelled Daniel with a look. "He has been a thorn in all our sides for millennia. Why are you defending him?"

"Because if you can do that to him, I'm afraid of what you might do to the rest of us," Daniel admitted.

Almega blinked. "You honestly think I did this in a fit of pique? Fortan has been driving everyone crazy for longer than I can remember. This time he's put an Eternal at risk. That is unforgivable. It's time he learned his lesson. I am tired of dealing with what amounts to a petulant child. He has informed all of us that we are inferior to him, and I have swallowed it. He has boasted about how wonderful he is in his trainings when he only ever chooses trainings where he has the power and influence to do things, and I have smiled and walked away. Not this time. Now, if you don't mind, I have work to do." He turned back to the console, effectively ending the conversation.

"Will you let me know...?"

"I promise, Daniel, the instant I have worked out the mechanics, I will call you back, but this is delicate work, and it will go a great deal faster without you watching over my shoulder!"

"Understood."

Daniel headed outside to the perfect gardens that surrounded Omskep – the building and its resident computer having the same name since, if you were in the building, you were in the presence of the massive computer and there was no separating the two. Alex had created a lot of the landscaping and Almega had added his

12

unique touch in various places. When it came to the landscape, Almega and Alex played off each other so well that Daniel sometimes felt jealous. Alex had suggested he join in, but he was loath to interfere. Yes, he could do it. He knew, privately, that he was exceptionally good at it, but if he did his thing, he'd leave Alex and Almega in the dust, and that wasn't fair. They derived so much pleasure from their creations, and they were appreciated by all the Eternals – with the exception of Fortan, of course, but even he grudgingly admitted that they were pleasant to walk in. Daniel was happy to sit back and enjoy their designs, rather than impose his own.

He wandered through the gardens, delighting in the scents and colours but constantly looking back at the imposing Omskep building, waiting for that mental nudge which was Almega telling him to come back. Since he could relocate in an instant, he roamed through increasingly diverse landscapes, finally reaching the lake and mountains Alex loved. There, he sat down and stared at the view.

They'd get Alex out. Of course they would! Anything else was unthinkable. Staring at her prone body these last few days had upset Daniel more than he cared to admit. The thought that she could remain there like that for the rest of eternity was abhorrent. If Almega didn't find a way to get her out, Daniel determined two things would happen: firstly, he'd find a way to finish what Almega had started with Fortan because no Eternal should be allowed to continue after so heinous a crime; secondly, he'd find a way to get into the program himself. If Almega could get Alex out, that was the ideal but, if he couldn't, Daniel would rather be in the system supporting her than waiting beside her empty shell for the rest of time. If he was in the program with her and Almega eventually gave up and switched it off, they'd be none the wiser. One moment they'd exist, the next they wouldn't.

He fell to wondering what would happen to their shells here in Oestragar. Would they remain, side by side (he wasn't going to leave her alone) forever, or would the patterns dissipate?

Would Almega give up? He couldn't imagine that Eternal ever giving up, even if it meant every other Eternal was trapped. He chuckled somewhat darkly. At least they'd know who to blame, and it wasn't Almega or Alex. Fortan's existence would become untenable. He'd be a nothing, never going into any training, shunned by everyone, ignored and forever vilified for his stupidity. The Eternal who was constantly proclaiming his superiority finally revealed as having more air in his head than Gracti – an Eternal who was famous for consistently picking the easiest training sessions with all the narrative depth of a car park puddle. Daniel's mood lightened as he thought of the misery that was in store for Fortan. That Eternal had been the bane of his existence for as long as he could remember. Then he thought of Alex alone, caught in a universe she might not even recognise with none of the usual opportunities to master the basics, such as learning the language, and his smile fell.

He picked up a stone and tossed it in the water, watching the ripples spread out. Would Alex's involvement destroy the program? Whatever she was, once she'd figured out what was going on he had no doubt that she'd want to change some things, using her Eternal perspective to look for better options. As an NPC, would she be in a position to make changes that might affect the future of the program? If she did, what did that mean for their memories of events after her insertion? Would they alter in line with what their later selves experienced? Would some of those trainings suddenly no longer have happened?

Daniel's mounting concerns were interrupted by a call from Almega, and he promptly relocated to Omskep.

"Well?" he asked, worriedly.

"Good news and bad news," Almega replied. "The good news is, she's fine, back in our universe, and I think I've figured out a way to send you to her within the program."

Daniel nodded but, until he heard the bad news, he didn't know whether he should be celebrating or not.

"And?"

"Even once you're with her, removing her isn't going to be straightforward."

"You can't just yank her out of there?"

"I don't yank anyone out, ever!" Almega informed him. "When you go into a training, you are connected directly to your character and can only leave when the character dies. At that point, your energy has nowhere to go but back here. Alex's situation is rather different. The insertion was botched – thanks to Fortan's interference – and she was never attached to a specific character. That means there's no triggering mechanism to bring her here."

"Can't we just send the message telling her to come back?"

"It's not that simple. *She* can't. Omskep does the reintegration at the end of the training, but it needs the character you're playing to die to activate that process. Alex isn't *in* any specific character. She's free floating, which shouldn't be possible, and Omskep has no protocol to reintegrate for something that shouldn't happen in the first place. You might as well ask a horse to stop being a horse. There's no means to do that because it's not supposed to be possible."

"Then she just needs to find an elderly character, get inside and wait!"

"She'd be a squatter, not an occupier. The character would die, and she'd be free-floating again. I'm still trying to work out how to trigger the reintegration and, without her help, it's proving rather difficult. Even *with* her help it wouldn't be easy."

"And if you turned off the program?" Daniel asked warily.

"In the end, we may have no choice, but there's no guarantee she'll reintegrate into her Eternal form even then. She may be put on hold, as it were. Stuck in limbo until the program is reactivated. Aware, perhaps, of herself and the world around her, but unable to do anything."

"And I thought your description before was hell," Daniel glumly declared.

"Exactly. So... First things first. I've set it up so that she can see and hear you but no one else can. You won't be able to interact with your surroundings in there because, strictly speaking, you won't be real. More..." He paused, looking for an appropriate metaphor.

"A ghost in the machine?" Daniel offered.

"More or less. You'll be able to talk mind to mind the way we can in Oestragar so that, if she's in an NPC amongst others, there won't be any embarrassing conversations with thin air, and when she's not in an NPC, you'll be able to interact almost the same as you do here. However," and he raised a hand, "you will not be the same as her. I want to keep you rooted here. I've no intention of losing both of you, and," he continued, overriding Daniel who'd opened his mouth to speak, "I need you to be able to relay information from here to her and back again so that we can fix the system and get her out in one piece. If you go in the way she is, both of you will be stuck and I won't be able to fix it, so you need to stay rooted here," and he jabbed a finger at the floor to reinforce the necessity.

"All right, I get it!" Daniel assured him, raising placating hands. "How do we do this?"

Almega pointed to a spot in the room. "Stand there. I can then scan you and direct the image of you into the programme. Once you're in there, I can project what's happening around you in the program so that you can see it here."

Daniel went and stood in the spot. "How do I walk around?"

"Same as you always do."

"Yes, but if Alex is walking along a road or something, sooner or later I'll either walk into a wall or leave Omskep."

"Oh! No, the floor will adapt. You'll stay in the same place but the images around you will change to reflect what you would see if you'd moved position within the program." Daniel walked a few steps and left the circle. "It only activates once I've synched it all up and turned it on," Almega informed him.

"Ah!" He returned to the circle.

"Are you ready?"

"Very!"

Almega activated the controls and, within the circle, Daniel saw the view of the Omskep building fade.

Chapter 2

Daniel found himself on a street in (judging by the clothing) early 19th century London. Looking around, he spotted the wraith-like form of Alex, who was shadowing a rather well-dressed gentleman wrapped in a heavy coat and scarf against the bitterly cold weather. The man was walking with purpose, head down, utterly unaware of what was going on around him. Suddenly, Alex shifted inside him, and he changed direction, taking a side road that brought him to a mother, huddled in rags, rocking a baby. The gentleman reached into his coat, pulled out his wallet and offered a white five-pound note.

"Here, madam," he said. "Find somewhere warm tonight for you and your child. It's too cold to be on the streets."

The young mother, barely more than a teenager, stared at the note. "Sir! A shilling would buy me lodging for several nights!"

"Yes, but not for the rest of the month, and I would not have you freeze to death. This should provide you with food and lodging until the cold snap ends. Perhaps a chance for you to find work so that you can get back on your feet?"

"Sir, if I walk in with that, they'll assume I stole it, take it, and throw me back out onto the street! Where would a girl like me get money like that?"

"Oh, for..." The gentleman inhabited by Alex fumed and then seemed to come to a decision. "If you could afford it, where would you stay for the week?"

"There's a hostel with proper rooms instead of ropes, but it's four pence ha'penny a night."

"Right! Take me there!"

Daniel followed quietly, out of sight of the 'gentleman' in case Alex saw him, and watched as the girl led the way to a marginally more up-market area. They went inside and the gentleman explained he was going to pay for the girl to stay there. He got some rather unpleasant looks from the person in charge, which he pushed aside.

"I came across her huddled in a doorway without means to stay warm in these freezing temperatures. I do not know how she got into this state of destitution, and I do not wish to know, but as a Christian soul I believe it my duty to do what I can to help. To that end, I want both her and her child looked after. I don't want to see her out on the street for the next few weeks. Do you understand me?"

Daniel raised an eyebrow. Alex no more believed in a deity than he did but, given the time period and the fact that, until that moment, it was clear the owner suspected the gentleman she was inhabiting was the baby's father, it was probably the safest explanation.

"Yes, sir," the owner said, looking at the woman and child in a more benign manner.

"I may look in to check on you. I will pay to keep her warm and to support the child while she looks for work. Once she has a job – a decent, proper one, befitting a young mother – she is to stay here, warm and fed until the money runs out. Is that clear?"

"Crystal clear, sir!"

"I warn you now that if I discover you have overcharged or taken monies illegitimately, I will take you to court." The gentleman lowered his formidable eyebrows at the owner who nodded his understanding.

"Of course, sir."

"Very well. I am told that you charge four pence ha'penny a night." The owner nodded. The gentleman reached into his wallet and pulled out money. "This will last at least two months. If I see her back on the street before then, there will be trouble."

"Understood, sir."

The woman stared at the gentleman and then nervously looked to the owner who now smiled at her.

"Come on. Let's find you somewhere warm to bed down. I think a bath might be in order as well."

The young woman looked scared, but the old gentleman reassured her.

"It's only *hot* water," and he gave the owner a glance which was answered with a nod, "and soap. You'll stay healthier and be better able to look after your child if you're clean." He turned to the owner. "I don't suppose you have some clean clothes so that she may present herself rather better to potential employers?"

"We do, sir."

"Excellent. How much?"

The monies were exchanged, and an agreement struck as to the nature of the clothing, which was to include a cardigan and a coat to keep her warm. The old gentleman turned to go, then paused.

"Remember what I said. If I see her back on the street in those clothes within two months, I will shut you down so fast that you'll think you're on a racehorse!"

"Understood, sir. Come along, child. Let's get you cleaned up."

The young woman wrestled herself out of the hands of the owner and hurried back to the old gentleman. "Thank you, sir! Thank you so much!" she said. "I will find something. Perhaps then I could pay you back?"

The old gentleman shook his head. "If you end up with enough money to do that, find someone else on the street and do for them what I did for you. That will be payment enough."

"I will, sir! Oh, I will!" and she allowed herself to be led away.

Alex guided her unwitting helper back to where she'd found him and then stepped out, Daniel following a good distance behind. Absent of Alex, the gentleman paused, frowning, and looking around him. He pulled out his pocket watch and noticed that some time had passed. He also noticed his pocket was lighter but, since there was no one around him, there was no explanation he could offer as to how he had been robbed without his knowledge. Angry but with no recourse, he stormed off, leaving Alex smiling.

"What was that all about?" Daniel asked, stepping up beside her.

"Daniel! Oh, it's good to see you!" she cried. She went to hug him but found she passed through him. "What's going on?"

"My question first," he insisted.

"I got confused. I was here, then I was somewhere else briefly, then back in this universe in this time – which I knew wasn't where I was supposed to be – and, at first, it was weird and a little scary. I couldn't figure out how I'd ended up here as a free-floating agent, or why I could remember who I was." They headed out of the area towards the more affluent part of town. "Then I started thinking." When she paused too long, Daniel urged her to continue. "If there'd been a mistake – which there obviously had been – whatever I did here would have to be erased and Almega would have to install the backup from the system. That meant I could have some fun until someone came and fetched me out. So..." and she waved vaguely in the direction of the unintentionally philanthropic gentleman.

"He's going to call the police when he realises that he's been mugged."

"It's 1828, there *is* no police force. That starts in March next year," she replied smugly.

"Probably, in part, because of things like this!" Daniel pointed out. "And how do you know he could afford to give the girl that much money? Maybe that was his rent."

"I've been following him for two days. He's loaded, mean and tighter than a nun's –"

"OK, let's accept this man could afford it. What difference have you actually made?" Daniel asked, his practical side coming to the fore.

"I made a difference to her," Alex insisted stubbornly.

"Did you? Or did you just put off the inevitable for a couple of months?"

"A couple of months may be all she needs. At least it'll be a bit warmer by then."

"Alex, you're wasting your time! You can't make the differences you want to and, even if you do, as you just pointed out there's every chance that this program will be shut down, deleted and the original reinstalled from the backup. What's the point?"

"The point," she replied archly, rounding on him, "was that I was stuck in here with no way out and nothing to do!" She stepped toe to toe with him. "But now you're here, I take it I can leave?"

"Ah. Not quite," he replied, taking a step back. Daniel towered over Alex, but when she was in this mood, he felt the size of a mouse.

"What does **that** mean?"

"It means that we're still trying to work out a way to get you out. From what Almega tells me, the death of the host is usually the switch that activates your reintegration into Oestragar. The problem is that you don't have a host, which means that, as far as Omskep is concerned, you're not here."

"How did this happen?" she asked. Daniel explained and then raised his hands to ward off Alex's ire. "Where is Fortan now?" she demanded.

"Trapped in an energy bubble in his house. He can't leave the bubble or the house, and if he fights it, it hurts him."

She stared at Daniel. "Nothing can hurt us," she said flatly.

"Turns out Almega can if he's ticked enough."

"Really?"

"Really," he nodded. "It's actually quite terrifying."

"Sorry I missed it," she commented thoughtfully. "So, how are we going to get me out of here?"

"Almega is working on it, but he's open to suggestions," Daniel informed her.

Alex paced, her brain running through options. Finally, she paused and turned to Daniel.

"You say that the system only activates when the avatar dies, correct?"

"Yes."

"But we've been to the end of the universe when everything dies. Once everything is dead, any of us still in here should be automatically drawn back, shouldn't we?"

Daniel turned away and started talking. Alex assumed he was talking to Almega since she couldn't hear the other side of the conversation.

"Almega thinks it might be worth a shot, but it means we'll have to find a way to time jump, otherwise you'll have to live here as a disembodied spirit for trillions of years."

"That's going to get very boring very fast," she groaned.

"We can't fast forward this universe with you in it, but if we step you out of it and then back in, he thinks we might be able to leapfrog you, so to speak. Plus, you seem to have already managed it."

"I don't know what I did! One minute I was walking along a road, minding my own business and trying to figure out what had happened, the next I was lying flat on my back, my head spinning, staring at a green sky. I was just getting up to explore when the world shifted sideways, and I was in Victorian London. Quite a shock to the system!"

"Trust me, you jumped universes. Almega picked it up on his readouts," Daniel assured her.

"So, there's a way to step across to other universes that I don't understand but somehow used?" she clarified. Daniel nodded. "But not a way to get back to Oestragar?"

"When Fortan pulled his stunt, he was running multiple universes in parallel so that he could become other characters that this universe doesn't have."

"Riiiight."

"Now, those other universes are running alongside, but they're in a mess and every now and then they cross the primary universe. That's this one," he added for clarification, and Alex gave him a look which said, 'Yes, I know!'. "Anyway, he thinks he might be able to take advantage of one of those crossings, speed up time in this universe while you're out of it, then jump you back at the next crossing and so on."

"I'm going universe hopping?"

"Uh huh."

"To universes we've never visited to meet aliens we've never before encountered?"

"Yep."

"Great! Let's get started!"

"Woah! Almega has to calculate when the next crossing is, where it is, and then you have to be there at the right moment. That could be a week, a month, even a year from now."

"No, no, no, no," Alex replied, shaking her head. "These are programs. They answer to us, not the other way around."

"I think Omskep might disagree," Daniel began.

"Normally, yes, but this situation isn't normal. Everything's in flux, which means we can manipulate it."

Daniel looked over to the side, listening to something Almega was saying. "Almega says that unless you can teach him how to do it, he hasn't a clue."

"Come on," she replied, levitating and then shooting off. Daniel was temporarily at a loss but, knowing the circle could keep up no matter what he did, he joined her.

"Where are we going?" he asked.

"Almega can't hear me, right?"

"No."

"But he can see where I am and what I'm doing?"

"I guess. He can see the portal I'm using to interact with you."

"Ask him if he can see what's projected on the portal."

Daniel did so. "Yes," he replied. "That's available to him."

"Then we're going where there'll be someone with paper, working alone, who can be hijacked."

"And where is that?" He looked around. They seemed to be heading for the docks.

"Shipbuilders' drafting offices. Lots of large sheets of paper and, at this time of night, not too many workers, but there might be someone or, failing that, a security guard I can usurp."

In her energy state, Alex could easily pass through the walls of the large building, and then move further in until she found where the draftsmen worked. It was dark, freezing cold and only illuminated by the moonlight that occasionally broke through the clouds and shone through the huge, panelled windows high up in the walls. Lines of silent, tall, clerk's stools and angled drafting tables stood in mute testimony to the industry that filled the room during daylight hours.

"OK, we've got paper and pens, now I need a worker. Any worker!"

The moon broke through the clouds and drew Daniel's attention. "Alex," he called. When she spun around, he pointed. "What about sleepy head over there?"

Alex followed his pointing finger and found a young man snoring against his drafting board. The stub of a candle he'd been working by had long since extinguished itself in a pool of wax, leaving him in darkness until the moonlight picked him out. She slipped inside, woke him up, fetched a new candle, and looked at the plans he'd been poring over until this late hour.

"Is it me, or is this ship going to sink?" Alex said, pointing at the flaws in the draft.

"First big wave, I'd say," Daniel agreed. "He was probably trying to get it done on a schedule and was too tired to see what he was doing wrong." He pointed at some other papers on the desk, and Alex pulled them out and flipped through them. "See? All the others are fine."

"What say we fix his mistakes by way of a thank you, then use him?"

Between them, they identified the small but potentially fatal errors in the young man's design and set about putting them straight. With that task done, Alex pulled up a fresh sheet of paper and, within an hour, had written down, in the text of the Eternals, the programming Almega would need to employ.

Programming for a computer as powerful as Omskep wasn't anything like the tedium of human programming, and Alex's approach was slightly different to that of Almega. While Almega would go inside and nudge, persuade or, occasionally, try to bully the computer to comply, for Alex it was more akin to storytelling. Alex was explaining to Almega how to interact with Omskep in such a way that the computer would happily carry out the corrections itself, rather than stubbornly resist all efforts. Hers was a more persuasive approach, applying psychology and reason rather than brute force, and thus was less likely to bring out Omskep's stubborn side, which was presently blocking all Almega's efforts. Most of the time, Omskep was happy to do as its Guardian requested, but once it was in this mood, only Alex seemed to have the right touch.

Once she was done and had checked her work, she stepped aside so that Daniel could focus on it and make it fill the area in which he was standing. Occasionally, at some instruction from Almega, he would lean closer to some section or ask for clarification. Finally, he reported that Almega understood, thought it would work and would implement it immediately.

Alex promptly shredded the sheet of paper covered in her handwriting. Not that anyone in this time could read it, but if it got into the wrong hands, someone might try. She put the tiny pieces in a bin filled with other torn papers, walked back to the desk, lay the young man down over his completed work, and stepped out of him.

The young man groggily lifted his head and blinked several times, then sighed, picked up his pencil and turned to his work. He stared at it for a moment, double checking. Yes, it was all complete. Yes, it would work. Yes! He could go home and get a few hours in his bed, which would be considerably warmer and more comfortable than his desk. Eagerly, he got off his stool, grabbed his meagre coat from the hook and headed out, the Eternals watching his departure.

"If he'd stayed, I could probably have improved on his design," Alex said thoughtfully.

"Not in 1828."

She shrugged. "Like I said, the system will have to be reset. Imagine the changes if I introduced some new concepts now that won't be introduced for a hundred years or more." She gazed at the designs and Daniel could see that she was trying to work out how she could use the pencils without a body.

"Think of the effect on our memories," he retorted. "Muck around in the other universes we haven't activated as much as you like, but let's keep it to a minimum in here. While it's still running, who knows what trouble you could cause for things we do in the future?"

"I've already done things here while I was waiting for you guys to get me out. Noticed any changes?" she asked.

"No," he admitted, "but you're doing small things that might not have any significant long-term effects. That girl might have found shelter somewhere else, or somehow survived. This boy may have woken up, seen his mistakes and corrected them. Please, just in case you touch on something that makes irrevocable changes, hands off!"

"Spoilsport!" She looked around. "Let's at least go somewhere interesting while we're waiting for Almega to figure it out."

They left the building, emerging high above the city. It was Christmas Eve and people were out and about, grabbing the last things they needed before settling in for the celebrations. Many places were still open, catching whatever last-minute business they could and, the Eternals knew, some would be open again on Christmas Day, including places with ovens where the poor would cook their food and then carry it as fast as they could through the streets to their homes.

"It's a scene straight out of Charles Dickens, isn't it?" Alex observed.

"Well, he was born in 1812 and he was in London by 1824. Scenes like this would have been familiar to him."

"As was the workhouse," she agreed, pointing to an example of same as they passed overhead.

"His father tended to live beyond his means and that was the penalty in those days. Not sure if that's better or worse than prison, to be honest. At least it didn't leave you with a permanent mark on your record; it was just embarrassing."

"And cold, and dehumanising, and potentially lethal if you were ill."

"Then be grateful you won't have to deal with it... in this training session, at least."

"I wonder what it would be like to be a member of royalty?" she mused as Daniel turned away to talk to

Almega. "Oh, wait, Victoria doesn't take over for another nine years. Right now, it's William IV." She shuddered. "No thanks. Don't want to be inside him! He's already in his sixties."

"Nothing wrong with older men," Daniel replied, returning to the conversation. "And William wasn't the worst King that England's ever had. He built up relations with Egypt for the Suez Canal, encouraged the independence of Belgium, and rebuilt relations with America after the Revolutionary War. OK, he hated Russell and other left-of-centre politicians, whom he deemed dangerous radicals, and he was sometimes called tactless and a buffoon, but he could turn on the charm when he had to. Given we want to avoid changing things too much, however, it's probably best to stay out of him."

"You know, if you'd stayed away for another few weeks, I could have done so much," she moaned. "Why'd you have to spoil everything?"

"For the sake of our memories and those of the other Eternals, I'll pretend I didn't hear that!"

"Can we at least take a look inside the palace and see what they're up to?" she whined.

"The kitchen will be preparing a ton of food for tomorrow, the royals will be reading or playing music or listening to someone else reading or playing music, and the scullery maids will be finishing up their duties so they can get to bed in cold rooms to be ready for the morning. What's to know?"

She turned on him. "Your capacity to take the fun out of things is quite extraordinary!"

"I'm being practical! We *must* take it easy here. I promise you, once you've jumped to another universe, I will be delighted to join you in rewriting it."

She settled on the top of St Paul's – by now a long-established feature of the London skyline, having had its final roof statues added in the 1720s – looking around her. The Cathedral dwarfed everything around it, in stark contrast to later years, and the view of smoking chimneys in the sharp winter air and ant-like people scurrying through the streets looked like something out of a Punch cartoon. "So, until then, I'm kicking my heels."

"Could take in a show?" he suggested.

"Nothing running in this time that would be worth sitting through," she replied, her tone morose.

"Hey! Just because it's different —"

"It's not different, it's simply a lot less sophisticated than the stuff that will come out later. When people like Gilbert and Sullivan appear for their equivalent of a musical, it'd be worth a visit, but the acting is still massively overdone and it's not like in Ancient Greece where that was the whole idea. And before you say it, the quality of orchestra players has to go up too. No one outside a school play would tolerate the standards accepted in this era. The bar kept being raised."

"The actors around now are supposed to be excellent. Garrick, for example."

"He's already dead, and no, thanks. Good by the standards of the time versus good by the standards of the future are two very different things. I looked before you arrived. Sorry, not my thing." She turned to him. "How's Almega doing?"

He glanced over his shoulder. "Still working on it. He's got a lot to input!"

"Is Omskep still being stubborn?"

"More... amused, I think. Almega's having to keep his cool and use your persuasive approach when his instinct is to go in there with a hammer. Omskep, on the other hand, seems to be sensing the dichotomy and is enjoying making Almega's life difficult just for the fun of it."

"I don't suppose he could apply my approach to persuade Omskep to get me out here?"

Another pause and a discussion she could not hear with the invisible Almega. "Apparently not. Sorry. Omskep's still insisting it can't find you in here, so there's nothing to take out."

"Oh, it knows I'm in here," she assured Daniel. "It's perfectly aware that I just delivered the methodology to Almega. For reasons of its own, it's refusing to play ball."

Daniel cocked his head at her. "Why would it do that?"

"You know Omskep. Sometimes, I think, it just likes to make our lives difficult. Perhaps for its own entertainment, perhaps just because it can."

"It's a computer," he replied, his tone derogatory. "What you're talking about requires emotions."

"You and I both know that Omskep's far more than a mere computer. It has its moods, the same as the rest of us. The only difference is that, ultimately, we have the final say, whether it likes it or not. Of course, *when* it succumbs is another matter. That it will is inevitable, but it could keep me in here for centuries before then, and I'm not prepared to put up with that."

"Neither am I!" he assured her. "I've no intention of sitting in Oestragar waiting on the whims of that machine and, while you're in here like this, no one else can use it either, so all the Eternals will get annoyed!"

"That's sweet of you," she smiled, then continued before he could reject the epithet. "In the meantime, I'm back to kicking my heels." She sighed slightly theatrically and tried to do just that. Unfortunately, the effect was marred by her heels passing through the roof. In truth, the fact that she was able to sit there at all was because she'd convinced herself that she could, but her feet dangling below her couldn't detect where the edge was, and so they failed to connect. "Can't even do that right!" she chuckled. Daniel's charming fury at her virtual incarceration had lifted her spirits.

Daniel jerked up, listened to an instruction from Almega and turned urgently to Alex.

"How fast can you move?"

"Where to?" she asked, floating upwards.

"Cumbria."

"Cumbria? Why there?"

"The crossover will happen in twenty minutes near a place called Little Salkeld. I gather there's a stone circle there –"

"Yes. Long Meg and her Daughters. It's opening in a stone circle?" She took off like a supersonic jet, Daniel having to focus hard to keep up with her. "Is it a weak spot in the ley lines or something?" she asked.

"No. Just where the paths between the worlds cross on this occasion. Could have been in the middle of the Atlantic, or Soho, or anywhere else."

"Bet this will cause a stir!" she said, adding even more speed.

"With any luck, the neighbours won't be around and, if they are, they'll see very little."

"You really are a downer, aren't you?"

"As little interference as possible, remember? If there's some spectacular show it'll cause no end of stories and that *will* change something."

"I doubt it," Alex replied. "It may be written up by someone – assuming there's anyone local who *can* write – but more likely it would be retold through the generations and put down to local superstition and ignored, like tales of dragons."

"But they *are* fantasy."

"In this universe," she corrected. "How do we know what the others are like? There could be anything. Do we know what Fortan was trying for?"

"He installed everything. Who knows? Perhaps when Almega lets him out of his cage, we'll be able to ask him."

"Over there!" Alex cried and headed downwards towards a circle of stones, presently being intermittently illuminated by the moon as it glinted through the scudding clouds.

"You've a good sense of direction," Daniel said, admiringly.

"I've been here before. A long time ago, but it did impress me. Plus, it's easier to find your way when you're above it." She landed and made her way to the south-west edge where the twelve-foot-high monolith known as Long Meg towered over the rest of the three-hundred-and-forty-foot-wide ring. Alex pointed to the cup and ring carvings in the monolith's sides. "One day we'll have to do someone in the megalithic or neolithic age and find out what those mean."

"Or just ask Omskep when it's in a better mood. Not a very interesting time, either" he said, settling down beside her. "Freeze or starve to death in winter, risk death while hunting for food the rest of the time, and always scrabbling to survive. I prefer later eras when we have some of the basics sorted out. There are more interesting things to investigate than the rudiments of mere survival."

She shrugged. "But less to worry about than later years. No middle-management to make your life a misery with paperwork for a start."

"Not with paperwork, no, but I'm sure the Chief's seconds could make life difficult anyway. Nothing really changes."

She leaned against the monolith... and promptly fell through it. "Well, that was embarrassing!" she said, picking herself up. "How is it that I don't fall through the planet?"

"I suspect it's because, in your mind, you can't and you never could, but now you've walked through enough walls and solid stone to know that that isn't a barrier. You *could* fall through the planet if you put your mind to it."

She focused and, briefly, began to sink, then she pulled herself up again.

"OK. That's enough. I've no desire to find out what it's like in molten lava!" She looked around. "What am I looking for? A door? A tunnel? What?"

"I have no idea and neither does Almega. We've never done anything like this before. What was it like when you moved before?

"Disorientating. I was so confused I don't know what happened."

"In that case, this time you'll learn something new!" Off her sour look he added, "Got to look for the positive, right?"

"Oh yeah," she drawled. "Right."

***

It turned out that what they were looking for was the feeling of being extremely drunk at the loudest party in the universe. For a moment, everything shifted and then, as the two universes fought with each other over whose patch it was, the dimensions spun, warped and twisted until Alex was starting to feel quite ill.

"Close your eyes and follow my voice," Daniel called. He was unaffected by the dimensional distortions since he wasn't actually there, which allowed him to see the crossover point.

"How will closing my eyes help?" Alex cried. "Everything's twisting, not just what I see!"

"Then just stagger over here as fast as you can!"

Squinting and blinking repeatedly through the twisting, morphing world she presently inhabited, she managed to half stagger, half crawl to Daniel who pointed to a tiny hole that expanded, warped, and contracted in front of her.

"Quickly! It won't last long!"

"It's too small!"

"You're energy. You can be as small as you want to be. Now jump!"

She knew she could not be hurt and, indeed, if she was somehow killed by this vomit-inducing distortion, she'd end up back in Oestragar. That being her ultimate aim anyway, she pulled herself together and jumped through the hole.

***

She lay on the ground of wherever she'd landed, surrounded by blessed silence while gently patting the ground to make certain it held still.

"How are you feeling?" Daniel asked solicitously.

"Like I've just been to the worst social event ever!" she replied, holding her place with her eyes closed. "Is it over?"

"Yep. You're in the new universe."

Very carefully, she sat up and looked around. "Is this prehistoric Earth?"

He pointed behind her. "Not unless the biology here is very different to that on Earth. Plus, the gravity is different."

She turned to see some very odd-shaped plants – bulbous, with blue leaves and little pods that opened to welcome insects that tapped on the petals. The insects, in turn, were also odd and more like helicopters than the bees she was used to. She moved forward to examine them in more detail. As she did so, one of the insects flicked its legs, catching the edge of its domed, helicopter wings. They spun and the insect leapt from the plant to another one, its flight gentle as a result of this bizarre addition.

"That answers my immediate question."

"Looks like that's a baby. The older ones don't need to kickstart it," Daniel observed, pointing to a much larger version. It was slowly spinning up the rotary extension and then, suddenly, it shot upwards. "Must have muscles or something in there that can turn the screw, as it were."

Alex shook her head. "I'd say strange world, but I'm sure if they saw bees, they'd wonder how they do it. What else is different around here?"

"Apart from the purple-tinted sky?" Daniel grinned.

"Yeah. Apart from that!"

"Well, you've an alien city over there," he said gesturing through the foliage.

Alex made her way through the heavy greenery to see a series of huge, glass domes that glinted with the reflected light of the star the planet was orbiting. "Looks like something out of a sci-fi novel," she commented.

"I wonder, sometimes, if the ideas our novelists get are some kind of bleed through from other universes. Maybe the fact Omskep has them in its memory, even if they're not active, allows some crossover?"

"In that case, there's going to be some spectacular novels in the Prime Universe once this adventure is over!" Alex chuckled.

"Ahh, but once it's over, all this will be deleted and the Prime Universe reset," Daniel replied.

"Yes, but with Omskep, the fact it was played out at all won't be forgotten. Looks like I'll have to do some more reading when I get back!" She advanced through the thick foliage to get a closer look at the city. "Why are they under cover? It's lovely out here!"

"High CO_2. Good for the plants," and here he gestured to the abundant evidence of same, "but the indigenous higher life form struggles with the heat and humidity. Inside those domes, it's all climate controlled and absolutely secure. No insects, no dangerous animals, no worries."

"That won't last!" she snorted. "Any higher being, once it gets too comfortable, finds reasons to wreck everything. It's almost as if they can't bear to have an easy life!"

"Keeps them constantly striving to get something better, I suppose," Daniel mused. "Still, it would be nice if they could go a few centuries before they start kicking off."

"As opposed to twenty-four hours? Yeah."

She'd picked up speed and now positioned herself outside the large dome that stood hard against the edge of the jungle. She peered through the glass at the creatures within, found an area that wasn't presently occupied, and moved inside.

"So, these are the intelligent species on this planet? A bit... pale and weak looking."

Daniel gazed around him. The creatures were, indeed, very pale – a consequence, he suspected, of not getting access to the star's rays. They seemed a little flabby around the gut and lacking in muscle-mass, with spindly arms and legs, making him wonder how they had survived long enough to evolve to this point. Then again, with everything done for them, having muscles could be a disadvantage. They were about six feet tall, a pale, watery greenish blue, with triangular heads, five limbs with a tripod arrangement for the legs, holes for ears, and large, black eyes. There also weren't that many around. Alex noticed one with a mechanical arm that was seamlessly attached to the body and worked, so far as she could tell, exactly the same as a real arm. She pointed it out to Daniel.

"Biomechanics is at a high level, then," he nodded.

A far greater number of the beings occupying the concourse were robots, scurrying here and there on various errands. Some were working in coffee bars or shops, some delivering goods. A small number appeared to be some kind of security force, but friendly and happy to give directions or advice when asked. Frowning, Daniel asked Alex to move closer to one of them.

"Why? We've never been here, so it's not like we can understand the language."

Daniel turned away for a moment and suddenly Alex became aware of a mental nudge from Omskep. She accepted it (you always accepted such messages. Omskep didn't do them often and, when it did, it was important or something you'd previously asked for) and realised the language files were being given to her. It seemed that, while Omskep claimed it didn't know where she was, it could still find her mind, which was odd but tallied with her opinion that the computer knew exactly what was happening and wanted it to continue for a while. Strangely, that made her feel better. It meant that, once Omskep got what it wanted, she'd be pulled out regardless of what Almega did or did not do to help her.

While she was pondering Omskep's nature, the files were absorbed and applied. Within moments, both she and Daniel could understand the conversation. They listened as the cops chatted to one of the citizens and then moved on to help someone else.

"That AI is remarkably well advanced," Alex commented. "Far more advanced than the rest of the technology here would suggest was possible."

"My thoughts exactly," Daniel nodded. "Not machine-like at all."

"How did they do that?"

As they mulled over the ways technology could advance differently on different planets, a couple of what the Eternals assumed were teenagers – judging by their noise and carelessness – came zooming around a corner on some kind of scooter. One of them crashed into one of the cops and sent it stumbling backwards. It lost its balance and fell, the neck striking the edge of a fountain and snapping rather spectacularly. Sparks shot from the break, the eyes flickered and died, and the cop went silent. Its partner promptly activated an alert which cordoned off the entire area, picked up the troublemaker who'd caused the accident, and cuffed him (or her. It was hard to tell for the newcomers) – the chain from the handcuffs attaching to one of the legs to effectively hobble the criminal who was then led off. A few moments later, two more robots arrived and collected the broken one to carry it away. A third cleaned up the remains and the cordon was lifted.

"I'm following them," Alex declared and put actions to words. As this was going to be Daniel's suggestion, he merely nodded and followed in her wake.

Within minutes of leaving the more public areas, the group came to an elevator. They carried the broken robot inside and headed down into the bowels of the dome. There, the robot was put on a gurney and then pushed along a dull, unpainted corridor with utilitarian lighting, to what appeared to be a repair shop.

Inside they found a number of bits of robots – arms, legs, torsos, but no heads, which Alex found curious. Two of the aliens – called Parchti in their native tongue – looked up from their work, which was presently re-attaching an arm to another robot. The previous one looked like it had encountered a mincer from the state it was in.

"Oh dear," the older one said as it walked over to look at the damaged security guard. "Don't think there's much we can do with this one."

The younger one finished inserting a screw, checked his work and nodded to the robot. "Back you go. You're all fixed."

"Thank you," the robot said. It rose, moved the new arm a few times to make sure it worked properly, nodded its satisfaction, and left, the door sliding shut behind it. The young Parchti strolled over to join the supervisor and winced when it saw the damage.

"Can we put the head on a new body?"

The supervisor shook its head. "No. Look. Servos have been mangled, casing's cracked and leaking." It turned the robot's head to show the damage and Alex inhaled sharply.

"That's blood!" she cried, pointing to the trickle that was now slowly making its way through the cracks.

Daniel leaned down, using his Eternal sight to look at the blood's structure. "Hmm. Mammalian, at a guess."

"They're using a mammal's brain inside a robot? That's... That's horrible!"

"Answers our question, though. How are these so much more real than usual robots? Because they *are* real. Animal brains running a mechanical body. Still very high tech but fits better with what we've seen of the technological level of this species. Making a mechanical brain think and act realistically under all circumstances is an almost impossible task. Using a mammalian one short-circuits those issues provided you can link it up, and they've clearly mastered that."

"Is it one of them?" Alex wondered.

Daniel shook his head. "That blood contains different elements to those common on this planet. I think they've caught them somewhere else."

"And removed their brains to turn them into slaves? What kind of a species is this?!"

"I'm not sure the ordinary Parchti know what's going on inside those robots. They certainly seemed keen to keep the natives away until they'd cleaned up the mess, and that was done very quickly."

Alex leaned in, her energy passing through the supervisor to examine the casing around the head.

"Double lined," she murmured. She pulled back, again passing through the supervisor who was unaware of the incident. "Whoever designed this was trying to make sure there were no leaks."

"And the robots clean up fast so that they can catch any problems before the truth is revealed," Daniel nodded. "Someone's determined to hide the truth."

"Worth investigating, I think," she said, eyeing him. "Don't you?"

"Definitely!"

"It's no use," the supervisor declared, straightening and getting the kinks out of its back. "Detach the legs and arms and throw the rest in the burner. At least we can get the metals back."

"That means we're down a security guard," the younger Parchti said as it collected its tools to do as requested.

"We've a delivery of heads due tomorrow. I think the dome will be fine less one security guard for a few hours. If there is any trouble, they can activate one of the ones in rest mode to pick up the slack."

"I thought they needed the full six hours of rest mode?"

The supervisor shrugged. "They're a little sluggish with the processing, but they can manage, so long as you don't do it too often."

The junior dipped its finger into the blood leaking from the head. "What is this stuff?" it asked.

The supervisor shrugged. "Some kind of chemical wash to keep the parts protected? I don't know. Not my department. I just attach them."

"So, they don't know what's happening either," Daniel surmised.

"Ever looked inside to find out?" the junior asked.

"Nope. Against company policy. Proprietary hardware and software. You open a head casing, and it sets off every alarm in the place. Next thing you know, you're out of a job and out of the dome. The end." He picked up the head which had been separated from the torso and carried it to a conveyor belt. Immediately it detected the weight, the conveyor belt activated and carried the head towards a hatch which opened, briefly, and then closed again. Alex passed through the hatch with Daniel and followed the head. It rumbled along until it reached a second hatch. Alex stuck her head through and instantly pulled back.

"It's a furnace," she explained. "The supervisor was right. They melt the heads down for the metals, such as they are."

They watched as the head passed through the hatch and then, to their horror, heard a scream.

"Was that...?" Alex asked, hardly daring to speak her fear aloud.

Daniel had gone pale. "Yes. It was still alive and knew what was happening to it."

"How? The head functions were inactive."

"Not all of them, it seems. We need to find out where they're getting those brains from."

"The supervisor said they're expecting a delivery tomorrow," she reminded him.

"Which suggests the ship delivering them is either due to land soon or has already landed. Time to find the space port!"

***

The ship's engines were still cooling in the early evening temperatures as large crates were removed and taken into a warehouse. Warily, but knowing only she could do it, Alex put her head into one of the crates, then pulled back with a shudder.

"There are at least twenty heads in there," she told Daniel.

He quickly looked around at the crates filling up the warehouse and those still aboard the ship.

"That means we're looking at around two thousand or more victims. What are they using them for?" he wondered. "There aren't that many jobs left, surely?" He paused, looking between the ship and the rapidly filling warehouse. "Go into the ship. See if you can find out where they came from."

Alex walked inside the ship and went up to the cockpit. There, a pilot was shutting things down in careful sequence. Quickly, she slipped inside the alien and then, with a little help from Daniel, who'd flown spaceships in some of his trainings, managed to bring up the navigation screen.

"Different solar system," he mused. "Takes them most of a year to make the trip there and back."

"You can lose a lot of robots in a year," Alex said.

"Which means they're stocking up. How are they preserving them while they wait for the bodies?"

"Back to the warehouse?" she suggested.

"I think so."

Alex left the pilot, who frowned at the readouts that were lit up.

"What the...? I turned you all off!" With a growl, the pilot went back through the shutdown procedure while Alex and Daniel passed through the cargo bay with its ghastly load and went into the warehouse. There, the boxes were being prised open, revealing a network of tubes attached to the heads – presumably providing the oxygen and nutrients required to keep them healthy. One by one, the heads were disconnected and reconnected to a rack connected to a cylinder, giving the effect of heads on sticks. Once each rack was full, it rotated to expose another. When every rack on a cylinder was full, the mass was wheeled into another building where tubes were connected to the cylinders. Some other Parchti workers were taking note of the numbers on the spikes that supported the heads, and the readings from the machines that were now connected to them.

"Check four eight five," one of them yelled. "I'm not getting any readings."

A worker found the right rack and rotated the heads until they found the one delivering the faulty readings, then checked the connection.

"Try it now!" the worker yelled, having tightened one of the tubes.

The one on the computer refreshed the screen and nodded. "That got it. Six seven six isn't giving me a reading either."

Another walk through the racks, another rotation, another bout of tightening.

"How about now?"

"Nope. Nothing. Looks like it was disconnected for too long. Throw it out."

The head was removed from the rack and tossed from worker to worker until it was put on another conveyor belt. Alex was in tears.

"They don't care!"

"They don't know," Daniel gently pointed out.

"Look at them! Even if they did know, do you think that would make any difference? To them they're just parts!"

"I think we need to go to the planet they're using to source these brains and check out their original owners. They might not care about dumb animals, but the way these are working tells me they're anything *but* dumb. They're holding intelligent conversations. Know a lot of oversized mice that can give you directions, even if they are aided by a specialised computer? It has to understand the question and respond to it appropriately, and they are. Plus, the fact they're not transferring the brains on *this* planet tells me that they don't want the natives to know the process. Perhaps that's the trick to putting a stop to all this?"

He turned to Alex and took a step back. Her face was thunderous.

"Oh, we're putting a stop to this all right!" she declared. "They want servants, they can make their own, entirely automated, or hire their own species as staff and pay them properly. This... This is... vile!"

"No argument from me," he assured her and turned away briefly to talk to Almega. "All right," he continued, turning back, "Almega says the next crossover won't be for a while, but it will be on this planet, so we have to be back here in time. I've asked him for directions. Because Omskep doesn't presently recognise you as existing within this program, you can't simply be relocated unfortunately. You're going to have to fly there."

"Recognised me enough to deliver the language files!" she complained.

"That you exist is not in question." He cast around for a suitable metaphor. "If you were a laptop, I could still send you a file provided your IP remained the same. Where you are on the planet at any given moment is irrelevant. You remain you and so Omskep can send the files; it's that you're here and not in Oestragar that is the issue." He gave her a rueful grin. "And you've still got to make the journey to that planet."

"Under my own steam?"

"Unless there's a spaceship about to head out, but that would take six months. I don't think you want to be hanging around these guys for that long, so..."

She released a long-suffering sigh. "Tell Omskep that, whether it likes it or not, I *am* here and mighty ticked off!"

When Daniel merely raised an eyebrow, she nodded. "I know. Lead on, Macduff!"

***

Even with Alex's ability to go at a velocity that would put the most advanced space-faring races throughout history to shame, it still took over a day and, by the time they arrived, Alex felt the need to pause and catch her breath.

"You're an Eternal," Daniel said, fists on hips as he looked down at her. "A: You don't need breath, and B: You don't need rest."

"Humour me. I feel like I've just expended a lot of energy. Feel free to explore," she said, waving him off.

"I'm tied to you. I can't go anywhere until you do."

"What about when you first came looking for me? You kept your distance then!"

"You noticed me, huh?"

"Of course I noticed you, but I was busy with that tight-fisted old gent and couldn't take time out to say hello."

"I can go a little way, but there's nothing around here except rocks, plants, a few trees and some..." He squinted. "Well, I'm assuming they're birds." Alex looked up and he pointed.

"Definitely birds, if birds include anything that has feathers on any part of them. Not necessarily on the wings, though."

"Looks like its avian ancestors got a little too friendly with a bat. That shouldn't happen. Why use skin when you've got something lighter that works better?" Daniel wondered.

"Annnnd that's enough rest for me!" Alex said, standing up. She knew what Daniel could be like once he'd got an idea in his head. "Let's go and explore."

They started on the ground, but it soon became clear that they'd landed in an area that was largely uninhabited.

"Those bat-birds. They couldn't be the source, could they?" Alex asked.

"No. Appearances to the contrary notwithstanding, those are standard birds – in the brain department, at least. We're looking for something with a community and, based on the level of intelligence those robots evinced, some kind of governance."

"Buildings, then?"

"Not necessarily. They may live underground – I know I would if I had those brain-nabbers after me – but there'll be quite a few in any given location."

Alex paused, gazing around her. "If the Parchti are killing them and putting their brains into electronic heads, that's not something you can do overnight. Not that many, anyway. That means there must be a factory around here somewhere. If we can find that, maybe they'll have maps or, if the natives keep moving to avoid them, we could listen in and see where they think they are?"

"Good idea. Hang on, I'll see if Almega can find it for us." After a brief consultation, Daniel turned back and pointed. "That way, about two hundred miles."

"So why did he give us this point to land in?"

"He gave us the whole planet. You were the one who decided to land here. C'mon."

***

It was horrifyingly easy to find the Parchti base, once they were in the right location.

"I think I'm going to be sick," Alex groaned.

"Way to warn the locals not to come anywhere near!" Daniel agreed, eyeing the row of heads, minus the back, that had been put on sticks, and the pile of decapitated bodies off to the side of the building waiting to be taken to the incinerator, which was belching smoke.

"This is horribly familiar," Alex said, gagging.

"Well, we now know what their victims look like, I suppose," Daniel offered. Alex gave him a sharp look.

"There's nothing we can do for the dead, but now we know who to look for among the living. We need to see the process they're using."

"What's to see? They lop off the back of their skulls, extract the brain and shove it in a metal box!"

"But what else is inside the metal box? How much is them, and how much is the machine? They can't kill them before taking out the brains because brains die very fast, so how are they doing this?"

"If you think I'm going in there to see them surgically remove a brain from a living animal, you're out of your mind!"

"But we need to know how they're stopping them from revolting," he reasoned. "Think about it. If you woke up and realised your body was now mechanical, much larger and stronger than the one you were in, and you're surrounded by the people who put you in there, would you serve them drinks or direct them to the leisure park?"

"Probably put some kind of inhibitor in them," she reasoned, but she sounded unsure.

"That's one effective inhibitor! They're not telling anyone what they really are, they're polite, friendly, and accommodating. Emotional inhibition might explain some of it, but not all of it. Something's been removed."

"Apart from their whole body?!"

"Something in the brain. If we can fix it so that isn't removed..." He left the suggestion hanging.

"How about I stand outside and *you* go look?"

"Won't work. If they're removing something, you're going to have to step inside one of the operators to stop it."

"I can't stop all this!" she argued. "I'd have to stay here for years!"

"This is industrial. They're not doing it one at a time. They must have a machine doing it, but machines with this level of skill have operators and programs. Operators can be inhabited, and programs can be changed." He gave her significant look and she stared at him for a moment, then all the fight went out of her, and she turned to the building and took a deep breath.

"Erasure, after we're done, may be needed," she informed him, and headed into the facility.

"For both of us," he quietly agreed, following her.

***

The inside of the facility was clean and looked more like a hospital than the 'factory of death' Alex had expected based on what was outside. There were also robots in the building, but these were clumsy compared to the ones on the Parchti home world.

"They're making the things. Why don't they use them?" Alex wondered.

Daniel shrugged. "Maybe they're struggling to keep up with the demand at home?"

"How long have they been doing this? If they're shipping two thousand every year, surely they've got to reach saturation point sooner or later?"

"As we saw, some don't make it to the planet, others get damaged there, and we only saw a tiny part of one dome. There were lots more, and plenty going on underneath the ground as well. Plus, for all we know, they've got some in another part of the planet doing mining, farming or other jobs. Humans found uses for millions of slaves for centuries. Didn't matter the colour or language, there was always someone willing to use other people." He looked around. "They're capturing and keeping them somewhere, but where?"

Alex began to explore, Daniel poking his head into some rooms while Alex walked through the walls to check others. One of the rooms Alex unwittingly walked into was the surgical section. She withdrew almost immediately, her colour pale.

"You're right. It's industrial and mechanical," she said, swallowing repeatedly. "They're bringing them in from that direction," and she pointed to their left. They followed one of the Parchti until they reached the holding area.

They found cage after cage in a massive warehouse. The cages were strong, one for each animal captured. Many were presently empty, suggesting the hunters were probably out looking for more, but some were occupied. The mammals huddled in the cages, whimpering and frightened. Some reached through the bars to others to offer comfort, while some lay curled up, shaking and rocking in terror. Alex cocked her head and realised there was a noise that was probably beneath the hearing of the Parchti. The mammals were all talking.

"Can Almega get us the language files for this species?" she asked.

Daniel looked off to the side and soon Alex got the upload from Omskep – a part of her privately wondering if she could change her equivalent IP address once she was back in Oestragar just to mess with the computer. She had to adjust her hearing to listen because most of the speech was in a register outside her normal range, but once she'd done that the wails, cries and repeated pleas for mercy whenever a Parchti walked in were so loud that she soon found herself crying.

"Alex," Daniel said gently, "if we're to help them, you've got to switch off."

"And be like their captors?" she snarled, turning on him.

"No. To be what they need you to be if we're to put an end to this. This isn't our universe, so we have the power."

"Can't Almega re-write it so the Parchti never find this planet in the first place?"

There was a pause and then, "Apparently, they found the method and were looking for brains that would work. They weren't bothered where they got them from so, even if you stopped it here, it would happen somewhere else."

"Then stop them from going into space!"

"They do some good in other places. We don't want to stop that," Daniel replied.

"No amount of good would offset this nightmare!"

"I don't think they can hear them," Daniel mused, watching the way the workers delivered basic food and water to the captives. "They don't realise they're highly intelligent. They know they're smart enough to work in their machines, but the rest is put down to instinct because they're not picking up the language."

"They can operate linguistics from inside the machines. That should tell the scientists that they're dealing with an advanced species," she argued.

"We need to see those helmets!" Daniel declared. "They must be stored somewhere around here."

Alex watched as several of the cages were moved to another section of the room. There, the walls of the cage were contracted until the creatures were squashed between them, and they were injected. Once unconscious, the bodies were put face down onto a conveyor belt, the heads supported in a box-like frame, exposing the back. She closed her eyes and walked away.

By following more Parchti workers, they found where the robot heads were stored. A row of them were being prepared for the animals that were presently having their brains removed. They were in a sterile unit with the front, facial features removed and waiting beside each head. Alex and Daniel investigated them in detail, looking at the connections and the electronics within to see if there were any inhibitors or computer processors that might be taking over tasks and would explain the docility of the captives once they were inside. They found none.

"You realise that can only mean one thing?" Daniel said, once they'd finished their investigation.

"Strictly, two," Alex replied. "Either the mechanics are in the body of the robot, not the head..."

"Except they're happy to recycle those, and something like this is too important to risk having an old version running."

Alex nodded, sadly. "They're removing parts of the brain."

"Sorry, but we're going to have to watch the process."

"From the computers, I hope. Watching lasers cutting into a living brain, I wouldn't know what I was looking at anyway."

They followed the Parchti workers taking the heads to the new victims of cerebrectomy and found a roboticised setup with some Parchti watching computers. As the latest victim – the back of whose head had already been removed to expose the brain – was rolled into position, the computer scanned the brain, identifying various parts. The operator very carefully outlined the areas concerned with long-term memory, double-checking some parts that weren't as obvious that a machine might miss.

"So that's how they're doing it," Daniel grunted. "By removing the long-term memory, the animals don't remember who they are, and they have to rely on the memory stored in the robot."

"But they leave the short-term memory so that they can have a conversation and speed up everyday tasks," Alex agreed. She was examining the computer that was being used, while assiduously avoiding looking at the animal presently having everything that made them them surgically removed. "I think I can reprogram this. The problem is, it knows it must remove something, so I can't simply tell it not to, and anything that's removed will cause a problem if there's not a mechanical alternative."

The machines were fast and soon the present run was complete. The brains had been put into the new heads, the faces reattached, and the lot connected to machines that provided oxygen and blood to the living part of the machine. While this was happening, Alex and Daniel retired to the front entrance where they could talk without seeing the horror.

"We can't remove short-term memory instead. They wouldn't be able to act or think quickly, and these guys are going to have to move fast once they know what they need to do," Alex pointed out.

"Motor control is the same," Daniel agreed. "Plus, they need to be able to see and hear to do their jobs and put this right. We need to find something that isn't vital, but there isn't anything!"

"Except emotion," Alex groaned. "Once they're in there, they're never getting out again, so having a sex drive with no outlet would be frustrating. If we designate that area to be removed –"

"But without the emotions, why would they care to put a stop to this? They need the anger; the sense of wrong done to them."

"But if they're really angry, they'll trash this place before they can get to the Parchti planet and let the natives know what they've been supporting. I think, once the Parchti back there realise what they're doing, they'll demand it be stopped."

"Don't be so sure," Daniel replied. "Since when did morals get in the way of convenience for most advanced species?"

"This isn't like arguing vegetarianism," Alex countered. "These are clever animals with language, a social structure and emotions."

"Most animals feel some kind of emotion," Daniel said. "Fear is needed to make them get out of the way of predators; a sense of familiarity and concern to protect offspring and sexual partners; something like happiness to keep them going; pleasure associated with sex to make breeding worth doing..."

"But there are levels. A plant can be wired up to a machine and we can hear it scream when it's cut, but that's not enough to put anyone off eating it. Most draw the line at hurting things that can talk back to us. That's what the Parchti need to learn – that they're killing something that can reason, discuss and interact in a civilised manner."

"We're assuming that based on what we heard from them in the cages," Daniel cautioned. "We've not seen what they're like when they're free."

"They're not going to be that different!" Alex replied. "They'll still talk to each other, care about each other... All the things we saw evidence of in the cages will exist outside. The level of it may be different, but the fact they were doing it at all tells us that these animals... Oh, what are they called?"

"Djaroubi."

"Right. The Djaroubi are advanced. Too advanced for any civilised animal to consider what's being done to them as acceptable. If I walked into a field and suddenly found I was having a detailed discussion with the cows, sheep, pigs and chickens about the state of the world or the moral consequences of eating them, I'd turn vegetarian. The fact that we can't understand them, and they show no evidence of higher intelligence, makes it easier to see them as food."

"Also, the fact that other creatures see them that way," Daniel pointed out. "Foxes, wolves, and the like."

"Wolves see humans as food. Not really an argument!" Alex pointed out, then fell back to her musings. "A higher-order species finding out that they're mutilating another higher-order species should stop them. Question is, how to do this?" She paced. "If we remove fear, the drive to procreate and some but not all of the emotions, put together those might be enough to replace the mass identified as long-term memory, and none of them are any use to them once they're inside those robots."

"Fear of being decommissioned if they misbehave will keep them alive long enough to do what has to be done," Daniel argued. "If they don't care, they'll go rogue immediately."

"All right, "Alex said, frowning as she went through their options. "All the sex drive, because that's useless and it's cruel to let them feel the drive without the equipment to satisfy it. Some of the other emotions but not all of them and, dammit, *some* of the long-term memory, but not most of it. We have to make the Parchti think they're still removing the same thing and, if the amount removed is too small, they're going to realise something is up."

"Can you distinguish early memories from later ones?" Daniel asked. "If you can remove those laid down most recently, that's a lot of trauma they can live without."

"The Parchti scans are good. Not sure they're *that* good," Alex sighed. "It's going to be a little hit and miss on that front. Still, the most recent memories will give a slightly different signature. I might be able to do it. Which means," she continued, turning to stare at the wall that led to the operations section, "I'm going to have to get inside one of the operators."

"Better to do it sooner rather than later," Daniel said. "You never know when you'll have to get back to the Parchti home world." He paused, summoning the name. "Narzhin," he finished.

Alex went to walk through the wall, then paused. "This is a side universe," she said, looking at Daniel. "We need never visit or have anything to do with it."

Daniel raised an eyebrow. "You and I both know that now we're aware that these other universes exist, we'll all want to play in them. If we're to play in this one, we can't leave it like this. Neither of us could be Parchti, knowing what they're doing, and I certainly don't care to be a Djaroubi when you end up a slave. We have to fix it, and we can't do that once it's running as a primary. We're only getting this pass because of the unusual circumstances. I'd say that means we need to make the most of them, no matter how bad it is."

"Yeah, but I'm getting all the bad!" she grumbled, then pulled herself together and headed towards the operations centre.

With the hunters out capturing their next group, the operators were taking a break. Alex identified one that seemed suitable and, when he paid a visit to the toilet facilities, watched until he came out and then slipped inside him, redirecting him to the computers. There she used her skills in programming to examine what was happening and the source of any updates to the system.

"All right," she said to Daniel, once she was certain they were alone. "The updates are beamed from Narzhin via some kind of subspace connection, but they seem to be happy with what they've got and haven't updated for months. That gives me two choices. I can try and program it here, but we don't know when they're going back to work, and I can't be caught doing it. Alternatively, we go back to Narzhin, we find where they write the originals, rewrite it there overnight, then beam it out."

"But if we do that, we'll have to come back out here to check it's worked," Daniel warned. "We may not have time before the next crossover."

She sat at the programming desk, drumming her host's fingers on the table. "OK. I could block updates from Narzhin. If I don't do that, the instant they realise there's a problem they'll send out a fix and we'll be back to square one."

"But they'll see they've not received the update and look to find out why not," Daniel said.

"Give me some credit. I can write a program that can analyse the update and install everything that doesn't override my changes, including the update number." She paused, "Or *only* the update number if that's all that's left." She leaned back in the chair. "But this is not going to be easy and will take me several hours to program, and that's if I pull out all the stops and work the avatar at Eternal speeds, which will leave it exhausted when I leave. Plus, while I'm doing it, no operations could be carried out, and they're going to wonder what's going on."

"How about putting your avatar to bed now, while it's quiet, and waking it up after everyone else has gone to bed? That way you can work through the night when no one else is around." Daniel suggested.

"Assuming they don't work shifts, that might be our best option," she agreed.

She leaned forward and spent a little time scanning through the programming to make sure she understood how it highlighted the areas the operators had to mark. By the time she was done, she already had the beginnings of a code building in her mind and, while her avatar excused itself and headed for bed, she continued working on it. Daniel, wisely, left her to it, withdrawing to Omskep to see if Almega could help speed things up. As it turned out, there was another aspect to the conversion process they had not encountered, so Daniel set about preparing for that whilst leaving Alex to mentally structure the new programs they needed.

Once everyone had gone to bed, Alex roused her avatar and took it back to the computer room, closing and locking the door behind it. She then sat down and began by inserting the program that would block updates from the home world. If she didn't have that in place, the rest would be a waste of time. Then she worked on a replacement for the main program that, instead of identifying one spot, would identify others and no more than ten percent of the long-term memory (primarily the most recent additions) to make a total that was the same size as the original. Luckily, the brains were extremely tightly organised, so the resulting coloured pattern, while subtly different to the original, looked the same to a cursory examination and could be excused as their finding a new source of Djaroubi from a different genetic line.

It was nearly dawn when she finished her coding and checking – a feat that would have taken a Parchti or human equivalent months of work – and then she sat back and released a satisfied sigh.

"Done it!" she declared.

"Not quite," Daniel said, reappearing at her side. She reached for the keyboard to check her code again. "No, not that. That's fine, but there's another part of the conversion process you need to address," he explained.

"What? Where?"

"You can't do any more tonight, and your avatar needs some rest after that workout. Get him/her/whatever to bed and I'll show you."

Once her Parchti host was tucked up, Daniel led her to another room where the boxes containing the severed, robotic heads had been positioned. They were in front of a screen which was telling them a story about a massive disaster that had killed most of their species. However, their 'kindly' friends, the Parchti, had seen what had happened and managed to rescue a few of them. Sadly, the video claimed, their mangled bodies were in too bad a state to be preserved but, wanting to save the species, the Parchti had found a way to preserve their brains and give them new bodies. In return, all they asked was that the creatures come to Narzhin and contribute to that society. There, they would have a home, their bodies would be maintained, energy supplied freely (which was a replacement for the food that they no longer required), and they could have their choice of jobs. As their own world was, according to the film, on the brink of extinction, it was a better option than staying here. A number of opportunities were flashed up and film footage of robots working in and amongst Parchti side by side. These were real robots, the viewers were informed, merely doing their jobs but, as the viewers could see for themselves, they were allowed to roam freely alongside the Parchti, and the same would hold for these poor, rescued souls. The film finished by explaining that they now had individual screens they could activate using their thoughts so that they could examine and choose any job, and then would be provided with the information required to do it. If, on the other hand, they would prefer to die, the Parchti would, regretfully, honour their wishes and shut them down as painlessly as possible.

"Some sales pitch," Alex squirmed. "There's a lot of psychological trickery being used there. They've put a great deal of emphasis on how kind and considerate the Parchti have been, putting themselves out to help the beleaguered Djaroubi, the implication being that if their victims don't offer something by way of payback, they're ungrateful wretches."

"I wonder if they do turn off those who beg to die," Daniel mused. "Or do they program them for the worst jobs away from the natives?"

"If they're too mentally distraught, I suspect they simply switch them off," Alex replied. "A mentally unstable being inside a very strong robot would be a dangerous combination. Otherwise, they probably strip their mechanical memory down to the barest of essentials and leave them the most menial tasks." She watched as one of the Djaroubi examined the options on offer. "I can't change the main film, but I think I can add something to these ones. Some subliminal messaging? I've a feeling that, once they've decided on a career, everything but the stuff suggesting they're lucky to be alive and should be grateful, will be stripped from their memories, leaving only the training sessions intact. There's a lot of information being downloaded. It looks like they can literally take their pick and know everything they need to know about any given subject."

"How are they understanding all this?" Daniel asked. "It's not as though it's in their native language and, so far as we know, the Parchti don't speak Djaroubi."

Alex frowned. "Unless they do." She turned on Daniel. "It could be that whoever creates these things knows full well what this species is capable of, has translated the language, and is using that translation as an intermediary between the Djaroubi brain and the Parchti communications package they end up using inside the robot. They'll think they're speaking their native tongue and, miraculously, the Parchti understand them, but it's all translated into Parchti." She thought through what she'd seen of the inside of the helmets. "There's enough electronics inside these things to bridge that gap. They may not even see the Parchti world exactly as it is. After all, a mortal creature's understanding of their world is entirely dependent on what information the brain receives."

"The brain in the vat," Daniel nodded.

"Exactly. The software filters what they mustn't know, adjusting everything to fit the narrative. If they talk to another of their kind, what they hear and what is said may be quite different."

"Right now, when they encounter another of their kind, they probably think they're talking to a mere robot. It would be a sensible security measure as well as enabling the Djaroubi to integrate seamlessly with the natives."

Alex nodded. "Whatever goes in or out is automatically checked by the software to make certain it passes the censors. A Djaroubi could scream their nature and experience at the top of their voices, and what came out would probably be a patriotic Parchti song!"

"Which means that they have no idea how many of their own species are on Narzhin," Daniel agreed. "You're going to have to figure out a way to stop the installed software in the suits from distorting what they see and hear."

"One thing at a time," she replied. "I can't do that here because the helmets have already been completed, and they're not connected to a computer I can program. I think we may have to trust the Djaroubi to figure out how they're being lied to, and how to fix it."

"How? If they do pick up something they shouldn't, it's wiped from their memory before they can act on it," Daniel grunted.

"With the new program, their own memory will be preserved, so the erasure of records on their internal computer memory storage won't be a problem, but I need to use this to let them know what's really going on, warn them to play act until they're on Narzhin, and *then* find a way to tear down the entire system." She let out a whoosh of air. "That's a tall order! If any of them react immediately, the Parchti will destroy the lot and reinstall the software from backups. I can wreck the backups so that they have to wait for hard copy to be delivered from Narzhin, which would slow them down, but once they've wiped and rebooted the computers, the process will start all over again." She stared at the blank screen, searching her mind for a solution. "We can't have anything the Parchti can see or hear, but the Djaroubi hear in a different range. Perhaps I can take advantage of that and combine it with the subliminal programming?"

"Not tonight," Daniel told her. "Your avatar needs to sleep if it's to do work in a few hours."

"I could use a different one," she began.

"And explain its work on the computers how, exactly? No one can be allowed to see your avatars working. That means that even if you use another one tomorrow night – and I suggest that you do, or they'll wonder why the first one keeps getting a very early night – you can't do anything more now. It'll be wake-up time in under two hours and that's simply not long enough for what's needed here."

"But they'll be bringing in more Djaroubi for conversion!" she cried.

"I know, but this has been going on for years and, as much as I feel for them, the needs of the many must outweigh the needs of the few in this instance. We cannot risk your avatars being seen, especially if they're not programmers. If a Parchti spots what your avatars are doing, they may become suspicious, undo all your arduous work, and there may not be time before the next crossover to fix it."

"If I don't do something quick, they'll have time to half-convert the next load. Those Djaroubi will find themselves inside a box without a body, fully aware of who and what they were. It'll drive them insane."

"You kept a backup of the original program, right?" Daniel asked, worriedly.

"Carefully hidden in case something went wrong before we left, yes. I never delete the original until I know the new one works so that I have a point of reference to fix any errors, but I thought we'd have more time!"

"We don't. As soon as the operator walks into the computer room, take him over, restore the old program temporarily, and the next group will simply have to suffer the same fate as their forbears. After tomorrow night when you've fixed the training sessions, reinstall the new program and, with any luck, there'll be time for us to check it's all worked before we have to head back to Narzhin for the next crossover."

"I don't mind missing the crossover if it means I can make sure this works!" she replied, stubbornly.

"The next crossover may not be for centuries. We can hop fairly fast if we follow Almega's plan, but if we miss the window, there's no telling how long you'll have to wait for the next one. He's juggling a lot of universes and getting them to line up within the same galaxy is tough, let alone on the same planet. We have to stick to his plan if we're to get you out of here." He stood, toe to toe with her, taking in her fuming expression. "Alex," he reminded her gently, "they're programs, remember? Unless we live their lives, they'll remain programs. I absolutely agree with you that this is horrible, but you're risking your own existence for something that isn't yet real. *If* you fix it, we may well come here for training and be the first ones who get the upgrade and change everything, but we can't do that if you're still stuck in here."

"But they're —"

"Programs," he insisted, lifting his hands to place them on her shoulders. At the last moment he remembered he couldn't do that and, giving her a rueful shrug, let them drop back to his sides. "Keep reminding yourself of that. If you get emotionally involved at this level then you'll never fix it and I, for one, have no intention of being Parchti or Djaroubi while this..." He turned blazing eyes on the warehouse that held the captive Djaroubi. "...This filth is still going on," he finished.

"Fortan would!" she snorted.

"Only if Almega ever lets him out, which isn't looking too likely in the near future, I assure you."

They went back to the computer room, Alex pacing agitatedly while they waited for the morning shift to come online. Daniel stood by the door, watching for a likely candidate.

"Here comes one. Get ready!" he warned.

"Any others?" she asked.

Daniel looked as far as he could down the corridor. "Not yet!"

"Right!"

The operator scanned their access card, walked in and Alex immediately stepped inside. It was the same operator she'd been running that night, which made it easier.

"Keep watch," she said, sitting the operator down, "and warn me if anyone's coming."

In a matter of moments, she'd swapped the programs, making sure the new one that would give the Djaroubi their chance was as well-hidden as the backup had been. Just in time, she shut down her command level console while the door opened to allow another operator to enter.

"What are you waiting for?" the new Parchti asked. "Get it started. We've a long day ahead of us."

Alex got the operator going, then stepped out, leaving it staring, for a moment, at its hands.

"You feeling all right?" the other Parchti asked.

"I think so. Just had the oddest feeling. Like I just did all this and now I'm doing it again."

"You did. Two days ago. Now get on with it!"

Alex turned to Daniel.

"I do not wish to see that horror played out a second time, and there's nothing more I can do here until this evening. Let's go and find some free Djaroubi and see what they're like when they're not wrapped in metal and circuitry."

"Amen to that!" Daniel fervently agreed. They left the building.

Chapter 3

The Djaroubi had moved repeatedly, in an effort to escape their hunters, so it took some time for Alex and Daniel to track them down. They used the Parchti trackers, initially, listening in on their discussions and identifying the clues that led them to each new Djaroubi territory. Once they knew what they were looking for, it was painfully easy to find their targets, telling them the new group would soon follow their fellows into robotic captivity.

"Can we warn them?" Alex wondered.

"Not easily," Daniel said, looking around at the Djaroubi pups playing a game of hide and seek. The animals were similar to otters but larger and without the webbed feet. They were perfectly capable of swimming and, based on the activities of the pups cavorting in a nearby river, good at it, but it wasn't their preferred home. "You'd have to get inside one of them and then use them to alert the others that the hunters are on their way, but how would they know unless they'd ranged far afield and beyond their usual territorial limits?"

"They must be aware of the Parchti hunts. Surely, they'd have lookouts further afield as a consequence?"

"They probably think they're safe, this far away from the processing centre," he said, his tone glum.

"None of the Djaroubi are safe on this planet. The Parchti will keep capturing and converting them until there are none left!"

"I know that, and you know that, but they don't."

"Could I get inside one of them, send them a bit further afield so that they can see the hunters, come back and warn them?" she suggested.

"Let's listen in, first. Apart from spotting the threat, if they're to beat the Parchti, they'll need to fight, and I don't see any weapons, do you?"

"Looks like they rely on teeth, claws and hiding," she admitted.

They walked into the Djaroubi communal area and then noticed they could hear loud voices coming from underground.

"Sounds like someone's upset," Daniel observed. "I think that's where we need to be."

Alex morphed her size to something more appropriate for the smaller space, then focused and dropped through the ground, emerging in the middle of a debating chamber just as one of the Djaroubi jabbed a finger towards another, passing straight through her. She frowned at her unwitting assailant, stepped aside and listened.

"You think we'll be safe?! They're capturing tribes all over the planet!" the finger jabbing Djaroubi cried.

"Herrass, you need to calm down. The aliens are far from this place," the tribal leader commented calmly.

"Not for long," Alex muttered.

"Then at least allow me and a few others to stand sentry to warn the keroo when the aliens are getting too close so that the females and children can escape! It's all I ask!"

"We cannot allow that," the Chief replied. "It would scare the cubs and females, leaving them thinking we are constantly at risk of attack."

"You are," Alex muttered.

"The thought is far better than the reality of getting caught by the aliens. I have seen the heads on spikes and the bodies. They're killing all they capture and ripping out their souls!"

"Not exactly," Daniel edited, "'though as good as."

"You were told not to go near the alien camp!" one of the other seniors growled.

"Why?" Herrass asked, turning on the speaker. "Too harrowing? Yes! And yet you, all of you," and his paw stretched out to encompass all the members of the hierarchy, "refuse to take proper precautions so that we may avoid the fate of other keroo!"

"If the aliens see you and follow you back, it will be you who endangers the keroo, not us!" the Chief yelled, his temper finally snapping.

Herrass stared at him. "That's what you're worried about? That I or the others who agree with me are too slovenly, too careless to dodge the alien hunters? Do you think I'm a week-old cub?!" Herrass was at his wits end, tears forming as he tried to find a way around his Chief's intransigence. "If you won't let us keep watch, at least let us make weapons so that we can fight and protect the keroo to give it time to escape!"

"We have weapons!" one of the leaders declared, unsheathing his claws and baring his teeth.

"And much use they've done the other keroo," Herrass shot back. "Do you think they didn't fight with everything they had? Do you think they meekly submitted to having their souls removed from their bodies? Oh, you may be certain they fought with tooth and claw to preserve their souls, and yet still they were taken. We need weapons that can be used at a distance. When we get too close to these aliens to use what Geshall gave us, they take us. There are empty keroo all over the place! Good Chiefs, good fighters, and all taken."

"Geshall will protect us!" the Chief cried, "And you forget yourself! Do not question what Geshall has in store for us. He knows what is right for us!"

"Being captured and having your soul removed, this is right for us?" Herrass gave a derisive snort. "Are you certain it is Geshall who is calling the shots here? Perhaps Artak is on the side of the aliens, attacking his brother through us. If that is so, we must fight to protect what Geshall created."

"You are not a sakto leader. You have no right to interpret the will of Geshall!"

Herrass looked at the sakto, the equivalent of a priestly class amongst the Djaroubi. "Do you believe Geshall would allow any keroo to be destroyed completely and their souls stolen like this?"

"If they violated Geshall's commands, then yes, and they would deserve their punishment," one of the sakto replied calmly.

Herrass shook his head. "All of them? You honestly believe that every other keroo deserved their fate and we will be spared? I'm telling you, they violated nothing. They were good, fair, but as blind and ignorant as you of the threat these aliens represent. And, like you, they placed their faith not in early warnings, weapons or even escape. They placed everything in the paws of a God who has deserted us!"

"ENOUGH!" The Chief rose to his feet and bore down on Herrass. "You will be escorted to the boundary of the keroo. You are henceforth banished!"

There was a collective intake of breath. It seemed that this was the ultimate sanction amongst the Djaroubi.

"Good! I welcome it!"

"Your partner will stay with us," the Chief finished on a sneer. "She does not lack your faith. She deserves the protection of the keroo."

With a speed that even the Eternals found shocking, Herrass unsheathed his claws and went to strike the Chief, but the older Djaroubi was quick to see the danger and dodged the slashing paw. Before Herrass could strike again, two beefy Djaroubi had seized him and forced him onto his belly. The Chief looked curiously at Herrass.

"You would strike your Chief?"

"You don't deserve to be Chief if you allow your keroo to be captured by the aliens!" Herrass managed to get out, while his face was pressed into the dirt.

"You should consider yourself lucky that Djaroubi do not kill Djaroubi, or I would order the guards to tear you to pieces." He went back to his seat. "You have shamed the keroo and insulted Geshall. Your crimes have been witnessed. There is no defence." He turned to the guards. "Take him to the border and see that he does not return." He paused and then added, "And make sure he goes alone. I will not have him infecting anyone else with his heresy." Herrass was lifted from the floor and forced from the meeting. Alex and Daniel following on his heels.

"They have a faith, then," Alex commented.

"Much good it does them in these circumstances," Daniel replied. "Putting their faith in divine intervention when they need far more practical solutions."

"Looks like you've found your avatar," Alex grinned.

"He must be caught, though. We can only change this as avatars if we are converted to the robots and survive the journey to Narzhin."

Alex shuddered. "What a horrible training!"

"But worth it if we can put an end to this."

Ahead of them, Herrass was arguing with the guards.

"I am permitted to say my goodbyes. That is the law!"

The guards looked at each other. It was clear they thought this was a bad idea, but the law was the law and, until it was changed, they had to obey it. They changed direction and frog-marched Herrass to a tree with a hole in the base. Herrass shook off his guards, got down on all fours and scurried into the hole.

"Be quick about it, Herrass," one of them yelled. "And don't even think of escaping with your family. If you do, we will hunt you down. Your partner will be brought back in shame. Even her cubs will not be allowed to speak with her!"

Alex and Daniel followed Herrass into the set. Another Djaroubi, a female, hurried to greet him.

"Did he listen?" she asked, breathlessly.

"I've been banished."

"He can't do that! I will talk to him!" She went to leave but Herrass caught her paw. "He means it, Gilesh. It's been witnessed and confirmed."

"Then I'll gather the cubs and we'll go with you!" she declared.

"Your father insisted I go alone and, if you try to come with me, the guards will bring you back in shame."

"Oh great. Dad's the Chief!" Alex groaned.

"Bet Herrass and his father-in-law have been having ructions ever since the day Gilesh and Harrass met," Daniel agreed.

"Probably had someone 'more suitable' picked out, and her decision threw all his plans into disarray."

"Naturally."

Herrass and his partner were holding each other close, the female in tears. She pulled back.

"I'll wait until it's dark," she sniffed. They can't watch me all the time."

"Gilesh, the aliens are on their way here. I..." He looked around to make sure the guards weren't listening, then shrugged and decided he no longer cared. "I went deep into the jungle and found their camp." He quickly raised a paw when she went to speak. "Your father said that if I went in search of them or we posted guards, that would bring them here. What was I to say? It's too late?"

"Get a move on in there!" one of the guards called.

"Herrass! What are we to do?" Gilesh was clearly very aware of the consequences of being captured and it scared her so much she was visibly shaking.

"I don't know," he said, sadly, stroking the fur on her cheek, which was wet with tears. "No one has ever survived their onslaught to tell us their approach."

She sniffed deeply and patted his chest. "Then *you* must do it. You must stay close enough to see what they do, then get to the next keroo in time and warn them."

"You think that Chief will listen to an outsider? I couldn't even get your father to listen to me!"

"You can only try." She took a deep breath, nodded to herself and leaned forward to whisper in his ear. "Just as I will try to join you once father takes his guards off me."

"Gilesh! If you do that, we will never be allowed to speak to the cubs again!"

"If the aliens catch us, will the situation be any different?" she asked, her head cocked to the side. "Once he has calmed down, I will speak to father on your behalf. In the meantime..." She jerked her head and Herrass turned to see one of the guards had come into the set.

Herrass closed his eyes, nodded to the guard and embraced Gilesh once more.

"My love... Whatever happens, I will find you," he murmured.

"Not in this life you won't," the guard said, pulling the two apart. "Come on!"

Herrass was escorted into the jungle. When they were a few miles from the centre of the keroo and on the border of the tribal grounds, one of the guards poked him in the back.

"On your way. If you're ever found on keroo land again, you'll be slashed so badly you'll wish you were dead," and the guard unsheathed his claws and bared his teeth.

"I'm not worried," Herrass assured him. "With the aliens on their way, you will not be around to make good on that threat."

"You'd better hope you're wrong," the guard replied, "else your partner will be dead too." He gave Herrass a contemptuous look, turned, and together the two guards made their way back.

"I'm very much afraid I'm not," Herrass groaned.

"He's not, is he?" Alex asked Daniel.

"Nope. From what Almega can tell, they'll be here by tomorrow evening. Not enough time for Gilesh to argue with her father or for the guards watching her to be removed. They're all captured."

"And Herrass?"

"He's nearby, despite the injunction, and tries to fight when he sees Gilesh being taken, but the Parchti use an odourless gas when they begin their assault. It leaves the Djaroubi dopey, weak, and easy to catch and transport. Any who are too old, too young, or infirm are killed to stop them warning anyone else."

"Including…?"

"Including Herrass and Gilesh's cubs, yes. They're all killed."

"We've absolute proof this is a highly evolved, intelligent society," Alex said, watching Herrass disappear into the jungle. "Now I need to add the bits to the training videos so that they remember that and free themselves."

"Do you know how you're going to do it?" Daniel asked as they took off to head back to the Parchti base.

"With the language uploads I know how to speak Djaroubi. The problem is that the Parchti don't have the vocal cords to do it. None of the Djaroubi survive long enough to record the message, and it would be next to impossible to explain to them what they need to say and who to in the short time they have. That means I need to find a recorder, record the message using a Parchti, then find a way to change the pitch so it's at a level that the Djaroubi can hear." She shook her head at the complicated task. "After that, I need to upload the file to every single training session on offer, so that it's embedded into their knowledge of whatever job they decide to do. That bit of memory won't be wiped because it's needed if they're to do the jobs the Parchti need them to do, and the Parchti won't be aware it's there because they can't detect it unless they know what they're looking for. If I insert it several times in the training, then every time they access the file to do their jobs, they'll be reminded once again of who they are, what's been done to them and what the Parchti are really like. It's the only certain way of putting an end to this once and for all."

***

Alex found a digital recorder and, in the absence of a dedicated software feature and with a little help from Almega via Daniel, created a pitch shift on a basic audio editing software that could get the level at the same pitch as the Djaroubi used.

"The big question is, what do I tell them?" she asked.

"The truth?" Daniel suggested.

"I mean, what do I tell them that won't freak them out and send them into a catatonic fit?"

"Start with the bad news and get it over with. They've been captured by the aliens and put into a robotic head that will, in due course, be attached to a robot body on the alien's home planet of Narzhin. That their senses can't be trusted and some of them need to learn programming and electronics so that they can correct that and see and hear the world as it really is, rather than the way the Parchti want them to see it. That the ordinary Parchti don't realise that they're sentient and intelligent because they can't hear them. That some friends have adjusted the process used to keep them as slaves, so that they keep most of their memories of who and what they are, know what's happening, and can work to stop any more Djaroubi from being captured..."

"Wait! Wait! I need to write this down!"

"You'll remember it. You're an Eternal, after all," he told her. "That they need to lie low until they're safely on Narzhin, have fixed their own systems and then find whoever's behind this, put a stop to it and let the Parchti know what they've been doing. That they need to remember that most of the Parchti are innocent and honestly believe they're simply robots, and the only ones they need to take down are the ones behind all this. That if they attack the Parchti en masse, the chances are that the aliens will take their revenge on the rest of the Djaroubi before finding another planet with brains they can use. That the future is in their paws."

"Just that, huh?" she deadpanned, raising an eyebrow at him.

"In your own words, of course," he added. He managed to hold the straight face for a few seconds longer, then the quirk of his lips gave the game away. "Look, you asked!" he defended.

"I'll work with it."

***

Sitting in the cabin of the Parchti she was inhabiting with the recording downloaded into the augmented audio software with its pitch adjuster, Alex managed to create the speech and figure out a way to insert it into all the training programs. Then she put her Parchti to bed so that he'd be alert when the time came. It helped that the hunters had yet to return with the new captives and many of the Parchti involved in the procedure were taking the opportunity to relax and enjoy a little down time. That her own Parchti was spending inordinate amounts of time asleep in his cabin went without notice or comment. It seemed that, provided he (or she. Alex still couldn't work out the gender and, for all she knew, the species were hermaphrodites) was available to work when the time came, that was good enough.

When she was satisfied all the Parchti were asleep, she roused hers and took it to the computer room. It took a few hours as she not only had to insert the speech into the trainings but check the Parchti themselves wouldn't be able to hear it. She added warnings before and after the speech to remind the Djaroubi that, if they wanted to put a stop to this, it was imperative they not let their captors know that they were different, and then work quietly, and in secret, until they were ready to reveal themselves. Failure to do so would ensure their instant destruction and all the software running the conversions would be overwritten to return it to factory standard. Once that was done, she reinstated the brain surgery programming so that, with the next batch, they'd keep their memories both of their previous lives and of what had to happen next. At the end she sat back, her Parchti aching all over from the hard work it had been doing.

"I need to put this one back to bed," she told Daniel, leading her avatar back to its room. Once it was tucked up in its bunk, she re-emerged, feeling triumphant. "Now all we have to do is wait to see if it works!" she declared. "Of course, the problem will be that Herrass's tribe will only be the first of the new shipment captured, and they need to survive long enough as heads to get to Narzhin. As terrible as it sounds, it would be better if the Parchti caught more Djaroubi faster on this occasion. The longer our tribe is kept waiting, the more chance some of them will freak out and give the game away."

"You're right," Daniel nodded. "That is terrible, but I think it must be done."

"How?"

"Simplest solution? We identify the location of a few Djaroubi keroo, then you get inside one of the Parchti trackers so that it can point the way. Most of the delay is caused by their having trouble finding them, not in the capture and relocation."

"Oh no! That's horrendous! I can't be responsible for all those murders!"

"They're programs, Alex, until we get inside them, and we will be," he reminded her. "It's no more unpleasant than shooting zombies in a video game."

"You know as well as I do that it's more than that!"

"Not until we step inside. Alex! This is important! If they're to be saved, this must be done!"

"Their god really is as vicious as Herrass suspects," she sighed, heading out towards the Parchti hunters' camp.

"I think Herrass lost all faith a long time ago," Daniel said, floating alongside her. "And we're not gods."

"Relative to them, we're as good as," she replied, zooming off.

Since they knew where the camp was, they quickly found their targets. Alex got inside one of the trackers. It had identified Herrass's tribe, and the attack was already being prepared, but Alex planted some ideas in its head as to where they would find two more tribes. While the hunters prepared their knock-out gas and cages, Alex led the tracker to the other two sites. Upon its return, she abandoned it and watched as it eagerly reported what it had found.

"I guess now we have to wait to make certain they capture enough," she groaned. She felt sick to her stomach as what she'd been forced to do.

"We can't," Daniel told her sadly. "The gate on Narzhin is going to open. If you leave now, you'll just about make it if you go at maximum velocity."

"What? No! We have to know whether or not it worked! If it doesn't, this universe isn't going to be worth jack to anyone."

"I'm sorry. We must go, now!"

Alex was torn, but Daniel was insistent. Reluctantly, and with much cursing directed towards Omskep, Alex headed back to Narzhin.

"Look at it this way," Daniel suggested as he travelled alongside her. "At least you won't have to watch those keroo being converted."

"I was trying not to think about it," she snapped. "Certainly not my part in it!"

"We'll more than pay for that when we become Djaroubi and lead the fight against the Parchti. As you said, it's not going to be a training most would leap at, but we now know just how important it is, so we have to."

"It's going to be terrifying," she agreed, already anticipating being in one of the cages and knowing what lay in store.

"But we'll get through it, and we'll stop it from happening to anyone else. And after that, the other Eternals might enjoy being Djaroubi. If they turn out to be mostly decent – apart from whoever came up with this nightmare – they might even enjoy being Parchti."

"Fortan would enjoy being Parchti without worrying about that!" Alex snorted. The space around her was dark since she was going faster than the speed of light, but she seemed to glow with fury. "And if he does, I'll be tapping Almega to find out how to trap him again!"

"I've a feeling that talent is reserved for the Guardian of Omskep," Daniel replied. "If we all had the skill, I think I would have trapped Fortan eons ago and put him out of our collective misery!"

Alex grunted her agreement and continued her impossibly fast journey back to Narzhin. She arrived barely in time at the crossover point and dived through the gap just as it was starting to close.

***

"We're back on Earth?" she asked, looking around. A lot of it seemed familiar, but other parts were strange. The sky was blue, there were snow-capped mountains in the distance, and she was lying beside a river with trees and grass that were all the right colours but, looking more closely, they were subtly different. A nearby tree that looked like a pine, on closer inspection proved to have not pine needles but instead thousands upon thousands of tiny balls arranged in lines. The blades of grass were thicker and had different colours top and bottom so that, when the wind blew, a meadow that was dark green before shifted to a more turquoise-blue hue and back again. It was mesmerising. She looked at Daniel who shrugged.

"It's supposed to be, according to Almega, but it clearly isn't. He's trying to figure it out."

Alex picked herself up. "Would be nice to land on my feet at least once!" She dusted herself down, although that was more from habit. In her present form, she was not susceptible to dust or dirt. "Any idea how far ahead I've moved?"

"According to his charts, about six-hundred-and-fifty million years."

She blinked. "*That* far? Better make the most of this, then. In another three-hundred-and-fifty million years the sun will be around ten percent hotter, and the oceans will boil off, so it doesn't look like I'll be coming back here if that's the size of the leap I'm making." She turned around, admiring the view. "Looks like humans sorted out the pollution and energy problems... Assuming humans are still around and didn't destroy themselves, leaving the planet to recover on its own?"

"Almega's still trying to figure out why this isn't quite right. I suggest we fly up and take a look around to see if we can spot evidence of civilisation."

Together, they flew up... and then further up until Alex could look down on the continent.

"None of this is familiar. The continents have changed," she observed. "However, given that's the equator, the area where we landed should have been desert." She orientated herself. "Which means that must be the Iberian peninsula, though it doesn't look like it, and it's now attached to what was Morocco. We came from over there, which is, or was, roughly Algeria, in the middle of the Sahara."

"Someone passed geography," Daniel grinned. "But yes, it is looking rather different. Like a second, very green Pangaea. Good different, though. Perhaps that's why the plants look odd? Some kind of genetic alteration to help them thrive in a more arid environment?"

"With a fast-flowing river running through it? That's far from arid," she replied.

"I meant before." He shrugged. "Maybe we just missed the rainy season? Or perhaps they created the plants and, in combination with climatic changes, the desert was wiped out?"

"Something isn't right here," she insisted. "Let's go and visit England. We both know what that should look like."

"Assuming it's not vanished into the sea?"

From their height, it was an easy matter for Alex to reorient herself and then arrow towards what had once been the United Kingdom. It had, indeed, been eroded, but bridges had been built over waterways and seas, connecting islands that had once been part of the mainland, while the mainland itself was now attached to France in places. When she landed in the middle of a lonely track in the area of the South Downs, still high enough to be above water, she noted the grass and trees were once again different to those she was used to.

"Either some chemical company's GMO ran amuck, or this isn't Earth. It's similar, but it's not the one we visited before."

"Parallel version?" Daniel suggested. "Except, it's in the exact same space-time location as ours, and Almega's convinced it's the same universe."

"Where are the people?" Alex wondered. "Maybe hiking's gone out of fashion. We need a town." She rose once more and headed for the nearest conurbation. "Let's see if the dominant species is still human and, if it is, are they different."

They floated above a town.

"I wonder if this was Lewes?" she mused.

"The River Ouse would have swallowed it whole," Daniel commented. "This is probably an extension, or a new town relocated once the river expanded to form that lake." He pointed.

"Hmm. Very hard to figure out where we're at with all the changes. Still, it's the people we need to check."

They landed in what appeared to be the town centre.

"Looks pretty much the same to me," Daniel shrugged. "Must be a student town, though. Rather a large number of people in their late teens or early twenties. Also, they're a bit taller than during our last visit."

Alex squinted at the people, her eyes going up as a man, who must have been close to seven feet eleven inches, strolled past.

"A *bit* taller?"

"Yes, well, you always get outliers," he admitted. "Generally, they seem to have gained around ten centimetres or so. Not outrageous, but impressive."

Something seemed off. She tried to move into one to check them out and passed straight through. She tried another with the same result and turned to stare at Daniel.

"They're not real!" she gasped. She tried another, then another and yet another, each with the same result. "None of them are real!"

Daniel had been listening to two ladies chatting. "Certainly sound real," he said. "Unless it's some kind of script they run every day."

"But why?" Alex asked, moving around, trying to find a genuine human in amongst the fakes. "Who's it for if there aren't any actual people?" She looked around, trying to find something, anything to explain what was happening. That was when she noticed that every single person was wearing the same band on their wrist. Curious, she bent over someone who was sitting on a bench, reading something on a tablet, and examined the internals of the band. "There's a *lot* of electronics in here," she declared as Daniel walked up to find out what had caught her attention. "I wonder if..." A moment later, she vanished.

"Alex?! Alex, where are you?"

The man whose band she'd been examining lowered his tablet, turned to Daniel and winked.

"Alex?"

'The reason they talk like real people is because the consciousness is stored in the band,' she said, availing herself of the Eternal's natural telepathy. *'At some point or another, this was a real person.'*

"Could it still be? I mean, could they be staying at home and sending themselves out to work or something?" Daniel asked. The idea held some appeal, especially if you could double up and remember both experiences. Part of you lazing on a hot beach, the other version freezing in a boring office. If the two could be connected, at least you might be able to regulate temperature. He shook his head. As if holograms felt temperature variations. Get a grip, Daniel!

'Interesting idea but no, I don't think so,' Alex replied, unaware of his internal monologue. *'It's very hard to read the data on this thing, and I don't want to push too hard in case he notices me as a separate thing and not a temporary glitch, but he has a pretty clear memory of being about to die, then waking up in this form.'*

"That's... different. You'd better get out of him before he realises it's more than a glitch."

She did and, for a moment, the man blinked repeatedly and looked around him, then he stared at the band and tapped it a few times. A thoughtful stare at the pavement was followed by him pressing something on the tablet. It folded itself up and vanished. Then he stood up and headed off.

"Probably going to have a stiff drink... or whatever counts as one for these things," Daniel commented, watching the man's departure. He turned to Alex. "If he was dying and now is walking around, does that mean all the people around us are dead?"

"Definitely looking that way." Alex's voice was muffled as she explored another band. She withdrew. "Different cause, but a similar memory for this one."

"So, someone, somewhere is taking people near death and relocating them into... what? Hard holograms?"

Alex passed her arm through a couple of people who were walking past. There was an almost imperceptible fizzing at the edges as two energies interacted. "Something like that," she nodded.

"And is it something they wanted, or something forced on them?"

"For those who were still aware up to the moment of transition, I don't get the impression of fear or that anything was wrong. A lot of them were in agony, angry, and struggling to think much beyond 'will it make the pain stop?', and now they seem quite satisfied with their new condition. It's... a little weird, though."

"What do you mean by weird?"

"It's akin to a computer chip. A very advanced one, but still a computer chip, so the emotions aren't exactly right. The memories from before the transition are as they should be, but after that..." She shook her head. "There's something you would call a feeling because it doesn't fit under any other category, but it's not human emotion or even what we feel as Eternals. It's... muted? Much quieter than in a real human. For some of them, it's so muted as to be almost gone completely. Still," she continued, looking around. "It doesn't seem to be perceived as a problem because many of them were quite elderly when they passed."

"Old people still have feelings!" Daniel insisted.

"Yes, of course they do, but it's not the raging, hormone-driven focus you get in teenagers. They're not upset that they're unemotional. They seem to be taking it as par for the course."

"Look around you," he said, a sweep of his arm encompassing the passing citizenry. "They're all young."

"When you were in an old body, did the person inside feel old?" Alex asked, cocking her head.

Daniel thought about it. "No," he admitted. "Most of the time I felt like a young squatter sitting inside a decrepit mess, peering out of the two holes provided for that purpose."

"Exactly. I think the hologram manifests the age they felt, not the age they were."

"That's remarkable technology," he admitted. "It does, however, leave a huge question. Where are the real people? Did we somehow stumble on a town given over to the holograms?"

"It might make sense to keep real humans and holographic ones apart," she returned, thoughtfully. "You wouldn't want to get into an affair with someone who appears young, then find out they're actually in their nineties, not real, and incapable of having a family."

"If they look like they're twenty-five, does their mental age matter?"

"It wouldn't bother me," she replied, "but it might bother some. Plus, they'd probably not be very interested in the latest music or getting drunk as a skunk at a frat party and acting like an idiot."

"I wasn't interested in that even when I was young!" he protested.

She turned on him. "You're trying to tell me that in all the trainings you've done, you've never got drunk?"

"Of course I did! I said I wasn't interested in it; I didn't say I'd never done it. You get dragged into things, sometimes, whether you want to or not."

"Hmm." She raised an eyebrow, but his demeanour remained stolid. "I seem to recall you staggering home from a do and knocking over a lamp."

"Alex! That's got to be over a hundred trainings ago! How is it you can remember that and not what you did last week?"

"Perhaps because you burnt the house down, with us in it!"

"Once! That one time, and you've never let me forget it!" he sulked. "And I didn't ask to get into that state. My friends were celebrating my new status. I didn't want to look like the miserable supervisor who suddenly cuts off all his friends because he's got a promotion!"

"We didn't even get to enjoy it for one day!"

"I said I'm sorry! I've said it a hundred times. I'm sorry, OK?"

She held his look for a few seconds and then, "You are so easy to wind up," she laughed.

He baulked, then gave her a reluctant nod.

"Back to business," she continued. "Perhaps, somewhere else, there's a town where real people can be found. We need to find out who and where."

She checked a few more of the bands and noticed that they all had memories of one place. "I think I know where we need to go," she smiled.

Still smarting from the reminder of his somewhat ancient error, Daniel stuffed his hands in his pockets. "Oh?"

"Those that weren't already comatose all have a memory of what I think is a university campus."

"One we know?" he asked, cheering up at the thought of perhaps seeing what had become of an old stomping ground.

Alex shook her head. "Never heard of it. Greystones University?"

"Nope. Not one I've encountered. Where is it?"

She stuck her head into a few more bands, finally stepping back thoughtfully.

"If the brief glimpses are anything to go by, roughly where Durham was."

"Hmm. Well, I guess it is a few hundred million years in the future. We shouldn't expect such places to have lasted."

Alex nodded, but kept her mouth shut. Even in the more highly educated people she'd explored, there was no sign it had ever been called anything else. Still, as he said, expecting records to go back so far was asking rather a lot.

"Trip to Durham, then?" she asked.

"Is it still called that?"

"Dunno, but I've picked up a sense of where it is and what it looks like now. Can't say I recognise any of the buildings, but the locale is vaguely familiar."

"Meaning?"

"North East England."

"After you, then," he said, waving her on.

***

It took rather longer than the Eternals thought it would. The shape of the British Isles had changed so much that it was hard for Alex to orient herself to find such a relatively small target. The city had never been that big even in her time, being dwarfed by the nearby towns of Newcastle and Sunderland. Indeed, it only had the honorific 'city' because it had a cathedral. As for the coast – which might have provided a clue – where once soft beaches had been, now the sea had worn them back until it had reached more resilient rock, changing the landscape significantly, and tectonic shift had changed the country's angle to the continent. With Alex's internal geography still rooted several million years in the past, that made finding the location harder. The River Wear had vanished altogether (or, perhaps, changed its route to the sea), denying Alex that easy marker from above. Eventually, though, they managed to track down the city – now very different to the one she'd once known.

"Where's the cathedral?" she wondered as they dropped down into the space that, in her time would have boasted that ancient building.

"Six-hundred-and-fifty million years, remember?" Daniel replied. "Expecting a building that was a thousand years old when you last visited to keep going for that long is asking a bit much, don't you think?"

84

"No cathedral, no castle, no old buildings at all, and this place was full of them."

"Again..."

She stood on what, in her past training, would have been the green swathe known as Palace Green, and looked around.

"Nothing. None of the buildings I knew are here, nor any sign they ever were. Not even a mound of stones or a placard."

"Between your last visit and this time there may have been devastating wars, global catastrophe from meteor strikes, some ice ages, you name it, and we've seen the tectonic shift. If you think about it, it's astonishing there's still a vaguely recognisable country. There may even have been a period a million or so years ago when it was all underwater, so the fact that you could navigate yourself here at all is amazing."

"Ask Almega to check we *are* in the right place, would you?" she asked.

Daniel did, but Almega was still trying to make sense of what he was seeing. "He says it is, but it isn't at the same time and it's driving him nuts. If you don't mind, having seen what he can be like when he's angry, I'll stay out of his way!" He looked around at the people who were walking around the small park to visit shops or sitting on benches to enjoy the sunshine. Again, he noted a lot of the wrist bands. "Are there any real humans left on this planet?" he wondered.

"We need to find out what's going on, here," Alex declared. "This is very, very wrong!"

"Where do they do the conversions?" he asked.

"I think it was on the old science site, but now I'm completely lost. Hold on." She rose to take in the view. "Found it! It's over there." She pointed and took off, Daniel quickly coming alongside her. They flew up the hill to the south-east until they reached the location. There they found an imposing building, as tall as the cathedral had once been, with glass towers and a magisterial front entrance. Alex nodded. "This is what they had in their memories."

They stood in front of the grand edifice, looking around. Once again, they saw that there were plenty of young people wearing the bands, but no one else.

"There has to be someone, somewhere who's real!" Alex snorted and headed inside.

***

It took a while, but they finally found the room where the conversions took place. Unfortunately, it was dusty and didn't look to have been used for years.

"Someone else took on the job?" Daniel suggested.

"And left the equipment here? Why not move it?"

"It's a bit big to just ship out," he replied, taking in the house-sized scanning machine.

Alex was exploring the internals. "It's intact. Nothing's been removed, not even the smaller bits." She stood back and took in the dimensions of the machine versus the dimensions of the doorway. "The building's older than the machine," she began.

"You're sure?"

"Definitely. Which means it had to be built in here. If they could put it together, then they could take it apart and move it somewhere else. Why leave it here? And why mothball it? Are there no more humans left to convert?"

"That's a scary thought," Daniel winced. "But why? The planet seems clean, fit and healthy. In fact, it's cleaner than I've ever seen it. Why would people need to be converted?"

"Perhaps the reason it's cleaner is because everyone *was* converted?" Alex suggested. "But when? This," and she waved at the machine, "has been shut down for years." She paced, thinking things through. "The building's still here, and the machine, plus lights," and she indicated same, "which means power. That all suggests that there are people still doing work in this building who might explain some of this. We need to explore."

They did, going from floor to floor and through empty offices until they found some busier areas. And in one of them...

"I've found a real human!" Alex cried. Daniel spun around to see Alex pointing to a woman who was working away on some extremely complex formulae. She was considerably shorter than the holographic people, and looked to be in her sixties at least, with white hair and a lined face. She was using a sheet of paper that allowed her to cleanly write, erase, and copy-paste using a pen, and all while the results were printed up on a floating computer screen that cleaned up her handwriting and made it legible. She finished with the paper, stood up by leaning on the table, and shuffled over to gaze at the clean readout on the screen. She manipulated a few parts, paused to consider, put one back where it was originally, and then tapped the side of the screen. Immediately, the formulae were converted into an active simulation, which the scientist gazed at with interest.

"I think," Alex said after watching for a while, "that she's trying to find a way to reintegrate the holographic humans." She paused, watching one bit closely. "Oh!"

"What?" Daniel asked.

"If this is right, then I know why there are so few real humans."

"Which is?" he nudged when she continued to watch the new data simulation mesh with ones that were already in the computer.

"This bit," and she pointed to a section of the screen the scientist was focused on. "Recognise it? That's the bit of DNA code that's concerned with fertility. Look at her! She's determined that this, above all, must work, and the fact that it's not is frustrating her. That tells me it's very important." She turned to Daniel. "I think, for some reason, all the humans have become or perhaps became sterile!"

"And they made them into holograms until they could find a way to fix it? Isn't that like trying to crack a nut with a hundred-pound sledgehammer?"

"Perhaps they tried to fix it and ran out of time?"

"But why preserve old people who were dying? Why not youngsters?"

"I've not checked everyone! There may well be those, too, just not in the town we checked. Keeping all of them gives you a large gene pool if they can be reintegrated." She paused as an idea struck her. "Or!" she cried, "Or the older people may have been more willing to convert, given they were dead anyway, and the young may have preferred to live their lives as real people first. I know I would, especially given the loss of emotions the conversion seems to cause. After all, if they ever figure out how to give them bodies again, they can make them young. Their DNA patterns have been recorded and, so far as I could tell, any anomalies caused by illness or age have been corrected. They could be reincarnated as fit, young humans." She stared at the old woman. "If they have all their memories, mentally older people would probably be easier to handle than a load of teenagers. A solid basis for a new population."

"This is never going to work, though," Daniel muttered, looking at the formulae. "She's hitting a wall when it comes to full transference, in large part because the holo-humans already lost some of themselves in the initial transfer. She needs to guarantee a one hundred percent transfer rate of what's left to make this work, and it's not going to happen."

Alex nodded idly, having already determined that, and continued to gaze at the simulation. She turned and doubled-checked the formulae on the sheet. "I need to find out more," she declared and stepped into the scientist.

Almost immediately she stepped out again, staring at the woman.

"What? What is it?" Daniel asked.

"That was... horrible!" Alex declared, squinting at her target and shuddering. She felt like she needed to take off several layers of skin, if she had any. "She's much older than she appears. I'd say at least a couple of hundred years, which should be impossible. She's got a lot of mechanical replacements so that, appearances to the contrary notwithstanding, she's more android than human." She turned to Daniel. "And despite the calm outward presentation, she is scared out of her mind!"

"Of what?"

A light started flashing in the corner of the floating screen that the scientist was using. Within moments, the present display was shut down, the electronic paper erased and then covered with a different set of formulae, a tiny crystal doubling as portable data storage was removed from the computer and became part of a ring the scientist was wearing, and the new formulae from the electronic paper appeared on the screen. By the time the door was opened, the scientist was bent over a completely different problem.

"Just a theory," Alex said wryly, "but I'm guessing it's this woman."

"Or whoever she represents," Daniel nodded.

"Oleana," the new woman said. "How are you getting along?"

"I think I've almost cracked it," the scientist, Oleana, replied. "Just need to run a simulation..." She activated the simulation on the floating screen and the two looked at it together.

"Very good," the other woman nodded, approvingly. "All those cyber implants of yours haven't dulled your wits, I see."

"Experience counts for a lot," Oleana admitted. "You said that if I did this for you, I could see Miyok alone for an hour."

"I did indeed," the other woman said, pulling a rather less impressive thumb drive from her pocket and downloading the solution before erasing it from the computer and the paper. "And, once you've had your time, I have another problem for you to solve." When Oleana looked crestfallen, the woman continued. "Cheer up. It'll mean more time with Miyok." Oleana perked up. "Oh, yes. The bosses are pleased with you. You've behaved yourself, done as you were told. They think you have earned a little more latitude." She narrowed her eyes. "I suggest you don't screw it up!"

Oleana sighed. "Can't you just let him go? I've been working for you for fifty-five years. For other corporations for over a hundred years. You won't let me die and you won't convert me. I've solved every problem you've given me. Isn't that enough?"

"My dear Oleana, don't be silly. You know the sentence. He stole the future," and she gestured to include the building as a whole. "That's the greatest crime anyone could ever commit. He's never going to be allowed to leave." She gave the older woman a hard look. "And you helped him. You've a fine mind, which we need to solve the problems we have, but you don't get off that easily. It was a life sentence, remember?"

"This is at least two lifetimes!" Oleana argued.

"OK, I hate this one already!" Alex muttered, pointing at the women Oleana was talking to.

"Can't say I'm wild about her myself!" Daniel agreed.

"And, as he explained at the trial, and I've told you repeatedly since then, it wasn't about stealing the future," Oleana continued. "It was about changing it and making it possible for us to save the ordinary people. I'm just about the last real human left on the planet, unless there's some indigenous tribe living underground out of sight of the

90

scans. The people deserve a proper life again, not this... this half-life we've given them! I'm certain I can fix it all if you'll let me, allowing everyone to be re-integrated into bodies that work properly. Then they can live their lives, have children, and die in peace."

The other woman snorted. "And have them messing up the planet again? Don't be ridiculous! This," and she indicated her wrist band, "was supposed to be reserved for the elites, but your husband put paid to that. Still, he did the World Government a favour. They'd assumed they'd lose more than half the consumers, but Miyok preserved them and created new markets, and all of it digital. No packaging, no need to pay manufacturers, and the AI can do most of the work, so they don't need to be paid either, and all the humans have to do is behave themselves and they can have whatever they want!"

"I know!" Oleana snarled. "But it's never theirs and can be snatched away in an instant! The people no longer need to be fed, there's no need for waste clean-up or clothing, all the energy is redirected to your server farms..."

"Not mine! The corporations' server farms," the other woman corrected.

"You told them they'd be happy because they'd get so many choices, but they're time-limited and dependent on an inhuman system!" She pointed at the woman. "Even you, Sagea! You're as much a victim of this as anyone else!"

"I'm no victim!" Sagea snarled. "I paid my dues for conversion, and I wanted it! I think I look pretty good for two hundred and twenty-five. Better than you, certainly!"

"You know full well I have no control over that – because your bosses have denied it to me!"

"The price you paid for crossing the wrong people," Sagea replied, offering a smile that had nothing to do with humour.

"She's enjoying this," Alex observed. "What a malicious bi –"

91

"So, somewhere around two hundred years ago," Daniel interrupted, keen to get them back on track, "for some reason, the elites were made into these holo-people. Meanwhile, the rest of the human population had become sterile and were dying off. Along comes her husband," he pointed to Oleana, "and finds a way to mass convert people."

"I suspect he stole the method, and they somehow found a way to build it," Alex said, still fuming at Sagea's callous attitude.

"And nobody noticed that they were building something the size of a house, with all the power it would require to run it, and with queues of millions outside the doors?"

Alex paced. "Maybe... Maybe he was a whistle-blower? He alerted the news media, or whatever they have now, to what the elites had planned, and that forced them to make the option available to everyone?"

"That would make more sense," he allowed.

"And you can bet whatever you like that anyone who was deemed a troublemaker was simply allowed to die."

"Of course," he nodded. "The perfect opportunity to get rid of unwanted humans. They don't have to actively kill them; they simply don't allow them to live. Criminals, troublemakers, and those who simply refused to conform. A kind of social credit system where the penalty for breaking the rules is death."

"Thing is..." Alex said, her mind whirring as she went through everything they'd witnessed. "Doesn't this all strike you as a bit, I dunno... Backward?"

"What do you mean?"

"We're millions of years in the future, but there are still shops, offices and labs. Even in my last training, shopping centres were dying and most of it was done online, and these holo-humans don't need anything physical. Everything they need can be delivered digitally, so why shops? Shouldn't they be made of energy and out amongst the stars or something?"

"Well, they've got the 'made of energy' sorted," he replied.

"Yes, but it's second-rate. The emotional quality is largely absent – apart from this one, who seems to have her vindictive levels set to max. I've not seen any animals, not even a dog being walked. And what about the aliens? Have you noticed? There aren't any, yet we know from our trainings that humans encountered them millions of years ago."

"We've seen the end of the universe. We know humans do all those things in time," he reminded her.

"But this doesn't seem to fit with what we saw," she insisted. "It's like they've taken a wrong turn, gone down a blind alley and then got stuck."

"We don't know what happened between your last training on Earth and now. Perhaps they advanced a lot, then there was some terrible disaster that set them back massively and they had to rebuild from scratch?"

"Possibly, but they'd have to be sent back to the stone age repeatedly for that to explain this situation after a million or so years."

"Maybe the most recent disaster happened five hundred years ago?"

"No," she replied, shaking her head. "This is wrong. The timeline is wrong, the people are wrong... Nothing about this fits with anything we saw before or after."

The two women were still talking.

"You have an hour with Miyok," Sagea informed Oleana. "I suggest you make the most of it." She swept out of the room. The door locked automatically behind her and Oleana made her way as quickly as her damaged body could carry her to a section of wall. A tiny door opened revealing a wrist band attached to a chain. She pulled it out – the chain extending easily – and quickly activated it. A young man appeared. He was tall, like all the holo-humans.

He had four fingers on each hand and his bare feet showed the little toes had vanished. At first, Alex thought he might have lost them in a fight, but then she double-checked Oleana and realised that she was the same.

"The residual digits have been absorbed," she quietly commented.

"Had to happen eventually," Daniel nodded. "All the little toe seemed to be good for was finding the edge of furniture when you walked around barefoot!"

Alex winced. She'd lost count of how many times she'd done that. Shaking her head, she returned to her observations. Miyok was handsome, but how close his holo-version was to the original was up for debate. He saw Oleana and instantly wrapped her in his arms.

"How long has it been?" he asked, smothering her wrinkled face with kisses.

"Two years," she replied, responding in kind. They held each other tightly, revelling in the moment.

"How long do we have?" he asked in her ear.

"An hour. Less now."

"Then let's not waste any more of it." He glanced around the room.

Oleana took something from her pocket and surreptitiously attached it to his wristband before speaking. "They're getting something, but it's not us. I hacked their bugs and now they'll get the same thing if they check your band. We just need to keep our backs to the camera above the door so that they can't see our lips." They were still hugging, their mouths close to each other's ears, hair and kisses covering their words.

"Got it," he nodded.

They parted and she led him to some chairs which they put together so that they could stay touching each other while they were talking, and their faces were turned away from the camera.

"Any joy?" he asked.

"I can't do it. The damage that was done in the first download was too great."

"Is that across the board, or do the top dogs get a free pass?"

"What do you think?" she asked, stroking the side of his face.

"I should have just stolen the plans, not forced them to release them!" he snorted.

"And how were we supposed to build one of those things and get the entire population of the country, let alone the rest of the planet, to it in time?"

"I should have found a way. I'm sorry, I let you down," Miyok groaned, bowing his head.

Oleana bowed hers until they were touching, forehead to forehead.

"You didn't let anyone down. You gave them a chance," she insisted, her fingers stroking the hair at the back of his neck. "It's only a shame that this planet will be empty of people soon."

He drew a deep breath, raised his head and kissed her forehead. "How long?"

"Based on my research, another ten years at the outside. After that, the degradation of the records will be beyond retrieval. There have already been some glitches, although naturally they've covered them up."

He nodded. "Naturally." He sat back, angling his body carefully. His prison clothing was minimalist. A thin shirt and some shorts. If he was human, he'd be freezing. He picked at the hem of his shorts. "What about your other project?"

"I wish I could show you," she replied, her face lighting up. Suddenly, she appeared so much younger. "It's an amazing world with so many advances, but so overcrowded. Once we are all gone, this place will be perfect for them. They will bring so much with them, too!"

"But not the politicians. Please, not the politicians!" Miyok begged.

"We can be selective. No politicians, no crooked corporate heads, none of that. Oh, I wish we could be here to see what this world will become, but it's time to end this."

"How bad is it getting?" Miyok asked, his fingers twined with hers.

"So many," she sighed, shaking her head. "They cannot switch off because the band knows what they're thinking and stops them. When they wake up, a little more of them has been removed. Most of the people are little more than zombies now, dutifully buying what their media tells them to buy, and going where they're told to go. We are becoming more and more machine-like every day."

"Except for the elites, of course!" Miyok snorted.

Oleana caught his face in her hands. "Even some of them," she assured him. "They say that they want to live forever, but it's too easy. There are no challenges, and they couldn't rise to them if there were. Why do you think they have preserved me? I have begged them to let us go, but they refuse because I am the only one who can still think clearly enough to solve their problems for them." Tears were leaking down her cheeks and Miyok gently wiped them away. "But now I make it clear that I will only do it if they allow me to see you."

He nodded, smiling, his own tears matching hers. "I have missed you so much. They lock me in the band but I'm still aware. The only thing I wait for is when they release me to be with you."

Oleana looked around, briefly, then leaned close. "I made contact!"

Miyok stiffened. "You did?"

"Um hmm. And I talked to one of them. She's a good person, Miyok. You would like her."

"Only if she's like you," he assured her. "Is she interested?"

"Very much so. They can travel across the universe, but most are too poor, and their world is busy and noisy.

She says there are many who would welcome a more peaceful life with space to move."

"Not too many, though," Miyok warned.

"No. Enough to do the job and get them started. No fewer than five hundred. Anything less than that and they risk genetic drift." Miyok nodded. "She thinks no more than a thousand. That should allow some choice and ensure a healthy population. She wants to make certain that they're the right ones, though, and that will take time."

"How long?"

"At least a year. Probably two."

He nodded. Trying to identify genuine people who weren't trying to sneak in under the guise of believing in the new world and instead wanted to use it to line their own pockets would not be easy.

"And the world!" Oleana continued, still lost in whatever she had witnessed. "She showed me, walking around with a machine so that I could see it for myself. I could ask questions and she answered them. She introduced me as a friend from another country – a country that was poor and had been left behind – and that allowed me to talk to the people in the streets. Ask them questions!"

"We were right, then? The language…?"

"So far as I could tell, identical," she nodded. "Seeing and hearing about their advances! I think, if we had not become trapped in a digital reality, we might have managed many of them ourselves, but the others?"

"What are they talking about?" Alex wondered as Oleana continued to wax lyrical about her talks with someone else.

"I guess they have gone out into the stars and found another species that needs a new home," Daniel replied. "If she's right, in ten years there'll be no humans left on this one."

"An alien species that speaks English? How does that work?"

"I have no idea," he replied honestly. "Perhaps they found one of the spaceships that was sent out into the universe during your last Earth training session, learned the language and adopted it."

"Do you have any idea how unlikely that is?"

"And yet it seems to have happened," he shrugged. "Fact, as they say, is stranger than fiction."

"So, they're handing over this planet to a limited group of new tenants?"

"A carefully vetted, very select group of new tenants," he corrected.

Alex shook her head. "No! This isn't what happens! We've been to the future and there are humans there, which means these ones can't die out."

"Maybe there is an underground tribe they missed?" Daniel offered.

"We're the ones who are missing something," Alex insisted, shaking her head. "Different plants, slowed advances, and somehow, without spaceships, they've made contact with another world, done it so well that they can communicate in real time across light years, and they found probably the only other planet in the universe that has aliens that speak English? Come on!"

Daniel turned, suddenly.

"Almega says there's a crossover due and we need to head out."

"Without solving this one? Oh no! I need to find out what's gone wrong here!" she insisted.

"He's put a marker in it. We can live it and find out directly, but if we don't go right now, you'll be stuck here for thousands of years with no humans, no animals and nothing to do. Do you want that?!"

"The aliens will be here within a couple of years, before these beings are 'switched off'. I'll have company."

"Alex, it won't be enough to keep you going for millions of years. Also, the other Eternals would get pretty annoyed with you given that, so long as you're here, they're trapped without training. Do you really want to face them when you do, finally return, and explain how you just *had* to know?"

"Aww, nuts!" She watched Oleana and Miyok whispering to each other, words of love and affection interspersing their plotting. Half of her wanted to stay to find out what species they had met, but Daniel was urging her to hurry. She had so many questions and not getting any answers was driving her mad, but there was nothing that could be done about it.

"We come back, right?" she snarled.

"Yes! Yes! Now come on! We're running out of time!"

***

Emerging above the building, Daniel pointed and they headed to a hill, overlooking the city. With the towering glass and steel that now filled the area, the view was a far cry from that which Alex remembered.

"It's going to land here?" she checked.

"Yes."

She looked around, thinking of the conversation she was now missing. "Well? When?"

"Any… minute… Now!"

As before, the ground seemed to shift and the deafening roar surrounded her. The tunnel was ahead, floating in mid-air, but there was something else. In the walls of the tunnel, distorted but clearly visible, was the view from the hill, except it kept changing. One second it was the one she'd seen when she arrived, the next it was an open plain with a river running through it and no sign of human habitation now or ever. Nothing but trees, birds and bizarre wildlife, the like of which she'd never seen before. Another shift and she was staring into empty space. Stars, the sun, but no sign of Earth at all. Another, and it was a town but a very different one with floating buildings and some kind of aerial transport. For one brief moment she saw the view she recognised, including the cathedral and the castle, both still standing, before it shifted again to show recreated versions clearly made of steel or something similar. She paused, frowning as she tried to make sense of the multiplicity of images.

"Get in there!" Daniel yelled.

She jumped.

***

She still didn't land on her feet.

"What was that all about?" Daniel asked, appearing beside her. "Why didn't you just jump in the instant it opened?"

She was still getting over the nausea the trips encouraged, leaning on one arm and trying to pull herself back together. After a few breaths she shook her head and squinted up at him.

"Didn't you see them? All the different places, one on top of the other?"

"What places? No!"

She pulled her knees up to her chest, her brain mulling over what she had witnessed.

"Is Almega still confused?" she asked after a pause.

"Yes. Very!" he confirmed, after a glance over his shoulder at something she couldn't see.

"Ask him if it could be the same Earth but a different, overlapping possible world. Not a branching version, but a membrane one."

There was a brief pause and then Alex could almost hear the exultant cry across the connection as Daniel relayed her message and then turned, smiling at her.

"Well done! He says you're quite right. Same location, same universe, but a different possible world." He looked off to his right, then nodded. "He says that now you've spotted what the problem was, and he knows what he's looking for, he's finding endless layers of the things."

100

"Explains what I saw," she nodded. "Could make it a little difficult to get back there to find out what happened, though."

Daniel listened to Almega for a moment. "What?" He turned to Alex. "Hang on a moment. I'll be right back." He vanished.

Alex stayed where she was. The jump had made her very queasy, and she was still mentally exploring the discussion between Miyok and Oleana.

"I wonder...?" she murmured, her eyes closed while she pictured the possibilities.

Daniel reappeared.

"You won't have to worry about finding that one again," he began.

"Because Oleana was working on making a path between the universes," she finished, nodding to herself.

He blinked in surprise. "How did you figure that one out?"

"Oleana was talking about the other person she had contacted. Whoever it was couldn't be alien because, despite your suggestion, that simply wouldn't happen. Ergo, how would they communicate? And how would they get to a level where the advances of the other world were comprehensible in so short a time? Combine that with the different views I was getting in the tunnel..."

"Ahh. That's why I couldn't see it," Daniel nodded. "Not being really there, I'm not privy to what that looks like."

"Or sounds like?" she asked, carefully standing up.

"For me, I'm aware of a point which looks like a black hole. Not a spatial phenomenon type," he added quickly. "A literal black hole."

"Yeah. It doesn't look like that." She dusted herself down. "And if you got the sound, Fortan would be complaining about the racket."

"*That* loud?"

"Yep. The combination of aural and visual distortions is what's making me feel ill. If I was mortal I'd be throwing up and then having to lie down for a few days every single time."

"I'm sorry. I honestly didn't realise it was that bad," he admitted.

"Next time Fortan or one of the others decides to mess around with Omskep, let's hope it's you stuck in here, then you can learn first-hand!" she grumbled.

"I think Almega is putting extra security around Omskep to make certain this never happens again." He watched, worriedly, as Alex staggered a few times before pulling herself together. "Are you...?"

"I'll be fine," she replied, waving a dismissive hand.

She looked around. Wherever she was, it was a jungle. She suspected that, were she physically present, it would be humid and, given the size of the insect that buzzed past her, she'd be eaten alive. She cocked her head, hearing a strange sound, and headed through the trees (literally, in many cases) until she reached the edge of a massive plain. She gazed, dumbstruck, at the sight before her.

"I thought we were jumping forwards in time?" she said.

"We are," Daniel assured her.

"Dinosaurs?" She pointed to the herd of brachiosaurs that were making their way to a watering hole.

"From the looks of things, on this planet they never got the meteor."

She lifted herself up so that she could cross the distance more quickly, Daniel beside her, as eager to get a close-up view as she was. Arriving, she dropped down so that she could get the full effect.

"I'm in a film!" she cried, gazing up at the swaying head of one of the beasts, which was over thirty feet above her. "Ahh, this is wonderful! I get to see them and I'm in absolutely no danger, which I would be in if I was in an avatar on this planet."

"Unless you were in one of them, of course," Daniel commented.

"Are they intelligent?" she asked sharply. That would be a different training session!

"No. They may have been around a long time, but they're still running more on instinct than intellect." He took in her expression. "Feel free to step inside and see for yourself."

She did. It was an interesting experience. The animal was very aware of the movements at the edge of the plain and the calves amongst the herd which would be a target for the hunters. This was a matriarchal society and Alex's avatar was listening to the sounds made by the primary female. Basic commands that indicated what they should do if the distant hunters decided to attack. For now, however, the herd was calm, and the hunters in the trees seemed more interested in the aurochs grazing on the other side of the river. There was something else, though. The herd members were also watching the skies and, listening in to the emotions of her host, Alex got the impression that the real danger was perceived to come more from there than from the ground, which struck Alex as most odd.

She stepped out of her host and found Daniel was floating by the sauropod's head.

"Well?" he asked.

"You're right. Conversation amounts to 'Danger! There! Protect calves! Fight!' and not much more beyond 'I'm hungry' and 'I'm thirsty'. There's something in the trees over there that she's aware of but doesn't see as much of a danger because there are some aurochs grazing rather closer."

"Aurochs?"

"Well, very large bovines with big horns? Around six and a half feet tall? They're over there. Look." She pointed and Daniel zoomed his vision so he could get a better look.

"You're right. They're pretty close to Earth aurochs, but on Earth they only came on the scene long after the dinosaurs had left. With all these lumbering beasts, I'm surprised they evolved so much and weren't simply wiped out."

There was a loud crash and a massive therapod charged out of the trees and snatched up one of the older bovines while the others fled in panic, sending clouds of dust in every direction. The massive cow was barely a snack, gulped down within two chews, and now the therapod, which Alex labelled akin to an allosaurus, picked up speed, arrowing towards the sauropod herd and its small number of calves.

The sauropods closed ranks, presenting a united front to the carnivore. They roared and swung their necks, carefully keeping out of reach of the snapping allosaurus. A couple on the flanks did a lumbering turn, watching the allosaurus all the while, and now brought their tails into the fight, forcing the carnivore to step back to avoid a bruising or bone-breaking hit. A few others now moved forward, the tree-trunk legs making the ground shake. They might not have the carnivore's teeth, but they had bulk and a herd of them all moving steadily towards the therapod was enough to make it pause. It had lost the element of surprise, if it ever had it, and the herd was big enough that even with the group roaring and screaming their defiance at the predator, there were still plenty to protect the calves who huddled close to their parents.

The stand-off seemed to be insoluble. The allosaurus was clearly still hungry and was gauging its chances, its head weaving left and right as it sidestepped the swishing tails. Suddenly, a roar split the air and a shadow passed over the group. Panic seized the sauropods, now torn between the threat on the ground and the threat from above. One of the slightly smaller sauropods, but not a calf, was suddenly snatched upwards, roaring and screaming. Whatever had seized it disappeared into the clouds. There was a pause during which everything on the plain could hear the cries of the sauropod from high above but could not see what was happening. Suddenly, the screaming stopped abruptly. A few moments after that, it reappeared in free-fall, crashing into a boneless lump on the plain. The allosaurus dashed towards the downed giant, seeing its chance to get something if it moved fast enough, Alex and Daniel following to see what was going on. Behind them, the other sauropods took the opportunity to withdraw and put some distance between themselves and their would-be attacker.

At nearly thirty miles an hour, the allosaurus crossed the plain to the dead sauropod quickly, but not quick enough. The killer appeared through the clouds and alighted gently beside its kill.

"Oh. My... Am I dreaming?" Alex breathed.

"Nope," Daniel replied, the smile on his face so wide it reached from ear to ear. "You finally got what you wanted, Alex."

"And this was inside Omskep all along," she nodded, her eyes sparkling. She watched as the beast tore up the dead sauropod. With a little effort, it bit through the base of the long neck and threw it at the allosaurus, the latter eagerly snatching it up. It ran off with its prize between its teeth, the ends hanging down and brushing the bushes as it disappeared into the trees. The trail of blood and gore caused other creatures, which Alex smilingly identified as deinonychus antirrhopus – the very large raptors of popular media – to come out of the trees, snatching and licking up any dropped morsels before following the allosaurus. A roaring, crashing noise indicated the allosaurus was not about to share and the raptors quickly exited, heading for the aurochs who were slowly reassembling. There were easier meals to be had!

Meanwhile, back on the plain, the aerial attacker used teeth and front claws to grip and lift the rest of the carcass into the sky. There, with great, lumbering flaps of its huge wings, it headed off to the mountains.

"Finally!" Alex sighed, and took off, Daniel quickly coming alongside.

"I guess that explains how the aurochs survived," he observed. Alex looked at him. "That dragon is smart. It knew the allosaurus needed food and it shared a very meaty chunk of its dinner. Probably flew over the allosaurus' nesting site and saw it had young. Looks to me like the dragons are farming the dinosaurs."

"Farming?"

"It didn't take one of the senior matriarchs. It identified a surplus male the herd could do without and then shared the kill with a beast that could help keep numbers down. After all, you don't want all the plant food to be eaten. That would kill the planet as surely as any extra-terrestrial event." He looked around. "I'm guessing this plain used to be a lot smaller, but the brachiosaurs and aurochs have slowly cleared it."

"No wonder the sauropods were more frightened of what came from above than below," she nodded. "Pretty horrible way to die, though!"

"Oh, I don't know. No method is clean, and the dragon and allosaurus have as much right to live as the herbivores. Needed, too, for a balanced and healthy ecology. I think the dragon killed it before it dropped it, anyway. The bellowing stopped rather suddenly. Dropping it guaranteed it was dead, the bones were broken, allowing access to what's inside for smaller teeth, and a ground dweller got a brief look at the view from above. Probably better than having your stomach ripped out or being burned to death."

"You think they can flame?" she asked, eagerly.

"I guess we'll find out."

The dragon had dragged its haul into a gap in the mountain, and Alex and Daniel quickly followed. Landing on a very flat, very well-cut ledge, they walked through an arch and stared.

"What the…? Daniel breathed.

"No way!" Alex agreed.

Chapter 4

Alex and Daniel stared at the clean, elegant, spiral pattern of dragon residences inside the mountain.

"These aren't dragon caves," Alex said at last, once she'd turned a full three-hundred-and-sixty degrees to take it all in. "This is a dragon apartment block!"

"And not made by dragons," Daniel added. "Those big claws couldn't do the fine work needed for that level of electronics." He pointed to a forcefield across the entrance to one of the caves.

For a moment, Alex feared that they were being held captive. Then one of them calmly pressed something, turning the field off, and walked inside, reactivating the field once they'd passed through.

"It's a hot day," Daniel nodded. "I'm laying odds those are designed to stop the heat inside the cave becoming oppressive."

"So, another species was once here, and the dragons took over their apartments?" Alex wondered.

Daniel pointed to the ledges, which were perfectly sized for the massive beasts.

"No. I think these were built for the dragons initially. The ledges are exactly the right size for a dragon to stretch out on if they want to laze in the sun."

Alex had noticed something going on in one corner and she went over. This, of course, forced Daniel to follow, but he wasn't disappointed.

"It's a classroom!" Alex cried delightedly. "But what are they using?"

She floated amongst the whelps. The very youngest had trays filled with damp sand, into which they were carefully inscribing the letters the teacher was demonstrating, which made sense. The older ones had something very different.

"OK," she said, staring at the tools being used. "I kinda get the supersized marker, but that's thicker than any paper I've ever seen, and it's not made of wood pulp."

"And the marker can be erased so that they can reuse it," Daniel commented, as one of the adolescents frowned at their work and did precisely that.

"These guys are very intelligent," Alex declared, "but still not capable of the stonework and electronics they're using."

"Whoever made this stuff is still around, too," Daniel added.

"Why do you say that?"

"Well, it's that, or they left yesterday. Everything is working. The dragons couldn't repair it, but it's all in perfect order. That means someone's maintaining it."

"The dragons have another species as a servant?" Alex replied, disappointed.

"Not necessarily. Until we find out who the other species is and see them interact, we won't know for sure."

Alex looked around. "Hang on. Where's the brachiosaurus gone? That's too big a meal for one of these." She spied an arch and a few tell-tale blood marks on one side. "There! Looks like they took it that way." She headed off, Daniel forced to reluctantly turn his back on the class.

"I wanted to find out what they were writing," he grumbled.

"Better ask Omskep to give us the language files, then," she suggested in a very practical tone. "You won't get anywhere without them."

By the time they arrived at the rather imposing entrance to what was clearly a palace structure, both of them had been given the means to understand the dragons. They walked inside.

Their path led down through a wide, clean, smooth tunnel, then opened out into a massive room, presently filled with dragons.

"Where's all that light coming from?" Alex wondered, noting the large circles in the ceiling. "We're right inside the mountain!" She went up to one of them and peered inside. "I'll be!"

"What?"

"Mirrors to redirect sunlight during the day, but there are also electric lights hidden in there for the evenings."

"Definitely another, much smaller species," Daniel said. "The dragons would struggle to get their claws into that space."

"Except for the very young ones," Alex nodded. "And while they're smart, they're not electronic engineers." She motioned to the parliament of dragons. "I think we should listen in, now we can."

They moved fully into the room and Alex walked through the dragons, who all had their backs to the entrance. Once in the middle of the group, she found it was a meeting. Off to one side was the carcass, presumably for the attendees once the meeting was over.

"Politicians get the treats, as usual!" Alex sighed.

"Nothing stopping the other fully grown dragons helping themselves," Daniel pointed out.

"Unless there are rules against it!"

"Why not wait and find out? You're assuming a lot."

"Because we've seen it over and over in other species," she explained.

"Even so, we don't know, so let's wait before we make any assumptions."

Alex tuned into the dragon conversation, which was taking place at a much lower pitch, even lower than that of the Djaroubi.

"Thank you, Carthak. If you and Brethik take the whelps out for their training, that'll give their parents a bit of a break for a few days!" There were chuckles and nods all round. "Prathak, how's Methik doing?"

"Seyuwenwi found him some tasks that allow him to feel wanted without putting the varn at risk," Prathak, a large green dragon, replied. "He wants to help, but he's so clumsy he causes disaster wherever he goes. This way, he feels proud of himself and the rest of us aren't constantly chasing after him to fix the mess!"

"But someone's keeping an eye on him, right?" the one who seemed to be in charge asked.

"Of course! Just not obviously."

"A pity his parents didn't allow a scan of the egg before he hatched. They might have been able to do something then," the leader sighed.

"It happens," Prathak shrugged. "Less often, of course. The records tell us that this was commonplace at the old Selesis varn, but now? Methik was just unlucky."

"Make certain he gets regular time at the lightning seams. I'm told that will help his muscle development." The other one nodded. "Right. Before we dig into that delicious lunch Garthik was kind enough to collect for us... The brachy herd. Can we help ourselves to a few more from there?"

"I think so," Garthik nodded. "The herd's getting large, and they've some healthy young. The older ones are a bit tough to eat, but I think it's time some of them were taken out to allow the younger ones a chance. No one here will object to some roasted meat for a change."

"The T-Rex?"

Where Alex had cocked her head at 'brachy', both she and Daniel jerked up sharply at that human term.

"I made certain it got the neck," Garthik assured the leader. "Should keep the young happy for a few days. The raptors are circling, though. I think we need to remind them of their limits again. We need a few more of the larger carnivores to keep the balance right."

"Ask some of the females to take a few of the raptors out. They're less likely to get clawed, given the raptors won't see them coming."

"Couldn't we just flame them?" one suggested.

"No," the leader replied sternly, shaking his head. "My ancestors were quite adamant about that. We only flame them when they're either attacking or we have no other choice. It's a horrible way to die and, while I agree they're a menace, they're only doing what they need to do in order to survive. The numbers are going up again, though, and we don't want them wiping out the buffalo. The whelps depend on those and, frankly, I like that meat, too! The varn won't object to raptor meat for a few weeks if it's spread out."

"If we could throw in a garga from time to time, they'll be very happy!" Prathak sighed.

"How are they doing?"

"We're finding very few, and those we do find are far too young and small to be taken," Prathak replied. "They've learned to stay away from the beaches, which is good for the whelps and the humans..." At that, both Alex and Daniel turned and stared at each other. "And our females have more chance of capturing them, because the instant they see our shadows on the water, they go down so deep we can't catch them, but there are so few of them. I don't understand it. We've deliberately avoided them, limiting our hunting to one every few months for a treat, but their numbers have dwindled almost to nothing. No bodies on the beaches; nothing in the water. It doesn't make any sense."

"Can Mara and her team give us any help explaining that?" another asked.

"No idea. Why don't *you* ask her?" Prathak said, a chuckle in his voice.

The leader gave the two a quelling look but seemed to find the comment equally amusing.

"I heard they've had some trouble with a big one attacking the underwater tunnel to Crada," Carthak said.

"Especially when one of us is aboard!" a female commented. "I took the trip last week to see my brother. I swear, the garga that attacked could have swallowed the entire train in one gulp! I have no desire to see that far down a garga's throat ever again! It takes longer, but next time I'm using the landing stages!"

"I wonder if the humans could persuade that one near enough to the surface for us to take it?" the leader wondered. "That would serve us and them."

"Been a while since we had a big feast," another nodded. "I think you'll be using a Darthyn Spear, though. A garga that big, the hole will be deep and well protected."

The leader looked at the female, who nodded solemnly.

"I'm not exaggerating, Darthak. Ask the humans to show you their recordings. It was huge! I'm not even sure a Darthyn Spear would be enough."

Darthak mulled for a moment. "If it's that big, perhaps it would be better to let the humans deal with it. We have more than enough creatures against whom we can pit our wits. Attacking something –"

"Several times the size of any one of us," the female supplied helpfully.

"Even bigger than the one King Darthyn took down?" Darthak asked.

"The humans still have the skull of that one preserved at Crada," the female nodded. "I've seen it. Bigger than that."

"Woah!" Carthak murmured in a low voice. "That really *is* a monster!"

"I'll talk to the humans," Darthak nodded. "Perhaps we can work together. If they can stun it enough and send it to the surface, we could finish the job and have it for the Inter-Continental."

There were grunts all round although, judging by the looks on some faces, even if it was stunned with human weapons or drugs, none of them were keen to take on the beast.

"The dragons are huge. How big must this garga be to scare them?" Alex wondered.

"Big enough to swallow a train, apparently."

"Yeah, but how big's the train?"

"Any other business?" Darthak asked.

"If you're going to talk to the humans, could you ask them to send one of their tech support to my cave?" Carthak asked. "The computer's acting up."

"You need to stop whacking the keyboard every time it frustrates you!" Darthak laughed. "Mine's still going strong. I'll be talking to Mara this afternoon, so I'll ask then. C'mon. Let's eat."

As the dragons descended on the brachiosaurus carcass, Alex and Daniel were left looking at them in bewilderment.

"Dragons using computers?" Daniel said, his tone expressing his astonishment.

"I'd like to see that, I must admit," Alex chuckled. "This is a remarkably civilised society," she continued. "You were right. I shouldn't have assumed."

"I'd like to see this garga they've got to face," he admitted.

"Sounds like we need to go to Crada, wherever that is, and check out the old skull. At least that'll give us an idea."

"Or we could just go underwater and look for it."

"Across the ocean? A rather large area to investigate, don't you think? Besides, while we're in one section, it could double back. We'll never find it." Alex pointed out.

"They said that they've some kind of underwater train that seems to attract it. Maybe we should find that?"

"I think we should follow Darthak to his meeting with the humans – assuming he's going immediately after lunch, and we have time?"

"Almega's still trying to persuade another world to cross over and intersect with this one," Daniel said after a pause while he checked. "He says we've plenty of time. Omskep is being a little stubborn."

"Tell Almega to thank Omskep for me!" Alex grinned. "After the last two trips, I'll enjoy taking a pause here. Plus, I want to learn more about these dragons and their life on this planet." She looked over at the feasting beasts. "While they're eating, why don't we explore?"

The two looked around, noting the tunnels that led off the open space. As the dragons were on the right, they headed to the first available tunnel on the left.

"Oh yes!" Alex cried, looking at the text carved into the walls. "Motherlode!"

Daniel read a few sections. "It's the archive recording the history of this varn. We should be able to get all the information we need in one hit."

Alex looked from one side to the other. "You take the right, I'll take the left. Bet I can beat ya!"

Using their talents as Eternals, it took them very little time to race down the tunnels, absorbing the information as they went. When they reached the section where King Warzak, his daughter, Princess Eyowenwi and her partner, Darthyn, from Crada varn, defeated Mazik and his pet raptors in battle, and then led the Selesian dragons to the new varn, Alex stepped back and whistled.

"Sounds like the sort of thing we'd do," she commented, pointing at the text. Daniel paused for a moment to read her side and then nodded.

"Certainly the sort of training we'd take," he agreed.

There was more to the archive, and the two continued their path along the records until they reached blank walls awaiting their inscriptions. Alex did get there first, but only just.

"Humans, from this universe, and aliens working together as equals," Daniel smiled. "It *is* possible!"

"Waste scales for the stuff the dragons need, plus a load of improvements. And the humans are quite advanced. Electricity providing lighting, long distance communications using in-ear speakers and mikes, forcefields to protect the dragons from the heat in the summer and wet during the rainy season, scanning of eggs to make sure the young are healthy, DNA correction if there's a problem..."

"Hence their sorrow that Methik's family didn't allow that," Daniel agreed.

"If he was brain damaged due to the egg being dropped or kicked early on, there might not have been much they could do beyond abort it. They don't lay many eggs, which means neither parent wanted to risk that."

"And neither wanted to admit being responsible for accidentally damaging it?"

"They might not have," she shrugged. "Sometimes, it just happens."

"But the varn is going out of its way to protect him and make sure he feels valued. That's an advanced social order right there," Daniel smiled.

Alex nodded. "An electronic 'pen' to carve the walls so that they can make their records easily even in the hardest rock, special paper that can be handled by dragons without tearing, but which is still biodegradable."

"No polluting energy sources, either. Everything here is dependent on high-quality solar panels hidden in the mountains with excellent batteries."

"Which they need, since it looks like quite a few dragons have computers now," she added. "Although they seem to be reserved for those who have an interest in being part of the leadership group." She jerked a thumb over her shoulder. "The dragons back there."

"And anyone can do that, provided they study, work hard and have proved to everyone's satisfaction that they care about the varn, not themselves. Plus, you can raise an issue directly with the leader. You don't have to go via intermediaries."

"Humans should do that with their politicians!"

"Plato advocated it," Daniel nodded, "but no one seems to have taken him up on the suggestion. I wonder if the humans ever loaned the dragons a copy of The Republic?"

"The dragons got there first," Alex grinned. She turned, taking in the vastness of the archive. "I really like this setup. Once we've fixed the Djaroubi and the holo-humans, we should come here for a vacation."

"Might be a little boring for us, given they've got everything running smoothly."

"I could stand a little boring in my trainings from time to time," Alex replied stubbornly. "We don't always have to be the characters who rush in and save the day!"

"We're not. We've been peasants, civilians on the home front, farmers, a couple of shopkeepers in Ancient Rome, office workers, IT support, ordinary soldiers, and teachers, amongst others. Yes, I've been a pharaoh and you've been a queen, but neither of us did much saving the day then, either. Most of what we do in trainings is run-of-the-mill, trying to figure out who we are and why we're here, or merely to pass the time. Every now and then we find something that we feel needs fixing and we go in and fix it, but as a percentage of our trainings it's small. Maybe one in every twenty or thirty?"

She stared at him. "I'm telling you that I want to do one here. Yes, after we've fixed the other stuff, but don't think I'll forget. I've wanted to live with dragons for as long as I can remember. I don't know why, and it doesn't make sense, but I fell in love with them. When I found out from Almega that there were none in the entire universe, I can't tell you how disappointed I was."

There was a catch in her voice. Daniel reached out, then pulled his hand back when he remembered he couldn't offer any physical comfort. She gave him a half-hearted smile for his efforts.

"But now Fortan's opened this up. Being an idiot, of course, but it's still a good thing. I've had some incredible trainings, but this was my dream. Can I have my dream? Please?"

"Absolutely," he assured her. "When we've done what has to be done, we'll come straight back here. I'll book it with Almega the instant we get you out of here."

A smile, wide and bright lit up her face and Daniel found himself glowing inside.

"Yes!" She punched the air. "Let's go check out the rest of the palace!"

***

They walked through the large room once more and noted the dragons were about halfway through their meal.

"We are quick, aren't we?" Alex said.

"And they're slow eaters," Daniel returned.

They headed into another tunnel and found the private rooms that King Darthak and his partner, Queen Hyawenwi used. In one of them was a computer whose bulk would have filled most human living rooms. The keyboard was as long as Daniel was tall, but there were only a small number of buttons. One of them, Alex noted, was 'print'. She looked around and spotted a large thermal printer against the side of the room.

"A dragon computer," Alex nodded, imagining Darthak working at it.

"With a verbal and, I think, eye-tracking command interface," Daniel said, pointing to the headset suspended from the ceiling.

"Makes sense. I can't see a dragon getting much beyond hunt and peck typing methods!"

Another room, that was now empty, looked like it had been used as a nursery.

"I remember this from the archive!" Alex cried. "The more recent reports said that their whelps, a male and a female, have recently been sent to Crada to make connections with that varn."

118

"The two varns have definitely merged here," Daniel nodded. "The names are a dead giveaway on that front, but their leadership structure too. They've blended Selesian and Crada approaches into a democratic monarchy that works remarkably well. It's still hereditary, but the young are trained and disciplined so that they know they have a duty, not a privilege."

"And whatever they gave Eyowenwi to fix her leg seems to have become part of the royal genes," Alex added. "They always have twins. Unusual for these dragons. It's amazing there are so many of them given all but the royals only lay one egg. Some don't have offspring at all."

"But they live a very, very long time," Daniel said. "If they bred the way humans or most other species do, Mithgryr would be overrun. If the numbers got too low, I'm sure the humans could increase their birth rate, but the royals always have an heir and a spare and then choose which one is most skilled, works hardest, and shows the greatest dedication to the varn. Darthak was the second of the two to stick his head out of the egg he and his brother came in, but his brother, the one who captured the brachiosaurus –"

"Garthik," Alex provided.

"Yes. He was more interested in exploration and training the young in survival techniques. Not that Darthak's a slouch in those departments, but he's better at the diplomacy, record keeping and that sort of thing. Garthik finds the latter, in particular, incredibly tedious."

"I'm with Garthik," she nodded.

"Both of them also did their time on Crada, where Darthak proved to have a knack for picking up the ancient languages and spent a lot of his time in the Crada archive."

"And Garthik?"

"He learned how to hunt and take down garga."

"Those things again. We really need to get over there and take a look."

Daniel grunted his agreement, and they exited the quarters. The dragons were almost finished, so they hurried into the last tunnel.

"What is this?" Daniel wondered, looking around.

The room was dark with a very flat, round, white area on the floor. Above it, Alex noted a lens in the ceiling. At that moment, they heard Darthak.

"I'll just check the humans aren't out exploring. Be right back!"

He lumbered in and an image of the valley was instantly projected onto the floor.

"Computer, zoom in on the human camp," Darthak said aloud in English. The image instantly shifted, showing humans young and old around and inside a camp with electrified fences. A few were armed, keeping an eye on the local fauna, but it appeared that the carnivores had learned to avoid these small creatures with powerful weapons, and the guards looked relaxed. A few more were in towers, watching further afield.

"It's the camera obscura!" Alex crowed. "Warzak mentioned this in his part of the record. He used to love coming here and watching what was happening. Some of his paintings were based on what he saw in this room!" She noted Daniel's blank expression. "My side of the archive," she explained.

"Ahh! King Warzak was an artist?"

"A very good one. His work was auctioned on Earth for exorbitant prices. The humans thought they were based on his views while flying over his land, but most of the aerial ones were done in here."

"Clever dragon!"

"Computer," Darthak said. "Contact Mara."

"Hey, Darthak," came a voice out of a speaker in the wall. "I'm glad you called. How may I help you?"

"Is it all right for me to pop by for a visit? I hear you have a problem with a giant garga, and we'd be interested in helping."

"Very much so. I was going to contact you on that very matter. Besides, you're always welcome," the friendly voice replied. "You know that!"

"Oh, and Carthak's broken his computer again."

"We'll have to make him a steel keyboard!" Mara laughed. "I'll see what we can do. Our technician will need a lift to the varn."

"I'll take him back with me. Carthak can return him to you when he's done. It's the least he can do by way of payment."

"Fair enough. I'll be waiting for you."

The call was ended. With a chuckle, Darthak left the room and, a few seconds later, the obscura switched itself off.

"Motion detectors by the door," Daniel commented as they followed Darthak out of the room and then through the long tunnel leading to the outside.

"I wonder if that's for everyone or just Darthak," Alex said as they passed through the main bowl. When Daniel raised an eyebrow at the non sequitur, she added, "The camera obscura. I was wondering if it turns on as soon as it detects any dragon or only Darthak."

"I'm getting the impression of a very open but respectful society," Daniel replied after giving the question due thought. "I think it would activate for anyone passing through that doorway, it's just that most don't invade the King's private spaces. They stick to the main room."

"Dangerous if someone had it in for the varn."

"A good thing they don't have to worry about that, then."

Several dragons gave Darthak respectful nods which he returned in kind. He paused to chat to a few, listened to their problems and then used his comms to contact others who came to help resolve whatever was causing the issue. He passed through the opening in the mountain that marked the entrance to the varn, opened his massive wings and dropped off the ledge, Alex and Daniel flying alongside him. Sneakily, Alex positioned herself so that it looked like she was sitting on Darthak's back.

"Tch, tch!" Daniel scolded. "Getting a lift from a dragon is an honour. They're not a taxi service."

"They are for whoever's fixing their computers," she pointed out.

"You would have thought they'd have installed an elevator so that the humans could get in and out on their own," he mused. "Instead, they demean themselves becoming a transport service."

"I think that's part of the deal, keeping the dragons and the humans separate. An elevator would allow the humans to go in and out of the varn whenever they wanted, instead of whenever the dragons wanted." She floated off Darthak's back. "I so want a picture of that!"

"Now that you've done it, I'm sure Almega can pull it from the program."

"And *that's* why I did it!" she smiled.

Darthak banked, circled, and dropped down to land in front of the gates of the compound, where he politely waited until one of the guards urged him inside.

"Mara's waiting for you in her office," the guard told him as Darthak, with his invisible entourage, walked into the human camp. He made a beeline for a particular building and very carefully tapped on the door. With his huge size, his light tap was a very loud thud. A few moments later, a redhead emerged, smiling.

"Hey, Darthak," she said. "I guessed you'd want to see the footage we got of that giant garga."

"Yes, please."

She activated a device in her hand and an image appeared. "This was the latest in a number of attacks. When we were told how big the thing was, we put holo-cameras inside the train tunnel to catch it all."

There was murky darkness for a while and then something huge attacked the tunnel. Mara froze the holo-film and ran it back to just before the garga opened its giant maw, so it was in full view. "We did measurements based on those markers we put in the tunnel to gauge size." She tapped the image and it morphed to show this new creature beside a dragon. The garga's mouth was easily big enough to swallow the dragon whole in two bites.

"That thing is *huge!*" Alex gasped.

"Length is a bit harder to estimate because the cameras didn't capture it all," Mara continued, "but based on the head to body-length correlations of ordinary garga, this appears to be around four dragon lengths."

"By the stars!" Darthak breathed. "None of us can take on such a beast!"

"No," Mara agreed. "However, we're hoping you'd be happy to eat it. Especially with the Inter-Con this week?"

"Hmm," he grunted, still staring at the size comparison.

"We can't leave it out there," she continued. "At that size and with nothing left in the ocean to get rid of it, the stench would quickly become horrendous, and its rotting corpse would poison the water for miles. We don't have the equipment here on Mithgryr to fetch it back to the coast, which means we need dragon help."

"How did it grow to be that big?" Darthak wondered, pointing to the hologram in which the representation of the dragon, which appeared to be him, looked like a toy next to the garga.

"We think that this might be the very same garga that Darthyn and Eyowenwi reported attacking the train tunnel when it was first built. It's now several hundred years older and, as you can see, still going strong. Dragons are a vital ecological tool to deal with these but, for centuries, your species lost the talent to take them, and they got out of control. The problem with the garga is that, once they grow to this size, there is literally nothing on the planet that can kill them outside a submarine volcanic eruption, and that will only work if they're on top of it when it blows. We've also got evidence that this thing is eating all the fish and has now turned cannibal."

"That would explain why fewer garga are being caught by our hunting groups," Darthak nodded. "We thought we had hunted them too much."

"It's definitely not you," she assured him, "and it has to be removed before it does irrevocable damage to the marine ecology. That would have a devastating effect on Mithgryr's ecology as a whole. At the moment it's contained within the waters between here and Crada, but it's running out of food and will be forced to explore the seas on the other side of the continents."

"How do you plan to do this?" Darthak asked. Alex and Daniel leaned closer because they were equally interested in the answer.

"It seems to be attracted by the train's vibrations. We've paused all trains passing to and from Crada until this is dealt with. As it attacks closer to the Selesian end of the tunnel, we're taking point on this, but Crada is helping with supplies. To maintain the train tunnel, we have mini submarines with articulated mechanical hands that allow operators to effect repairs. We're using some of those to install torpedoes in and around the area it typically attacks. When we're ready, we'll send an empty train down the line to get its attention. When it attacks again, we'll let loose with a salvo of torpedoes."

"You're using human weapons, then?"

"In part. We didn't want to, and we were going to ask the dragons if they could deal with it directly, but this size? No. It has to be torpedoes."

"Will there be anything left for the feast?" Darthak asked, his tone depressed.

"Ahh, that's the bit where we think you can come in. These torpedoes aren't loaded with massive explosive warheads. Instead, they have two components. One is a tranquilliser. The idea is to get the garga groggy enough that it can't fight back too hard. The other is an inert gas that will be injected into the body to bring it to the surface. If this works, the dragons can make repeated attacks with larger versions of Darthyn's Spear until one of them hits its mark." Darthak looked uncomfortable with the idea. "I know, it's cheating, but no dragon could defeat this as it is, not even Darthyn, and it has to be removed. We could use heavy yield explosives, but we really don't want to introduce such weapons to Mithgryr even once. Plus, they would obliterate the garga, sending rotting bits of carcass onto all the beaches for months. If it hadn't already decimated the rest of the garga population, they'd clean it up, but there aren't enough big ones left in this area to deal with this. With rotting flesh attracting insects and mould, we'd have to bring in other human solutions to deal with *that*..." She made a circular motion with her hand.

"I understand," Darthak nodded. "Even so, many of the dragons would consider your use of drugs to undermine the garga's ability to fight an example of cheating."

"Using a Darthyn Spear is also cheating," she pointed out. "If you want to be a purist, anything shy of taking this thing on directly and losing many dragons in the fight would be cheating." She restored the comparative images of garga and dragon and pointed. "Do you really think you can take this on without it being drugged? If you can, we'll drive it to the surface and let you deal with it."

"I don't," he admitted, "and we were going to ask you to stun it, so I shouldn't be complaining. Will the drugs affect the meat?"

She shook her head. "We've some that will have the desired effect, but they then disintegrate without leaving a trace." She looked slightly uncomfortable. "It's based on something used against enemy combatants in wars on Earth. We know it has no effect on humans and we've triple-checked to make certain it can't hurt dragons. If one of you somehow managed to get a mouthful of the stuff neat and undigested, you'd feel queasy and sleep well, that's it, but within thirty minutes it dissolves no matter where it is. That means that once it's on the surface, you'll have around twenty minutes to take it down. That's allowing for its ascent from the bottom."

"And it won't just explode when it leaves the depths?"

She shrugged. "Never seen one do that. They have ways to combat the effects of sudden decompression. A bit of evolutionary genius we're envying, I must admit."

"I need to talk to the varn," Darthak declared. "If I gave you a lift, could you bring a larger version of this," and he pointed to the floating hologram, "to them and show them what we're up against?"

"This," and Mara indicated the small tablet she was holding, "can blow the video footage and holographic comparisons up to life-size. I can put your entire varn inside the tunnel so they can see it for themselves, to scale."

"Excellent. When?"

"Right now, if you want."

"When do you plan to attack the garga?"

She flicked the tablet to some readouts.

"The last of the torpedoes is being put into position as we speak. If you say no, we'll have to swap them out for warheads, which will take another seven moons or so, and then try and figure out a way to clean up the mess, though I've no idea how. If you say yes, we can go tomorrow."

Darthak cocked his head at Mara.

"You assumed that we would say yes and prepared without asking us," he pointed out, a low growl in his tone.

"I was about to when you called. I don't like to keep dragons waiting, and we all know that you like garga meat, so it seemed likely you'd want to be a part of this. We're used to delays, but we know that once you've made up your mind, you want to get on with it." She tapped the tablet. "We got this footage a few weeks ago. We've been working on the best solution ever since, and we knew that if we didn't include the dragons, you'd be angry. Assuming dragon support seemed the most politic approach to take. I'm sorry if we overstepped the mark."

"Hmm." The dragon slowly nodded his mighty head. "Perhaps, in such matters, it would be wise for us to learn more patience! If the varn had learned of this beast when you got the footage, I've no doubt word would have got out. Then some group of young bucks keen to prove their courage would have set out to taunt it without the first idea what they were truly up against, and we'd be mourning them all by now. You have probably saved dragon lives, and for that I am grateful. However, in future I would prefer it if you alerted me immediately to such problems. I can keep it to myself perfectly well."

"Noted. Do you think you'll be able to persuade Garthik to be a little less reckless this time?"

"If I wish my brother to sit beside me at the feast, as opposed to becoming one for the garga, I have no choice." He paused, considering what he'd seen. "I'm not sure even a Darthyn Spear would be enough for this. Do you have something we can use?"

Mara nodded. "One of the other things we've been working on. If the varn's in agreement, your hunters can come down and collect the weapons this evening." She noted Darthak's expression. "Only four with any explosive capacity. From a few other bits of grainy footage that we got as the garga swam away, the back of its head is surrounded by accretions, and they're quite deep. They'll need to be blown away so that you can get at your target. The rest of the spears are the old-fashioned variety of which Darthyn would have approved. It's the same spring-loaded approach, just with better springs that can be fired repeatedly, and the spears are separate rather than attached. We didn't want any of you to be stuck unable to escape because the spear got caught."

"Thank you for that," he said. "I'm happy to present this to the varn, if you are?"

"In that case, let me see if Akira has managed to finish Carthak's new keyboard. I spoke to him after your call, and he assured me that he had already prepared most of it, ready for the next time Carthak managed to break his. He should almost be finished. Ahh!"

Darthak and the Eternals turned to see a young man emerging from another building.

"Can I have some help?" he called as he struggled under the weight of the oversized keyboard. "This thing's heavy."

Darthak muttered a word and then spoke more clearly. "Carthak? Would you please come to the compound and help Akira with your new keyboard? He can't manage it and I need to bring Mara back to the varn. She has something to show us all." He nodded at the response he received in his ear and muttered the word again.

"Some kind of verbal on-off switch for the comms," Daniel commented. "Makes sense."

"You wouldn't want private conversations broadcast across the varn," Alex agreed.

"Carthak is coming down so that we can carry the pair of you and that keyboard back," he informed Mara.

She looked at Akira who nodded. "We'll get our harnesses," she said, and hurried back inside.

***

"OK they've more guts than I have as a mortal!" Alex commented as the dragons carried the humans hanging from straps around the dragon's necks back to the varn. The straps were attached to harnesses that the humans wore on their backs. Their legs dangling in midair, the humans seemed unfazed by the precipitous drop, showing total faith in their dragon carriers and their equipment. Akira's view was slightly impeded by the keyboard that Carthak carried in his front paws, but the dragon was careful not to let his prize wallop his passenger.

They arrived at the ledge and Darthak motioned that Cathak should go first. Carthak carefully took position above an indent in the mountainside that appeared to have been created precisely for this purpose. The platform here had a strong fence surrounding it. Akira pressed a button on his harness and lowered himself to the platform while his dragon maintained his position with great sweeps of his wings. Akira then released his harness and dropped a foot or so to the ground. The straps that had held him to Carthak were sucked into the backpack as Akira walked inside via a small side tunnel, followed by Carthak through the main entrance, proudly carrying his shiny new keyboard and grinning. The same process was repeated for Mara.

Once inside, Carthak led Akira across the floor of the varn to his cave. As he was on the second level, Akira had to climb up a slope, but he seemed happy with the arrangement and, with long strides, quickly reached the cave and disappeared inside.

While that minor matter was being dealt with, Darthak called a meeting of the fighting members of the varn. Much to the Eternals' delight, this included many females.

Darthak whispered his 'mike on' phrase, and then carefully placed one foot on a stone, which depressed. Now his voice rang out across the area easily, while he spoke in his normal voice.

"We have a problem with a garga. It is eating all the other garga that we might enjoy, and every other creature of the deep. Its size is greater than even that which Darthyn faced so many turns ago, so I have decided we should work with the humans to defeat this threat." There were mutterings around the varn. It seemed the dragons felt their courage and ability was being denigrated. Darthak raised a paw. "I know. I felt the same way until I saw what we faced. I have asked Mara to show you the film the humans took from the train tunnel." This seemed to cheer up the disgruntled dragons. Films were, it seemed, rather popular in the varn.

Mara, looking very tiny amongst so many massive beasts, walked to the middle of the open space and switched on her tablet. The image appeared and she zoomed it several times until it filled nearly half the bowl.

"This is lifesize," Darthak explained as the holo-video began to run. "You are inside the train tunnel that runs between here and Crada." Again, the murky darkness and then...

"Woah!" several cried, one almost falling over backwards as it tried to get out of the way of the holographic beast.

"Do we all agree this is not a beast that we can take on alone?"

The image of the garga next to a dragon was blown up until the dragon was the same size as Darthak. Many of the watching dragons had their mouths open in shock.

"Agreed!" several shouted.

Next to her, Alex overheard one mutter in dragon tongue, "I wouldn't go near that thing without help if my life depended on it! That's insane!"

"The humans are placing projectiles along the tunnel where the beast strikes. All train communications between Crada and Selesis are on hold until the garga is removed. The projectiles contain two things. One is a drug to make the beast dopey enough for us to have a chance. It will not kill it," he emphasized. "That is *our* job!" There were some muted agreements. With the size measurement still floating in the air, some were wondering whether they would have a chance even then. "The second will force gas into the beast to drive it to the surface so that we can get at it."

"Darthak," Garthik said, climbing onto another platform and operating the speaker for himself. "A Darthyn Spear will not be long enough to penetrate this beast's brain. How are we to take it down? Are we to try and tear it to pieces?"

130

"Mara informs me that they can offer us something even more powerful. Provided we can get our claws over the hole at the back of the garga's head, we can fire it and it will penetrate. We will all be so armed so that we can make several attempts and, due to the risks, instead of a retracting spear, these are separate. We will not be trapped by our weapon against the beast's head."

"What about the growth around the hole?" Garthik pressed. "With something this age, that will be like rock and hard to break through."

Mara trotted over to Darthak and said something. He nodded and straightened.

"A small number of the spears will have some explosive – Mara tells me they are no larger than the smaller fireworks they display at their New Turn celebrations that we all enjoy. The humans think it should be enough to blow that away." There were growls from many of the surrounding dragons. "If this were a normal garga, we would not need it but, on this occasion – and since we are not in competition with another dragon – I believe we may be excused using a little extra human ingenuity. We are not going out there to prove a point about our courage or skill. We are going to remove a threat to the whole of Mithgryr. Under such circumstances, refusing human tools is foolish. In addition, our time to attack is quite limited."

"How limited?" Garthik asked warily.

"Less than half an arn," Darthak replied. "After that, the drugs will start wearing off, the gas will dissipate, and our quarry will be able to fight back with force or sink below the waves."

"How did Mara know what the problem was?" Alex wondered. "Human ears wouldn't hear most of this."

"She's got an earpiece in," Daniel replied. He'd been watching the human leader and noted the way she occasionally pressed on her right ear. "I assume it's connected to a translation program that's probably running on that small box on her belt." He pointed.

"Ahh. And an arn is the dragon equivalent of an hour?"

"More or less. They never used to bother, but interacting with humans so much, they needed more fine-tuned temporal measurements than morning, afternoon and evening." Alex raised an eyebrow. "My side of the archive," he explained.

"I know," Darthak said as the members of the varn expressed their horror. "It's a very limited time, but I'm prepared to lead the attack if any would care to follow me?"

"No!" Garthik cried. "You are the King! We cannot risk you. *I* will lead the attack."

"I no more wish to risk my brother than myself," Darthak replied.

One of the females stepped up and asked Garthik to stand aside. Reluctantly, he ceded his position so that she could be heard.

"With all due respect, Darthak," she began.

"Uh oh," Alex chuckled. "He's in for it now!"

"You are a fair garga hunter, not a great one. Frankly, you would get in our way."

"Geiriss..." Darthak began.

"By all means come to watch, but we would all feel safer if you stayed out of our way!"

There was laughter and nods of agreement.

"As King, I cannot ask you to do what I will not do myself!"

"We do not doubt your courage, and you're not asking, we're volunteering." She looked around the group. "Right?" There were more nods, this time sombre and determined. Several took a step forward, signifying their status as volunteers. Others followed until the entire group had taken the step, each one of them holding their heads high. Geiriss turned back to Darthak. "And, if anything should happen to any of us, then knowing that you are here, watching over and protecting those we love will give us peace. You are a great leader, Darthak, but only a fair hunter. You do your job well. Please, let us do ours." Darthak hung his head, clearly unhappy with the decision. Geiriss turned to Mara. In English she asked, "When will you need us?"

"The torpedoes are ready when you are," Mara replied solemnly.

"Where?"

Mara tapped her tablet and an image of the planet appeared before them. She zoomed in until they could see the target area, several miles from the coast and circled on the map.

"The garga attacks the train here. It's deep water and there's a continental shelf about thirty dragon-lengths away. We think that may be where it lives."

Daniel leaned down. "Just over half a mile away."

"Thank you," Alex replied, honest enough to admit that she struggled a little with spatial measurements. "It can probably feel the vibrations caused by the train and comes out to complain about the noise!"

"Or, since it's seen dragons inside from time to time, that this would be good eating if only it could break through. Especially now it's eaten everything else."

"That's one very wide, very long train."

Daniel nodded. "The tunnel must be at least the width of a six-lane motorway. Quite a feat of engineering."

"As an Underground for dragons?"

He shook his head. "I suspect it's used more for the transport of scales and equipment, with occasional dragon guests. It would make sense. Crada is a two-day journey by air for a dragon. I gather the train does it in a matter of a few hours. They can literally go to Crada, attend a meeting, and be back in Selesis varn in time for supper."

She cocked her head at him. "Your side again?"

"Um hmm."

"It'll take us an arn to get there from here," Garthik commented. "Around half that if we gather near Padzak Rock." He pointed to a spot on the coast where a small isthmus of land ended in a rock big enough for a couple of dragons to lie on if they curled their tails around themselves. "If you alert us the instant you detect the garga..."

"We have sensors. We'll know the moment it's coming into range. At that depth, and assuming our torpedoes hit their mark, it'll take it under a quarter arn to be forced to the surface."

"And it'll fight not to do that," Geiriss added. "That'll tire it and give us more time."

"We can stay circling for at least four arns if necessary. It's boring and we want to be as alert and strong as possible when we attack, so we don't want to be out there for that long if we can help it," Garthik commented. "How long after the train departs until it reaches this point?"

"Around a third of an arn," Mara replied.

Garthik gave a firm nod. "In that case, let us know the instant the train departs. We'll set off from Padzak Rock then."

"What happens if the torpedoes miss?" Geiriss asked.

"Then it'll take us a few days to reset to try again," Mara replied.

"I suggest we collect our weapons from the compound, do some practice so that we all feel comfortable with them, and then all get a good night's sleep," Garthik said loudly. "Don't eat heavily. We'll need to be light and manoeuvrable, not weighed down with dinner." There were nods all round and the dragons set off to collect their armaments and, perhaps, find some small meal to keep them going until the next day.

Darthak watched them go, then leaned down to Mara.

"The torpedoes won't miss, will they?" His tone suggested he knew full well what the human weapons were capable of.

"No," she admitted. "They've got sonar and other sensors to keep them on track. Every one of them will hit its mark."

"Any danger one might come out of the water and find a dragon?"

She shook her head. "One, they don't have air capabilities. Two, all your dragons have comm units. Anything wearing one of those will be rejected as a target. They've also got a distance limitation. If they go more than a mile and don't find their target, they'll automatically return to their launch point."

"Thank you for not mentioning that," he grunted.

"Of course."

"Neither side wants human superiority advertised," Alex commented thoughtfully. "That would explain Mara comparing the charges on the spears to fireworks – something associated more with entertainment than destruction. If the dragons knew the true power of human weapons it would change the balance of power."

"Darthyn was aware of it," Daniel said. "Eyowenwi also made an oblique comment on it in the archives, and we can see Darthak knows full well the dangers, but they don't advertise it publicly or in the records. That's probably because the varn archives are open to all."

"So long as the bulk of the dragons are unaware that the humans could wipe them out easily, they're equals. As soon as the dragons realise that they're hopelessly outmatched, even if the humans continue to behave themselves, there'll be a sense of being under a cloud and there on sufferance, which would be unforgivable to the dragons." She glanced at Daniel. "My side, although only if you read between the lines and already know about human weapons. A normal dragon unaware of such things wouldn't interpret it that way."

"They've both signed a very carefully worded treaty," Daniel added. "If the humans ever start throwing their weight around, they have to leave, permanently. That keeps them in check."

"Whoever helped with that did a good job, then," she nodded.

"A Crada leader, Gorthan, and a diplomat and teacher from Selesis, Padzak, together with Darthyn and Eyowewi," he explained. "My side!"

"Ahh! Padzak's Rock. That explains it. He must have hung out there at some time." She sighed. "I wish we could just merge our memories the way we usually do."

"Eh," he shrugged. "We're managing. It's not ideal, but between us we can do it."

"A good thing it was you and not Gracti," she replied, referring to the Eternal famous for her careless attitude to just about everything.

"Hmm. Or Hentric?"

"Don't!" she cried, raising her hand and waving it away. "Just... Don't!" The thought of the practical joker of the Eternals being involved in this was too horrifying for Alex to contemplate.

"Looks like there'll be nothing else happening until tomorrow morning. How about we fly over to Crada, take a look at the garga head there and see what the fuss is about?" he suggested.

"The holofilm was quite scary enough," she replied, "but yes. Besides, since their great leader, Darthyn, came from there, I'd be interested to read their archive."

"Uh, Eyowenwi was the leader," Daniel said as they shot into the sky. "Darthyn was the warrior but left the ruling to her. And you're assuming Crada is as diligent in recording their history as Selesis."

"Darthyn took over after Eyowenwi's death, until one of his offspring was ready to take over completely," she corrected. "Which means he did both. And I get the impression the dragons on Mithgryr are keen to record everything."

***

136

"Yeah, I wouldn't want to face even this one tired and hungry," Alex said as she stood in the shadow of the huge garga skull that stood beside the entrance to the human compound on Crada. It was encased in some kind of weather-proof, transparent substance, akin to Perspex but much tougher and capable of withstanding being knocked by a brachiosaurus.

"And this is small compared to what they're up against," Daniel said on a low whistle. He walked around to the back and pointed. "That's the hole they have to get the spears through."

Alex joined him. "It'll be larger on the bigger beast, but not by much. That's a very small target." She stepped back, taking in the entire head, which towered over her. "And Darthyn took this one down on his own. I'm impressed."

"They usually use their claws in the hole, but the garga build up a protective surround that gets thicker and deeper as they get older," Daniel commented, pointing to the growth on the back of the skull. "That makes it much harder. In the new one, that protection will probably be around a foot deep by now. Perhaps more. No wonder they need the fireworks."

A dragon flew overhead, heading for a spent volcano. "The Crada varn looks to be over there," Alex said. "Shall we?"

They set off in pursuit.

When they arrived, the first thing they noticed was that this was a far more rustic affair than the Selesian varn.

"This was dug out by dragons," Alex commented as they looked around. "Humans built Selesis after the dragons were forced to abandon their original varn because there were no lightning seams. Here, this is the original. Thousands upon thousands of years' worth of dragons hewing the rock with their own claws."

"Not as sleek as the Selesian varn."

"No, but more dragon, less human. I like it. Sort of like the difference between a new apartment block and a

Tudor building. The apartment block has all the fancy new additions to make life easier, but they've no character." She looked around. "Hard to spot which one is the leader, though."

Daniel glanced off to the side and asked Almega, then turned back. "Almega says it's one of those three up there," he pointed.

The two floated up and, after a little exploration, found the leader's cave.

"Ooh, I like the natural lighting," Alex commented as sunlight was replaced with the phosphorescent glow of some natural fungi.

Daniel had found the Archive.

"This one's in a slightly different language to Selesis, but they've a common root. Ready?"

"Ready!"

Again, they raced each other through the archive, which was much more meandering than Selesis and, when they reached the more recent tunnels, they noticed that they had been dug below the earlier ones, doubling back around the bowl of the volcano. As they neared the end it was to find a Crada dragon carefully scratching the most recent reports into the rock with her claw.

"Pyrutha, are you down there?" a voice called.

"Where else would I be?" the female called back. "Come in, Mathyn." She paused in her work, checking what she'd carved, then turned in the tunnel to face the reddish dragon who'd just arrived.

"What can I do for you?"

As the two dragons discussed training schedules for the whelps, and what sounded like a case of typical teenage rebellion that was causing upset, Alex and Daniel shared what they'd learned.

"Crada is a lot more traditional than Selesis," Alex commented. "The humans have offered to dig their tunnels for them and give the leader the electric pen to carve the walls, but they've insisted on sticking to the old ways."

"They were the first dragons the humans met," he nodded. "That encounter did *not* go well."

"Humans being idiots, or dragons?"

"Humans, but then the dragons began to think they'd win a fight and things got within a..." he glanced over at the chatting dragons, "a dragon's scale of all-out war. Somehow, and I don't know how, it was resolved and they got over it." He looked at her, but she shook her head.

"Not on my side."

"Hmm. Seems to have been deliberately glossed over. Strange." He shrugged. "Anyway, in general, the humans stay down on the plain and the dragons mind their own business. Pyrutha has regular meetings with the present leader of the humans, though. A man called Lucas. And no," he added when he saw Alex's look, "since the dragons don't use last names, there is none provided. He's a fully qualified doctor and has fixed a few injuries caused by raptors on the younger dragons, as well as helping the older ones with the pains of living such a long time, which makes him a welcome visitor. From time to time, they work together on projects: exposing more of the lightning seams, providing support in exploration when the dragons find something new, and in negotiations over medications and trade with the Great Desert dragons, who are very insular."

"The youngsters see challenging a pack of raptors as a rite of passage, which I guess makes sense. A good thing they'll never run out of the lightning seams, given how important the digestion of the rock is to create dragon fire and for general health." Now it was Daniel's turn to cock his head. "The new Selesis varn has more than it knows what to do with, and the humans have analysed it. They can now provide an equivalent that the dragons find quite tasty with a good flame. It's a natural consequence of seismic activities on Mithgryr, though, so new veins do grow if they're left alone long enough. A big seam was also found during the excavation of the lower archive."

"Ahh!" he nodded.

"There's another archive in an abandoned varn," Alex said. "They found it during the time of Gorthan and Darthyn. Should we take a look at that one?"

"I think we've probably got enough. The key events that have affected this planet are included in the Crada Archives. The rest is the very early history of the dragons before humans came on the scene, and we read quite a bit of that in here. Of interest to the dragons, undoubtedly, but for us I suspect it would be rather akin to reading diaries from the Stone Age. Are we likely to want to visit so far back?"

"Probably not," she admitted. "From what I've read so far, it seems pretty much the same problems over and over, and we can download it in Oestragar when I get back anyway." She took a deep breath and let it out with a whoosh. "We've hours before the attack on the garga. How about we check out what's happening in the human compound?"

"Or you could step inside a dragon and see what it's like?"

Her eyes glinted. "Not this one," she declared, pointing at Pyrutha. "Too important and she's not outside. I need one free to fly."

They exited the archives, floating upwards through the rock until they reached the lip of the old volcano. Alex led the way to the old varn and the two were suitably impressed by the mass of fungi that hung from the roof, lighting up the cavern like chandeliers. A couple of dragons were in there, exploring the older archives, and a few were taking the opportunity for a quiet nap in the caves, but none were eager to go for a flight. Returning to the main varn, they watched until Alex identified a female about to go out hunting.

"If I sit in the back of her mind, she won't know I'm there and I'll get to see the world through her eyes."

Quickly, Alex got inside the female, positioning herself so that she was aware of everything through the senses of the dragon, without impeding her. Zayenthi, with Alex aboard, opened her wings and Alex could feel the muscles tense ready for the all-important down stroke. Then they were off. Zayenthi quickly topped the crater and headed out across the forest that surrounded the mountains and then down towards the plains. There, she hovered, checking out the menu. Nothing seemed to particularly appeal, so she went westward towards the sea.

"I think she's going for garga!" Alex crowed to Daniel, who was floating alongside.

"Hopefully, nothing too large," he replied.

"No. She seems quite confident of getting what she wants easily. That beast clearly hasn't been decimating this side of the ocean yet."

"It's a big ocean," he allowed.

Alex, looking through Zayenthi's eyes, could see a few smaller garga that wouldn't have been a major threat even to an adult human, 'though they might have given them a nasty bite. Zayenthi continued to fly out across the waves, occasionally looking back to make certain that the land was still in sight. Finally, she settled on an area and looked carefully into the depths. Seeing nothing, she lowered herself, circling and watching intensely until a dim glint of movement under the surface caught her eye. She rose, circled again, dropped down and let one leg drag in the water briefly before quickly ascending. This tease was offered several times before a decent sized garga took the bait. It leapt from the depths, barely missing Zayenthi's leg. She wheeled and dove, her talons sinking into the flesh that was trying to disappear back into the water. Holding on, she dragged it backwards through the waves towards shallower water. The garga tried to curl around and get at her but, being buffeted by the waves and occasionally shaken by the alert dragon, it kept being stalled.

Once in the shallower water, Zayenthi released it, circled around and, as the garga tried to force its way back into deeper water, she descended and stuck a claw into the hole at the back of its head. Blood instantly coloured the water, turning the formerly white wave crests pink. The struggles continued for a short while, then died down, then stopped.

Zayenthi still hovered, watching.

"What's wrong?" Daniel asked.

"Nothing wrong," Alex replied. "She's simply making certain it's dead."

Sure enough, as Zayenthi closed ready to retrieve her prize, the garga reared up one last time, it's mouth open and teeth bared, but it was a weak effort that the dragon easily dodged. The garga flopped into the lapping waves, mouth open, eyes unseeing.

Inside her head, Alex could feel the thrill of the hunt that had coursed through her host slowly ebb to be replaced with satisfaction. There was enough here for her, her partner and their whelp, and she could use the head to teach her son the trick with garga. Not that he was old enough to try it, but sooner or later he would, and Zayenthi felt it would be better if he learned how to do it properly. There were classes where the whelps were instructed how to deal with garga, raptors, buffalo and even the brachiosaurus, but they never waited to be taught. Every one of them wanted to prove themselves early, which meant parental instruction was vital.

The garga was a good size – about fourteen feet long and about three and half feet in diameter for most of its body – and Alex could feel the strain on Zayenthi's wing and leg muscles as she carried it back to the varn. When, with a final push, she managed to get over the lip and dropped down towards the bowl, there were a few cheers from the other dragons.

"Well caught! Are there any more out there?" one cried.

"Mostly too young to bother with," she replied.

"Where were you fishing?" another yelled.

"Just below Garth Point," she called back.

"Try the other side next time," the dragon replied, pointing to the East. "There are a lot more over there."

"Thanks!"

"I was wrong. That giant garga they're about to deal with really has done a number on the garga population between Crada and Selesis," Daniel commented.

"Yes. Zayenthi is thinking that she needs to let Pyrutha know there's a problem with the garga on that coast."

Zayenthi landed on a ledge outside one of the caves and her partner and whelp both came out eagerly, looking at her prize. Alex noted that her partner, Jerthan, had a sprained wing muscle, which is why he hadn't come out hunting with her. It was healing, and they were both looking forward to Lucas coming by in the morning with more medication to help ease the pain, but Jerthan had tried flying earlier and only made it worse, so he was now confined to quarters. The two nuzzled and Jerthan congratulated his partner on a fine catch. He then quickly separated the head from the body and placed it to one side. Using it for instruction was something they'd both agreed on. Zayenthi asked that they make sure they left enough for her and then flew to Pyrutha's cave. The leader was now in the front of the cave, working on her own computer using a headset similar to that which Alex and Daniel had seen at Selesis.

"Pyrutha," Zayenthi said as she stepped inside. "The garga off Garth's Point are getting very few and far between. There were hardly any of the larger ones and I swear there were hundreds of them a few months ago. We haven't eaten that many."

Pyrutha nodded. "You're not the first to notice that. I've spoken to Selesis. Apparently, they've an absolute monster that's devouring everything. A hunting party is going to attack it tomorrow."

"I wish I'd known," Zayenthi moaned. "I'd have been happy to help."

"The Inter-Continental Feast is in three days. I think they're planning on using it as the centrepiece. Are you coming?"

"Only if the train is running. Jerthan still can't fly far. Strictly, he shouldn't be flying at all, but you know how he is."

"I spoke to Lucas. He's got some injections he says should fix the worst of it, but even so he'll need to leave the flying for at least a couple of days. The train's been off because this giant has been attacking it. If Selesis is successful, there will be space for some of us aboard. I'll make sure Jerthan is one of them."

"Can Garthan travel with him?"

"How old is he now?"

"Eight turns."

"Frightening how fast they grow up. Feels like only yesterday he was picking eggshell off his hide! He's certainly not old enough for a two-day flight, so yes, I think so. I'll let Lucas know."

"Thank you! They'll both be thrilled. They were afraid they'd miss it this year and Garthan enjoyed it so much last year when it was here. He made some good friends and he's eager to catch up with them."

"Use the communal computers. At least he can chat with them using those."

"A lot of friends were made last year. Garthan can't compete with the older dragons who want to chat to their potential mates," Zayenthi replied sadly.

"Hmm. Perhaps we need to have times for each group so the youngest get a chance? The older whelps do seem to be hogging that cave rather a lot." She nodded to herself, made a note and then turned to Zayenthi. "You've a garga you'd best get back to before Jerthan and Garthan devour the lot, and I've some reports from OSROM I need to digest so I can sound vaguely intelligent when I speak to Lucas tomorrow. Go on."

Alex grinned. OSROM, or the Outpost for Scientific Research and Observation, Mithgryr, was the first human settlement on the planet and its past leader, Dr Susan Santos, had been part of the events that led to the new Selesian varn. It was good to know it was still going strong.

"Thank you, Pyrutha. Garthan and Jerthan will be thrilled. They were so afraid they'd miss it this turn."

She turned and left the cave, her heart soaring. She alighted on the ledge to her own cave and noted that there was still a good chunk of garga left. She walked in happily, Alex quietly slipping out at the same time.

"Feel good?" Daniel asked.

"They are very smart and, despite Pyrutha making notes, they all have prodigious memories. It's quite astounding." She glanced at Daniel. "And yes, flying as a dragon felt wonderful! Come on, let's look in on the humans."

***

The local star, which the locals called Syr, was setting, and lights had been switched on in the human compound. The electrified fences had also been activated, and the gates closed and secured. Some guards stood in the watch towers and on the gate, giving the whole a rather uncomfortable appearance, but then a child ran out and yelled up to one of the guards that she had some hot coffee for him, and he beckoned her up the internal elevator. When she arrived, he gave her a hug, gratefully accepted the coffee and chatted with her for a while before she said she had to return to the main hall because they were showing a film she wanted to see. With another hug and a kiss, he bid her goodnight and, when she emerged at the bottom, reminded her that tomorrow he wanted to hear all about it.

Alex and Daniel followed the child into the main hall. There they found music and laughter and the enticing aromas of hot food. A few minutes later, a greying man got up onto the platform and called for silence.

"Not too many notes, you'll be glad to hear." There were some scattered cheers. "Yes, thank you! All right," he looked down at his tablet. "First, yet another reminder that there's a raptor pack living in the forests to the south and no one should be going anywhere near there without armed protection. Actually, there's no reason to go anywhere near there at all – Stephen, that includes you! Pack it in!"

A teenager shifted uncomfortably while his friends shook their heads and then gave him a friendly slap on the back.

"No, no. Don't encourage him!" He looked sternly at Stephen. "I don't want to keep sending out guards to risk their lives because you want to explore. Move to Selesis and make it their problem. I'm sure the T-Rexes over there would find you a tasty snack!" He frowned and the teenager nodded. After fixing him with a glare, Lucas moved on. "Second: the garga on the East coast have been much reduced due to a giant garga that's settled itself between here and Selesis. Tomorrow, I'm informed, the torpedoes will be launched against this monster and a team of dragons will try to take it out. Now, based on the recordings I saw, this thing dwarfs the garga head at our gate, so brace yourselves. There may be dragon deaths." There were many sharp intakes of breath and muted mutterings. Several looked upset at the thought, proving that the humans viewed the dragons as friends they cared about. "It's the annual Inter-Continental Feast on Thursday and I'm sincerely hoping it will be a joyous affair, but I'll let you know, when we do, exactly what's happening. If it goes badly, the feast may be cancelled." There were low groans around the room. "I know, I know, but if they lose dragons they may not be in the mood, so

146

be kind. If and when that beast has been removed, the train connection between us and Selesis will be restored. I know it's been a pain having that shut down, but the creature has been attacking the same spot over and over and we don't want to risk it being weakened. We've maintained watch and repaired any cracks, so don't worry. We won't all be getting impromptu swimming lessons the next time we visit!" There were a few laughs at this, but more looking at each other worriedly. "However, in order to keep it secure from attacks we might not so easily repair, the moratorium was required. Selesis and Crada will do a scan of the entire tunnel before any trains are allowed to pass through carrying humans or dragons. If there is the slightest suggestion of danger, we won't use the train. That means I'll have to ask Pyrutha if any of the dragons would be willing to carry us in gondolas using the landing stages." More groans. "I think, given the importance of I-Con for both groups, she'll say yes and probably be the first to offer her services, but let's not make any assumptions. If they are required, remember that it's a two-day trip in cramped conditions so dress appropriately and remember to bow and say thank you to any dragon who volunteers. This is not something they like doing and it's only because we help them that they're willing to do it at all." He looked down at his notes. "Oh yes! Would whoever it is who's throwing toilet roll on the electric fence stop doing that? You're not only risking a short, you're attracting the raptors. That puts all of us in danger. I know it makes pretty sparks but this is not a game. Those fences are there for our protection and the threat is not imaginary. Understood?" The humans looked around, trying to spot who might be the perpetrator, but no one stood out. Even Stephen looked horrified that someone was doing this. "All right. Tonight's film is one I know we've all been looking forward to since those film makers visited us five years ago. I'll hand you over to Robbie."

Robbie, who turned out to be a she, nodded her thanks and bounded onto the stage as Lucas quietly stepped down.

"OK, we all know what this is about, but a few warnings first. There are some pretty graphic scenes during the battles, so all I can say to you is that if you don't care to see injured dragons and humans, you might want to give this one a miss." She paused, but no one moved. "OK, I've already watched it. A few minor characters have been amalgamated, as usual, but I have to say it's remarkably accurate. I think TIS funding and knowing that the dragons would watch it made the film makers a little more careful!" Laughs all round and a few cheers followed this comment. "We're the first humans to see it and the film makers are keen to hear what we think, since we're considered experts on dragons." She rolled her eyes. "If we want this thing to succeed on Earth and out in the other colonies, we need to tell them why we like it, so sing out on social media. There are several soundtracks and, of course, the usual interactive view that'll be available on your computers after I-Con so that you can experience it as any of the main characters..." She noted a few looks. "Yes, that includes Raethyn and Mazik, you sick people!" A few of the teenage boys pumped the air while Alex and Daniel looked at each other in shock, realising what the film was about. "Why anyone would want to know what it's like to die so horribly is beyond me! The dragon soundtrack will be used at I-Con, so remember to pack your translators if you want to watch it again, but for tonight, it's all in English." A cheer went up. "I've created a small handout highlighting any historical alterations and additional information. Just message me and I'll send it out." She took in the eager response of the audience. "Or I could just send it to everyone?" There were nods all round. "OK, I'll do that. It's three hours long so there will be a fifteen-minute intermission to give everyone a chance to use the facilities and grab a drink. Remember, this is an immersion film but, obviously, we can't go full size in here and we'll be using audience view." Awws were heard from many parts of the room. "But," she cried over the noise, "but it *will* be full size for the feast, when you and the dragons can walk around in it." More cheers followed this announcement. "So, tonight please stay in your seat. You can zoom in on details when you get your own copies, all right?" Nods and a few urging her to get on with it were the welcome response. "OK, for the first time ever, welcome to Dragon Liberation!"

The lights switched off, plunging the room into total darkness, then the film started.

***

Flying back to Selesis, Alex and Daniel were buoyed by both the film and the very positive feedback from the audience. Reading about the events and seeing them in three dimensions were two very different things. They noted that the fight with the giant garga was watched with an intensity it probably would not have received without Lucas' earlier warning regarding the events they were about to witness in the waters around Selesis and, even though it was a film, it was quite terrifying enough.

They whiled away the rest of the night and early morning with quick trips to Heyo and Narga, the satellites that orbited Mithgryr. The humans had outposts on both, allowing low gravity experiments as well as monitoring Mithgryr's weather patterns, storing excess scales and supplies until collection, and even providing a hospital facility for injuries that would repair better without the stresses of gravity. The latter were, naturally, rare, but even some dragons had visited to see their planet from above. Alex and Daniel knew that there was another science research facility underwater between Selesis and Crada, but there wasn't time to visit that, and so, after a brief flight over Selesis to the far coastline and back, they made their way to Padzak's Rock to prepare for the day's events.

The hunting dragons had already gathered and the tension in the air was palpable. Darthak was there, but Garthik was quick to remind him that this was not his fight, and he was to stay out of harm's way.

"Garthik, may I remind you who's king?" Darthak said.

"I know who's king," Garthik assured his brother, "I just don't want it to be me! Anything happens to you, I'll be holding the fort until your whelps come of age and have been properly trained. If you think I want to run this place for so much as one day, you're tserit-ridden!"[1]

Darthak was about to respond when the call came through. "The train has left," he announced. "You should get out there. The humans will tell you when you're in the right place."

"All right!" Garthik roared. "It's time to go. Everyone got their spears?"

Every dragon held up their dominant front leg. Strapped to each was a small holder threaded with two spears (no feathers and nearly as long as Alex was, normally, tall) attached to a mechanism strapped to their paws. The dragons had practised over and over before sleep and throughout the morning. Not that the system was complicated. All they had to do was get that paw over the opening in the back of the garga's head and flex whichever claw had been designated as their preferred trigger. Using old garga skulls that had been kept by the teachers to instruct whelps on how to kill them, the hunters had practised over and over positioning, firing through the hole and reloading their weapon until they could, quite literally, do it with their eyes closed. They now knew exactly where their paw needed to be to ensure a

---

[1] Tserits are bugs common to Selesis. They lay their eggs under dragon scales and then eat their way out. The open sores lead to infections and loss of scales, as well as mentally debilitating illness. The scientist daughter of Darthyn and Eyowenwi, Zohawi (who was given her own dragon-adapted lab by the humans), invented a shower to kill them that the dragons use after hunting or training expeditions deep in the jungle.

clear shot into the garga's brain. They had all been sent out with two 'spears' strapped to the firing leg, and an extra two on the other leg in case they missed. Garthik had nominated himself and four others he trusted to carry the explosive versions that would be used to clear the accretions around the hole.

"When it comes to the surface," Garthik continued as the dragons lowered their legs, "let me, Parthak, Brethik, Geiriss and Hayuwi check out the back of the skull. If the build-up is large, we'll use our spears to shatter that away so that we have a clear shot. If we're really lucky, one of them will do the job for us. If it doesn't, each of us can take a crack, but make sure you are cleared to attack so that we don't get in each other's way." There were nods all round. "Let's go!"

They set out, their invisible chaperones flying alongside them. They found the spot easily as great, growing balls of gas were bubbling up to the surface. Their wings flapping with powerful strokes, holding them in position, the dragons looked down, trying to see the garga through the sputtering, boiling water. The rush of bubbles increased, erupting across the surface, churning the water and then, suddenly, the garga was there! On and on it rose, water cascading down its flesh until its head was finally clear of the water and splashes. Its eyes, dazed and filmy, looked around in confusion and then it spotted a dragon. Instantly, it lunged. Geiriss, who'd been closest and was in danger of becoming dinner, rippled and vanished, much to the surprise of the Eternals who, with their extra sight, could still see where she was with a little adaption. She then executed a spectacular dive and flip, flying under the beast's throat to come out the other side, ascending as the garga crashed back into the water. Garthik now swooped down to examine his target. Something akin to barnacles as well as some seaweed surrounded the hole, making it inaccessible. Garthik dived at his target and fired his first shot slightly off where he guessed the hole might be, and at an angle in the hope that the explosion would shatter the beast's protection. He only barely withdrew his paw before the spear went off, shattering one side of the garga's shield. The hole was now visible, but so hard up against the shield that it was impossible to position the next spear.

Parthak now took his flight in. He slapped his spear against the target and another section of protection was blown away, but it was still not sufficient. Brethik now made his bid, but the previous attacks had alerted the garga to the danger. It turned and snapped, Brethik barely making it clear. Hayuwi, on the other side, took her chance, landed on the back of the beast and fired her spear. The garga turned. It was sluggish thanks to the drugs the human torpedoes had injected into its system, but it was angry. Its head whipped from side to side as it tried to throw off its attacker, and the spear exploded, right under Hayuwi's foot. She cried out in pain, leapt free and with great strokes of her wings rose higher and higher, the garga following her upwards, its great maw wide. More and more of it emerged until over thirty feet of the beast was out of the water with no end in sight, still chasing the bleeding Hayuwi who was struggling through her pain to put a safe distance between herself and her attacker.

"Why doesn't she vanish?" Daniel cried.

"She's bleeding a lot," Alex replied, equally caught up in the events. "She would still be visible because of that, and she needs all her energy to escape that thing!"

Hayuwi's explosion had done the trick. The hole was now completely exposed, and the rest of the hunters could see their target. One by one they flew down and attacked, sending their spears at the hole as the garga twisted and turned in the air, snapping and roaring its defiance.

"Concentrate!" Garthik yelled as many hit the surrounding area instead of going into the hole. "Make your spears count!"

Parthak focused and made his second attempt. He managed to land and was about to release his second spear when the garga shuddered, throwing him off. It turned and snapped, taking off the tip of Parthak's tail and ripping a hole in one wing. Parthak struggled, tore himself free but now he couldn't fly. He clung on with everything he had, knowing the cost if he let go. Garthik made a dive and the garga turned and snapped again. He managed to dodge the edge of the tooth, but barely, his side now badly bruised. Suddenly, Darthak was there.

"I told you to stay away!" Garthik cried, anger and pain mixing in his voice.

"I intend to. Let me bait him while you take him down."

"My King!" Garthik cried, fear and desperation colouring his tone.

"Your brother!" Darthak replied. "Now do what must be done, and be quick. The drugs are wearing off and I don't think Parthak will survive if this thing goes underwater."

The garga seemed more alert and Garthik realised there was no more time. While Darthak danced in front of the beast, teasing and goading it to keep it out of the water as far as possible, Garthik flew up out of sight. A few moments later he dropped down like an arrow behind the garga's head. Parthak had used his time chewing and tugging out the spears that had missed their mark, leaving the hole open and exposed.

Garthik and Parthak's eyes met.

"Do it!" Parthak whispered.

Garthik slammed his paw against the hole and pulled the trigger. There was a short pause and then a little blood appeared at the mouth of the hole. Cursing that the membrane was too thick, Garthik was reloading when the dribble became a spurt, shooting blood in an arc from the back of the garga's head and staining the water. The garga began to drop and Darthak swooped around and down, grabbing Parthak as best he could in his claws.

"Help me!" he cried.

A couple of the other hunters joined him and together they lifted Parthak free of the writhing, thrashing garga.

"You two, get Parthak home," Darthak said, pointing to the hunters. "Hayuwi, go with them. I've ordered up the varn to help us bring this beast back. Tell them to home in on my comms."

Hayuwi nodded and followed the others, grabbing Parthak's tail in her three working claws to help share the load. Behind them, the garga threw itself to and fro, trying even now to attack the enemy that had long since sealed its fate. It began to drop, and the other hunters followed it down.

"Wait!" Darthak yelled. "We know they always have a last attack. Don't become like Raethyn. Keep your distance. There's still enough gas in it to hold it near the surface for a little while."

The hunters quickly responded, putting some distance between themselves and the wallowing beast. It was just as well because, a moment later, it lurched out of the water with an almighty roar, hurling itself at one of the hunters who, thanks to Darthak's warning, was already out of reach. It crashed back into the sea sending a massive wave, twenty feet high, surging towards the shore.

That wave, in turn, helped the rest of the varn to congregate around the dying garga. As soon as it stopped twitching, Darthak and Garthik fastened their claws into its neck behind its head. Others quickly attached themselves, pulling more and more of the garga free from the water until over a hundred feet of the monster was hovering above the waves and still more was being picked up as dragon after dragon found a space and added its claws and wings to the effort. Together, with the garga hanging below them, the dragons headed back to Padzak's

Rock, but Alex and Daniel remained where they were, staring after the departing victors.

"Three hundred and forty-five feet in total. It was a monster all right. The other garga will now be able to grow up and swim the oceans. They'll still be occasional dinners for dragons, but that's a small fraction of the total and the dragons are careful in their husbandry. Only the oldest end up becoming dinner." He turned back to Alex. "It'll take a while for Parthak to recover, but the humans look after him, just as they looked after his great-great-great grandfather, back on Crada," he smiled.

Alex blinked, her eyes shining. "You mean...?"

He nodded. "Parther's descendant. Just as brave as his ancestor."

"And Hayuwi?"

"She'll have a couple of steel toes, like Darthyn, and be proud of them. She's a descendant of his and Eyowenwi's, and Geiriss is the descendant of Vieriss, Eyowenwi's maid who ferried the messages from Padzak to Maewi, Eyowenwi's mother, without ever letting Mazik or even King Warzak know what was happening."

"They are amazing creatures," Alex breathed. "I wish we could stay for the feast."

"I know, but the tunnel is opening any second... now!"

The hole appeared in the surface of the stained water, whirling and roaring.

Alex took one last look around the open ocean and the distant group of triumphant dragons, returning with their prize to Selesis. "I *will* be back!" she declared, and leapt through the sparking, shuddering gap.

Chapter 5

"Oof!" Landing on a very solid metal floor forced the outburst, even though Alex couldn't be hurt by the landing. Having people walking through her was rather disconcerting, however, and she quickly shuffled over to the side while she adjusted to this new world. It was certainly a busy and very crowded one!

As her ethereal stomach and brain settled to receive the new input, she realised that the slightly disjointed feeling was part of her surroundings.

"I'm on a spaceship," she muttered, getting up.

There was some form of artificial gravity, but it was a rudimentary type, based on rotation rather than energy fields. Not being fully 'of this world', Alex was aware of a disjunct between what she was supposed to be feeling and what her Eternal senses told her was really going on.

"I need to get outside," she declared. There was no sign of Daniel, but she had no doubt he'd join her in due course no matter where she was. With that in mind, she deliberately passed through several bulkheads until she was outside and could see the ship for what it was.

Massive, was the first word that sprang to mind.

It's a multi-generational ship,' Daniel's voice said in her mind. She was in space, after all, so there was no point in his using standard speech. She turned to see that he had materialised on one of the antennae. He floated down to stand beside her. *Theoretically, it was aiming for one of the planets in the constellation of Lyra, which is over a thousand light years away from Earth.*'

So, we're back in our original universe again?'

'Um hmm, but a catastrophe set humanity back massively, then stalled it for a bit before they slowly got back on course.'

'Hence the need for an old-fashioned, multi-generational ship,' she nodded. 'How far ahead have I jumped?'

'Almega's done you proud. You're another few billion years ahead. He thinks that one more jump out and back again, and that should do it.'

'Hate to point it out to Almega, but the universe carries on for trillions upon trillions of years.'

'Yes, but for a large portion of that there's no life in it. We only have to get you to a moment where there's no other life in the universe, and that happens long before the end.'

'That's a relief!' She motioned at the ship. 'That far ahead and they're reduced to ancient technology like this? That would be like fiftieth century me making flint arrows to catch my dinner. Worse! What happened?'

'The usual. War, politics, some natural disasters and changes, then a run of humans who started what amounted to religions, except without that label, which attracted the rich and powerful. World government and ways to force conformity now being in place, there was no one who could gainsay them. They demanded people conform to what they labelled the 'right way' or lose their privileges –'

'Privileges?'

'What they could eat, buy, where they could live or go, that sort of thing. As a result, people did conform for centuries. Knowledge that was accurate but didn't fit the narrative was over-written and lost, but the people were happy, and life was good, so no one cared. Then another disaster struck which the new religions didn't foresee and couldn't deal with. The world government was overthrown, the new religions abandoned, and they went back to something more primitive and worked their way back up.'

'Sounds horrible. Glad I missed it. Is this their first attempt to get out into the universe again?' Alex asked.

'The first to leave, not the first to arrive. This one started the journey using cryostasis to get them most of the way there, then woke up the colonists when they were within twenty-five years of reaching the planet. That was a hundred-and-eighty-six years ago.'

157

'Did it hit something and get thrown off course?' she asked, confused.

'No.'

'Then how come it hasn't arrived?'

'A very good question.'

'To which we're going to find the answer, right?'

'I'm hoping so. It's a bit of a mystery. The silly thing is that in the time between the Argo launching – yes, they named it after the Greek myth – and now, other ships, with faster engines and utilising some wormhole shortcuts, got to the planet and have been there for several hundred years. They've sent out numerous rescue missions but there's no sign of this ship anywhere near the route it should have taken and, space being rather big, they've not been able to track it down.'

'Aren't they sending out distress signals.'

'No.'

She noted the antennae which stuck out at various angles across the rotating body of the spaceship, looking like a rather spartan forest in winter.

'Electrical or mechanical malfunction?'

He shrugged.

'Almega can check the program, right? Is it ever found?'

'No. That's why I was a little late getting to you. Almega was scouting out ahead through the program but, in its present form, the Argo vanishes without a trace.'

'Ooh! A really big mystery!'

'And one that, right now, you're in a unique position to solve,' he grinned.

'OK. I suppose the first stop will be to check whether they think they're sending out any signals at all. After such a delay, they ought to be, but if someone's decided not to do that, we'd then have to investigate why.' She looked along the three miles-long ship. 'Is the bridge at the front, the middle or what?'

'Just behind the front of the ship. The prow is filled with sensors and the energy relays needed to push aside space debris.'

'Right!' She headed off and, as she neared the front, dropped back inside the ship.

Since the bridge was not in the nose, it was entirely dependent on screens to show what was in front of it. Males and females were monitoring, but in a routine way. There were none who were demanding why they were no closer to their target planet than they had been a month, a year or even a century ago. Indeed, there was a strong sense of being satisfied with the routine, which Alex found both confusing and worrying.

"No one seems to care," she commented as she watched the officers going about their business.

"It's as if this," and Daniel waved his arm to encompass both the bridge and the rest of the ship, "*is* the job – coming in, doing your shift and going home – not getting to the planet at all. Life has become living on a spaceship, not using it to travel to another planet."

"This is several generations in. They've never known anything else." She went to the comms section to check it out. "According to this, they're sending out a message in all directions."

"I think you need to check the links between this console and the external antennae."

"That is going to take forever!" she groaned. "There must be hundreds of miles of connections."

"Start inside the console," he suggested. "Check the message is reaching the relays and that the connections to the wiring are all working."

"And how am I supposed to do that?"

"Let's assume the worst: the system was sabotaged to prevent external comms."

"Why assume that?"

"Because there's no evidence of damage to the external parts of the ship. That means either they've fixed it remarkably well in deep space, or there was no such damage. If the problem didn't originate from outside, it must be from inside. One antenna failing or even a few of them is a relay or wiring fault that, for some reason, no one's detected. All of them going down is something else, and the fact that the comms officer seems unaware of it would suggest deliberate and careful sabotage. Now, they could do one box at a time, but that's a lot of work and you wouldn't want to be caught doing it. Therefore, we need to look at the nexus points that everything is dependent upon. Those are the weak links. This console is the first and, frankly, probably the easiest to sabotage. That means you need to look inside for broken or cut wires, broken solder, data cards that aren't locked into place, or whatever it is they're using in there."

"How could anyone sabotage this with all these people here?" she asked, sticking her head into the console to look at the insides.

"All you need is one shift with not enough officers, and whoever's in charge sends the newbies out for a coffee or on other errands." He paused and then added, "Or it was a holiday and he told them he'd man the bridge while they all went off and had a good time."

"He?" she asked.

"Could be a she," he agreed, "but disconnecting the ship from rescue puts women and children at risk. Most women wouldn't do that."

"Neither would normal men!" she replied, her voice slightly muffled. She withdrew her head. "I've just had a thought. It was supposed to be in space for fifty years, it's been out here for nearly two hundred. What are they living on? There's a lot of people aboard."

"They've got hydroponics. Even fifty years would need more than basic supplies, and I'm guessing they snagged a meteor or something for water and recycle wherever they can."

"Medicines?"

"I imagine they ran out of those a long time ago, but some plant-based cures would still work, provided the population is healthy."

"Don't get sick, huh?"

"Pretty much!"

She went back inside. "I can't see anything wrong in here, but I'm not the engineer. Can you come in and check?"

"Shrink yourself down so you're fully inside with room to move."

She did so, and he appeared beside her at the same size. Telling the cockroach-sized Alex where she needed to be, he travelled alongside, examining everything in detail. When they reached the end, he shook his head.

"There's nothing physically wrong in here, which means either they've been cut later, or this is a programming issue. It's simply not reporting what's really going on, but to check that, you'd have to take someone over and run some software of your own."

"That wouldn't be too hard," she mused. "All I'd need to do is get the raw address ID of the antennae and then ping them, but independently of the system software so that it doesn't realise it's being checked and gives an honest report."

"Where would you get the original ID from?" Daniel wondered. Alex was the software genius. His expertise lay more in the engineering and hardware, and he was more than happy to bow to her talent in this case.

"When they were initially installed, the system had to find them and then patch them through with a more natural name." She exited the hardware and expanded to her normal size, turning to point to the touch-sensitive panel. "Now, instead of some meaningless string of numbers and letters, it becomes antennae array one though twenty, forward and aft antennae arrays, and a couple of backups." She pointed to the relevant panels, all of which presently indicated that they were working correctly. "That means I have to get to at least one of the antennae and find out what it calls itself."

"Will you be able to do that without inhabiting someone?"

"Why?" she asked.

"If we're to come back and fix this, we'll have to be one of these characters, and until we find out what's going on, we won't know who may be trusted to get them to their destination. Any of them could be guilty."

"Or none of them," she pointed out.

"You've turned around since the dragons," he commented with a smile. "There you accused them of all sorts of things."

"None of which proved true," she replied. "They were honest, honourable, courageous, fair and caring of others. They restored my faith in sentient creatures."

Daniel looked around the bridge. The residents were young humans, albeit very pale ones after years in space, with all the foibles humans were heir to including, he strongly suspected, greed. He sincerely doubted this predicament was due to mere accident.

"I'll do my level best to find the answer without inhabiting any of them," she said, noting the look of doubt on his face, "but that's going to make it hard. Let's go find us an antenna and get its address."

"There's one right in front of you," he said, pointing. "If any of them are easy to trace from start to finish, it has to be the ones on the prow."

Without hesitation, she walked through the shift commander and two other humans, several banks of computers and screens, and out through the hull. She then checked the antenna and examined its computer components. Seeing data stored in the hardware without using a computer was far from easy and she paused, mulling over the thing until an idea occurred to her. At that moment, she disappeared.

"Alex? Where are you?"

'Pure energy inside the hardware,' she replied in his head. *'I'm just following the information paths. They're all working perfectly.'*

'That means no one's cut the power, just the signal,' he said.

'I'm following the signal.'

162

There was a long pause. Daniel knew roughly where she was because he was dragged along beside her as she made her way through the wiring, even though he couldn't see her. Suddenly, she stopped. There was another pause, then she reappeared.

"Behind that bulkhead there's a box," she said, pointing. "All the connections for the antennae go via that box, but there's an extra chip that doesn't belong. It's feeding false positives back along the lines." She looked at Daniel. "You were right. This is deliberate sabotage. Whoever did this originally knew what they were doing and knew the consequences. There's no way they could have wired it all up as well as they have without being fully aware of what would happen."

An alarm went off. Alex and Daniel jumped slightly at the sound, but the people on the bridge appeared unfazed. The Commander stood up.

"All right, time to lock it down. We don't want Sector 3 to wreck it, do we?" There was nervous laughter at that comment. "Make sure everything's secure and the automated systems have been engaged, then you can get back to your Sector."

"Dunno why the Captain doesn't just space Sector 3 and have done with it," one muttered.

"Because we're decent!" the Commander replied sternly. "It's not their fault they went bad, and we can't expect them to stay in their cabins for the rest of their lives." His expression shifted to a pleasanter one. "At least we know who to blame if we find chaos when we wake up, and there's nothing we can't fix, right?"

"No, sir!"

The crew, all in their very early twenties barring the Commander, went about securing the bridge. When they were done, they all stood to attention at their posts while the Commander checked each one.

"Excellent! As ever, Sector 1 shows how it should be done. Now off you go! Enjoy your evening and make sure you're safe in your cabins at curfew. I don't want to lose any of you!"

"Sir, where are Sector 3 due tonight?"

"No worries, lad," the Commander replied in a kindly voice. "The Officers have got them contained away from your Sector, but just in case any manage to sneak through, I'd rather they weren't given easy targets, all right?"

"Yes, sir."

"Off you go, then. See you bright and early tomorrow."

The crew saluted and then left the bridge, chatting and joking with each other as they made their way along the corridor and then into elevators with green lights above them on the starboard side. When all had left, the Commander took one last look around, pressed a button by the side of the elevators that closed the bridge hatch, got into a different elevator, and departed, the lights on the starboard side now turned red while those on the port side switched to green. The bridge was eerily silent.

"They leave the bridge unmanned for half the day?!" Alex said, shocked at the idea. "No wonder they missed the planet!"

"Automated systems should alert them if they're anywhere near something habitable," Daniel said, "but with the antennae down, how would they know? It's not like they can look out of a window."

"At least it gives us some peace and quiet to examine this addition," she said, bending to look around the section that hid the device. "It's been well covered. The entire bulkhead looks like it's been replaced."

"Easily done with a twelve-hour or more window," Daniel nodded. Off Alex's questioning expression he added, "Humans naturally fall to a twenty-five- or twenty-six-hour day if they've no clocks or daylight to tell them otherwise, so it might be a thirteen-hour break if they've decided to follow biological preference. In deep space you can easily do that and just set the clocks accordingly."

"Maybe I could use one of their bodies while their brains are asleep?" she mused.

"If there was a clear bad guy in here, I'd say go for it," he replied, "but you know the rules. You can only have one Eternal using a given body during any training. Two us in the same avatar won't fit, even in your present form, so we need to be certain that we're not going to want to live that life before you help yourself."

"Sector 3 sounds like a viable source. We'd better find them and get back up here before –"

The ding of the elevator interrupted her. The Eternals watched as a new bridge crew, equally smart but in their late twenties or early thirties, entered the bridge and took their positions.

"All right, crew!" the new Commander smiled. "Let's see what damage Sector 3 did this time, shall we?"

"Sir!"

The crew took their positions and reactivated the machines. Within moments, the helm called out.

"Sir, they've changed our course!"

"Of course they have," the Commander sighed. "Put her back on track, Ensign." He turned to the rest of the crew. "As usual, the subversives are undermining our efforts. Looks like we'll always be taking one step forward, two steps back."

"What the...?" Alex muttered, looking from the immaculate crew to Daniel. "I thought this was Sector 3 and they were the bad guys?"

After a few minutes, the crew confirmed everything had been reset and they were ready to get on their way.

"Excellent. Two minutes thirty-two seconds. I'm impressed. Next time, we'll see if we can get it down to two-minutes thirty, eh?" The crew grinned and nodded. "Which is the best Sector?"

"Sector ONE!" the bridge crew cried.

"Open her up, helm. Let's see if we can make up for the damage Sector 3 caused."

***

The Eternals left the bridge, now thoroughly confused.

"It explains why they're not reaching landfall. The bridge crews are working against each other, each accusing the other of being the problem."

"And they're not talking to or seeing each other," Daniel agreed. "They don't realise what's happening."

"I'm not sure even the Commander knew," Alex said. "Talk about the left hand not knowing what the right is doing."

"But the Captain of the ship should be overseeing all this and keeping them on course. Where's that character?"

"Unless the Captain's the problem," Alex returned. "It would make sense. Keep the crews fighting against each other and the Captain stays in charge. The instant they hit landfall, he or she is out of a job."

"For nearly two centuries? That's either an extremely long-lived Captain, or something very odd is going on," Daniel replied.

"Time to check out the ordinary people aboard this ship and then, I suggest, we find where the senior officers hang out," she nodded.

"Why not check out the senior officers first?"

"Do you know where they are?" Daniel had to admit that he did not. "We'll probably stumble across them as we explore the ship, but I want to find out if there *are* any insurrectionists aboard, or if it's all invented. Also, how come the groups aren't talking to each other. How are they being kept apart?"

"Port and starboard seem to be two routes," Daniel said, pointing out the two lines of elevators to the bridge.

"On a ship where the habitable areas are in the rotating section? Which is port and which is starboard there? One minute you're to port, the next to starboard. No, there's more to it than that, but I agree the different elevators lead to different sectors. Let's check it out."

166

Eschewing the elevators, they floated down through the floor until they reached the middle of the ship.

"Port or starboard?" Alex asked, pointing first left, then right.

"The first crew we met seem to have been from the starboard. It'd be a way to orient ourselves."

With a nod, the two walked and floated through bulkheads and across elevator shafts until they finally emerged in the habitable part of the ship.

"This is more or less where I landed," Alex said. "Looks similar, anyway."

"Pretty packed, too. There are a lot of people aboard this ship. How are they managing all this?" Daniel wondered.

Alex pointed. "And with burger bars?" She sniffed the air. "That's pork rather than beef, but it's definitely meat."

"Maybe they've advanced enough to make faux meat that's actually convincing?" Daniel hazarded. "I can't see them raising pigs anywhere aboard. There's not the room."

"Unless they live with them," she offered. "It's all very strange."

"This is the right level, though. Look," Daniel said. "There's our crew."

In amongst the civilians, most of whom were clad in basic, shabby, blue overalls, the smart blue and gold uniforms and caps of the bridge crew stood out. They were laughing and joking with each other and being treated respectfully but not fearfully by the citizens.

"It's not the military that's the problem, then," Alex commented. "I was afraid this was a mobile military dictatorship."

"There's more than one way to control people," Daniel replied, sadly. "Let's look at another section."

***

They held their relative position in space and allowed the rotation to bring them to another sector. This one was silent. Not a person anywhere. Alex looked into a few cabins and found the residents very soundly asleep. Much younger than the two previous groups, the Eternals now realised the sections were divided by age. With no one getting in their way, they checked ingress and egress and found everything was sealed. It seemed that nothing was to disturb people while they were on their rest period.

Another dose of holding while the core rotated and they reached the other active group, but these were in their morning rather than their evening cycle. This appeared to be where the new crew had come from since everyone was in the same age bracket of late twenties, very early thirties at best. Another pause and another sealed and silent deck, but this time the silence was due to a rest none would awaken from.

"They're all dead!" Alex cried as she went from room to room, checking on the occupants. "Every single one of them!"

"How?" Daniel wondered.

Alex checked, using her past trainings in medicine to find an answer.

"It's a combination," she declared at last, wiping her face. She'd been poking her eyes inside the bodies to see what had gone wrong. Naturally, in her present state, she was not covered in gore from head to foot, but the feeling remained. "Tell me I've not got anything on me?"

"You're all clean, I assure you," Daniel replied.

"Good. All of them have severe damage in their lungs. That suggests something was released into the atmosphere on this deck which isn't anywhere else."

"Something like carbon monoxide?" he asked.

"Probably very similar, but without the blue discolouration. Whatever it was, it's highly poisonous and killed them in their sleep but," and she raised a finger, "on top of that, they're only just thawing out. I think this deck has been exposed to space for some time to keep them from rotting, but the door or vent or whatever, was closed a few days ago and the bodies allowed to thaw slowly. Based on the condition of the ones I checked – and obviously I've not checked them all – in a few more hours they'll all start to decompose."

"The air in this ship is recycled," Daniel mused. "The hydroponics section provides it, and at least some of the food they need, but sooner or later the stink will reach the other decks. It has to."

"If I were living on one of the other decks and suddenly found the air thick with the smell of rotting meat, I'd be very, very worried," she nodded. "I think it's time to find where the Captain and his cronies hang out."

"Agreed!"

***

The senior officers had their own section of the ship, which was far less crowded. The mean age of said officers was considerably higher than that of any other section of the ship, with all the highest ranks sporting grey hair and the lines of age.

"No one else on this ship is past their early thirties," Alex said as yet another elderly officer walked past. "The dead were the oldest and they were still pre-forties."

"Rank hath its privileges, it seems," Daniel nodded, his tone thick with sarcasm.

"The question now is, what are they going to say about the dead in that Sector? I assume they know about it."

"Oh, they most certainly know. They've probably been on ice for months if not years."

"Accident or deliberate, do you think?"

"Whether it was an accidental discharge from the engines or deliberate murder is irrelevant, it's how they're going to sell it that's the key and, given they're being thawed, they're going to be doing that very soon. If it was accidental, they need to assure the thousands in other sections that they're not going to suffer the same fate. If it was deliberate..." He gave her a knowing look.

169

"Let's find out where they decide such things."

It took a little while, but in the more spartanly populated sector, following the groups of senior officers who all seemed to be headed in the same direction seemed a good bet, and so it proved.

Arriving at Command and Control – also known as C&C – Alex and Daniel passed through the myriad officers. Some were writing reports, some chatting, some delivering more reports on everything from relatively minor illness and injury (someone had a broken wrist as a result of some ill-judged horseplay, while another needed a wisdom tooth removed. There were several pregnancies), to food supplies (meat supplies were running low), water reclamation, air purification, duty rosters, maintenance of everything from engines to latrines and endless others. Daniel nodded as he listened to it all.

"Same as everywhere else. The information must always be available the instant it's requested. Whether or not those in charge care to avail themselves of it is, of course, another matter entirely!"

They passed through the crowded outer areas moving closer to the inner sanctum. Guards made it clear visitors were not welcome. The Eternals ignored them and passed through the doors unmolested.

"All right, which Sector is getting the news about Sector 4?" the Captain asked. He was an elderly, thick-set man with greying temples, wearing glasses that he kept taking off as he looked up from his reports to fix the other officers with a rather intimidating glare.

"Three is next up," one reported. "One and Two will still remember the last time they had to deal with one of these, so it has to be Three. Besides, they're the oldest, so it'll be their turn next."

Alex and Daniel looked at each other.

"It happens on a regular basis," Daniel murmured.

"I've a horrible feeling about this," Alex said.

"Have we enough children in One and Two to move them over once Four is cleared?" the Captain asked.

"We will have by the end of the week," another officer reported, "And there'll be more within the month. Frankly, One and Two have been crowded for over a year, so they'll welcome a bit more cabin space."

"All right, I'll make the announcement. What did we use last time?"

One of the officers checked his notes. "A sortie to a planet to check whether it was habitable. We put the deaths down to a disease that spread quickly."

The Captain put his glasses on and checked his own records. "That makes this one a space-faring animal, I believe? Haven't used that one for ages. Vaguely remember Captain Braken using it when I was a young lieutenant."

"I have the speech for you, sir," the other officer said, handing over a sheet.

"Excellent." He perused it briefly. "Shouldn't take long to memorise it and make it sound spontaneous." He turned to another officer. "Are you ready?"

"Very much so," the officer nodded. "Everything is in perfect working order and ready to run. I'm sure hydroponics will welcome the fertilizer."

"Absolutely," another nodded. "We're almost out."

"Oh, great," Alex muttered. "They're using the dead to fertilise the food!"

"Waste not, want not," he replied with a shrug. "Ultimately, the bodies are the same as any other. One assumes human waste is also used, and I doubt that's advertised, either."

"Amazing that people can be conned into thinking such a relatively small, enclosed location could possibly support so many in deep space without that," she agreed. "Still an unpleasant thought, though."

"I'm more concerned that they seem to be deliberately murdering the citizens for that purpose on a regular basis.

Except for here, no one in the ship is older than their thirties, and the low end of that."

"They're killing anyone over thirty to provide fertilizer for the crops and free up space inside the ship? Seems to me I've heard something like this before," she growled.

"I've a feeling it may be more than that," he replied, turning pale. "After all, they're serving what smells like pork."

"They're feeding the bodies to the pigs?"

He turned and gave her a very solemn look. "I've a suspicion there are no pigs."

She, too, went pale. "Oh no! They wouldn't! Would they?"

"I appreciate there are some here who dislike this aspect of our maintaining our position," the Captain said, as though he'd overheard their discussion. Alex moved forward and waved a hand in front of his face, and then poked it through the Captain's head. He didn't react. "However, we all know that we cannot sustain a large, elderly populace. Even we," and his circling hand encompassed the rest of the table, "are putting a strain on ship's resources. If most are to survive, we have no choice."

"You could try staying on course and getting to the planet!" Alex yelled in his face.

"Sir, mightn't it not be time to find a planet and settle?" one of the younger officers suggested.

"Thank you!" Alex snarled, still glaring at the Captain.

"Nice idea, Jackson, but with the antennae out, we don't even know where we are."

"Perhaps we could fix them?" Jackson suggested, looking around at the other officers who either glared at him or suddenly found the desk they were sitting at fascinating. "Or not? It was only a suggestion."

"I don't think Jackson will be at the top table for much longer," Daniel commented, noting the expressions of some of the senior officers.

"And they can't afford to have someone who knows as much as he does blabbing to the plebs," Alex added, shaking her head. "He'll literally be fertilizer."

"Or worse," Daniel grunted.

"I assure you, it's been tried," the Captain smiled, although it never reached his eyes. "Being new, you wouldn't know that, but I assure you that we've thoroughly checked every one of them, and the wiring between the antennae and comms. Whatever's wrong, it's beyond our understanding. Anyway," he continued when Jackson opened his mouth, "that's not our immediate concern. Anything else I need to be aware of?" A chorus of 'No, sir,' and shaking heads followed this query. "In that case, I have a speech to make. If you gentlemen would excuse me?"

He rose and the others quickly stood up and saluted as he left the table. He reached the door, paused and clicked his fingers as if remembering something.

"Oh! Filton, Keel, and Stanton. Would you mind joining me? I want to discuss some new protocols."

"Yes, sir," the three senior officers said, following him out. In their wake, Alex and Daniel also followed.

The three walked down a gangway and into a room that the Captain carefully unlocked. Once all three were inside and the door was closed, the Captain turned on Stanton.

"You said he was one of us!" he roared.

"I believed he was, sir. He passed all the tests," Stanton replied.

"Then I suggest we revise the tests. He's clearly not suitable. Add him to the Section 4 casualty list," he said, turning to Filton, "and be discreet!"

"Of course, sir. Where should he be found?"

"Oh, put him in bed with four of the males and let someone else find him. That way, if anyone does query what happened, we'll have a suitably degrading cover story that we won't even have to spread. He caught the bug because he was enjoying an orgy with older men in the affected Sector."

"I believe he has a girlfriend in Sector 2," Keel said. "She might be suspicious."

"Then put him with a bunch of females!" the Captain shouted. "Then his girlfriend will be disgusted and spread the news for us! Honestly, can't you think for yourself?"

"I'll do it right away, sir," Filton assured the Captain, giving Keel a filthy look.

"Be sure no one else sees you. I can't afford to lose half my staff!"

The two men left and the Captain sat down at his desk and read the speech. It claimed they had encountered a strange, alien creature. Shaking his head, the Captain inserted 'in an abandoned ship' and continued to read. Said creature was investigated, as was the ship, but subsequently, many of those who'd been aboard fell ill. The sector was immediately quarantined to ensure no one else suffered. Sadly, this resulted in a one-hundred percent mortality rate in the sector. To ensure no one else clearing up would suffer the same fate, the sector was opened to space and then fumigated. All those doing clear up would still be required to wear hazmat suits, but that was just a precaution. Once the area had been thoroughly cleaned, it would be made available to children aged fourteen to sixteen years, with the first choice of cabins given to those children who did well in their tests and joined the Corps.

"Covering all his bases," Alex said, having read the entire speech over his shoulder. "Sector 3 gets clean up duty – although, of course, they think they're Sector 1 and they're clearing Sector 3." She shook her head. "They'll be carefully monitored with a big show of suits and masks when there's nothing there to catch, while at the same time the kids are encouraged to do well in the tests to get the best cabins."

"I wonder if that's the same sort of test Jackson just failed?" Daniel mused.

"Probably. They're clearly identifying a particular type. Most will remain at ground level and be executed with everyone else, but a select few will get promoted. I'm guessing promotions go to those who are amoral, non-empathetic, narcissistic..."

"We've encountered this kind of selection before," Daniel agreed. "It doesn't bode well for anyone."

"And for what?" Alex asked, pacing the cabin. Since it was relatively small, she kept passing through the Captain's desk. "So that they can keep their little fiefdom? What's the point?"

"They must realise they've already been overtaken, and that the planet has been settled," Daniel replied. "They may have detected it the instant they came out of cryo and the then Captain, or one of his officers, decided they'd rather stay in command than be a technologically backward bunch of hicks to the established settlers."

"And once they started harvesting the Sectors, there was no going back," she nodded. "How would they explain how they survived? They'd be facing court-martial at best, imprisonment for the rest of their lives, or execution for what they've done."

"Alex, stop walking through his head!" Daniel said. "It's really distracting."

"Sorry," she replied, settling on one side of the cabin. "How are we going to fix this? Anyone who realises what's happening or even suggests how it might be solved is instantly removed, and if an entire Sector realised it, they'd be wiped out."

"At one point, all the Sectors could be reached from all the others. The only reason the officers have managed to maintain control is by keeping the population divided. They all think they're Sector 1, and that Sector 3 are responsible for anything bad or counter to what they've been told to do. I bet the Captain's speech claims it's Sector 3 that's been wiped out!"

"It does," she nodded. "According to him they were 'taking the opportunity to redeem themselves in the eyes of the rest of the ship.'" She carefully leaned back against a bulkhead, reminding herself that it was solid. "Without a Sector 3 to blame, I wonder how they'll explain course corrections when they take over on the bridge?"

"Sector 2 suddenly become the bad guys for a bit?" he suggested. "Or maybe they tell them they're renumbering the Sectors and they're now Sector 1 and need to uphold the high standard?"

"Hmm. Would make sense. Anyone but Sector 1 is the bad guy, but everyone's told they're Sector 1. What were you saying about the Sectors being connected?"

"Taking out one Sector is possible, but if they could find the old hatches and reconnect, the officers would suddenly have four Sectors all kicking off, especially when they find out what's happening to the dead..."

"And their burgers?" She shuddered, took a deep breath and released it slowly, trying to drive out the image in her head. It wasn't easy. "All right. Let's see if we can find the hatches. They'll be in more or less the same place in each Sector, so we might as well start with this one."

She started to head out, then paused, turned and stepped into the Captain.

"Alex, what are you doing?"

There's no way either of us would want to live this life, so I can explore,' she explained in his head. *'Ugh. We were right, he's a psychopath... or a sociopath? I can never keep those two straight.'*

"Psychopath," Daniel replied flatly. "This one can pretend to be caring when it suits him, turn on the charm, and look the part whenever he's on show. Sociopath is the unofficial term for antisocial personality disorder. Sociopaths struggle to hide their emotions, get angry and lash out, even when it's self-destructive. This one doesn't seem to have any compunction over killing several thousand people in one hit and wouldn't understand why anyone else is upset. To him, it's a practical solution to a problem – how to feed thousands with limited supplies. Classic psychopath."

She stepped out. "I was wondering if he might be a robot, he's so cold-blooded, but no, he's human, just a remarkably unpleasant one." She watched as the Captain made some more notes. "Do you think I could step inside him during the announcement and spill the beans then?"

"Wouldn't work," he replied, shaking his head. "There'd be rioting and people would be killed, but ultimately the military would say he went mad, and that obviously they wouldn't do that as it's insane. For all we know, they do have some pigs they leave on show, pretending they're part of a team that's the source of the meat, and eventually everything would calm down and things would carry on as before."

"Yeah, but the next time an entire Sector is wiped out, they're going to remember and ask questions," she pressed.

"And they'll have prepared answers," he assured her. "It's a closed system. They can remove anyone they suspect of causing trouble or spreading what they would call 'misinformation'; they completely control the narrative, and they've been at this successfully for nearly two centuries. Sectors have no communications, so they could wipe one out, not say anything, and the others wouldn't even know it had happened. In fact, given it looks like they're killing them when they hit their thirties, I suspect most aren't reported. They probably do just vent them to space and throw the bodies out. There aren't any windows so no one's going to see. This time they need the bodies, so this time they'll tell the people because they need help taking them to wherever they take them to start them on their path to..." He took in Alex's green expression, "ah, processing," he finished. "Our best bet is to get all the Sectors connected so that they can talk to each other and be aware of what's happening."

"On that note, *we* need to find out what's happening. How come no one realised they were being poisoned in their sleep? How come not one person out of thousands was awake? Doesn't anyone aboard get insomnia from time to time?"

"Good question," he conceded. "If they can kill an entire sector of people in their sleep, and not one person fought it, that means they're doing something else first."

"Some kind of knock-out gas every night?" she suggested.

"Or at least injected into the room when they need to quietly kill someone. We need to find the controls for those and adjust them a bit, and you'll need to get inside someone to do that."

"Yes, but it'll have to be someone in *this* Sector, and we both know we're not going to fix this as a psychopath."

He couldn't argue with that. "Why not use Jackson? They're going to kill him anyway, but with your talents he could dodge that fate a little longer, and he's the only one we've seen who seems to have any qualms about what's happening."

She shook her head. "They'll be watching him like hawks. Unless I make him kill them, he won't be left alone long enough to do anything. I need someone high enough to have access and trusted enough not to be questioned."

"Won't be trusted for long if they see the one you choose somewhere they're not supposed to be."

"Then we need to find the point from which they control the air vents, and then I'll have to inhabit someone who's already there."

***

Hunting through over a mile of cabins and compartments was a long and tedious task made quicker because of Alex's ability to fly through bulkheads so that she could pass from place to place in a direct line. Doing this, she swept along each side of the central gangway, and then focused on the mass of rooms behind and around Command and Control.

"Found it!" she cried as she floated into a nondescript compartment. She stepped outside and noted that the hatch was secured with a keypad and a retinal scanner. There were no guards because only the people who were supposed to be in there would be able to enter, but that meant whoever she used would be registered and traced.

"I think I can screw with the electronics so that the record of who did it isn't passed on," she said, examining the internals of the keypad and sensor.

"Can you make it so anyone can get in? It doesn't look like people go in there until they intend to use it."

She continued her examination and then stepped back thoughtfully. "I might be able to flash my own energy in the wiring to wreck it so that they have to send someone down to fix it. The problem is that there'll be a very short window between my wrecking it – assuming I can – and the arrival of someone to investigate. In that time, I have to find someone, get them in here, make the necessary adjustments and get them out."

Daniel looked around. He spotted a camera. "You'll need to wreck that, too," he said, pointing.

"Great!" she sighed, going back into the compartment.

She examined the setup. There was a computer. On it, every cabin aboard ship could be marked either individually or in groups or by sector. Once that was done, a lever was pulled, releasing engine fumes into the marked cabins. A sign proclaimed 'No less than ten seconds. No more than twenty seconds'.

"Excess exposure to the engine fumes is not wanted," Daniel commented.

"Probably leaves evidence that others can pick up easily," Alex replied, still exploring the computer program. "If I mess with this, they'll find it easily and put it back. The program's too simple to hide it." She walked over and stuck her head through the bulkhead to examine the pipes behind the lever. "This has been jerry-rigged, with an extra hose connected." She pulled back and examined the bulkhead. "All we need to remove this is a screwdriver, but I doubt any of the officers would carry such a thing in their pockets."

"No," Daniel agreed, looking at the screws that held the bulkhead in place, "but they might carry the equivalent of a Swiss Army Knife. Assuming we can find such a one, how could they stop the hose from releasing the gas into this compartment? The instant they find a dead officer in here and the lever still on, they're going to realise what's happened."

Alex traced the hose back until she found where it connected to the exhaust pipe from the engines. It was quite close to the outer bulkhead that separated C&C from the next Sector. She stuck her head through.

"That's the Sector where I arrived," she commented. "The bulkheads are strong but they're not that thick."

"They're made of titanium and are quite thick enough to protect a sector if another was open to space." He joined her as she stood with her right leg in C&C, and the other in her landing Sector. "Nearly two centimetres. That's thicker than the hull of the space shuttles that were used at the end of the twentieth century, and they had to withstand re-entry. This ship never lands. It was built in space and is designed to stay there, so the worst it ever has to withstand are small pieces of space debris. An internal bulkhead this thick is overkill."

"But it would protect the crew if the ship was forced to land, right?"

"Assuming the impact didn't kill them? Yes," he confirmed.

"Maybe that was the idea? Or perhaps they thought that after they'd reached the planet via shuttles or something similar, they could bring the ship down by remote control and salvage the extra metal?"

"Refined metal would be a valuable commodity for a community starting out on a new planet," he agreed. "Finding and extracting ores, and then turning them into something useable is time consuming in the extreme."

"Can it be cut? I mean, if we can't find the original hatches, or they've been covered up, could they cut their way through to the next sector?"

"They'd need a tungsten or titanium carbide drill, or a drill bit with a titanium aluminium nitride coating, or something even better."

"What about a plasma torch?" she asked.

"That'd do it too. Be a bit messy compared to the proper tools, but it would work. Why?"

"Because I saw some plasma torches as I was checking out the rooms back there," and she jerked a thumb over her shoulder towards C&C. "Probably used for external repairs and to seal the internal hatches. If there was some way those could be relocated into another Sector, like that one," and she pointed the other way, her arm vanishing through the wall, "we might kill several birds with one stone."

"Two problems with that," Daniel said. "Firstly, physically getting a load of plasma torches past the guards at the exits to C&C without them noticing is going to be practically impossible. Secondly, alerting someone on the other side that they're available, without condemning whoever gives the heads up to a very early death, is also going to be a tough call."

"We'd also need whoever gets them in the other sector to have a deck plan of the ship, showing precisely where the old hatches are located," she mused. "Otherwise, there would be a risk of them accidentally going through an outer bulkhead and suffocating the entire Sector."

"Three problems," Daniel corrected.

"What about if we used their intention to send Sector 3 into Sector 4 to do clean up while wearing hazmat suits? They're not going to be collecting the suits from in here;

the suits will be taken to them. It'd be easy to hide plasma torches in loads of bulky hazmat suits and get them past the guards."

"All right, let's assume you inhabit someone, print off some deckplans, and manage to hide the plasma torches. They're going into Sector 4, which is to be handed over to the kids."

"Even better! They get hidden in one of the air ducts. We know the kids won't be singled out for destruction for nearly twenty years. Plenty of time for someone to find the torches, the deckplans, and a summary of what's happening and what they need to do about it."

"What if they don't find the plans?" he asked reasonably.

She paced, staring at the deck. Finally, she looked up. "We can't try it now. They'd just kill whoever I inhabit to share the information, or shut down whichever sector gets it and kill them as well. That would be the end of any insurrection and the slaughter continues. That means we *need* to be here and know every detail of what's happening. We need to be organised, and we need to ensure all the sectors are connected before the move on C&C so that, shy of exterminating the entire civilian population, there's nothing command can do to stop it. With that in mind, and given this is not our proper training universe, ask Almega if we can plant an idea in our own heads to be realised when we're, I don't know, twenty? Twenty-five?"

"Why so late?"

"If we don't get it right, we're dead, but then we're dead at no more than thirty-two anyway, so at least we'll have had a bit of a life."

He turned and talked to Almega for a few moments while Alex tapped her foot impatiently.

"Maybe," he said at last. "A subliminal message planted in our dreams of a specific room location might be possible. If it's got positive associations, we may well be drawn to it."

"If that's all we can have, it'll have to do!" she nodded. "And, if we succeed, get rid of the command staff, and get the ship to a planet, we'll have a proper life."

"Hmm. Might be an idea to be vegetarian, though," he replied.

"Oh, yeah. Ugh! Do you think they've enough tablets to offset the deficiencies?"

"Almost certainly. Once meat became available, they wouldn't need to call on the stores, plus there'd be a few of faiths that don't allow their members to eat pork."

"Guess we're coming back as one of them, then!"

"That, or we're going to be very hungry for most of the training," he nodded.

"OK, I know how I'm going to get the plasma torches into the sector. The question now is, where am I going to hide them?"

"Put them in the air vent for the cabin one of us occupies, it'll help block any noxious fumes. Might hold it long enough for us to escape?"

"Hmm." Alex went into Sector 4, walked around a bit until she identified a cabin that wasn't being watched by cameras (a necessity if they were to live this gruesome life) and went inside. A woman lay dead on the bed.

"Pardon me," Alex said, rising so that she could take a look at the air vent. She cocked her head as she looked inside. "Hang on!" She shrank herself and vanished into the air duct. *'I think I've found out how they can easily kill the civilians when they're in their cabins, and there's no sign of a struggle.'*

Daniel appeared beside her. "What is that?" he asked, staring at the small addition.

"At a guess, I'd say it releases something soporific. Just enough that they go to sleep quickly and easily. What C&C do to them after that is up to the senior officers, but their targets can't fight back."

"Two hundred years of practice, I guess they learned from their earlier mistakes," Daniel winced.

"Talk about cold-blooded," Alex agreed. She examined the switch that had been added to the air vent and pointed to a date mark. "Looks like they refill it after each extinction event." Daniel raised an eyebrow at her choice of language. "I'm trying to put some distance between what we're talking about and the emotional force of it," she explained. "If I think about this in too much detail, I'm going to be sick." He nodded. He was feeling the same. "On a practical point, this," and she pointed to the switch, "means I'll have to make sure I also take over someone after they've done refreshing them, so that I can come back in and turn them off. We can't risk our avatars being drugged and killed in the night."

"Why not just take over the person doing it?" he suggested. "That way, rather than trying to explain why you've got a ladder and your face buried in an air vent, you're simply doing your job."

"Good idea! If they go in at the same time as everyone else when they start cleaning up, maybe I could make them the one taking in the hazmat suits with the hidden payload?"

"Are they going to hand out the hazmats in here? If they're claiming this is the dangerous area, surely the suits need to be put on outside it?"

She stared at him for a moment, then buried her face in her hands.

"Oh no," she groaned, shaking her head as she realised that he was quite right. "I was assuming they'd suit up in this sector, which would allow us to get the torches in without being seen. If they're suiting up outside, the whole plan goes to pot."

"We'll think of something," he offered gently.

"It's impossible!" she cried, throwing her arms wide. "C&C have everything locked down so tightly that there's no way to break in without breaking everything! And we can't do that because if we turned the exhaust on C&C itself and killed all those lunatics, the people would starve in their Sectors. To pull this off I need to be in about a dozen different people at the same time. I can't do it! How can we get them the necessary tools, tell them what they have to do and why, *and* protect the people while they're doing it so that they can get together and throw off these monsters? It's impossible!"

The two stood in depressed silence, realising the enormity of the problem.

"What if..." Daniel said at last, then went silent.

"What if what?" she snapped.

"Perhaps we're looking at this the wrong way?"

"What do you mean?"

"We're assuming we'll be inside. What if we're outside?" When she continued to look confused, he elaborated. "We can't fix this from the inside because it's too rigid. If we break one bit enough to do the job, we break it all, and they're dead either way. Instead, what if we got them in the path of another ship? If they were unexpectedly found and someone from outside realised what was happening?"

"And how are we to do that when C&C keep reversing course and stopping them from ever getting anywhere?"

"The navigational controls are all computerised. They can't see where they're going. They have to rely on the computers to tell them. You're a genius when it comes to complex programs. If you could rewrite the navigation so that they stay on course..."

She shook her head, staring at the floor. "I'd have to be inside one of them hacking the system, and the bridge has cameras everywhere. They'd see."

"Then how about we find another ship that isn't so controlled and redirect their systems instead?"

Her head jerked up. "Does Almega know exactly where we are?" she asked.

He turned, briefly, then turned back. "Yes. He has our exact position and the area the ship keeps covering."

"Where's the nearest space highway?" she asked, her hope rising.

Another pause. "About five thousand miles, bearing one-twenty by forty-six degrees. The Argo is holding below and to port of the major shipping routes, and far enough away that they're not picked up by sensors."

"Where's the nearest ship with the means to deal with this?" she demanded, her tone determined.

"The Invincible, an Earth-based explorer and troopship, travelling to the Lyra constellation to investigate another planet. It's slightly off the usual route because of its destination."

"Sounds perfect! Point me to it!"

***

In the vastness of space, trying to find one relatively small ship (although it was still massive in human terms) would have been impossible had it not been for Almega's excellent directions. Once inside, Alex looked around and took a long, deep breath.

"All right. This I can work with! Even better, if I do this right, we won't have to do a training here at all!"

"Can't say I was looking forward to it," Daniel admitted.

"Nor I!"

She headed for the bridge and checked out the navigational computers, helm, and then headed for the sensors. After a thorough examination, she pulled her head out of the console and examined the interface the officer was using.

"Based on their present heading, they'll only miss the Argo by a couple of thousand miles and this thing has two sets of sensors, one of which has a reach of several hundred miles. If I can nudge her off course a little and then a little more, those sensors will pick up the Argo. After that, they can do the rest."

"How are you going to nudge them?" he asked.

"Sensor ghosts," she grinned and stepped into the seated officer. It took no time at all to have the officer 'accidentally' trip detection of the first 'ghost'.

"Helm? I'm picking up something to port," Captain Saunders said, checking his own readings. "Navigation? Are you getting that?"

Alex stepped out of her officer who shook herself and checked the readings.

"Yes, sir."

"Any idea what it is?"

"It's not sending out a signal. Could be an asteroid?"

"A little close to the space lanes for us to ignore it. All it would need is a tap and it could become a hazard. Better check it out. Helm, adjust course to intercept."

"Adjusting course. Coming about to two-eighty by two-six-five."

Alex got back inside the navigator and created another reading right on the edge of the sensor readings, but this time indicating it was a ship. She stepped out again.

"Navigation, are you seeing what I'm seeing?" Saunders asked.

"Yes, sir. Looks like it might be a ship," Alex's officer replied.

"A ship? That far off the space-lanes?"

The helmsman turned in his seat. "Sir? Could it be the Argo?"

The Captain's eyes glinted. "Worth checking out, don't you think? A two-hundred-year-old mystery solved?"

"Yes, sir!" the helmsman responded with a grin.

"Follow the readings. Is it giving off any signals?"

"No sir," the navigation officer replied, "but its antennae could be broken."

"No signals, no readings... Could explain why it got lost and why we couldn't find it. Increase speed."

"Aye, sir."

Once again, Alex stepped in, but this time the Argo itself was identifiable at the far end of sensor reach, it was just a matter of making sure the navigator spotted it.

"Navigation, what is going on?" the Captain asked. "Nothing moves that fast!"

"I don't know, sir. Some kind of sensor ghost? I am getting something else, though, and this one is definitely a ship."

"I see it. If this is another ghost, then we'll turn back. Lay in a course."

"Aye, sir," helm responded, feeding in the coordinates that would point them directly at the Argo.

"That should do it," Alex smiled, the tension leaving her.

"You've still got a while stuck in this universe until Almega can persuade another to create a crossover point," Daniel said.

"Good. I want to see those monsters get their comeuppance!"

"This one's not jumping sir, and it's definitely a ship."

"Does she have power?" the Captain asked.

"Yes, but she's not broadcasting on any frequency."

"Why would a ship not broadcast her location?" Saunders mused.

"Getting more sensor readings..." the navigation officer said. "Over three miles long, indications it's using the old ion and plasma propulsion systems." She turned in her seat. "Sir! It *is* the Argo!"

"Excellent!" Saunders muttered. "Master at Arms," he continued, raising his voice so that the officer standing at the security console could hear him.

The officer snapped to attention. "Sir!"

"I'm going to need a squad. We don't know what we might encounter, so be prepared for anything and arm yourselves. Stun setting only, please. I'd prefer not to kill the survivors if there are any."

"Sir, there might be aliens..."

"Then even more reason to leave your weapons on stun. Last thing we need is to be court martialled because one of the crew got scared and fired off at something that turns out to be friendly."

"But sir –"

"Stun only, Mr Bracket! If they turn out to be dangerous, then you can up the power levels. Understood?"

"Yes, sir," Bracket replied.

"And take Mr Hong with you." He turned to his First Officer who had stood up the instant his name was called. "Stay in touch. I want to hear what's happening over there. Any sign of trouble, get back in the shuttle and come home."

"Sir, we're going to have to cut through the hull. We can't signal them to let us aboard, and the Argo's shuttle bay wasn't designed for our bigger shuttles. It won't fit."

"Then take along something to repair the hole with when you're done. If there are any left aboard, they probably won't all fit in the shuttle, given you're taking a squad, and we'll need to tow her to Lyrosa shipyard so that they can disembark and be checked. If there aren't any, the authorities will still want her towed there so that they can find out what happened. Either way, she's not going anywhere with a great big hole in her side."

"Understood, sir."

Hong and Bracket left the bridge. The navigation officer continued to monitor the sensors and, as the Invincible drew closer to the Argo, suddenly started tapping her board in an agitated manner.

"Something wrong, Ensign Toledo?" Saunders asked.

"Sir! I'm picking up lifesigns!"

"Glad to hear it," Saunders replied laconically. "How many?"

"I'm trying to... this is impossible!" she muttered.

"What is?"

"Over eight thousand are aboard, sir."

Saunders leapt from his chair. "Eight *thousand*? On that thing? They must be cheek by jowl. And what the hell are they eating?"

"Um..." Toledo looked very uncomfortable.

"Spit it out, Ensign!"

"Sir, I'm reading another two thousand dead and, from these readings, they're being taken to what looks like a food processing plant."

"Commander Hong!" Saunders yelled over the comms.

"Sir?"

"Take every shuttle, load them up with as many men as you can and some medics. You've eight thousand people aboard and another two thousand that are being chopped up for food!"

"Oh, God! Understood, sir."

"At least they now know what they're getting into," Daniel commented as they floated out of the ship and slipped into the first of the departing shuttles. Inside, Hong asked to be directed to an area with minimal life readings – preferably not anywhere near the meat processing facility. Their shuttle was guided to a cargo bay which, for now at least, was empty.

"Set her down as gently as you can," Hong told the pilot. "If we can get aboard without them even realising we're here, that'll make it a lot easier."

"Where are the others going to land?" Daniel wondered as the shuttle settled very gently on the outer hull of the Argo.

Alex went outside and saw that each of the shuttles was connecting via a hatch to the next and the next, forming one long line.

'Wonder why they developed that trick?'

'Perhaps for emergency evacuations?' Daniel replied. *'Or assaults where there's limited accessible space on the target ship?'*

Returning to the inside of the shuttle, she saw that a hatch had been opened on the side allowing it to connect to the others, and a long line of troops could now be seen

190

waiting to enter the Argo. Meanwhile, a floor baseplate had been removed exposing another hatch and, poking her head through, Alex could see that a seal had been connected to the Argo and a very precise laser cutter was slicing a hole into the Argo's hull faster than a tin-opener on a can.

"Definitely done this before," she stated.

A light went from red to green and a crewman spun the hatch wheel, lifted the hatch slightly and then slid it to one side, leaving the hole with nothing blocking it. Master at Arms Bracket checked his weapon and dropped through, quickly followed by several other crewmen, before the First Officer joined them.

Inside the Argo, the crew of the Invincible formed up in the silence of the empty hold.

"No internal sensors in here," Bracket muttered. "Didn't they have them two hundred years ago?"

"This ship set out long before that," Hong reminded him. "They were in cryo for most of the journey. Remember?"

"Even so, basic cameras? And in such an overcrowded ship, who leaves such a large space empty?"

The medics had finally made their way through the opening into the Argo. Every one of them, Alex noted, was wearing glasses. That seemed odd given no one else on the crew needed them. Then she realised they weren't for visual correction. These were scanners that allowed the wearer to focus on particular bits of information and have the image adjusted to show it or print out the details on the lens. The lead medic looked very concerned.

"Commander Hong? I thought the dead were in another part of the ship?"

"They are," Hong confirmed.

"Then that's not the first mass death they've had. This area, while it's been cleaned, is filled with evidence of human blood."

"Filled?"

"Commander, trust me, if you sprayed some Aminophthalhydrazide around here and turned on a UV-A, it would light up like a disco."

He handed over his glasses. The commander put them on and looked around the cargo bay.

"Woah!" Hong picked up his foot and noticed traces were now on the sole of his boot. He removed the glasses and handed them back to the medic.

"Commander?" came the Captain's voice from the comm unit on Hong's belt. "What's going on?"

"We're just about to advance, sir, but it looks like that wasn't the first mass death they've had aboard."

At that moment, a door slid open and a man entered pushing a rack filled with trays. The trays, in turn, were filled with meat patties. He looked up, saw the strangers and dashed back to the door, trying to shut it before the soldiers could advance. One of the crew fired a stun shot, knocking the man down. While one medic saw to him and another checked the trays, the soldiers quickly and quietly advanced into the ship.

***

"You can't do this to me!" the Captain of the Argo yelled as soldiers fitted security bracelets to his wrists, which were held behind his back.

"Does anyone outside of this section know that you've been feeding human flesh to them?" Hong demanded.

"Of course not! It would have caused panic and more would have died." The Captain fixed Hong with a cold look. "We had a choice, Commander: recycle everything, including ourselves, or die."

"I note you all made sure that you weren't for dinner!" the senior medic snorted.

"A few had to carry on to maintain command and keep the secret. To do what had to be done. There are eight thousand, four hundred and twenty-three humans aboard this ship, doctor. A ship designed to carry no more than two thousand. What do *you* suggest we should have done?"

"Get back to the space lanes? Fix your antennae so you could send out a signal? Keep going in one direction long enough to actually get somewhere?" Hong replied, listing the things his team had discovered as they took over the ship. His anger was now boiling over. That the senior officers showed not one whit of guilt over what they had done left him horrified. "Oh yes, we scanned your equipment and your systems once we took the bridge. Your antennae have been deliberately sabotaged. None of your ordinary crew members even knew they'd been backtracking for nearly two centuries, or that their sensors were sending false information, or that their comms were useless. They are not at fault."

"No, they're not," Captain Saunders said. He'd left the Invincible docked outside and come aboard to see for himself those who'd carried out this nightmare. "Get the others out of here," he told Hong, "and then get back to the ship. I want to talk to this officer alone."

Bracket motioned to his team to escort the senior officers from C&C.

"Where to, sir?" Bracket asked.

"The hold we left empty to bring back samples from the new planet. There's not enough room in the brig for this many, and that hold has plenty of security. Strip them, search them, give them something to wear and I want monitoring and forcefields at maximum. Understood?"

"Yes, sir!" The rest of the Argo's officers were led out. A few struggled but it was quickly made plain to them that, if they kept it up, they'd be stunned and carried back. With that warning, they all sullenly complied.

Hong turned to Saunders. "Sir. You really shouldn't stay here alone with this... person."

Saunders levelled Hong with a look that silenced the First Officer. "I believe the manacles will hold, Commander Hong. I would like Mr Bracket and a team to remain aboard to monitor our introduction to the rest of the population and keep guard on the lower ranks of C&C that we've got locked in one of the holds. However, so far as we can tell, the rest of the ship's complement are innocents. Dr Havarade and his medics should also remain." He turned to the doctor, who had been treating some minor bruises and cuts sustained by the Invincible's crew when they took over C&C. "Can you get together a team of psych officers to help us introduce ourselves?"

"I'll have them here within the hour," he assured Saunders.

Saunders turned to the Argo's captain. "As for you, Captain...?"

"Blake," the Argo's captain replied.

"Very well. You and all the senior crew who were in on this will be taken to Lyrosa to stand trial for your crimes."

"Crimes?!" Blake spat. "We've saved over eight thousand people! We deserve medals!"

"And needlessly murdered many thousands more," Saunders replied calmly. He motioned to the security officers standing either side of Blake, who manhandled him into a chair. Another security officer brought a rather more comfortable one for Saunders, who sat down and activated his comm to record the conversation.

"How did this happen?" he asked.

Blake rolled his eyes, making it clear he didn't believe Saunders was interested in the truth.

"I genuinely want to understand," Saunders told him. "I've read the biographies of your ancestors. Everyone did. None of them were psychopaths, which means all this," and he waved a hand, indicating the Argo, "happened as a result of events. Tell me those events."

Alex and Daniel found positions from which they could listen, equally interested in the answer.

Blake cocked his head, narrowing his eyes at Saunders, but Saunders merely leaned forward and urged him on.

"I'm recording everything we say here," Saunders said, pointing to a small camera he was wearing above his uniform breast pocket. "Now's your chance to explain how you became this. It could go well in your defence if you're honest. We will be checking the Argo's logs but right now I want to hear how you understand it."

Blake sat back, winced when his manacled wrists got in the way, and gave Saunders a pointed look.

"They'll stay on until I'm satisfied you can be trusted, Captain Blake. Now tell us what happened."

There was another pause until Blake recognised that he'd be stuck here until he told the story.

"The first captain of the Argo, Captain Lanos, woke up and realised we'd been overtaken by latter settlers and a civilisation now existed on the planet," Blake began. "The signals were coming in thick and fast from Lyrosa. He immediately sent out a signal, begging for someone to come and rescue the Argo, but there really had been some damage done to the comms system and the signal wasn't sent. He got a team together to fix it. While they were doing that, his First Officer, Commander Milkov, realised what would happen. The ship had been the height of technology when she set out, filled with the top brains of the time ready to start a new life on a new planet. Now they'd been left behind, not by weeks or months but by hundreds of years. He realised they'd never catch up and they'd be a joke! Akin to a sixteenth century scientist or physician waking up in the twenty-first century. He tried to explain this to Lanos, but the captain wouldn't listen. Lanos said that even a top scientist would rather be alive and work on a checkout than dead in space. Milkov and a few others got together and talked about it, decided that no, they didn't want to become beggars or a joke on late night chat shows, so they staged a coup. At that time, we had animal embryos that were going to be used on the new planet if no indigenous life was found, and we did raise them, but there wasn't the space for them *and* crops we could eat in hydroponics, and so, bit by bit with heavy rationing, they ate them. The crew were scientists and officers, not farmers and they made mistakes that ultimately prevented further births and so, eventually, the meat ran out, but we already had a large population, and it was growing. They looked around for another uninhabited planet that they could settle where they could use their skills and make a new life for themselves, but our sensors couldn't reach far enough and the Argo hadn't the power to get there even if they could." He leaned back, closing his eyes as he remembered the records. "It was decided that it would be better to stay out here, away from everyone and just die quietly. To that end, the antennae connections were sabotaged so that no messages would get in or out, and they settled down to finish their days amongst the stars."

"Lanos was prepared to do that?"

"Lanos and those who sided with him were all dead. They were killed during the coup," Blake replied flatly.

"Ahh. Carry on."

"You can't order people to become celibate, and forced sterilisation was deemed an unacceptable breach of their human rights. So, the population was ordered to use prophylactics. They were told that the Argo would never reach another planet and no more should be condemned to die here; that if they didn't rein themselves in, they'd run out of food and die even faster, but still more were born."

Saunders nodded. Trying to get humans, especially young ones, to abstain from sex in an enclosed environment with little else to do was a lost cause, and even the best prophylactics failed, assuming that, in the heat of passion, the couples remembered to use them in the first place. "Then there was an uprising. The Argo was low on food supplies, people were beginning to starve, and tempers were running high. A few took over the bridge and found that there were no working communication systems, and no evidence of other planets. They'd thought

196

the officers were lying. Now they realised they had no way to escape. They were desperate." He stared at Saunders, his eyes cold. "They killed themselves rather than face the future."

"And you used their bodies to solve the food shortages," Saunders nodded.

"No. Not then. There was a funeral, but then the senior officers realised the bones could be used as fertilizer and food was needed, so instead of shooting them out into space, they were recycled."

Blake paused until Saunders prodded him. "What happened next?"

"They couldn't risk another insurrection, so the sections were sealed in the night while everyone was asleep. When they woke up, they realised they couldn't go beyond their section of the ship and they couldn't get to C&C or the bridge, both of which were heavily guarded. A few tried to destroy the ship. That's when they discovered the fuel exhaust could knock people out. Some of the people trying to smash through the hull in Sector 2 broke through an exhaust pipe. At first, they were just asleep, but no one noticed what had happened. By the time they did, the entire section was dead. Some officers went in and fixed the pipe, and then they realised that if they extended it, they could feed it through to the air vents anywhere in the ship and make sure people were unconscious when... certain things had to be done."

"Like carrying dead bodies through?"

Blake nodded. "The meat processing facility was still accessible to Sector 3 at the start. It was only later it was sealed off. A few woke up and they could smell the machines had been used. The officers came in to find people licking up the blood and grabbing whatever meat had got snagged in the gears. They were literally starving. They didn't know it was human and the officers didn't tell them. Instead, the officers claimed they'd been working on speeding up the growth of some pig embryos that had been found in storage and were going to release them early. That's when the burger bars opened."

"And then you ran out," Saunders said.

Another nod. "There'd been some problems with Sector 3. Where they'd been eating the bits of raw meat from the processors, including brains, it affected them. It took a while, though not anywhere near as long an incubation as is usual. The scientists theorised that the long period in cryo and the malnutrition had made them highly susceptible. What should have taken ten to fifteen years, took less than a year, and then they showed signs of suffering from kuru."

Saunders cocked his head curiously.

"It's a form of transmissible spongiform encephalopathy. It's caused by proteins in the brain that..." His hands twisted and turned as the non-scientist tried to explain what he'd read. "They somehow fold differently and then cause all sorts of diseases. Symptoms include tremors and loss of coordination, as well as uncontrollable laughter. Someone in Sector 2, perhaps several of them, had the brain damage, and then Sector 3 – the first Sector to be given the burgers – got it too."

"Consequently, they were also murdered?"

"Yes, but this time the heads were removed to make sure no brain matter would get into the meat. The processing section was sealed off, Sector 3 was cleaned thoroughly, but it was announced to Sectors 1 and 4 that they'd tried to destroy the ship, which gave Sector 3 its bad reputation. After that, anything that went wrong aboard was always Sector 3's fault."

Saunders nodded. "Carry on."

"They left some of the damage so that the new occupants could see the officers weren't lying. Even showed them some selected footage that had been recorded."

"Which didn't show the burger bar, I assume?"

"Like I said, selected. They explained that, since there was now room, children would be allowed to live in the abandoned Sector. There, they'd be trained to take over running the ship since the officers were getting old. They were given the clean meat and, when they didn't get kuru, the burger bars were opened in the other sectors. Each sector was told it was unique, special and valued, and getting this rarity as a treat for working hard and not giving in."

"And now they couldn't talk to each other, they had no reason to doubt it," Saunders added thoughtfully. "How do you move them from sector to sector if all the connections are sealed?"

"There are narrow air ducts that have to be left open. This was why only the children were allowed to pass through as they're the only ones small enough to do it. The duct is opened, the children crawl through and, once they're all inside, grating is placed across the ends. Within a few years they're all too big to do it anyway."

"You were sending adults to clean your most recent slaughter when we arrived."

"We temporarily reopen the hatches between the sectors when we have no other choice. Most of the time, the only route is via the old air ducts, and it gives us a reason why children are separated from their parents."

"But C&C can get access to all sectors?"

"C&C is in the core. From there, you can get anywhere."

"What happened to Sectors 1 and 4?"

"In time they got old. Some died naturally, some agitators met with accidents a little earlier but, in time, they all passed. The problem by then was that they were too old. Everyone had got used to the meat and the poor quality of the new stuff wasn't good enough. Even so, it was better than nothing."

"That's when the maximum age for those outside C&C was reduced to no older than thirty?"

"Initially, it was forty-five. It's been dropped as the population expanded," Blake clarified. "It's now between thirty and thirty-two."

"And what do over eight thousand people do aboard a ship like this?" Saunders asked.

"Oh, there are classes in every subject the original settlers knew anything about. Sometimes they are asked to help clean up a sector –"

"When there has been 'an accident' or an unusual encounter?" Saunders asked, resting his elbows on his knees and raising an eyebrow.

"Of course. There are so many civilians now that the officers can't handle it on their own. No sector does it more than once and it's always the oldest sector that's given the duty. That way, when they die, the event is forgotten and the story can be reused somewhere else."

Saunders sat back, folding his arms. "You know what gets me about all this, Blake?"

"That's Captain Blake, Captain Saunders."

"No, I don't think you're entitled to that honour," Saunders dismissed. "What gets me is how calm you are about mass murder and cannibalism."

"I just explained to you why it happened, and it's all I've ever known. Why should it bother me?"

"You weren't bothered when you found out you'd been eating not only other humans, but possibly your own parents?"

"There are societies on Earth that did that as a ritual. The word kuru comes from the Fore People of Papua New Guinea. They would eat their dead in the belief it freed their souls. Kuria is the Fore People's word for 'shake'. In Russia, back when the people were starving, they ate their neighbours and even other family members. People don't talk about it, but that doesn't mean it doesn't happen. There's no other source of protein aboard ship and without pills to make up for the nutrient deficiencies caused by an entirely plant-based diet – and a limited one at that – the people would have died a long, slow and painful death before you found us. You may not care for it, Captain Saunders, but it kept us alive."

"Because you were scared of looking backward to the citizens of Lyros? That's the sum total of your reasoning. You were afraid you'd look like hicks, and everything else that has happened came from that initial assumption – which was wrong, by the way," Saunders added as he stood up.

"Wrong? You mean the original settlers would have been welcomed back into the scientific communities as equals immediately?" Blake scoffed.

"The Argo was the only ship ever to experience long term cryostasis and do so successfully. No other managed it, although they tried. Whatever was done aboard this ship, it worked and got you to within fifty years of your landing. A lot of scientists are very keen to find out how. They would also have liked to examine the original crew to find out what effects it had on their minds and bodies. They were so certain you'd be found in time that an entire academic centre was built, ready to receive you, with offices, nice houses for your ancestors to live in, honours and awards because of your courage and pioneering approach. So many papers, so many books, so much fame... And you threw it all away to become this."

He turned and walked away, leaving Blake staring after him.

"You're lying!" Blake yelled after him.

"I wish I were," Saunders sighed and walked out.

***

"Almega's managed to persuade another universe to cross over just ahead," Daniel warned Alex when the interview was over.

"Where?"

"Just a few light years away, but we'd better hurry."

They left the ship, Daniel pointing Alex in the right direction. Going at top speed, she reached the area of empty space and then hung, waiting in the silence.

'What happens to the passengers aboard the Argo now?'

'It's mixed,' he replied. 'The senior officers, like Blake, go through a rather protracted trial, but that interview is used a lot. It's clear they're also victims, of a sort. They were so utterly convinced of the uselessness of trying to return to the rest of the human race that their actions could be called benevolent, but their utter refusal to even countenance the idea that their passengers should have a voice and the option to choose differently went against them. Like many politicians, they thought they knew best and, for the most part, they were wrong.'

'For the most part?'

'People did struggle accommodating a group who'd been cannibals, albeit unwittingly. When they discovered what they'd been eating, the vast majority of the Argo civilians refused to touch anything pork-like ever again or turned vegetarian. A tiny few had got the taste for it, which was a bit of a problem. Every time there were murders in their vicinity where the body couldn't be found, they were immediately interviewed in case they'd eaten the evidence. A couple had taken the opportunity, but most hadn't, and the repeated targeting caused some to commit suicide, even though they were innocent.'

Alex winced. 'Was Saunders telling the truth? Was there a place prepared for them?'

'Oh yes! The Argo Institute was a thriving scientific community. As it turned out, the training the Argo civilians went through to pass the time was actually very good – a credit to the advanced status of the original settlers. Some of them not only managed to catch up quite quickly but went on to become senior professors in their own right. They had all the basics down so well they could outstrip many of their Lyrosian fellows who'd become used to relying on computers to remind them of stuff they'd either never studied or had forgotten. Argonauts – yes, they got that nickname – became well known for their disciplined mental acuity and their ability to combine ideas in their heads rather than depending on computers or mobile devices. Not that they didn't leap on those with alacrity now that they could. Energy on the Argo was a valuable resource. Hydrogen scoops and other particle collectors gathered what was needed for everything. They had solar panels, too, but their location in space meant there was very little light to collect, so those took a long time to charge the batteries. As a result, the people had to get very good at remembering. They had restricted access to the computers, and they couldn't go back if they'd missed something until the next day. They did have very basic tablets to do their work on, charged by the lights that had to be on inside the ship, but the original settlers had filled the computers with facts, not fun stuff, and there was limited space in the memory cores, so the civilians weren't allowed to fill them up with anything that didn't advance discovery.'

'Ahh. No gigabytes of cat memes, then!' Alex chuckled.

'No. They'd also made discoveries of their own.'

'Really? I'm surprised.'

'Why? Eight thousand people swapping ideas are likely to come up with something original if they've a good grounding, and their progenitors were some of the most advanced minds on the planet when they left.'

'It's just occurred to me. I didn't see anyone with any disabilities aboard the Argo.'

'There was a deliberate euthanasia programme when any were born with mental or physical defects because there wasn't the space or the resources available to give to them, so any faulty DNA was eradicated before it spread.'

'Ouch! Doesn't surprise me, given what else they were doing, but that's still horrible!'

'Agreed.'

'I imagine they weren't too tolerant of disabilities when they reached Lyrosa,' she mused.

'They adapted,' he shrugged.

'Did they ever find out why their system of cryostasis worked when none of the others did?'

'Yes. One of the original team had spotted the problem just before they set out, but she forgot to email it and her notes were lost due to a fire at her house the day after the Argo launched. Nothing sinister,' he added when Alex looked at him sharply. 'She'd left a power-outlet on, and it shorted. She had it on her personal tablet in storage and it was uploaded to the Argo's computer when she woke *up, together with some other ideas. They really were quite brilliant people. The new system was employed from then on and worked well.'*

'A pity their brilliance didn't extend to realising they'd still be appreciated despite their long hiatus.'

'A mix of imposter syndrome and a few very persuasive doubters in an echo chamber. After a while, they all became convinced they'd be seen as useless.'

Alex felt the tunnel opening.

'Any idea where I'm going next?' she asked as the blank area of space was suddenly filled with the swirling route to the next universe. The fact that they were in space did, however, mean that the deafening roar was silenced, for which she was most grateful. Before Daniel could answer, she was sucked in.

Chapter 6

'*Oh, not again!*' Alex thought as she realised that she was about to slam into another spaceship. She deliberately focused on passing through the hull, slowed her progress, and righted herself so that she landed lightly on her feet in the middle of what appeared to be the bridge.

She dusted herself down – more from habit than need – and looked around. Human*ish* was the first thought that struck her. The bridge crew were bipedal with two arms and a fairly standard arrangement of ears, nose and mouth, but their faces had more of a muzzle on them than humans and, when one of them reached up to flick a switch, they revealed a flap of skin that attached the inside of the arms to their sides while leaving plenty of space to manoeuvre.

'*Half human, half bat,*' she decided.

The commanding officer pronounced a series of clicks and whistles, further reinforcing the bat-like aspect of his physiology, but as Alex did not presently have the language files, she had no idea what he said. Someone at one of the other stations briefly responded, there was a slight shifting sensation, and suddenly the view on the screen changed from space to something else.

"They're using a type of spatial warp," Daniel explained as he appeared beside her. The language files followed hard on his heels, courtesy of Omskep. "Rather than scrunching space up and riding the wave, they twist it, open a hole, jump inside and then navigate to their exit point. Not easy to do," he added thoughtfully, "which means this is an advanced species."

"Called?" Alex prompted.

"Vynarians," Daniel replied. "This bunch decided to leave the home planet, Vynar, and seek out another more suited to them."

"What's wrong with their own planet?"

"The usual," he shrugged. "A small number garnering all the power and money, while everyone else struggles to have a life, as opposed to an existence. They've found a planet with significantly lower gravity, that they think will be ideal. Their skin flaps allow them to glide, but they're more like flying foxes than bats."

"Ahh. No powered flight."

"Not on Vynar, no. On the new planet, they almost certainly will be able to."

"How many aboard?"

"In total, about seven hundred, which is enough to start a new colony safely. Apparently, there was quite the rush of volunteers when the idea was first mooted, allowing them to pick the strongest, most intelligent, most adaptable and, amongst those, the ones least likely to complain or cause ructions in the group. It won't be easy for the first settlers, and they'll doubtless encounter some things they can't even imagine now, so the last thing they needed was people who were picky or likely to demand rights and privileges that might upset others. If anyone can make it, it's this lot."

"How long until we arrive?" the Captain or, in the Vynarian tongue, Korstan called. One of the flight officers responded.

"Eight yix, twenty-two krix."

"About seven hours," Daniel translated.

"Thank you," Alex smiled.

"Time enough for you to get to know some of the crew and passengers, at least," he added.

Alex checked out the bridge and found both the equipment and the crew clean, advanced and efficient. Looking closely at the crew themselves she could see that they had slitted eyes which could adapt to a wide range of light, as well as, judging by one of the crew, the ability to see very clearly in the dark. The female was examining something in a scanner that covered her eyes but, when Alex peered inside to see what was so interesting, she had to adjust her eyesight significantly to pick up the tiny bits of dark rock in the black mass of space. Nevertheless, the crewmember calmly noted each one and highlighted certain of them for the ship to scan. What she was looking for Alex wasn't sure but, whatever it was, she hadn't found it yet.

Their ears were quite large relative to their heads, were placed higher than on a human, and could be angled to scoop up whatever sound they needed to hear. Their noses were quite sensitive to a wide range of smells. One crewmember advised another officer to lay off a certain kind of food before coming on the bridge, but Alex couldn't smell anything until she expanded her range substantially although, without getting inside one of them, she couldn't tell the full extent. They had a fine layer of fur on their faces and hands which was so pale it was easy to miss it, whiskers on their muzzles, and the end of their fingers were large and appeared to have a suction cap that could be closed while they were operating the computers but opened when they needed to pick something up. She wondered whether their feet had the same adaptation.

The bridge had artificial gravity. The route off it, on the other hand, did not. Akin to an elevator shaft, but without the elevator, the reduced gravity meant they could, quite literally, drop from one deck to the next with no effort, while little effort was required when ascending. She suspected the crew jumped from level to level in the manner of their ancient ancestors travelling from tree to tree.

Navigating her way along corridors and between the decks, Alex explored with Daniel by her side.

Finding some Vynarians in an almost pitch-black gym practising fighting, confirmed both her assessment of their eyesight (not something bats usually excelled at), and proved that they had very acute hearing. Some fought wearing masks that prevented them from seeing, but it didn't stop them finding their targets, high-pitched squeaks echoing around the room as they sought their opponents and attacked them with enthusiasm.

"Nice mix," Alex observed. "They seem to have got all the smarts of the humanoid side and all the sensory talents of their ancestors, plus they've offset some of the weaknesses."

"According to Almega, some of that is a result of genetic engineering. However, it seems to have worked out rather well for them."

"If they could do that, why didn't they add greater musculature so that they could master powered flight?"

"Birds and bats are very light, with hollow bones. That hollowness is at the cost of the immune system developed by most mammals. Powered flight also requires a more pronounced breastbone to support the muscles. The Vynarians evolved to keep the immune features and the slightly flatter chest which, in turn, has limited their flight. Simply put, they're too heavy, and the size of the wings, protruding breastbone, and corresponding musculature needed to manage powered flight would make them clumsy with everything else. Hence, they decided to look for planets with lower gravity."

"If you can't change yourself, change your world," she grinned. "That's a new approach!"

"They're very advanced, but I imagine it's easier to relocate than to try and reduce the gravity on your own world."

"Just a bit!" she agreed. "But, in that case, why aren't they all relocating?"

Being Eternals, Alex and Daniel could see in the training room despite the darkness. The skill demonstrated by the top tier fighters was impressive, even if it did occasionally make one or other of the Eternals wince when a blow hit its target.

"It's a new world with unknown dangers. In time, I've no doubt, a greater proportion of the population will move but, for now, it's more about exploration and feedback to the home world. They need to learn exactly what they're dealing with."

"I take it they have no compunctions about destroying life on other planets, then?"

"Depends on the life. According to Almega, while there are mammals on the land surfaces of the new world, they're not the biggest danger, and the Vynarians are quite good at coexisting with other creatures, provided they're not a deadly threat or they can be suitably contained. They have colonies on some other planets, and they've settled in well with the local fauna and flora. Their ancestry and their skills with genetic engineering make them perfectly capable of adapting to local plants, insects and fruit as food. There is something on this new world that is a great danger to them, but he wouldn't tell me what it was. He seemed to find it intriguing. As we're stuck here for a bit, I think he wanted you to enjoy the trip, so he refused to divulge exactly what you're facing. Still, it's not as if it can harm you, regardless of what it is."

"But it will harm the Vynarians?"

"I think you can take that as a given. Not all aboard this ship will survive. If they did, new planets wouldn't need to be explored, merely conquered and occupied. The Vynarians don't conquer. They're more into peaceful coexistence. Not that they can't fight," he added as one of the fighters managed to land stunning blows on two opponents before turning on a third. "Oh, well done!" he cheered before returning to the conversation. "While they're not using them in here, they have sharp teeth and claws, plus manufactured weapons that can do everything from a simple stun to breaking down the atomic structure of an attacker so that they simply separate and vanish and, as we've seen, they're remarkably agile. They're a formidable enemy, but a useful friend."

"Sounds like my kind of people. An improvement on some we've met on this trip."

"It's not like we got to choose these ones. Normally, we don't get involved with less savoury characters on our trainings."

"No. We leave those to Fortan! How is he, by the way?" she asked as they exited the training room. Alex blinked a couple of times in the corridor's bright light, then continued her explorations.

"Still trapped, still raging about the unfairness of his incarceration, which makes Almega less inclined to release him," Daniel replied. "You'd think, by now, he'd recognise that the way out is abject apology, but you know Fortan. His pride and arrogance won't allow him to admit he was wrong."

"How about the other Eternals? How are they doing without their training?"

"Making it clear to Fortan how they feel about him, in no uncertain terms. He's learning just how much he's disliked, which isn't a bad thing, but he's still insisting everyone is in the wrong but himself."

"For an Eternal, who are supposed to be wise, he is remarkably stupid!"

"A point several have made to him, but he refuses to listen. At this rate, he'll be trapped in there for centuries!" Daniel's expression indicated that he wouldn't have a problem with Fortan suffering such a fate.

"How do the others feel about me?" she asked, worried they were blaming her for being stuck inside and preventing the reset.

"Almega has made it very clear that he was the one who put you in, unaware of Fortan's intentions, and therefore he should be blamed. He also gave a rundown on some of the things you've endured. Your last one made several feel quite ill and express relief that it wasn't them. They want you out of here as fast as possible, but they are keen to avail themselves of the extra opportunities."

"Let's hope they can!"

"In between helping you, and guiding the other universes to the crossing points, Almega's had time to play around. There are some restrictions, which is odd, and some trips are off limits. For example, the dragon world seems to be locked about ten centuries before your most recent arrival. He can't figure out why, but there's plenty to do there anyway, so it's hardly an issue."

"How strange. I was looking forward to checking out Eyowenwi."

"I know what you mean. Darthyn seemed right up my street but, unfortunately, that's in the no-go area. Besides, we already know the story."

"Assuming the film was accurate," she tossed over her shoulder as she walked into what appeared to be a sickbay. "I think there might be a couple from that training session in here quite soon."

She checked out what she could of the sensors and other equipment. "Really advanced. I'm impressed. According to this, they can regrow flesh, bones and organs on demand. Provided the victim of any attack is still alive when they find them, they've a good chance of survival."

Daniel frowned. "Perhaps it's some kind of very potent poison that affects them, then? Almega assured me there is a very real threat on the planet that the Vynarians aren't prepared for."

"Surely they did planetary scans before heading out," she said. "They'd have checked for deadly poisons in the environment."

"Whatever it is, they didn't spot it. They *did* spot that, thanks to the much lower gravity, everything on the new planet is considerably larger than they're used to." He chuckled. "The equivalent of a mouse is the size of a Labrador! Even so, they didn't detect anything lethal, so I confess to being rather confused."

"Intriguing. Should I go on ahead and explore?"

"There's still plenty of the ship and crew left to check in on and, by the time you've done that, I think they'll have arrived. Exploring a planet that you can't interact with might give you a false impression of the dangers, so probably better to wait."

She grunted and continued on her way, passing through a door to find herself in the galley. Two things struck her immediately. The first was that the protein part of their diet was very much alive and kicking (or crawling or flying) inside transparent balls into which the Vynarians flicked unusually long tongues. Said tongues must have been sticky, or had tiny suction cups similar to those on their fingers since, as soon as they touched an insect, their target was caught and couldn't escape. The second thing she noted was that, up until now, she'd only seen the more military side of the ship's complement. Here, she was encountering civilians. They were laughing and joking while their children ran around or chatted animatedly with their friends. They all looked fit, healthy and happy being in the relatively cramped conditions although, for a spaceship, there was more than enough room to move about.

"I hope they keep the kids aboard the ship until they know what they're dealing with," she observed.

"I'm sure they'll try. Keeping teenagers within boundaries for one extra second is a struggle for all species, though. I suspect one or two will find a way to sneak past the guards, and that may well prove their undoing."

"Why bring along civilians at this stage? Why not all military who can be trusted to obey orders?"

Daniel raised an eyebrow. "You've never been in the military, have you?"

"I did a couple of stints," she replied stoutly. He raised his eyebrows higher, dropping his head so that he was giving her a look that said, 'Seriously? Try again'. "All right. It was ages ago and I spent most of my time as an administrator. I did get onto the battlefield once, helping a senior officer who was doing a reconnaissance because he was the only one who knew the environment and what to avoid, and I certainly didn't go wandering off."

"Because you were a more mature female, seconded to a high-ranking officer in unfamiliar conditions where you deferred to his experience. Young males tend to be a little less disciplined." Now it was her turn to give him a look. "Yes. I was the same when I joined up as a teenager. I did things as a raw recruit that drove me crazy when I was an officer and saw new recruits still doing it." He sighed. "Mortals never learn. There's a reason for rules, even if some of the reasons sound stupid until you find yourself caught up in them."

"Which you did?"

He nodded. "And lived to regret it, which is more than could be said for some." He squinted at another ball of food. "Pudding, at a guess," he commented, pointing.

"They're part bat or flying fox. Could equally be the main course," she replied, noting the fruit inside.

"True," he nodded. He leaned over to examine the eating ball more closely. "Whatever they're using to preserve their food is very good. I could swear that's fresh off the bush."

"Might they have hydroponics?"

"On a ship this size?" He shook his head. "You need a very large craft – realistically, a space station – to have the room to run full hydroponics. It's usually used for both food and oxygen, but even if it's just food, with several hundred aboard you need a lot of trees and bushes to produce so much fresh fruit. Where are you going?" he asked, as Alex went over to a wall which one of the Vynarians was, apparently, talking to.

"I don't think it's fresh," she said, beckoning Daniel to join her. The Vynarian crewmember, who'd clearly just come off shift, chatted to a friend while he was waiting. Mid-sentence a slot opened in the wall, and he withdrew a ball full of fresh fruit with a few insects along for the ride. While the crew member walked away, still chatting with his friend who'd collected her own food ball, Alex stuck her head into the wall to examine the circuitry inside. "It's printing the food!" she cried.

"And the insects?"

"No. They're in boxes, but neither the fruit nor the vegetables are fresh." She withdrew her head. "There are containers that I assume have the raw particles needed, plus water, and the machine combines them into whatever they order."

"Efficient," Daniel nodded. "Perfectly good enough for a short flight, but I'll bet they're looking forward to real food once they get on the planet."

"They seem quite content," she commented.

"For a relatively short trip, I'm sure it's fine. Long term, they'll get fed up with it and want something real."

Alex looked around. No one seemed to be turning their nose up at the food. Indeed, they seemed quite eager, and a few came back for seconds.

"I don't know," she said, pointing to a child who'd brought back his food ball and placed it in a recycling receptacle before ordering a refill. The child's mother came over, cancelled the order, and grabbed his arm.

"You've had two helpings already! That's enough!" she said.

"Aw, Mogga. I like it!"

"So I can see, but you've had your lunch and it's time to get back to your classes." She shooed him through the door. "Don't force me to hold your hand and walk you into the classroom myself!" she added, wagging a finger.

The child cringed at the thought of such a humiliating spectacle and dashed off. The mother chuckled and headed off in a different direction.

"If the kids like it, I'd say it's passed the hardest test," Alex said.

"Or he may not have known anything else. Their home world is extremely overpopulated. They probably had to switch to these food printers a long time ago because there wasn't enough open land left to farm."

"And yet he really likes these ones? How are they different? And, if that's the case, they'd better be learning the basics of farming really fast." She headed off after the child to find the classrooms.

***

The classrooms used AI teachers and each child had a computer screen implanted into the desk, above which interactive holograms floated. The students wore glasses with bone-conducting speakers so that they could go at their own pace, while a couple of Vynarian teachers walked up and down, stepping in when a student struggled with some connection between concepts, or needed a different approach altogether.

Alex put her head through that of one of the steadier students – as opposed to one whose head was moving all over the place due to the subject matter, or because they were bored – to see what she saw. As opposed to the bare-bones hologram visible to those without the specs, what could be seen through them appeared so real that it was hard to remember that it wasn't. With a tap of a finger, the student could glide from tree to tree, seeing the world from above. Taps from two fingers produced a climbing mode, when the avatar they were using was too low and needed to gain some height, while their other hand controlled walking or running – something the Vynarian students were loath to do.

"This isn't the new world," Alex commented, revelling in the view. "The Vynarians can't do anything but glide, and the plants and animals are standard sizes. It's going to be very different where they're going, but maybe this is a history lesson?"

"Or another planet that was previously colonised," Daniel suggested. "I'm rather looking forward to seeing their reactions to this one, given what they're used to. It's going to be like living in a land of giants. Of course, unless they're remarkably active, they'll lose a lot of muscle-mass."

Alex pulled back from the mesmerising view. "Maybe they'll install something akin to the artificial gravity that they have here into the buildings?"

"That could get prohibitively expensive," Daniel replied.

"Is it, though? When it could mean the difference between survival and disaster, keeping those muscles could be worth their weight in any rare metal."

"It won't be a problem initially as they'll still be using muscles developed to deal with the artificial gravity aboard and the natural gravity on Vynar. Hopefully, by the time it is an issue, they'll have solved any problems."

"It's a big world they need to explore. If I were them, I'd keep pumping iron until I was certain I no longer had to. Of course, the weights will be insane compared to on their home world." She laughed. "Look, Mogga! I can lift a thousand pounds!"

"For them, one thousand two hundred and twelve pegrans," he replied, pronouncing the first 'e' as a long sound. "I suspect laziness will out in the end, though. It usually does. How about taking a look at the engine room? I'm curious as to the drive they're using."

While Alex wasn't nearly as interested as Daniel in the purely mechanical side of the ship's systems, she dutifully explored until they discovered the engine room. There, she floated in the middle of the room while Daniel eagerly

216

examined whatever he could, and she poked her head inside anything he couldn't immediately make out to give him greater access.

"Having a fusion reactor at the heart of things definitely makes life easier," he mused when he'd finished. "Plenty of power for everything. They've three different systems of propulsion –"

"Please, spare me the details," Alex groaned. "You know it's not my area."

He frowned at her, then sighed. "The warp-tunnel we've already seen, one for fast travel within a solar system, and one for station-keeping and manoeuvring that will double as landing thrusters."

"That suggests they'll be landing the entire ship, not just shuttles when they get to the new planet."

"Makes sense, if you think about it. They'll need a base with food, warmth, protection and supplies until they can set themselves up. Plus, shuttling down their medical facilities and science labs isn't really an option."

"Science labs? Haven't seen those!" she cried, and sprinted off. Now she could speak the language, she paused at a sign that pointed to various locations, identified where the labs were, and doubled back, dropping through the deck.

"You know, even if they used the warp system they employ within solar systems, it would take them generations to reach this planet normally, but with the... what? Hyperspace shortcuts?" He shook his head. "Whatever they call them, they reduce centuries of travel to weeks, days or even hours."

"I'm suitably impressed," she replied, although her tone indicated otherwise. "A long way ahead of the humans we were dealing with before."

"Totally different system and, I suspect, a slightly different physics in this universe, allowing things that couldn't be done in our old one."

"But humans find their own ways, right?"

"Hmm. Something similar but not nearly so efficient. The Vynarians really have solved the problem of intergalactic travel."

Alex had reached the door marked 'LAB 1" and walked in. When Daniel followed it was to find Alex pressed up against the wall, trying to avoid being walked through by the numerous Vynarians who were rushing around, preparing stuff ready for their arrival on the new world.

"I think we've found the busiest place aboard!" Alex declared.

"Trying to be organised and primed for whatever may assail them when they first land and go to look around," he nodded. "Systems for testing air quality, soil quality, myriad ways of testing plant samples..." He waved to the row upon row of computers and testing equipment on the tables. "They're not leaving anything to chance. My guess is a small, advance party will set out first and grab samples from everything they encounter while everyone else is kept inside the ship."

"No, no, no!" one of the Vynarian scientists yelled. "There's no more room here. Take that," and she pointed at the box the young assistant was carrying, "to lab two."

"I just came from there. They said they've no more room either."

"Then take it to lab three and, if they're full, keep it in your cabin until we have need of it." She turned to another assistant who was busy with what looked like some kind of microscope. "Who taught you how to set that up? We want to use it, not admire it! Look," and she grabbed a cable. "This goes in here and then, no, don't plug that in yet –"

"But Mydar Sagrit said you had to plug both in before the first scan."

"Sagrit!" the lead scientist groaned. "That explains everything. You were using the Mark 3's, weren't you?"

"Yes."

"Uh huh. This is the Mark 4. The initial self-testing and alignment is done automatically, you just have to put this," she picked up a piece of something transparent and highly coloured, and waved it in front of the young assistant, "here and then press this and leave it alone. It'll do the rest. When that light turns green, plug in the connector. Plug it in first and the computer will over-ride and we'll get false readings."

"What if it turns red?"

"Then you come and find me." The scientist looked around. "Fardish, you plug that in without engaging the safety and I will not be the one to deliver your charred remains to your mother!"

"Sorry, Mydar Gorshnat. I wasn't thinking."

"That sort of distraction will get you or someone else hurt or, possibly, killed. If you don't think you're up to focusing today, leave and I'll call in someone else to help. I can't be watching over everyone's shoulder."

"Evidence to the contrary notwithstanding," Alex muttered. Daniel smothered a laugh.

"I promise, Mydar, it won't happen again," the young male replied, shamefaced.

The Mydar, which was what the Vynarians called a professor, nodded, smiled encouragingly, and moved on, offering help and guidance, warning when someone was about to make a stupid mistake, and trying to be in fifteen places at once. To their credit, after this brief flurry of over-eager senselessness, the team settled down and, as Alex and Daniel watched, the lab setup came together smoothly.

"Look like they're ready for just about anything," Alex nodded approvingly.

"We will see," Daniel replied. "We're less than an hour from landing. I think things will be hotting up on the bridge. Shall we?"

Leaving Mydar Gorshnat and her team putting the final touches to their preparations, Alex and Daniel navigated their way to the shaft that led to the bridge and, eager to check her theory, Alex told herself that she was the same weight as a Vynarian and jumped from ledge to ledge. Daniel, amused, rose up beside her.

"You know you're not really the same weight," he pointed out.

"I just needed to believe it long enough to ascend the shaft the way they do," she replied. "Same way I don't fall through a wall if I believe it's solid."

He shook his head but allowed her fancy. "And?"

"It's remarkably easy and, in an emergency, probably very efficient. In most emergencies, the key would be getting off the bridge and into the life pods fast, and you can certainly do that using this," and she waved at the shaft. "Plus, if you're late for work, you just pull a bit harder to rise faster, rather than being dependent on slow elevators."

"Or even fast ones that have to come down again," he nodded.

They walked through the doors onto the bridge and realised that the ship had come out of its hyperspace (or whatever the Vynarians called it) jaunt and was now bearing down on the planet.

"Commence scans," the Korstan called.

"Haven't they done that already?" Alex wondered.

"Many times, I would imagine, using probes, but probes are limited. Now they can target specific regions in more depth immediately if they detect something anomalous. Plus, things can change. They want to know the weather for landing, more details about the atmosphere, any trace elements that might cause a problem to any of the passengers and crew, evidence of any other aliens who might have found the planet –"

"Sir! I'm picking up a spacecraft on the surface!" the scanning officer called.

"Where?"

Details were input and navigation adjusted their trajectory until they arrived at the planet and took up a geostationary orbit above the alien spacecraft.

"Any signs of life aboard?"

"None, sir."

"That's odd. Any signs of life anywhere nearby?"

"No lifeforms except the ones already logged, sir."

The Korstan frowned. "Well, they didn't just take wing and vanish into space. Where are they?"

"Perhaps their ship developed a fault and another one came and picked them up?" the First Officer suggested.

The Korstan looked dubious. "Any sign of a problem with the spaceship?"

"Scans show no obvious issues, sir," the officer at the scanner reported.

"A mystery to be solved, then. Finish your scans. When the labs give us the all-clear, set us down near the other ship. Let's see who tried to beat us to the punch."

***

The lab efficiently dealt with the flood of information and, in due course, Mydar Gorshnat reported that, based on the information collected, there were no immediate dangers to the passengers or crew, and they could safely explore without facemasks. From the sighs of relief around the bridge, Alex guessed that they found the facemasks excessively limiting, given their acute sensory abilities.

"It would also make it very hard to live down there," Daniel added. "Their very first scans would have been to check that sort of thing, so this was confirmatory rather than a discovery. Their relief is because they now know their trip wasn't in vain."

"Ahh."

"Helm. Now that Mydar Gorshnat has given us the go-ahead, complete atmospheric insertion and set us down near the alien craft."

"Aye, sir," the officer at the helm replied.

A low alarm sounded, which was probably more than loud enough for the Vynarians.

"Brace yourself," Daniel warned. "Even with state-of-the-art dampening, this will be a little rough."

Alex noted the officers in their various positions pressing a button which sent straps across their bodies to hold them in place. A few seconds later, she could understand why.

"OK, that's enough," she declared and floated out into space to make her own way down, landing lightly near the other spacecraft. They noted that its hatch was open.

"That's weird," she commented. "A new planet, unknown life forms you wouldn't want to come aboard. Why would they leave the hatch open?"

"Thought they were coming back and then didn't?" he offered.

Alex looked over as the Vynarians landed. In the process, they'd crushed quite a few massive plants and burned some of the ground, but the ship itself was fine. Doubtless the first team would emerge soon. Alex was torn between investigating the abandoned alien mystery alone and waiting for the crew to do it.

"They'll be here soon enough," Daniel assured her. "As much as they want to investigate the planet, they won't be able to resist finding out who this was."

Sure enough, within a few minutes two things happened. First, a forcefield was switched on around the ship, securing it from invasion by insects or seeds until they knew exactly what they were dealing with, which Alex deemed a sensible precaution. Then a hatch opened. The field around the hatch was temporarily disabled as the crew emerged, armed with hand weapons and buckets of curiosity. The forcefield was then sealed. While one team began sampling anything and everything they could find in their immediate surroundings, noting where they found it, what it was and, by using scanners before taking samples, ensuring no one doubled up, a second team approached the abandoned ship.

One of them paused at the hatch, noting the bits of plants caught in the entrance.

"Either this has been here a while, or they dragged that in on their boots," she commented, getting a sample.

The team entered warily, the leader, who was the Vynarian's First Officer, calling out.

"Hello? Anyone in here? I am Merdan Varish of the Vynarian ship Zantor. Do you need help?"

A translator device on his belt repeated the phrase in a range of languages as they made their way deeper. They checked cabins, storage and anywhere else they could access, but found no crewmembers. They did, however, find equipment, supplies and other materials. When they reached the door to the bridge, they found more plant matter on the floor as well as scorch marks on the walls.

"Weapons fire," Varish commented, tapping one of the marks thoughtfully.

"But what were they firing at?" another wondered.

The Zantor's First Officer wasn't taking any chances. Using his comm unit, he alerted those outside taking samples. "There's evidence of a fight in here. Turn on your personal shields and keep all senses alert."

A chorus of 'yes, sir' came back. Satisfied he'd done what he could for now, he ordered another crewmember to open the door to the bridge. Using a handheld device of his own, the crewman successfully broke the lock and the team entered.

"I don't recognise the language," Alex commented as she checked out the controls.

"It's a big multiverse," Daniel shrugged. "It would be a miracle if we encountered a species in another universe using the same languages we know."

"Any idea who this belongs to?" Varish asked.

"Not a species we've encountered, sir," one of the crewmembers replied. "And this has been abandoned for a while." He scraped a finger along one of the consoles. "There's a thick layer of dust," he continued, showing the result to his commander. "I think we can safely take what they've left behind. It doesn't look like they're coming back."

Varish nodded and sent a few of the crewmembers to collect whatever they thought might be useful, check it to make certain it was safe, and then take it back to the Zantor. Other crewmembers set about accessing and downloading the ship's logs to find out what had happened, and Varish, after a brief glance, left them to it, happy that there was nothing aboard the alien vessel that they couldn't handle. Emerging into the bright light of the planet, he turned on his own personal shield and checked on the crew collecting samples, Alex and Daniel in tow.

"Anything interesting?" he asked one of them, who was squatting beside a plant.

"This is a smaller version of that," the ensign, or nefti in the Vynarian language, replied, pointing to a monstrous plant that towered above them. "But look what happens when I touch it." Gingerly, he reached forward and gently brushed the plant. The previously closed petals opened to reveal a rather intimidating maw which snapped at his quickly withdrawn hand.

"That's that?" Varish said, pointing from the tiny thing on the ground to the towering plant beside them.

"Yeah. You know what? I'm really glad that the big one can't bend down!"

"Are you certain it can't?" Varish asked, looking warily up at the green and blue underside that blocked the sunlight above him.

"I think, if it could, I'd already be shooting my way out of its mouth."

"Carnivorous plants," Varish nodded. "I wonder if that's what happened to the other crew?"

"Sir?"

"I'm not suggesting that the alien crew could fly, nefti, but it does give us fair warning when *we* do. The scans from our probes wouldn't have shown up anything like that and, if there's one, there may well be others that could pose a problem on the ground. Nature has a way of adapting to make the most of every opportunity. Has the team finished its collection?"

The nefti checked the logs that had been shared between the group. "Last one just finishing now, sir."

"Then let's get back inside the ship and see what the labs make of all this." He pulled out his comm. "Korstan, we've finished exploring the alien ship and collecting samples. Some of the plants here are carnivorous and a little snappy. I suggest keeping up the forcefield and guards to make sure none of our more adventurous students start exploring until we know what we're dealing with."

"Understood, Merdan. Do it."

"Yes, sir."

The nefti got to his feet and the teams made their way back to the ship. Alex remained outside with Daniel, examining the smaller version and then levitating until she could see the top of the larger one.

"The nefti was right," she said, pointing to the wide-open petals. "If it could have bent down, it would have had them both."

"Might it, or something like it, have been responsible for the other crew's hasty departure, do you think?" Daniel asked.

"This one, no. Something on the ground? Quite possibly," she replied as the plant slowly closed itself up again. "They're certainly going to have to be careful when flying with things like this around."

A very large insect, the local equivalent of a dragonfly so far as Alex could tell, but three feet long, buzzed nearby. The plant opened briefly and something long and sticky shot out and snagged the insect from the air, dragging it into the mouth before closing again.

"Yeah," Daniel nodded. "They're definitely going to have to be careful!"

"As much as I hate to say it," Alex said, "but I think the only way they'll be safe on this planet is if they keep these things in reserves where no flying is allowed." She looked about, noting the wide range of unfamiliar plants, some of which now took on a far more sinister appearance. "Or remove the lot of them."

"Be interesting to see which path they take," Daniel said. "It'll tell us a lot about what kind of a species they are."

Alex went back down to the ground and then stood there, gazing around her. The trunks of various plants, the occasional massive insect that, now the Vynarians had left, crawled out from between the leaves, and all bathed in the green light that filtered through the canopy. It made her feel like an insect herself.

"Amazing world," she commented, watching a meter-long millipede-like insect carefully skirt one of the nipping plants, "but not a very safe one."

"Is any world safe when you don't know the dangers?"

"No, but normally the plant life is only risky when you eat it, not when you walk by!"

"Want to explore a bit while they're doing their tests?"

"We could do, but I'm worried we'll miss something important, like what's in the alien captain's logs. Probably best to join them."

He nodded and the pair of them made their way through the forcefield and hatch into the Vynarian ship.

After they departed there was a brief silence, then something slowly pushed its way out of the ground towards the forcefield. When it tried to go further it was driven back. Brown tendrils, earth clinging to them, extended steadily in every direction, probing to find a way past, but there was none. There was a pause, and then more emerged from the soil, feeling out the edges of the shield and then building a wall of ever-expanding root systems, the base thickening to support the top-most, which now stretched to check the top of the ship. Once it had fully surrounded the Vynarian ship, the ground began to shift.

***

"What's that alarm?" Korstan Darizh asked. He was watching the alien captain's logs, but the translation program was still working and couldn't yet deliver the necessary information, so it was hard to tell what he or she was saying beyond the fact that, assuming the species had similar biometric responses to everyone else he'd encountered, the alien was scared.

"Sir, something's trying to penetrate the shield," the security officer replied.

"Really? Show me external."

The alien captain's face was replaced by a view of the world outside the ship, the wavering tendrils of whatever had emerged from the ground now almost covering the whole ship.

"What *is* that?"

"A plant life, sir," Varish replied. "We found some of that in the hatch wells of the alien ship."

Suddenly, the ship lurched and what had been interesting now became concerning.

"Let's see if we can put it off a bit, shall we?" Darizh said, his tone calm. "Ramp up the shield, Mr Previzh."

"Sir!"

Alex, Daniel and the crew watched as the forcefield was ramped up.

"No effect, sir," Previzh said.

"I can see that! All right, enough playing nice. Extend the shields, put them to maximum and fry whatever that is before it drags us so far underground that we can't get out."

Now the effect was very obvious. The network of plant life burned and vanished, the ship settling at an angle.

"Helm, lift us up and put us down on more solid ground, please."

The helm officer complied and soon the Zantor was several meters away from its previous location and standing on some rocks.

"All right. I think we can imagine what happened to the other crew. Now we need to see if this is something intelligent enough for us to talk to."

The officer at the sensors shook his head. "No sign of anyone operating that... whatever it was, sir."

"You're assuming it didn't operate itself," Darizh observed. "You're also assuming that any control would be above ground, but evidently it isn't. We need some probes that can dig down and find out what's beneath the surface."

"Given what it looks like they'll be up against, I suggest giving them some powerful forcefields of their own," Varish said.

"Agreed. See to it. If we're encroaching on someone else's territory, I'd like to know who or what we're dealing with. Is it sentient, or responding automatically to things like heat or pressure? Can it be reasoned with or is it instinctual? Also, while we seem to be relatively safe, I want the labs to test some of those tendrils. I want to know what it is and how it works."

"Yes, sir."

***

To say their work became feverish was an understatement. With every mind firmly fixed on the prize of living on a planet that would allow them greater freedom, finding out whether they were competing with an intelligent lifeform, Alex quickly discovered, was vital. She learned that they did have a rule that said that if sentient, intelligent life was found, they had to find a way of communicating and living together or leave. There were no other options. Members of the survey team, supported by armed guards, went out and delivered the adapted sensors to the ground where they quickly activated a system that drilled into the soil, tossing it behind them as they buried deeper. Returning to the ship, members of the team watched as the probes worked their way down while others examined the tendrils that had been separated from the host and left behind when the Zantor's shields kicked in and its engines moved them to safer ground.

Darizh moved from the labs to the probe feedback sections to those working on the translation of the alien captain's logs, 'though he had a feeling he already knew what the latter would contain. In the end, it was the lab that reported first.

"There is evidence of what amounts to neural connections, but very basic ones," Mydar Gorshnat informed him, the screen showing the tattered remnants of one of the growths. "The problem is that, by the time we got to it, it was dead, so finding out the nature of the connection – whether it's fast or slow, how detailed the information, that sort of thing – is impossible. We need to scan it while it's alive."

"Given what it just tried to do to our ship, I'm not sure that will be feasible," Darizh replied.

"The probe has the requisite sensors, if it can get close enough without being swallowed or crushed."

The Korstan and Mydar Gorshnat made their way to the lab annex that held the probe team, who were avidly watching their screens.

"Found anything?" Darizh asked.

"Oh, we've definitely found something," the head of the team, a Vynarian female called Feyerit, replied. "The problem we've got is that we haven't found the end of it, or a central, controlling area." She indicated the readouts with a hopeless shrug.

"It's a mycelium network," Gorshnat gasped after poring over the data for a moment. "And it looks like it may well cover the entire planet!"

"You can't assume it covers the planet based on what the probes have sent back so far," Darizh insisted.

"Look at it! The probe's still working its way through, and it's gone through a zerbit already!"

Daniel leaned down. "About half a kilometre," he translated in Alex's ear.

"Why is it that you can do that so easily?" she asked.

"Same way you're good with all computers while I have to work at it," he shrugged. "Horses for courses."

"Hmm."

"What we know," Gorshnat continued, "is that every planet that has this has it across all areas where there are plants, and slightly into areas where there aren't any but, as it serves no purpose there, it doesn't go any further."

"And what purpose does it serve for the plants?" the Korstan asked. "Apart from telling them to try and swallow us whole, I mean."

"That approach is unique to this planet, so far as I know. The mycelium network is normally a force for good on any planet."

"Treat me like I'm not an expert in biology," Darizh sighed. "We were attacked by these things –"

"No. These gave the instructions, but a different plant, probably a form of fungus, carried it out. This is the network, not the front line. That doesn't mean it can't digest anything that gets caught in it, but it's not normally the one bringing the stuff in. It's part of a symbiotic relationship with plants. It provides what it can from below and they support it in return from above – usually sugars and carbohydrates, although I'm not sure about this particular version. Might be into something a little higher in protein?"

"Murderous mushrooms. That's a new one on me," he grunted.

230

"It's not that simple. Look," and she zoomed in on the image. "Mycelia are made up of rigid cell walls, which allow them to move through soil and tough environments. They can break down pretty much anything once they surround it, which is why it tried to drag us down. It knows that, given enough time, it can always break through. They're fine, but mycelia can support up to thirty times their mass, which means that, with all this below us, we were nothing to it. They extend the area in which the fungi and other plants they're attached to can find water and nutrients by drawing in and funnelling what's needed along their systems. They bind to plants short of resources and fetch what's needed. In this case, given the size of it, probably from zerbits away. Basically, this is one big stomach, but with very basic lungs and a neural network."

"Can we talk to it?"

"No," she said, shaking her head. "It's not a higher order of intelligence. Thanks to the lower gravity and billions of years of evolution, this system is more advanced and faster than any I've ever encountered, but it's still not intelligent in the sense you mean. They can collect intelligence, such as the arrival of our ship, and order defences to kick in such as the... What shall I call them?" She cast around for a moment, then settled on an answer. "The liana that surrounded us. They also alert plants regarding any diseases to limit the spread, communicating ways to resist the attack and survive. Make no mistake, this is good stuff that helps whatever plants that grow on it, it's just that in this instance..."

"It's a little over-zealous?"

She nodded. "You've got plants that have learned to be carnivorous, probably because in this low gravity they can grow and use up nutrients much faster than on Vynar. All that was left to eat were the animals, insects, and each other."

"A little culling, then, might not be a bad idea? Not just for us, but for the planet as a whole?"

"Looking at the scans the ship did before we landed, there are very, very few animals on this part of the planet and the number of insects really isn't enough to support the plant life and deal with it properly. So, yes. I'd say if it doesn't want to wipe itself out, it needs to be reduced a bit and a greater variety of animal life introduced. One dead animal can provide nutrients for a whole host of things and, in all honesty, plants are carnivorous too."

"I saw that!"

"No, I mean generally. They feed off bones and flesh and whatever else presents itself as biologically digestible, they just don't normally directly attack other species while they're still moving, which is why they're seen as benign. However, if you've ever seen how quickly plants can take over and pull apart ruins, you'll know they're as strong as the most powerful predator – much stronger, in fact – just usually a lot slower."

"That means we need to clear the area of plants. That's not going to be easy," the Korstan mused.

"No, indeed. A sandit of soil on Vynar contains around ten zerbits of mycelium cells."

Alex looked at Daniel.

"Roughly one cubic inch contains around eight miles of them."

"That's the same as on Earth in our universe," she nodded, happy to be able to provide information of her own.

"Here, however," Gorshnat continued, "they're larger, so less per sandit but capable of ferrying more nutrients and more information." She turned to Varizh. "And considerably harder to destroy." She went to another computer and pulled up the external view. "See? Where we landed is already being restored."

"Blimey! That's ridiculously fast!" Alex said, looking at the space that had originally been charred by the thrusters. Shoots had sprung up everywhere. "The Vynarians can't

232

be caught outside on this planet. They'll be eaten within minutes!"

"And yet they didn't try to eat the teams," the Korstan mused, unaware of Alex's comment.

"Shock from the initial devastation wrought by our engines, I suspect," Gorshnat replied. "I doubt it will be so forgiving a second time."

"Hmm. I'd better warn the passengers and crew. Otherwise, you can bet some idiot will decide they've waited long enough and sneak out."

"Darizh," she said, reaching out to grip his arm and stall him. "I'd double the guard before you spread such news amongst the passengers, and, personally, I'd keep it quiet until I had a solution."

"Oh?" Darizh said, cocking his head to one side. "Why do you say that?"

"The thought that, after all this, they might not be able to settle here will be devastating. It's going to be hard enough to keep the crew from speaking but, if you're working on a solution and this does get out, you can tell them that to keep them from over-reacting. If you don't, I fear you'll have a riot on your hands, and all civilians will have to be locked in their cabins until we can sort this out."

"This group was picked because they were the least likely to do that," Darizh countered.

"And, as a result, they'll be slower, but if you think they won't react, you need to study more psychology!"

"Hmm. You're going to explain that to your teams here, right?"

"Already done," she assured him. "They know that the last thing any of us want is to be required to flash ID cards at every intersection or be denied free travel around the ship to see friends. Whoever's working on the alien log translations will probably need the same reminder."

With a groan, Korstan Darizh pulled out his comm. "Varish, are you going over the logs?"

"Yes sir. The translation program's finally cracked them."

"Excellent. I'll be right over. Keep the crew in there until I arrive, would you? I need to talk to them."

"Yes, sir."

Alex and Daniel followed Darizh to the room where the log was being translated – the feed to the bridge having been switched off when Darizh left. The area was only a few doors down from the lab, causing Alex to decide that the entire deck was mostly given over to research and analysis, which made sense.

"Korstan," Varish said, straightening as Darizh entered.

"At ease, Merdan. I take it he's talking about the carnivorous plants and their attacks on his ship?"

"She, we think, and yes. What our forcefield blocked, wiped them out. They were, quite literally, taken from their posts and cabins and sucked down, all while she was recording her last entry. They'd secured the doors, but that didn't stop it. Didn't even slow it down that much."

"All right. The crew members know not to tell the passengers as it will scare the whiskers off them. They came here to make a new life, and many sold up everything they had, so they've nothing to go back to. With that in mind, I would ask all of you to keep quiet about the problem until we find a solution."

"Is there one, sir?" one young nefti asked, his tone depressed in the extreme.

"According to Mydar Gorshnat, it's a bit out of control and, if it's not reduced slightly, the animals that still remain here will be eradicated completely, which will have major environmental consequences. The plants have grown too big, too numerous and too hungry and, as the animals are wiped out, many of the plants will die and perhaps all in a given species or two. With that in mind, we want to create an area free from the larger carnivorous plants and, until we tame it, the mycelium network below ground. An area large enough that it can support both us and some local

234

animals and less, ah, aggressive plant-life with, perhaps, a little help from us. This will give us the space to settle but, obviously, anyone going outside that space will be taking their lives in their own hands."

"How are we going to stop this?" the nefti asked, pointing to the video which showed the plant surrounding and carrying away the alien captain.

"Yes, thank you for that image," Darizh grunted, urging Varish to turn it off. "I was going to ask for suggestions."

Varish stared at the floor, running through options. "We could use the weapons system to cut through the soil so that the mycelia are separated from the rest of the planet to start with, and level the plants above ground to give us some space. If we drop some security nodes into the holes we can link them up to create a grid both above and below ground, blocking reconnection and limiting the spread of the jungle. What's left we could keep clear by hand. Then we could work with the lab to determine which plants won't eat us and allow them access."

Darizh paced as he thought through his First Officer's suggestions.

"I don't want to force animals to stay or go. Could the security nodes be adjusted so that the animals are free to move about – unless we identify one that isn't safe, of course – and stop our own people from wandering outside until we say otherwise?"

"On ground level, possibly. Animals and plants are two different things usually, although I'm not so sure around here, and we can program the nodes to block Vynarian DNA easily, but now they'll be able to fly..."

"Ahh. Hadn't thought of that. We'll have to install fence posts tall enough to connect across the top, too. Can we do that?"

"I think so," Varish nodded. "A lot of minerals and other resources will be available once we cut through the soil, given how deep we'll have to go, so anything we're getting short of can be sourced from there. We know the planet has all the resources we need in raw form, and we have the technology to refine it easily enough."

"What about a field to stop the ground being opened to suck us down to our deaths?"

"If we can manage above we can certainly manage below, it's just a question of drilling extra holes for the security nodes. As for the animals, in order to guarantee that the plants can't wander in, it might be better to provide raised gates above a closed network that we can monitor with guards. An animal wanders in through the gate, they're allowed to pass, a plant tries to crawl through, the guard takes them out. Initially, we can power the lot from the ship to give us space to work but, once we've established ourselves, we'll need to supply energy from elsewhere. The ship will need to maintain enough to leave if we have no other choice, so it can't simply become our power station."

"Oh, there's plenty of energy sources we can tap into," Darizh assured him. "With the plants down, the local star will provide more than enough, and we can make salicide batteries to store the energy at night. We know there's plenty of salts in the soil."

Alex looked at Daniel. "Batteries that use salt?"

"Not unheard of, and a rather more environmentally-friendly approach than the usual rare earths humans used."

"Efficient?"

"Given the technologically advanced status of the Vynarians, probably enough to keep going for weeks without sunshine."

"All right," Darizh nodded, straightening. "If anyone asks, we were on unstable ground, moved the ship when we started to sink in and we're re-scouting the planet to find a better landing place, all right?" There were nods all round. "I cannot over-emphasize this. If the civilians find out that this planet is trying to eat them, there's a good chance they'll panic and the whole ship will have to be locked down. So, if you want to be free to move and not armed all the time, keep your wings tight until we fix this. If it turns out we can't, I'll announce it to the ship myself."

A chorus of nods interspersed with 'yes, sir' satisfied Darizh that they understood the risks.

"Merdan. Let's get into space and cut ourselves a piece of land."

***

It took a while but, several hours later, the ship set itself down in a cleared space some distance from the original landing spot, the captain seeing no reason to let the civilians see what might happen to them if the local flora got the upper hand or, in its case, leaf.

Every plant higher than the tallest Vynarian was chopped down, just in case, and the teams, with their personal shields set to maximum, went out to explore and bring back any other samples that weren't present at the previous landing site. They found several. This site also boasted running water, samples of which were dutifully collected, tested, and found to be clean and safe to drink. If any tendrils of plant life tried to snag a leg or an arm of the explorers, the personal shields that the crew deployed immediately fried them, leaving nothing but ashes, the system being run by an AI that could tell the difference between an attack that needed to be repelled, and a collection that needed to be let through.

By the time the star began to set on the horizon, the ground security nodes had been inserted and attached to the ship's power relays. More had been attached to widely spaced metal posts, extending the barrier well above the tallest plants beyond the perimeter, although not yet sealed across the top. Guards and crew were left to monitor it all, allowing those inside to sleep without immediate fear of assault.

***

While the night watch took their places and the crew settled down to get some well-earned rest, Alex and Daniel went out beyond the secured area to explore. The planet's three satellites, which were small but close enough to cast light between them, illuminated their path although, of course, both Eternals adjusted their vision so that it might as well have been day. Alex took to flying once their immediate surroundings had been examined, the better to cover the ground. They eventually found what was left of the animal life on the continent eking out a living amidst the mountains on the edge of a rather desolate area with little water and hardly any plant life.

"They're a sorry-looking lot," Daniel observed. The mammals, lizards and even a few birds were moving about, nervous and afraid, and rather smaller than Alex had expected, given the size of the local insect life. Any sign of plant life was quickly dug up and eaten, and the keenness with which the animals patrolled their areas and removed plants suggested not only hunger but a desire to ensure no greenery was anywhere near them. In desperation, a few nibbled at the edges of the jungle, but it didn't take long for the news to be spread underground that there was a threat and a potential meal. One small mammal barely escaped with its life although, sadly, not its tail, which it sacrificed in order to make its escape.

"I hope the Vynarians find them and give them safety before they're all wiped out. I always thought plants were the good guys!" Alex said.

"Usually, yes, but here you've got a carnivorous diet combined with no self-restraint, no animal-husbandry, and not enough intelligence to realise that they need to tone it down. All they know to do is to eat, grow, and spread their seeds."

"Will the Vynarians limit their own spread, though?" she wondered. "They could do a lot of good for this planet, and stop it from killing itself, but if they go too far..."

"I don't know," he admitted, "but their attitude seems right."

"For now. What about later?"

He turned and consulted with Almega.

"It seems they've occupied a few worlds and been quite diligent when it comes to finding balance. To them, the whole point of a new world is all the new experiences, flora and fauna and the opportunity to learn. They can't do that if they simply wipe everything out and replace it with their own stuff."

"True, but if they plant something for their consumption that upsets the balance –"

He shook his head. "They're happy to adapt themselves, remember? They have the technology. They'll be checking out local plants, seeds, fruits and the like to see if there's anything they can eat without adjustment and, if there's not enough, they'll make genetic alterations to themselves."

"And if they can't, or doing so would have unwanted side-effects?"

"Then they'll have to decide whether to keep on printing food by extracting the necessary chemicals, or adjust the native plants to make them slightly more compatible, but that would be, according to Almega, the very last resort. He says that they're more likely to abandon the planet and look for somewhere else. They've done it before, apparently, but most of the time it requires minimal adaption on their part to accommodate most things. They're a pretty robust species."

"They'll have to be to survive this place!"

They continued to explore. Another mountain range housed more animals, giving Alex hope that it wasn't too late.

"They'll be sending out probes to examine the planet's ecology in detail once they've founded their first camp, and then some will be sent out to explore."

She shivered. "I hope, by then, they'll know what to avoid!"

"In most cases, yes, but their personal shields and weapons will also help. Your average rodent caught by one of the plants can't pull out a heated plasma or laser weapon and burn their way out. The Vynarians can."

"Could be rather exciting, being one of those pioneers," she grinned. "Feel like giving it a go?"

They'd reached the shore of the continent and were now flying over an ocean, which was teeming with fish and larger beasts that were the equivalent of Earth's whales, dolphins, seals and the like.

"They won't be able to get out here without a shuttle, and it'll be scary, but yes, I would!"

She pointed to a pod of dolphin-like beasts leaping out of the waves. "The plants haven't managed to take over in the seas."

"They need something to cling onto, although some may have adapted to floating in order to capture their prey. Seaweed and the like couldn't catch those characters even on this planet. It's too far down, leaving several hundred meters of water relatively safe. I imagine those or something else in the seas has evolved to attack and eat any plants that might cause a problem in large amounts."

"You'd have thought they would have done the same on land."

"The plants there may have got too strong a hold too quickly? The animals seem to be safe out here, though."

"Until you get close to the shore." She pointed at a furry, water-based mammal caught in a mesh of plants in the shallows surrounding an atoll. It was wriggling furiously in its efforts to escape. "Why doesn't it just chew the stuff off?"

"Go inside and help it," he suggested. "It's not like we're planning to come back as seals... or whatever that is."

She dropped down and entered the animal. There was a pause and then, with some difficulty, the 'seal' started to gnaw at the 'seaweed' that was trying to choke it. Soon it had severed the major branches and then wriggled away from the rest, quickly putting some distance between itself and its would-be diner. Alex emerged and floated up.

"The plants release a toxin to dull the brain activity of the animals to make them easier to catch," she said. "Took me a while to figure out why it couldn't think straight and then take over enough to get it clear." The seal had paused, floating on its back in the open water as it tried to gather its wits once more. "I *may* have left the method in its brain."

"Deliberately or...?"

"They need a break. At least if that one teaches others how to get out, they'll have a better chance of survival and, if the land animals are obliterated before the Vynarians manage to alter the balance, it means there'll still be some native mammals around."

"Hmm. Well, it is a side universe rather than the prime, which means you're allowed to make minor alterations."

"Just as well, given what I've done already!" She looked ahead, adjusted her eyes and pointed. "Hey! There are loads of animals over there!"

She took off, Daniel dragged along beside her until they reached another continent, this one still dominated by massive plants but here there were equally massive animals.

"This is what I was expecting before," Alex smiled.

"Fewer carnivorous plants," Daniel mused, "and the mycelia seem to be happy with what's being provided by the animals."

"Why didn't the Vynarians land here?" she asked.

"From above it probably looks more or less the same, and they wouldn't want to bother too many animals if they could help it. Still, if things don't go well where they are, it might be worth making certain that those checking the scans find this place."

"I'll see if there's a way I can make their computers spit it out in front of the right onlooker," she assured him. "Mind you, Mydar Gorshnat seems to be on top of things. I've no doubt she'll be making them go through everything with a fine-tooth comb. They'll probably find it without my help."

They landed and started to explore. Having ten-foot-tall bovines strolling along beside them was a little disconcerting, and other beasts had horns that curved the wrong way, to Alex's mind, pointing forward or down rather than back. She pointed to another beast whose massive teeth stuck out to the sides.

"If he ran through a herd of those," and she pointed to the bovines, "they'd all lose their knees!"

"Like one of those chariots with knives on the wheels in the films," he agreed.

"Presumably he uses those for defence rather than for eating."

"Unless he's carrying trays of food on them, I think we can take that as read."

The earth shook and Alex turned, looked up, and then further up.

"Wow. That's some kind of equine? Look at the size of that thing!"

At nearly twenty feet high, the horse-like beast was certainly impressive. Alex shook her head.

"I don't know what it's like on Vynar, but the Vynarians are going to have quite a culture shock when they find this place!"

"And before the plants took over, these were probably on the other continent as well," Daniel nodded, straining his neck to take in the details of the beast. "Do me a favour and go up so we can take a proper look, would you?"

She dutifully rose so that they could fully examine and admire the equine. Despite its massive proportions, in many ways it was a scaled-up version of the horses she knew from Earth. The head was broader at the top and the jaw and mouth flared out more at the bottom, giving its face an hourglass appearance. There was no mane, but it did sport a shaggy coat more akin to that of a collie. It had a tail, and it had two toes rather than one fused hoof on the end of each leg, but it was recognisable as the local equivalent of a horse. Its nostrils flared as it sniffed the air, but it sensed no threat and helped itself to one of the taller plants.

The Eternals explored further. A few hundred miles inland, where the trees kept the ground in a perpetual green gloom, they found pale creatures vaguely reminiscent of primates with huge eyes to help them see more clearly as well as large ears and nostrils.

"The eyes I get," she said. "In this twilight world you need all the help you can get to see, but the ears and nose?"

There was a cry and the primates all leapt into the trees and headed towards the source, Alex and Daniel alongside them. They reached a pond where a familiar plant was growing. One of the primates touched it and its maw opened and then snapped shut. The primates set upon it, tearing the plant apart and then digging down until the roots had been destroyed. They ate bits, then carried what was left to a pool of bubbling, yellowish water.

"Thermal spring," Daniel commented.

Alex adjusted her own olfactory senses and sniffed.

"Eugh! Sulphur!"

The primate threw the parts of the plant that they couldn't eat into the spring where they floated, briefly, then fizzed and disappeared into the depths, the primates hooting and screaming in delight.

"They know those things are bad news," Alex said. "Interesting. Either they were here once and these animals somehow managed to overcome them..."

"Seems unlikely, given what we've seen they can do at full size," Daniel replied.

"Or the primates came from the other continent at some time in their past, and the injunction to uproot and destroy these plants the instant they're found has become instinctual."

"It's doing everyone else on this continent a favour, though," Daniel said.

Another 'whoop, whoop' noise summoned them to another part of the forest and, now she knew what to listen for, Alex could detect similar sounds further afield from other groups.

"They seem to have taken on gardener duty," she said as another, slightly larger version of the plant was found. The primates revelled in certain bits of the plant and Alex began to get the suspicion that at least some of it had pharmacological features the primates enjoyed. One of the senior primates, who'd had a good chunk of the previous plant and this one, now lay down with a rather beatific grin and began snoring.

"He's stoned!" Daniel laughed.

"Explains why they're so eager to find the things," Alex agreed as the primate rolled over onto its side, wriggled a bit to get comfortable, and sighed, at peace with the world. "If the Vynarians examine this plant in more detail, they may find uses for whatever is in there."

"The plant probably uses it to drug its victims so that they don't fight back once it's got them," Daniel said. "You said earlier that the seaweed had a brain-numbing effect on the seal. For the plant, using such methods to prevent its meal attacking it would be better than torn and damaged parts that'll take a while to regrow."

"You're dead, but you'll be happy about it. Nice!" Alex said, wincing.

They continued through the jungle, noting that those primates not on 'dangerous plants' patrol (or, possibly, teenage drug addicts looking for a high!) were feasting on the oversized fruits that hung from the trees.

"The Vynarians really should have landed here," Alex sighed. "Everything they could ask for, from the looks of things."

"They'll find it, eventually," Daniel assured her, "but where they are they can do more good. I don't know how large the other continent is, but if it's the size of this one and those plants manage to spread, the planet will be destroyed. They're in the best place they could be. Even the damage they cause would be helpful if it gets the plants back under control."

"Maybe it's like Australia?" Alex suggested. "A continent with all the dangerous stuff concentrated into one area so that the rest of the planet can live in relative peace."

"Some have made it to this continent," he replied. "I don't think the planet will be safe until those things are under control. While the primates here are doing a good job, it's the Vynarians who'll make all the difference." He looked at Alex. "And yes, I will happily to do a training as one of them."

"Excellent. Shall we go back? The sun, or whatever they decide to call it, will be rising on that side of the planet soon."

They headed back and, upon arrival, found the Vynarians already hard at work clearing the space and finishing the enclosure. Once it was secure, and no one could fly out without permission, the captain ordered the ship to be unlocked and removed the guards, allowing the passengers their first chance to walk on solid ground for, presumably, weeks.

Korstan Darizh allowed them to walk around, stretch and take in their surroundings, a few jumping and floating down, revelling in the height they could attain, before he signalled for Varish to switch on the speakers.

"My fellow Vynarians. Welcome! We have arrived on the planet –"

The whoops and cheers drowned out anything else and a few of the youngsters managed to flap their wings hard enough to rise up, although they were quickly grabbed by their parents and yanked back down to earth.

"Yes, yes. We're here, however, we do have a problem."

Hushed silence followed that remark. Darizh explained, without embellishment, the situation they were in. There were a few mutterings, but the group knew there would be risks coming out here and, as the Korstan explained how they'd mitigated those risks (and hence the delay in allowing the passengers to disembark) several visibly relaxed, although not a small number gazed at the ground beneath their feet thoughtfully.

"With all this in mind, we ask that you do not, under any circumstances, leave the large enclosure we've created until we've made it safe. Any crew or scientists who have to leave to do their jobs must turn on their personal shields and set them to maximum before they leave – so make certain those things are charged fully before you go out – and all should be armed and prepared to fire. We're still examining the plants. I was informed this morning that one of them releases a toxin that puts its victim to sleep. I assume you inhale it, although we don't yet know for sure. I would therefore suggest filter masks should also be worn." He raised his hands when there were a few grumbles, his wing flaps catching the breeze. "I know, it's a pain, but if it saves your life and gives you the chance to escape, I'd say it's worth it. We can refine and adjust the rules as we learn more." Nods and a general air of compliance filled the space. "We think we've mitigated the worst of the danger within the barriers but, if you see the ground moving, don't hang around. Get out of the way.

Now we can fly..." and here he jumped and began to flap his arms. It was a little clumsy at first, but it worked and there were cheers as he rose high above the group, "that means you have more than one way to escape. This is new to us, and I'm sure there'll be some sore muscles until we get used to it," he continued, panting a little until he lowered himself to the ground, "but I'd say the more practice you can get, the better. Just remember you've only got about thirty-five yarits before you reach the roof, so try not to fly too high."

Daniel provided the answer before Alex could even ask. "About thirty feet or nine meters."

"Should be enough, I would think," she murmured.

"For the adults, yes. For the kids?" He pointed. A few younger Vynarians were already taking off. One, rather clumsily, tried to execute a roll and ended up crashing into the ground from fifteen feet in the air. He was quickly helped to his feet, assuring those watching that he was fine before trying again.

"And don't do stupid things like that until you've got your wings properly under your control!" the Korstan added, sternly.

"Sorry, Korstan!" the youngster yelled from just above the ship.

"Thirty-five yarits, remember?" Darizh yelled. "You'll get a visual and then an audible warning if you're getting too close. I don't want to hear those alarms going off all day and night!"

The youngster dropped slightly as the lights on one of the pylons flashed an angry red.

"I also don't want my medics dealing with avoidable injuries, so please be careful. Due to the lower gravity, your landings won't be anywhere near as harsh as they would be on Vynar, but land badly and you can still break a limb, and if you tear a wing you'll be down for at least a couple of estiz while it repairs."

"Around forty-three hours," Daniel said. "That's really fast, considering the repairs needed to make sure wind pressures don't tear them a second time."

"Fits with what I saw in the medbay. Effective medicine would, in most societies, be a priority, and I suspect those flaps of skin are easily damaged. They're quite thin."

"And if they use them to glide from point to point to get to work or school, rather necessary." He paused and turned towards the invisible Almega. "Ahh, your next tunnel will soon be opening."

"Where?"

"Not too far, this time. Just outside the fence and through those plants over there," he replied, pointing in the right direction.

Alex took a last look at the Vynarians, many of whom had found a space to practice in so that they could build up their skills and muscles for the adventures ahead.

"We'll be back," she muttered and passed through the fence without causing so much as a flicker.

There were quite a number of carnivorous plants outside the Vynarian enclosure and Alex couldn't help the feeling that they were trying to get *in*side in order to sample the food that was presently thumping the ground and filling the air with subtle but unfamiliar scents. Not that the Vynarians had an odour problem – far from it – but these plants appeared to be able to sense the presence of animals and were turning towards it.

"If I were a Vynarian, I would have made certain those security nodes could very quickly alert the crew to potential breaches," Daniel commented as another of the massive plants shivered and turned towards the noise.

"I'm sure they're being monitored very closely," Alex replied, passing through the stems. "There's certainly a lot to learn on this planet. Whoever goes out to explore will have their work cut out for them. I'm rather looking forward to it, even though it's going to be terrifying in places."

"Here you are," he said, stopping her advance. "It'll open right in front of you."

"Any idea where I'm going?"

"Not a clue," he replied cheerfully.

"Thanks for the help!" she returned, sarcastically.

The tunnel materialised, the roaring, nauseating, twisting pattern making Alex close her eyes and step through as fast as she could. Daniel vanished the instant she entered, looking to Almega to home in on wherever Alex ended up.

***

She found herself in amongst some plants in a rather marshy area. Wary, after the last trip, she rose up to make sure that nothing could suck her down, and made her way to the line of shacks and rather drier land off to the side.

'Looks deserted,' she thought to herself, stepping forward. The door to one of the shacks opened and a rather large rat emerged. It was walking upright and, as she watched, it slipped on some bizarre headwear and looked around. Then it paused and squinted in her direction. She moved and its head tracked her. She moved back and, once again, it followed.

"Can you see me?" she asked.

There was a pause and then an electronic voice emerged from a device the rat was somehow carrying on its waist.

"Human? The language is familiar, but what *are* you?"

"What do you see?" she asked, walking up to the animal.

"It's hazy and your voice is attenuated. I can only just hear you. Keep talking and I'll try to fine tune the equipment."

"Why is it that whenever someone says that, you suddenly find yourself at a loss as to what to say? I mean, yes, I'm speaking what you would call English, but only because I don't yet know your language. What are you?"

"Ah! Got it," the rat replied. "Much clearer. I think, in order to answer that, I'd need to take you to the lab, but I'm not sure security would let you through."

Alex walked up to and through the rat, who shuddered. She then turned around to look at it. "I don't think they can stop me," she assured the rat.

"But the lab is not only elsewhere on the planet, it's also in another time period. The only way to get to it is to pass through the gate and, without permission, you won't be able to. I mean, yes, you could walk through it, but you wouldn't be recognised so you wouldn't make the jump. You'll be in the same time and space, just on the other side of the gate."

"Ahh. That could be a problem."

At that moment, Daniel appeared beside her.

"He's an intelligent looking fellow," Daniel commented. "Why's he wearing all that get up?"

"I think it's a she, and she's using it to see me," Alex replied.

"What?! Impossible!"

"Do you have a name?" she asked the rat, who was looking around and fiddling with the head gear. "Mine's Alex."

"I don't suppose a name would matter much," the rat returned after a pause. "I'm Marique."

"Nice to meet you, Marique. Can you see my friend?"

"Ahh, I wondered who you were talking to. No. Whatever he or she is, they're not showing up. You are, but..." She squinted, although Alex was assuming that from the rest of her body language as her eyes were covered with the strange equipment. "Hmm. I suppose a hazy outline would be the best description of what I see. If I hadn't been testing the equipment when I walked out, I'm sure I would have missed you altogether, but you're clearer than you were. I might be able to tune you in better with time, but right now I think we need to talk to Berik."

"And who's Berik?" Alex asked.

"The closest thing we have to a leader."

Throughout the conversation, Daniel was staring at the rat and back at Alex. He went over to try and see what Marique could see but, being only a projection, he couldn't.

"They shouldn't be able to see you!" he cried. "You're effectively a ghost in the machine!"

"But to Marique here, a visible one," she replied. "And this species can do time travel," she added with a grin at Daniel.

"Oh, really?!"

Chapter 7

"How can she see you?" Daniel asked again as Marique excused herself and went into a broken-down shack.

"I do exist," Alex said, following the rat. "Presumably I give off some kind of energy that her goggles can pick up." She walked into the shack to find it empty and no sign of Marique. "Hey! Where'd she go?" Alex went into the air, scanning in every direction, but there was no sign of the rat. "She can't have run away so fast!"

"A route to another shack?" Daniel suggested.

Alex checked all of them, floating from one to the next through the walls at high speed, in the hope that she might find the rodent hiding inside one of them, but they were all empty. She returned to the first shack, scratching her head.

"This doesn't make any sense! A three-foot-high rat wearing glasses doesn't just disappear!"

"Or reappear," Daniel said, pointing behind Alex. She turned to find Marique once again outside the shack.

That was empty! she insisted in Daniel's head.

"My apologies for leaving, but I had to communicate with Berik. Since you cannot go to the lab, he and some security officers are coming to you."

"If you're going to try and corral me into some kind of cell, I've got to tell you that even with your incredible technology, you're not going to succeed," Alex replied severely.

"Oh, Berik knows that, but security likes to keep track of anyone turning up on our planet. You can't stop them coming out to take a look."

"Without your glasses, they won't see much."

"No," she admitted, sadly, "which means that, while Berik is talking to you, we will just have to wait." She looked up. "I do hope you will hang around long enough so that I can ask you some questions when he's done."

"Marique..."

'Be careful what you say,' Daniel warned.

"Ahh, I probably won't be able to offer much by way of answers. My species is so advanced, even compared to yours, and I'm sure you're wary of giving too much information to less advanced species?"

"Ahh, yes," Marique nodded. "We have very strict rules governing such things. I suppose it's not a bad thing to be on the other side for once and to understand how other species feel when we refuse to help." She sat on her haunches, cocking her head at Alex while she tried to refine the image. "I cannot quite clarify the image. Most annoying! What kind of energy are you, exactly?"

"I honestly have no idea," Alex admitted. "What kind do those glasses pick up?"

"Oh, all sorts. I've been expanding the range as a pet project for months. I thought they might be useful for some of our experiments. We can see things using the mathematics and the sensors, of course, but using these we should be able to see energy flows directly, which may well give us some new insights and allow us to make our inventions more efficient. I never thought a human would be the target."

"Ahh, I'm not, strictly speaking, human," Alex told her, very aware of Daniel's warning murmur at her back.

"Yet you speak the language of the humans."

"I speak a lot of languages. That one was just the one I happened to use. If you tell me yours, I could probably speak to you in your own language."

"That would require I tell you my species, and that's not my choice, I'm afraid. That will be up to Berik. He should be here any second now."

Sure enough, a few awkward moments of silence later a group of rats walked out of the woods, some of them armed with strange little spears.

"Ahh, Marique. Where is our visitor?" one asked as they neared. He was distinct from the others because he was wearing a jewel on a band around his head and another on his wrist. Now she looked more closely, she noticed the others had the wrist version – albeit with smaller crystals – but none the head band.

Marique handed the goggles to the other rat and pointed at Alex. The other rat, who Alex assumed was the leader, Berik, put on the goggles, looked around and then stared at Alex. After a few moments contemplation he walked up to her.

"I gather you understand the human language?" He didn't need any kind of translator. He spoke English as if it was his native tongue.

"I do," she confirmed. "But I'd be just as happy to use yours." Truth be told, she was surprised Omskep hadn't already delivered it.

"That might be difficult. We are telepathic," Berik informed her.

"Oh!" That explained Omskep's dilatory response. "In that case, I'm happy to continue in English."

"I do find it curious that your species used to speak so many languages on your planet, yet this one alone dominates off world."

"An accident of history," she told him, not certain that the history within this universe was the same as her own, although it was good to learn that humans had survived and spread to other planets even here.

"I really must read up on it," he said, thoughtfully. "I never seem to have time to explore all the other species we deal with in detail, and we're rarely asked to help humans."

"Too advanced?"

"Quite the contrary! Too behind in most cases, although they were late entrants to the technological race, and are catching up faster than any. They seem to figure things out well enough on their own, though. Oh! Where are my manners?! I am Berik, laughingly termed the leader of our species. We are Siphians. I would offer a paw, but I don't believe we can shake."

"No, I don't think we can. I'm Alex and my friend –"

'At the risk of sounding like a sitcom, don't tell him my name, Alex!' Daniel insisted. *'You've already told him too much as it is!'*

'Oh, come on! What's the harm in a name?' she asked.

'He's not going to be able to speak to me, so Fred will do or 'my friend', but let's not spill out too much information. This species is incredibly intelligent and, if we do come back here and someone mentions meeting an Alex and a Daniel, some part of our psyche might recognise the association.'

'You honestly think that's possible? We never remember anything from Oestragar once we're in training.'

'Sometimes it does happen. On those occasions, the Eternal's avatar ends up having a breakdown, a psychotic break, or turns into a raving lunatic. Let's not tempt fate!'

With a sigh, Alex turned back to Berik. "And my friend is even less corporeal than I am, so I suppose his name isn't particularly relevant. I might as well be making him up for all you know."

"And, appearances notwithstanding, you are not, and never were, human," Berik declared. Alex cocked her head at him, wondering how he had drawn that conclusion. "You are hazy, but you did not speak aloud, nor did your lips move, yet you communicated with your friend. That tells me that either you have some kind of implant, which humans can't do at present, or your species is also telepathic." He chuckled. "That or you're mad, but you don't strike me as the latter."

Beside her, Daniel thumped his palm into his forehead.

"Too smart! Way, way too smart!" he groaned.

Alex sighed and nodded. "Telepathic, and using a different system to your own, which is why you couldn't hear it. My apologies, Berik. I wasn't trying to cut you out

– that would be rude – but we have to be careful about how much we share for fear we upset things."

"That I fully understand," Berik assured her. "In our own business, we are very careful not to give our customers technological advantages that they have not already discovered for themselves. We combine the knowledge and technology they already have to solve specific problems, but we never give them more than they already have access to – we merely use what they have in ways they didn't spot. It's a delicate balance that garners us some enemies. This is why we are leery of novel or uninvited visitors. However, for the sake of the universe, we find it best not to hand over advanced technologies to species that are not technologically or morally ready for them."

"Exactly! For that reason, would you mind if we moved away and spoke more privately?"

"I don't think security would care for that... yet," he replied. "However, you may convince me. Let us continue. You are clearly a being of energy, which would suggest there is little that we can do to help you."

"Actually, normally I'm not in this form." She declined to add 'within a universe' for fear it would tell him too much. Eternals were beings of energy in Oestragar, of course, and could manipulate it as they saw fit, but within the trainings they had to be inside an avatar to have power, which was leaving her at a disadvantage.

"Oh?"

"Alex..." Daniel warned.

"If they're going to help us at all, they have to know something! It's not like they're in a position to emulate what we're doing!" she said aloud. She turned to Berik. "Please, I can't tell your species too much." She indicated Marique and the guards.

"They hear me, not you. Carry on."

Alex sighed. "Please don't freak out?"

"I am not in the habit of doing so," he assured her.

"Normally, I'd occupy someone. It's the only way I can be an active force. It doesn't hurt them in the slightest," she added quickly when Berik stiffened. "I sit in the background and watch through their senses, or I can take over and make them do things that will correct an error or help someone else."

"Really? And are you always benign?"

"I can honestly say that I have never deliberately hurt anyone or anything unless it was already hurting my, ah, carrier."

"And would you leave upon request?"

"Absolutely. I have no right to do otherwise."

"And what are you hoping we might be able to do for you?"

"This is going to sound insane," she began, waving a hand to shush Daniel. "I need to get far enough into the future that there is no life at all."

"On the planet?"

"In the universe."

Berik looked confused. "But you just said that you cannot act unless you are controlling someone else."

Another of the Siphians perked up at this and levelled his spear in Alex's general direction.

"At ease, Tedrus," Berik said. He looked at Alex who made shushing motions.

"Most species will panic, but we've been in the universe a long time," she began. So far as she knew, no Eternals had been in this particular universe but, if they decided to visit, it would be safe to assume that they would visit at various times and some might well be in the past, so it wasn't entirely a lie. "One of us might even be you, now," she continued. This was rather less likely, but not out of the question. "But as you are as you've always been, you wouldn't know."

"I think it's time to put some distance between us and the guards," Berik declared. "Tedrus, calm down!" he added when the security guard stormed up to complain.

"If Alex wanted to harm me, she would have done so by now and there's nothing you could do to stop her. If I should start acting oddly, *then* you may apply your spears." He put some distance between himself, Marique and the fuming Tedrus, and turned back to Alex. "I assume you feel pain when you..." He waved a paw.

"Very much so."

"Then I would suggest not doing anything to me because, believe me, those spears smart!"

"As I said, I wouldn't dream of it except to protect another innocent being, or because I've been given permission."

Berik sighed, turned and shooed the advancing Tedrus away before he got too close. "I am fine, my friend! Sit down. Alex and I need to talk privately." With an annoyed mumble, Tedrus went back and ordered his squad to make themselves comfortable. He settled back onto his haunches but remained alert and attentive.

"Now," Berik said, sitting back in the grass. "Please explain. You are confusing me. You are before me as a being of pure energy."

"I will explain Berik, but I need a promise, first."

"Which is?"

"That you do not share this with anyone."

"Alex! They're telepathic! How can he NOT share once he knows?"

"That's a fair point," Alex admitted, turning to Berik. "My friend has pointed out that, as a telepath, you might struggle to keep the secret, especially when you're asleep or when something else triggers a memory of this conversation."

"You are telepathic," Berik replied. "Do you broadcast those things that you wish to keep secret?"

"No, but we have rules and a great deal of discipline."

"Can you step inside my mind and look without taking over?"

"I can."

He took a deep breath and let it out slowly. "A show of faith, then. Look inside my head." As Alex advanced, he added, "Remember. Those spears are agonising."

"Duly noted." She stepped inside.

The first thing that struck her, once she'd connected fully to Berik's brain, was that it was remarkably well organised for a non-Eternal. There was a hum at the edges that she couldn't pin down, but inside it was carefully structured, quiet and without the normal internal chatter that plagued most species.

'Can you hear me?' Berik asked.

'I can!'

'Try to send a message to Tedrus or Marique, telling them to come over here.'

She did. It was impossible. Whatever method she attempted was blocked immediately.

'I've never encountered this in a being other than ourselves,' she admitted. *'How are you doing this?'*

'You noted those crystals I wear?'

'Yes.'

'They allow me to control the flow of information coming in from the Collective. You probably haven't even noticed, but I'm dealing with several issues in the lab at the same time as I'm talking to you.'

'You are?!' She looked around and found no evidence of same.

'I'm keeping them locked down. It is, after all, our private workspace.'

'What do the crystals have to do with it?'

'They permit me to send over much greater distances and make my brain a meeting place for our scientists to share ideas.'

'So that's the hum I can hear!' she cried. *'I can't make out what they're saying,'* she added when she felt Berik tense, *'but that there was something happening I did spot. It's like there's a party four doors down! Because your mind is remarkably quiet, it's a background hum that I probably wouldn't hear if your brain was like most species.'*

'Have you seen enough?'

'What if you're not using the crystals?'

'I would struggle to talk to the Collective. I could communicate with Marique, Tedrus and the guards because they're here and, since the gate is open, I could send a message to the lab, but I would not be able to perform my job as leader. An ancient ancestor of mine, by the name of Arren, developed this quirk of the brain that allowed him to compartmentalise and communicate what he wanted to whomever he wanted while keeping his own thoughts private. Once he was assured that he would not be made to suffer for this quirk, he permitted tests. We found the genetic adaption that allowed his ability so that we could give it to all, but we also learned that only his descendants adapted to it readily, if they did not already have it. Today, most Siphians are related to Arren and his partner Crique. The genetic advantage was too great, and we are keen to take every advantage nature grants us. Now are you satisfied that I can keep your secrets?'

'Having so many people sharing your headspace, I understand why you were more willing to let me in. I can't imagine Marique or Tedrus over there would permit it.'

'Tedrus would, if I asked it of him. He is extremely loyal. Marique might, once she knew you had already done it to me, but she is still a young scientist and has much to learn. Please leave, now.'

Alex stepped out, staring at Berik.

"Marique is young, and she created that?!" She pointed at the goggles, shaking her head. "If you're typical of your species...?"

"Oh, I'm not as smart as some, but I make a good leader, apparently," he shrugged.

"Then you guys have the most extraordinary minds I've ever encountered. You're the strongest telepaths and the most disciplined." She turned to Daniel. "Honestly, it's like a steel trap in there. No one and nothing is getting in or out without his permission."

"And can you trust him not to share it anyway?"

Alex considered what she'd seen in Berik's mind. Incredible intelligence, kindness, good humour, tolerance, a devotion to his people, and an even fiercer devotion to the idea that they were here to bring about positive change.

"Honestly, he's the closest physical being to one of us. In fact, he could teach lessons to certain of our number!"

"Ahh!" Berik said. "So, you do have members of your species who are not so benign?"

"He's..."

"An arrogant, self-righteous, conniving, low-level, trench rat!" Daniel supplied sourly.

"The reason I'm in this state," Alex said, giving Daniel a look. "He interfered while I was between lives and threw me off course. I don't even know where the person I was supposed to be is!"

"Might we help you find them?" Berik offered.

"In the entire universe? Besides, they'll be dust by now," Alex told him. "They were not an especially long-lived species, and I've been around a while."

"Please, explain further," Berik said, settling down into an even more relaxed position. Alex had done as he requested and not stayed after he asked her to leave. He'd sensed no malice while she was inside him, only curiosity, which satisfied him that she was, for the time being, safe.

"As I said, it was an accident. Normally, we know where we're going and who we're going to be in when we start, and we stay there until they die."

"What about the being you're inside? Are they not washed away?"

"Under normal circumstances, we enter right at the start of their lives. There never is anyone but us. We are born inside that body, live as that being and, when the body dies, we look for another life to live."

"Remembering all your past lives?"

"No. That would give us an unfair advantage. We block all memories until we're finished." All right, that wasn't true. They didn't actively block so much as simply not realise they had any other option, but Berik didn't need to know that.

"Then why can you not do that this time?"

"Thanks to that member of our group, I wasn't correctly inserted into a body. I'm not... attached, so anyone I go into, even one near death, when they die, I just float free and I'm back like this. However, we think that if I can get to a place where there is literally no life I can enter, I will finally be allowed to leave."

"You mean die?"

"From your perspective, I suppose so, yes," she replied.

"You said that you've been around for a long time. How long?"

"Hard to tell. What year is it by the Earth calendar?"

"Earth has long since ceased to exist. Its star is a white dwarf. Humans are on other planets now, and each has its own calendar."

"Do you know any Earth history?"

"Some," Berik replied. "Enough to know they have come a long way in a surprisingly short period of time."

"I first turned up just after the Industrial Revolution."

Berik blinked a few times. "That long?! No wonder you want to leave! But how can you be certain that you will not simply continue to float in eternity, now deprived even of the possibility of doing something to alleviate your boredom?"

"I can't," she admitted, "but my species isn't meant to be like this in the universe. We're supposed to be within a living being. We're reasoning that, with there being no physical opportunities left, my energy will... dissipate."

Berik stared at the ground, his demeanour distraught. "We... we have never helped someone to die! It's not in our nature. We try to help beings to live better lives."

"After all this time, you *would* be helping me. My species..." She looked about, trying to come up with a way of putting things that wouldn't give away too much. "We believe in reincarnation. I'm not being allowed to be reincarnated because I'm trapped. If I want to live a life again, I have to escape this one."

"And what of your friend? Wouldn't he miss you?"

"He understands. He's been by me all this time and yet, while we can talk and see each other, we can't touch or be together. It's... well, it's all got rather depressing."

"You wish to die because you're feeling depressed? We have some means to alleviate that emotion. The fact that you are telepathic will help there."

She raised her hands. "No!" she cried. "No," she repeated, more softly. "I understand, truly I do, but I must leave. If I don't, I'll never live again."

Berik leaned back, his tail wrapping around his back feet while his upper paws supported him. He stared at the puffs of clouds above him that inched their way across the sky as he looked for a solution.

"Making a time portal normally requires there be another one at the other end. We can travel back to certain times because we built portals back then allowing it, but we cannot go before the time of the first portal."

"Oh," Alex groaned, taking a position opposite him. "In other words, you can't send me into the future because you've not already been there," she groaned. She hadn't thought of that.

"I did not say that," Berik replied, straightening. "*We* cannot use such a method because we need the gate at the other end to reintegrate our particles from pure energy to matter in the exact same pattern that we held when we entered the gate. *You*, on the other hand, are already energy, and so have no need for physical re-integration."

Alex had been slumped. She was imagining more jumps, perhaps into scenarios even more horrifying than those she'd already encountered, before she could reach her destination. Now she straightened eagerly.

"Of course, we would need to do tests to make certain that you can use a gate, and the easiest way of doing that is by seeing if you can join us in the lab. After all, if we're to make this thing, we will need you nearby so that we may ensure you are able to use it." He stood up and dusted himself down. "Would you and your friend care to accompany me?"

She jerked her chin at Tedrus. "I've a feeling your Head of Security won't be too keen on my seeing your laboratory."

"Tedrus!" Berik called.

The Head of Security leapt to his feet and hurried over. "Sir!"

"For goodness' sake, my friend. How many times do I have to remind you? I'm not 'sir'! Berik will do perfectly well."

"But you're..." He withered under Berik's expression. "Yes, Berik."

"Alex will be joining us in the lab, assuming she can pass through the gate, which may not be as easy as it sounds."

"But you can't! She can't! We don't know anything about her."

"I know a great deal, now. I know her species is so far advanced relative to ours that there's really no comparison; that they live for billions of years; that this is not their natural state and, if she was in her proper state, she could be here, right now, and none of us would know about it. That means that others of her kind have almost certainly been to the labs and not only done no harm but, perhaps, helped. Anyway, I have promised to aid her and, to do that, she needs to get to the lab."

"S... Berik! I must protest! My job is to keep the labs secure. How can I do my job if you over-ride me?"

"And how can I do *my* job if you ban me from the lab?" Berik replied, calmly. When Tedrus spluttered, trying to express the difference, Berik patted him on the shoulder. "You're a good Siphian, Tedrus, but you can be a little over-protective. That's not a bad thing in security, but Alex is already here. If we don't find a way to move her on, she could potentially remain here, watching us all, for millions of years. Now, which option is the least troubling to you?"

Alex smothered her mouth to stop her laughter from being heard. She could see why Berik was the leader. While Tedrus fumed, Berik turned to Marique, removing the glasses and waving them in his paw. "Do you have the specifications for these?"

"Yes! They're in my house."

"Would you mind sending them to the lab? I think we will need several pairs and I think, with a little help, you can make them lighter and even more efficient." He reached out and squeezed her shoulder. "You've done excellent work on your own here, Marique. I can see you moving up fast, but you must learn to ask for help more!"

"I... I didn't want to bother anyone. They were really just a toy to begin with."

"Well, they're not a toy now. They're a very useful tool and we need to make them better. Do you have a name for them?"

"I just called them energy glasses," she shrugged.

"Perhaps, while we work, you will find an even better name, but energy glasses will do for now." Berik put them back on, adjusting them until he was satisfied that they were as comfortable as they were going to get. "And they definitely need some work when it comes to padding. I'll have a bald spot on my snout before this is over!"

He turned and headed towards the trees, beckoning Alex to walk alongside him.

"Your lab is in the forest?"

"No," he chuckled. "The gate to the lab is at the edge of the trees. The lab is in another time period and on the other side of the planet."

"Why the spatio-temporal separation?"

"Security. If someone should attack the planet, we have somewhere that we can escape to that they cannot possibly find."

Tedrus muttered something and Berik chuckled.

"He really doesn't like this, does he?" Alex said.

"Tedrus, if Alex can remain here for millennia, sooner or later she'll find the active lab merely by flying over the planet at the right moment. You cannot keep her out forever, so we might just as well let her in when we know what is happening and we still have some control."

Tedrus threw up his paws and marched ahead. One instant he was walking towards the trees, the next he had vanished.

"What the...? Where'd he go?" Alex asked.

"To the lab. He walked through the gate, probably to warn security about your imminent arrival."

"But I can't see a gate."

"Is it possible..." Berik began. He paused, tapping his snout a few times as he mulled ideas. Finally, he looked up. "You are a being of energy. I assume that means that you can adjust parts of yourself to whatever you require?"

"Yes."

"Can you adjust your sight? The gate is invisible to anyone who is not a Siphian, unless they're wearing a special tag, and since we cannot give you the tag..."

"Ahh. Hold on." She scanned up and down the electromagnetic radiation scale until she finally saw the gate shimmering into view. "Wow! That's really impressive. No living being would pick that up. How come you can?"

"The scientists who work there are given a subdermal tag once they are old enough to take up their post. To us, it looks like a normal gate."

"Do you have something similar in the shacks?" she asked, suddenly connecting Marique's comments about going to her house with the gate.

"Similar. We use trans-dimensional gates there, but yes, they are hidden in the same way. It allows us to give the impression of a formerly occupied and now abandoned planet to invaders, while we can all live in comfort. Any given shack may contain many entrances to different homes."

"Multidimensional accommodations! Brilliant!" She turned to Daniel. "We should do that and block you know who from ever darkening our doors again!"

"Almega says that if Fortan doesn't start taking some responsibility, he'll do the same to the Omskep building and good luck to the nuisance ever finding it again!" Daniel smiled. He evidently found the idea appealing.

Alex turned back to Berik. "All right, I can see the gate. How do I go through it?"

"Try?" Berik suggested.

She did but went no further than towards, and briefly through, the tree behind it that marked the edge of the forest.

"Hmm. I suppose we should be grateful that you didn't hurt yourself," he said as Alex walked back through to stand in front of him. "Clearly, the gate doesn't recognise you. One moment."

He seemed to be staring into space but Alex sensed he was talking to someone in the lab. A few moments later, another Siphian walked out of the gate with a sensor.

"Forgive us, Alex, but in order to allow you through, we need to determine the nature of your energy."

"Um... OK, I guess."

"Alex," Daniel warned.

"He's right," she replied. "If I can't walk through this gate, how can I use another to jump forward several billion or, better yet, trillion years?" She turned to face Daniel. "You originally said several billion, but if there's the tiniest possibility of life recurring, I'll be trapped. If we want to be sure there's nothing and no possibility of anything ever again, I have to get to the point in the universe where black holes have swallowed everything and even they've dissipated. That's trillions upon trillions of years in the future, most of it staring at nothing with nothing to do. If I can't walk through the gate, that's what I have to deal with. No thanks!"

Daniel sighed but held his tongue. Truth be told, he was curious. What were they, really? In Oestragar, the question wasn't even asked, so it would be interesting to find out. Berik handed the goggles to the scientist who put them on, adjusted them until they were as comfortable as they were going to get, and looked around.

"Ah! There you are! Nice to meet you. My name is Tarek."

"Hi," Alex smiled, waving.

"I'm just going to do a scan. This won't hurt a bit," he assured her.

Alex stood still while Tarek walked around her, waving his device.

"Fascinating," he murmured as he ran through his scans. "If I didn't know better, I'd say I was looking at something held together entirely by thought alone."

Alex blinked. "I'm sorry, what?"

"The electrical range is between what humans would call one and one hundred megahertz, but it hovers around forty megahertz most of the time, which is roughly the electrical signal in a brain. It's as if you were pure thought. Amazing!"

Alex suddenly noticed movement in the trees. She peered into the darkness, adjusted her eyes to see more clearly and stepped back quickly.

"Woah! That went a bit off the scale. What's the matter?" Tarek asked.

"The biggest spider I have ever seen in my life!" Alex blurted, pointing.

Berik and Tarek turned as the arachnid reached the edge of the forest.

"Karmiayaadoritchee," Berik said, bowing slightly. "To what do we owe the pleasure?"

Alex couldn't hear the arachnid's side of the conversation, although Berik spoke aloud – she suspected purely for her sake since the two were communicating telepathically – but the fact Tarek continued to scan her, unconcerned, while Berik was holding a civilised conversation allowed her to calm down. She wasn't scared of spiders, but having one appear that could look her in the eyes while standing on the ground was enough to make her wary.

The arachnid looked around, but it was obvious it couldn't see her – something else that helped to assuage Alex's fears.

"Our guest is a being of pure energy," Berik informed the beast, "which is why Tarek is wearing those goggles." A pause. "Yes, she is friendly and no danger to you or your family. She's asked us to help her with a problem she's having." Another pause. "I don't know. That is why Tarek is scanning her so that we can adjust." Pause. "We'll be away from the gate just as soon as we can get her through it, I promise you, and we won't go any further into the forest."

"Makes me want to go in there and explore," Daniel muttered.

"Because you're a polarity responder!" Alex replied.

"No more than you are. That thing is massive!" he added as the arachnid stepped forward, seeking to examine the space where Alex was standing to see if it could sense her.

"Alex, I know Karmiayaadoritchee is a little intimidating, but she is curious, and she cannot hurt you. Would you mind if she felt about?"

Alex gulped.

"It's all right," Daniel assured her. "Just close your eyes until I tell you to open them. You won't know she's there."

Alex stared into the eyes of the slowly advancing beast which stopped, politely, awaiting her permission.

"Oh, all right," Alex groaned and shut her eyes.

"Just keep listening to my voice," Daniel said calmly, aware that Alex was finding this extremely hard. "She can't hurt you and I doubt she will even sense you but, even if she does, it won't affect you and you can fly up or walk through her without any problems."

"That's easy for you to say," Alex replied, her face screwed up as she imagined Karmiayaadoritchee pressing mandibles against, or through, her body and 'sniffing' around. "You're not the one with a giant spider checking you out!"

"No, I'm not, but we both know it would make no difference. She asked permission and waited for it, so we know that she intends no harm. Even if she did, in your present form you could walk right through a star and not be affected. She's just a curious alien trying to make sense of what's got the Siphians excited. You didn't object to the Vynarians, humans or others walking through you or you walking through them, and this is no different."

"Feels different to me!" Alex insisted, fists clenched.

"Because she looks a bit different and she's not a fluffy mammal. Honestly, Alex! Are you becoming speciesist in your old age? Keep your eyes closed," he added when he realised she was going to go 'full Alex' on him.

"She's right in me, isn't she?"

"No," he lied. "But she is nearby and a face full of her might put you off your afternoon tea."

Alex began to jiggle on her feet, her fists clenched. "Tell me she's nearly finished!" she begged.

"Can you feel her?" Tarek asked. Being the one wearing the goggles, he was the only other being present apart from Daniel who was aware that Alex was starting to become stressed.

"No, but the idea is becoming unpleasant!" Alex admitted.

"I can appreciate that, but I can only assure you that the Vayuk and the Siphians have lived together on this planet for millennia and on our original planet for millennia before that."

"You brought them with you?" Alex gasped, still keeping her eyes squeezed shut.

"When our local star was nearing the end of its safe cycle, we explored the universe to find somewhere similar to our world where we could have the plants and insects we need without causing any trouble to local inhabitants. The Vayuk are expert gardeners, nurturing plants to feed their insects, which then grow big enough to be worthy meals for themselves and, as it turns out, us. They, in turn, provide us with what we require to maintain our telepathic abilities at the highest level. We could, now, do the job on our own, but it's tedious and time consuming and would take away from our scientific research, while to the Vayuk, it's their normal behaviour. With that in mind, we looked for a world as similar to our old one as we could find where both we *and* the Vayuk would feel at home. We chose a site that looked almost identical to our old home, tested a few plants that are vital to the insects we eat to make certain they would thrive here, checked to ensure the insects were as happy as we were and then explained to the Vayuk what was happening and asked if they'd care to come with us. The then leader of the Vayuk, Sharniayaadoritchee, descendent of Vermiayaadoritchee, who was the first Vayuk to communicate with us, agreed. We built gates on both worlds to allow us to transport everything from one to the other quickly and easily, set everything up almost identically to the way it was, and shut down all evidence of our activities, visible and invisible, on the old planet. There was one house, built for some humans who came to live with us which was not recreated, but everything else is the same, including the location of the wetlands for one of the plants, and the forest for the Vayuk." He paused and then added, "You can open your eyes, now."

Alex did so. The arachnid had retreated back to the treeline but was eyeing the space where Alex stood thoughtfully.

"Did she sense anything?" she asked.

Tarek consulted with either Berik or the arachnid, Alex wasn't quite sure, then turned back.

"She thinks she picked up a very faint energy outline, and she admits you are here because we're talking to you, but otherwise she says she'd think you were nothing more than a breeze."

"How I'm feeling right now," Alex grumpily agreed.

Tedrus reappeared through the gate.

"What's keeping you so long? My guards and I have been waiting on the other side for ages!"

"Well," Tarek said, shutting down his sensor, "we have a problem. The gate is programmed only to accept those who are tagged, which we can overcome, but it also requires a physical presence. If it didn't have that block, every drop of sunlight, sound or a stiff breeze would be rushing into the lab. Unless Alex can make a part of herself solid, she won't be able to pass through the gate and we won't be able to help her. Any gate we make has the same limitation."

Tedrus looked from Berik to Tarek and the ever-curious Vayuk who were all looking at the same empty space.

"May I try the goggles?" he asked.

"Certainly," Tarek said, removing them and handing them over.

Tedrus put them on and looked at Alex. "What, exactly, is it that you want us to do for you?"

"Jump me so far forward in time that there is no life left in the universe and I'm allowed to leave."

"Leave? Do you mean die?"

Alex sighed. She hated misleading them – they were such honest beings and deserved the truth – but no mortal creature would be happy if it knew it was a mere program in a very complex computer, which left her with no choice. "My species believes in reincarnation and that we never die," she replied, which was more or less true if you looked at the Eternals from the perspective of mortal beings. "We believe we are inserted into living beings at birth, and we stay with them until they die, learning from the mortal being's point of view, and then we do it again." Again, from the Siphian's perspective, it was the truth, which made her very convincing. "Because I wasn't put into a body this time around due to an accident, I've been moving around for billions of years, and I've had enough." Also true, but only from the perspective of an external time frame. Internally, she'd been doing this for the equivalent of about a week, which felt like an eternity to her! "So, I would say leave, you might call it death."

He cocked his head at her, and she got the impression he was trying to see inside her mind.

"You go inside other beings?" he checked.

"Um hmm," she nodded. "I went inside Berik before and left the instant he asked me to. That's the rule. I can't stay inside anyone if they don't want me there." If they knew about it, of course. The Victorian ship designer and the Parchti employee had no idea that their bodies were being used while they were sleeping, but she wasn't going to admit to those.

Tedrus turned to Tarek. "She needs something physical that she can be inside to pass through the gate, yes?"

"In sum, yes."

"And she won't be blocked by the gate?"

"She's almost indistinguishable from the electronic signals in your brain. The gate won't block those because that would kill you. The only difference is that she's rather larger."

Tedrus turned back to Alex. "Can you shrink yourself down?"

"Of course. I can fit inside the brain of a shrew if I have to. Even a flea, although it wouldn't be of much value."

Tedrus sighed and took off the goggles. "Step inside me, then."

Berik did a double-take. "Tedrus, you don't need to do that. I can carry Alex if that's what's needed."

"No. If anyone's going to carry her inside our labs, it's me. That way, if it all goes horribly wrong, I'm the only one to blame: not a scientist; not our leader." He stood firm, eyes staring ahead. "Well? Do it!" he ordered.

Inside his head Alex meekly replied, *I already did. Thank you, Tedrus.*

Tedrus swallowed a few times to calm himself, took a deep breath and marched through the gate, followed by Berik and Tarek. Daniel faded out while Karmiayaadoritchee, who knew the gate did not grant her species access, turned and went back into the forest.

***

I can step out now, if you want, Alex told Tedrus.

No. We use trans-dimensional physics. There are too many of us now to fit into one laboratory, so until we know you'll be staying in one section for some time, you'll have to stay inside me.

This is very kind of you.

It's my duty. No one else should be responsible if you prove a malevolent force.

A rather easily contained one, she replied. *You'd only have to go into an empty dimensional extension, order me out, walk out and shut the gate.*

Be assured, if you are up to no good, I will lock myself in there with you rather than risk your escape!

Understood. Um, it's going to be hard for me to answer questions if I'm stuck in here.

I will relay your responses precisely, he assured her.

Alex, though the eyes of her host, looked at the rather empty lab.

So, everyone is in their own dimensional bubble?

They are.

How many bubbles do you have?

As many as we need! he replied brusquely. Clearly, this was not a subject on which he was prepared to elaborate.

Berik stood in the middle of the airy room and Alex got the impression that he was sending out a call because, within moments, several Siphians appeared, stepping out of thin air – or so it seemed to Alex – and awaiting their instructions. She squinted at the spaces from which they'd appeared. There were no gates anywhere on the electromagnetic spectrum. One minute they weren't there, the next, they were, and Alex was at a loss as to how they had achieved it. While she was mulling over this, Berik explained, very clearly, what was being asked of them. One group was ordered to take Marique's goggles and refine them using the readings Tarek had obtained.

"That is top priority," he added, giving the scientists a significant look. They nodded and Alex suspected something else was afoot. "And I want a pair as soon as you can deliver them," he added.

He then explained that those same readings were to be given to a second group ordered to create a gate through which Alex could pass, and a third were to work on the temporal dynamics, figuring out how they could send her trillions of years in the future. Marique went with the group re-designing the goggles while Tarek went with the group working on the gate. Once again, they seemed to simply step into thin air and vanish.

"We used to do it all in this room," Berik said, turning to Tedrus but talking to Alex. "But our interests grew so varied, and our numbers increased. Now, this space is reserved for meetings, primarily."

'And when groups need to work together?' Alex asked through Tedrus who, as promised, relayed her question word for word.

"The dimensional rooms can be linked as required and, of course, they can have as much space as they require. Last time I checked, propulsion, astrophysics, ship design and engineering had a rather fine space-station in their section, around eight kilometres long."

Alex was taken aback. *'How are they going to get it out of there?'*

"One of the advantages of using trans-dimensional space is that the portals can be opened wherever we want. It's certainly cut down on delivery times!"

Alex could feel Tedrus's rising discomfort at the 'secrets' Berik was giving away.

'As Berik said, it could be delivered anywhere at any time. It's not as though I could find it or even get there unless you took me,' she reminded him.

'Which, I can assure you, I won't!'

Alex sighed, wondering what it would take to change his mind about her aims while simultaneously admiring his dedication to Siphian safety. If she had been a negative force, she had no doubt he'd throw himself into space before allowing her to do anything.

'There's nothing I can say or do that will convince you I can be trusted, so I'll shut up.'

He grunted but made no further comment, stubbornly holding his position. In her mind, Alex carried on a conversation with Daniel to while away the time.

'This is going to get incredibly tedious very quickly. He can't expect to stand here for days or weeks while they work on the problem,' she told him.

'I don't know. He strikes me as the type who would stand like Horatius on the bridge, all year and in all weathers if his boss ordered him to and he believed it was for the good of the group.'

'Got to admire his dedication,' she agreed. *'Even so, I wish we could see some of the things they're doing, the spaces they work in... I want to look around that space station they're building. It sounds amazing!'*

'Wonder who they're building it for?' he mused. *'Normally, from what Almega can tell, they provide help to crack scientific nuts, they don't usually do all the work. That would suggest the space station is for them rather than a customer.'*

'Experiments that require zero-G?'

'Could be, although an entire space station seems a little excessive.'

'Maybe they've had several different requests for help with such things and it was easier to build one than try to solve the problems theoretically,' she suggested.

'And rather fun that they can, and still walk home for dinner!'

"Alex, I know that you can't eat, but I'd like to chat with you, and I could use some sustenance. Would you care to join me?" Berik asked.

"I would love to," she replied via Tedrus.

Berik walked off and Tedrus followed. They soon arrived in a dining area where Berik sat down. At first, Tedrus remained standing but then, at Berik's insistence, he took a seat. Berik waved his paw over the table and a meal materialised in front of him. Tedrus, with a little prompting, did the same, but he kept himself to nothing more than a drink.

"I gather that you can make your host do whatever you want them to do," Berik began, garnering a sharp look from Tedrus, whose heart rate skyrocketed.

"I can but, as I told you, I don't like to do it without the host's permission."

"And the host is aware of your manipulation?"

"That depends on how much I take over. If it's merely redirecting a look or a subtle movement, they might be surprised it's happened, but they wouldn't connect it to another force inside them. If I took over more and they're conscious, I imagine it could be quite terrifying. If I take over completely, the host consciousness normally sleeps and is unaware of what they do unless someone tells them when I leave."

'Don't. You. Dare!' Tedrus fumed.

'Only with your permission,' she replied.

'Never –'

"In other words, if you took over Tedrus, we could talk privately, without the intermediary," Berik reasoned.

"You can't hand me over to an unknown force!" Tedrus roared.

"I would not be 'handing you over', as you put it. I would be asking you to step back and allow Alex to communicate with me directly," Berik replied reasonably.

"No! Absolutely not! If I lose control —"

"You're under the illusion that you have control in the first place," his boss replied. "If she wished, she could take you over at any moment. She refrains because you have asked or, more probably, told her not to, and she respects your request. Does that not tell you that she is safer than most of our customers? How many of them would respect your autonomy were they given the opportunity Alex has right now?"

"I can keep control of my own mind!" Tedrus insisted.

'Ah, no. Strictly speaking, that's not true. Berik is correct. I'm not doing anything because you told me not to.'

Berik noted the change in his security chief's expression. Shock, a hint of fear, then grim determination. "Alex just told you that's not true, didn't she?"

"I have complete control. Even if she chose to, she could not take over."

'Wanna bet?' Alex murmured.

"Arrgh!" Tedrus roared and stood up. "Very well. Make me hop on one foot!"

Berik, grinning, sat back to watch what happened.

'You are explicitly giving me permission?' Alex confirmed.

"I hereby give you permission to try and make me hop on one foot!"

'Very well.'

The next moment, to Tedrus's shock and Berik's amusement, he was hopping around the dining room on one foot. When he stopped, he resumed his position, arms folded, stomped his feet hard on the ground, and glared inwardly.

"Now try again!" he insisted.

Despite the barriers he'd put up – and they were formidable – Alex was able to control the muscles, tendons and nerves with no more issue than she had the first time.

'Having your personal barriers up doesn't stop me from operating your body or, as it happens, accessing your thoughts, although that would be rude in the extreme.'

"No! Get out of me at once!" Tedrus ordered and Alex obeyed.

'That was easier than I thought it would be,' she grinned at Daniel who shook his head but couldn't help smiling.

Berik, too, seemed to guess what Alex had done and struggled to contain his laughter. Tedrus, realising his mistake, looked around desperately.

"Where are you?!" he cried.

Alex stood right in front of him, then leaned into his head and whispered, *'Still in the room, never fear.'*

"You're in my head! I told you to get out!"

With a shrug, Alex walked away and sat down next to Berik.

One of the invisible gates opened and Marique came hurrying out.

"Berik, we thought these might be useful to you," she said in English without the aid of her translator, and handed over some smaller, far more refined, glasses. "The scanning is now automatic and responds to telepathic adjustments."

He put them on and, after a moment, turned and jumped slightly to see Alex smiling at him.

"Alex is sitting beside me, Tedrus. Calm down," he informed his distressed security guard.

"I stepped out when he told me to," Alex assured him, now audible to the Siphian Leader. "I just poked my head inside his to reassure him I was still in the room."

Berik explained this to Tedrus, then suggested he grab his drink and go check on the other departments while Berik talked to Alex.

"But..." Tedrus began, then his shoulders slumped. It was evident that there was, quite literally, nothing he could do when it came to Alex, and she had followed his instructions as promised. That left him capable of nothing more than standing around feeling silly. With a snort, he turned on his heel.

"Marique. I need a pair of those glasses!" he growled and, together, they stepped through a portal and vanished.

"Nicely done," Berik chuckled before schooling his features. "How was it inside my head of security?"

"He has remarkably good barriers. I suspect no other species would be able to get through them. He's also very disciplined, suspicious, but loyal to a fault. You've a good one, there."

"I'll let him know you approve, although I doubt he'll thank you for the compliment." He paused and sighed. "Ahh, Alex. I wish you would stay with us. Apart from keeping Tedrus on his toes, you've a unique perspective on the universe. It's a pity you want to finish it."

"As I said, while you see it as dying, we don't. For all I know, I'm already here, inside Marique or one of the others. The only two I couldn't be in now are you and Tedrus."

"He'll be relieved to hear that! So, you can't live as someone you've already been inside?"

"Nope. Can't have our energy twice in the same place and time. If I or any of my fellows were inside you or Tedrus, I couldn't have occupied either of you and I would have sensed the second presence the instant I tried. That doesn't mean some of us aren't already here, but we'd be the same as everyone else."

"Your species lives as other species as a matter of course?"

"Um hmm. It's a great way to learn. Yes, you can read the books and watch the films or whatever, but there's no substitute for being the people dealing with things. It gives you a perspective nothing else can."

"And you get to choose?"

"Oh yes, although we don't remember doing that until we're back home."

"Do you ever choose less savoury characters?"

"I don't and neither does my friend. As for the others, one of them might pick characters with power and a less than passing acquaintance with honesty, but even he wouldn't pick someone evil."

"Ahh, but evil people never think they're evil," Berik replied sagely.

"No, but we can see all of space and time and the consequences of what our characters do. That particular individual would not pick someone who deliberately and personally harmed others, although the consequences of his activities might hurt as a collateral effect. He doesn't take on military dictators or leaders who could give orders that directly hurt innocents. He prefers company CEOs, senior military officers and the like. And yes, they can cause a great deal of harm, but CEOs have to answer to shareholders, and officers to the chain of command. If either of those are crooked..." She shrugged.

"That would suggest that you have no freewill."

"Once we're inside, we follow the pattern. Personally, I prefer to know as little as possible. I find that, if I know too much, it puts me off. A character who ends up with a very good life may go through terrible things before they get there, and that can be overwhelming when you read about it all in one hit. When it's spread out over months and years, it's not so bad."

"I can understand that," he nodded. "But it suggests that we have no freewill either."

"You mentioned a couple of characters from your history, Arren and Crique. From your perspective today, you know what they did. Does the fact that you know because you're after the event mean that they had no freewill?"

He considered her comment and his face cleared. "No. What you're telling me is that, normally, you can see the whole of space and time because, from the perspective of the end, it's all already happened."

"Exactly."

"But if you can see all of time from the end perspective, why can't you go there now on your own? I could understand if you were inside a limited species, but you're in a pure energy form which is, I assume, your natural state."

Whoops! "Not quite my natural state," she replied carefully. "We set aside some of our power in order to step inside another. I set aside the power and then wasn't inserted, and I can't get my power back because the system, which stores it, doesn't recognise that I've 'died' since I was never 'born'. If I had all my powers, I assure you that I wouldn't be bothering you."

"Ahh. Now I understand." He stared at her for a moment. "In your full state, your powers must be formidable if you have left some behind and can still do what you do!"

"Another reason we're not a malevolent species. If we were, the universe would have ceased to exist a long time ago. That would not only hurt those living here, but us. We'd lose our way of learning."

"That I understand," he nodded.

Alex breathed an internal sigh of relief. Berik clearly thought her species had machines or some equivalent that could store energy during their trips, which was fine by her. "Um, Marique was speaking English when she came back, and those glasses appeared rather fast. Can I assume that as well as being spatially expandable, your workspaces can manipulate time?"

"Ahh. You noticed that. Yes. When I told them it was top priority, that meant that they were allowed to use temporal displacement so that the job could be done within moments for me but probably weeks for them. We don't do that often, for obvious reasons. You can't leave the lab while you're doing it, and you age disproportionately to your family. If we kept it up for too long, a scientist would end up leaving as a neophyte in the morning and returning as a senior scientist with greying whiskers by the afternoon. Not good for their partners. A few weeks or months here and there are forgivable in an emergency. Since everything depended on the data from those glasses and the readings Tarek took of you earlier, the others would be in the dark until that data was delivered. Marique clearly took the opportunity to learn English in her down time."

"And now I feel terrible," Alex muttered. "Your people shouldn't be aged trying to fix my problem."

"Oh, I wouldn't worry about it. Siphians thrive on learning new things. It's our entire reason for living. The more we learn, the happier we are." He dug into his meal.

'And finding a way to make your gate will help them to learn all sorts of new things they can use elsewhere,' Daniel pointed out. *'Which means you've changed them, and that's not good.'*

'Can all this be erased from the program once I'm back?' she asked. Marique and the others deserved to live their full lives, including the time spent with their families. Alex couldn't get over the feeling that, despite Berik's reassurances, she'd just stolen some of their lives from them.

'Given you weren't supposed to be here in the first place, Almega thinks there might be a way to reset it.'

'That would be great! Can he reset the dragon world so we can visit more of it?'

A pause as Daniel relayed the query. *'No. He says that whatever he does, that world has a permanent block on certain events. Seems to be a glitch in the program. Here, however, he thinks it'll be easy enough. Berik will never know you were here. This program only starts after they left their previous world, though, which is curious. Events before the move aren't available.'*

'That's a shame. Those days must have been amazing.'

'And a lot of very hard work. Even so, there are hundreds of millions of years available for us to explore.'

'Given how advanced these guys are, I'm surprised they still look like large rats. You'd have thought they would have evolved.'

'Ask him,' Daniel suggested.

"Berik. Not that I object, but why do your people maintain the appearance of rodents? I assume you could adjust your appearance by now."

"Oh, yes," he said, waving a fork. He emptied his mouth, took a sip of his drink and turned to her. "We did try it, millennia ago, but we found we missed our old look, and it's harder to hide from intruders if you look like something associated with advanced intelligence. As rodents, capable of scurrying on all fours, we're easily mistaken for ignorant beasts, which we find works to our advantage. For those doing long-term surveillance of a civilisation, we do change our appearance to match that of our hosts, but it's done with camouflage systems. Those same systems allow us to become invisible if things become dangerous. Even so, scratch the surface and our rodent form is underneath." He stared into space for a moment. "I suppose, in our own way, we're doing what you do, we merely retain our own character and knowledge while we're doing it." He picked up his fork again.

"No one else knows what a Siphian looks like, then?"

"Some humans did, once, because we had to help them out due to a bit of a mess where one of our creations to end a war was stolen and used as a toy. That was when we first allowed a human to live on our world. That planet has gone the same way as Earth, and their records were lost in the rather mad rush to escape. As a consequence, we're now safely unknown once more, and we intend to keep it that way." He took a mouthful and chewed for a moment. "Plus, there are lots of mammalian species in the universe, and rodents are quite common," he continued. "Even if they knew Siphians look like large rats, they wouldn't imagine us acting that way if they consider us at all beyond our deliveries. We're scientists and, so far as we can tell, each species assumes we look similar to their image of a scientist, which isn't usually associated with something that is a pest on many planets. Should an invader arrive, we normally go onto all fours and scurry about so that the invader thinks they've got a nuisance on their hands, rather than an advanced species. Something Marique should have done when she saw you."

"She was wearing the goggles. Even if she'd suddenly dropped to all fours, they were a bit of a giveaway that she was rather more advanced than your average rat."

"You have a point," he agreed and returned to his lunch.

"Now that Tedrus isn't censoring our every word, may I ask... Why are you building a space station?"

"Hmm? Oh, that's just a proof of concept."

"Proof of concept?! It's five miles long!"

"Well, yes. If you're to have working gravity and hydroponics, you need something that big. The final version will be roughly the size of this planet."

Alex blinked in surprise. "I'm sorry?"

He cleared his plate, and the table calmly absorbed it and his utensil. Grabbing his drink, he leaned back.

"Our last planet had a bit of a run-in with some unwanted visitors who thought we were dinner, and we've had a couple of near misses with this one, so we thought we'd build our own. The outer shell marking the edge of the atmosphere will be about, in your terms, ten miles above the surface, which will allow room for clouds and weather systems. Fusion energy will power light that will move around the inner surface like a... oh, what do you call it? Ah yes, sun! We'll live on the surface of the globe within that space and, with our trans-dimensional systems, we'll have all the space we require. Gravitational beams will be able to quietly nudge any deep space probes or observers aside without them realising there's a planet in the way because the planet itself will be invisible. We'll be able to put it deep in the space between galaxies and, hopefully, be left alone."

"Couldn't you just put everything inside one of your trans-dimensional spaces and do without the planet?"

"They require power, and power requires occasional maintenance. If a major power source failed, we could all end up flailing in a vacuum. Having our own planet is safer. Plus, the Vayuk need room to farm, and they wouldn't care for it. They have senses that would constantly remind them that they are within a simulated space."

"You'd take them with you?"

"We've built up something of a symbiotic relationship over the millennia. We respect their space, they respect ours, and they provide our food. They have a very different take on things, which is sometimes welcome and refreshing. We have a tendency to get bogged down in detail while the Vayuk state the obvious and wonder why we don't do it. It's not always the right answer, but Karmiayaadoritchee's suggestions can put us back on a more workable track. Plus, they deserve to live too, don't you think?"

"Absolutely!" she replied, although she knew she'd have to spend a lot more time with the Vayuk before she would be able to appreciate their value. Still, if the Siphians said they were good, who was Alex to argue?

"She has a very long name," she mused.

"Karmi is her given name. Ayaadoritchee is Vayuk for 'mother of all', which is what she is, now – literally in hundreds of cases, figuratively for the others."

'Hundreds of cases.' Alex shuddered slightly at the thought of so many Vayuk running and weaving their webs deep in the forest, then shook herself. They were not cute and cuddly, but they were intelligent and equally deserving of respect. Daniel was right. Apparently, she could be speciesist!

A thought struck her. "Hang on, that means you will still be there no matter how far into the future you send me!"

"No. There'll be no one left to help, and, eventually, nothing more to learn because the universe will have effectively closed for business. At that point I'm sure we'll simply stop having cubs and quietly die out, even assuming we're not sucked into a black hole or blown apart by a wayward star." He stroked his muzzle. "I think I prefer the idea that we die out from choice rather than violent accident." He shrugged. "Besides all that, our power systems will run out and there'll be no energy left in the universe for us to harness. The teams are working on sending you well beyond even the most fantastic calculations for the space station."

Alex was once again overwhelmed, this time at the thought of this incredible species seeing the end of the universe and choosing to die effectively, if not necessarily directly, by their own hand rather than be alone in the immensity of empty space.

"There's a thought. Have you tried inserting yourself into a black hole?" Berik asked.

Not on this trip, but... "Believe it or not, yes. It doesn't affect my species. I can stroll through the most damaging of black holes or stand in the heart of a star and admire the view – not that there really is one, but you get the idea. No effect at all. Bit bright."

Berik laughed but then looked at her thoughtfully. "Tedrus will be stunned to discover that he was holding something so powerful."

"Not powerful, though, am I? Yes, I can withstand pressures that can separate the atoms of anything else, but if you're alone and you can't do anything but watch, it's a gilded cage at best and gets very boring very fast."

Berik tilted his head and seemed to be communicating with someone.

"Is there a problem?" Alex asked.

"No. Tedrus wanted to come back, and I've told him rather firmly that I do not need his help and he's to support whichever group needs him the most. He's not happy," he added with a grin, "but once I explained how powerful you are..." He raised a paw when Alex once again tried to argue to the contrary. "I know, I know, but to him, your resilience to any force marks you as the most potent thing he's ever encountered. He seemed taken aback that you were willing to submit to his control at all and has finally accepted that you are not a malevolent entity. This leaves us in the happy situation of being able to talk in peace."

Without Tedrus's constant disapproval, and Daniel now satisfied that none of what they discussed would be remembered by the mortal participants, Alex was able to learn a great deal about the advances in Siphian technology. While she still maintained that her species was of this universe and merely energy wanderers who would re-incarnate if there were no more lives available to live (she didn't want to see the look on Berik's face if he learned he were a mere program), she was happy to fill him in on human history once she'd checked with Daniel to make certain that the events in this universe had paralleled those of her own.

"Do you only focus on the human population?" Berik asked.

"No, I've been many species, but I find humans interesting. Not anywhere near as advanced as you, of course, but that's probably because they allow politics to shape and direct science, rather than encouraging it to explore on its own. To be honest, I'm surprised your species doesn't go rampaging through the cosmos, given you could overcome any species without so much as bending a whisker. If humans were as advanced as you, I've no doubt that they would!"

"What would be the point of that?" Berik asked, genuinely confused. "As you said, how can you learn from something you've destroyed?"

"What is there left for you to learn? All the other species are so far behind you that you'd struggle to see them with a telescope!"

"The same could be said of your species, yet you do it. Plus, when you're struggling to find an answer with limited resources, free-thinking and open-minded species can become very innovative. They're constantly surprising us with problems we didn't even know existed. Solving those problems within the constraints of technical knowledge and available resources stretches us and keeps us on our toes."

She shook her head. "A species that delights in the sorts of things that drive other species crazy! I think you're almost certainly unique in the universe!"

"We've never encountered anything with a similar mindset," he agreed. "A pity. We could advance even more and faster with another species at the same level that enjoyed the same things but saw the universe from a different perspective. Not that we don't get that with other species as we solve their problems using their own technology, and the Vayuk, of course, whose farming allows our telepathy, but to have an intellectual equal we could spar with academically would be very satisfying."

Alex was confused. "What have the Vayuk to do with your telepathy?"

"Chemicals in the bugs we eat enhance and maintain the talent. While we can, now, produce the chemicals artificially in a stable form, the bugs are the healthier option for the cubs. We lace all our foodstuffs with the chemicals, but there's nothing quite like the raw version."

Alex shuddered. "Can't say bug eating appeals much."

"Do you eat?" Berik asked. "In your native form, I mean."

"For pleasure, yes. For nutrition, no. We don't need it. We always have all the energy we need."

Berik exhaled a low whistle. "A more primitive species would see your kind as gods."

"Which is why normally we make sure we're not seen. Had I known Marique's goggles would allow her to spot me, I would have hidden or simply stayed well away."

"And yet now you're talking to me and availing yourself of our talents."

"And now I feel guilty," she admitted. "If you want to pass on creating the gate..."

"Oh, no! That's not what I meant at all. I'm merely delighted that Marique *did* invent them. It gave me a rare opportunity which might otherwise have been missed. I can honestly say we have never encountered a being like you."

"That you're aware of," she corrected. "For all you know, many of your species and others in the universe that you've interacted with may have lived their lives with one of us inside them."

"That's a rather disturbing thought!"

"What would you rather: to die and that's it; or to die and find out that you have infinitely more opportunities to learn about the universe?"

"Oh, if you put it like that!" he smiled. "Now I'm rather sorry that you've proved I will never have that opportunity. Still, not that I believe it, but if there is something more once the mortal life ends, doesn't that mean you've stolen that person's chance?"

"We've been here, quite literally, since the dawn of time, although I admit we had no interest in living as single-celled creatures or plants. Once intelligent life started to appear, we got involved. For all we know, it was subconscious memories of former travels at different moments in time that gave rise to the idea of an afterlife. Despite the claims of various individuals to have witnessed the divine, when living those lives I'm afraid we never saw it or, if we did, it could easily be explained using more prosaic means – mild poisoning, mental health issues, dreams, or just a misunderstanding of natural events. The very fact that the number of reported miracles drops with the intellectual advance of a species should be an alert that it's less likely divine intervention, more likely local ignorance." She watched him digest this idea. "You know, you're a scientist and yet you seem to enjoy philosophy."

"There's a great deal of philosophy in our business. Mostly ethics, although metaphysics and epistemology do appear from time to time. I suppose that's inevitable when you occupy yourself with the building blocks of the universe."

There was silence for a moment between them. A silence that Daniel broke.

'Ask him if, now that Tedrus is away, he could show you some of their workshops,' he suggested. *'Even if it's just the ones working on the gate, it should be fascinating.'*

Alex passed on the message as her own. She didn't want to remind Berik that, wherever she went, her shadow – which the Siphian Leader could neither see nor communicate with – was tagging along.

"I suppose you could just as easily insert yourself into one of us without our even knowing you were there," he observed.

"Yes, but I wouldn't do that. It would be wrong on so many levels, not least since you've offered to help me. It would be a total betrayal of your trust."

"Ahh! The right answer," Berik smiled, standing up. "Please, hop in... although, given what you did to Tedrus, I would be grateful if that particular talent was not expressed through me. I do need to maintain the illusion of decorum."

Alex laughed and inserted herself into Berik.

'Comfortable?' he asked.

'Yes, thank you.'

'Do you wish me to hide your presence?'

'That is entirely up to you,' she replied. *'I trust you to determine what's best.'*

'Very well. Let's see how the gate is coming along.'

***

The physical gate was done and looked like it had been completed almost immediately. The problem was tuning it to recognise Alex's energy signature as a trigger. It was not, in fact, a physical gate. It was a plate on the floor that projected the gate's energy field and appearance above it. While Daniel – who'd vanished when she left the communal area and reappeared a few seconds after her arrival in the large lab – explored the gate and listened, so far as he could, to the technical discussions, the lead scientist, Arrit, explained to Berik the problems they were having.

"Because Alex is using the same energy as our thoughts, if it could take the thoughts without a body, it follows that it could, theoretically, take our thoughts away and leave the body behind which is, well, not a very nice idea, to be honest."

"And not something you'd want to test!" Berik nodded.

"Definitely not! If we do manage to crack it, it will be the most dangerous object we've ever created, and I would strongly recommend destroying it the instant Alex has passed through." He turned and gazed at the gate. "Assuming we ever get there."

'I can shrink down to fit inside anything,' Alex reminded Berik. *'And I can animate whatever it is from within. Is there something already dead I could occupy for the journey? An insect, perhaps?'*

Berik, keeping quiet the source of the suggestion, relayed Alex's comments to Arrit.

Arrit stared at his leader for a moment, smacked his forehead and cried, "Of course!" before diving back into the group and eagerly sharing the information. The others seemed equally delighted and, after a rather fevered discussion, Arrit returned with a huge smile on his face.

"We can do better than an insect. We weren't aware Alex had that ability, but that's opened up a raft of possibilities. Give us a little while and I think we'll have it cracked."

"Will you be able to test it? I would rather we didn't put Alex through the gate and then realise we've accidentally sent her backwards in time instead of forwards." Inside his head, he felt Alex's trepidation. *'Never fear,'* he assured her. *'We will make certain you go so far in time that, whichever way you go, there will be no living thing in the universe.'*

'I'm sure, but just in case the possibility of life is all that's required to keep me tied to this place, please make certain it's the right direction!'

'Of course.'

"Obviously we can't get a message from the future," Arrit replied, "but we can send one from the past, so we'll be sure to check. Sajen is our temporal-dynamics expert, and he can land us within a few microseconds of our target. She's in safe paws."

Alex relaxed. She could go through the whole, nauseating rigmarole all over again, if necessary, but the thought that the Eternals in Oestragar would be further delayed did not sit well with her.

"I'll check in on Sajen, then," Berik said. He turned, focused, sliced his paw through the air and a gap appeared, which he walked through.

'How are you doing that?' Alex asked.

'Trans-spatio-temporal dynamics, with the instructions as to where I want to be passed through the crystal,' he replied. *'Once it knows my target and has confirmed it's available, a movement opens the link between the two and we can walk from one to the other.'*

'That easy, huh?' She shook her head. Berik seemed to think that this was something straightforward. For an Eternal, it was, but for a mortal, material being it was a

monumental discovery. She imagined the effect on another species living on an overcrowded planet if they could simply expand their farming or housing indefinitely. It would certainly solve a lot of problems. It might even stop wars since many seemed to start over the matter of space or, more specially, prime real estate. The perfect farm, the perfect housing, the perfect facilities. The Siphians wielded energy like an Eternal, but with rather more purpose. She briefly considered promoting a Siphian training to the other Eternals so that they might improve their outlook, then dismissed it. The instant Fortan paid a visit, the Siphians would be doomed!

On the other side of the portal was what appeared to be a simple work room. Six Siphians were sat at a large table, three of them working on computer models and three with pen and paper. Daniel appeared beside her, shaking his head.

These guys are incredible. This room is three days behind the previous room and the dining hall which are, in turn, one-million, seven-hundred-and-twenty-eight years previous to the time when you arrived. To Siphians, time is literally just a number!'

'So why do they need the gate to get from their town to here?' Alex wondered idly, then asked Berik.

'The transtemporal portals are only good for fifty years at most, although we've never gone beyond six months. Anything longer than that requires the gates,' he replied. *'The lab is many centuries separate from the town.'*

'Ahh!' Alex nodded, then added, *'Thank you,'* but she found she couldn't take her eyes off the computer modellers. The computers themselves appeared to be telepathically connected, allowing data to be input without the need of a keyboard. The holographic screens floated in mid-air and were summoned or dismissed with a wave of a paw, each Siphian apparently in control of several different screens that they swapped in and out as needed. They could keep multiple screens stacked above, below or side by side in one location, or summon them from nowhere

and then dismiss them, seemingly into nothingness, when not required. One of them had six screens in two rows and was swapping data between them.

Meanwhile, one of the Siphians working with pen and paper scratched an ear, put his pen down and stood up. He walked slightly away from the table, waved his paw and a shelf of books appeared. He scanned through them and, not finding what he wanted, waved his paw upwards. Another shelf appeared. He did it again and found what he was looking for. He pulled out the volume, dismissed the bookcase back to wherever it had come from and walked back to the table, his eyes glued to the pages he was flipping through.

Berik cleared his throat. The Siphian with the book looked up, and Alex noted that his muzzle was greying.

"Oh, hello Berik. How may I help you?"

"Sorry to bother you, Sajen. I wondered how the calculations were coming."

"We can move her forward to the right time easily enough. Making certain she's not in a black hole or something equally disastrous is proving rather harder."

"Alex told me that she's stood in a black hole and in a star and it has no effect on her whatsoever."

Sajen stared at Berik. "Really? But... but those things separate atoms down to the most basic particles. No energy could resist such power."

"Hers, it seems, can. If she couldn't, she would have solved her problem aeons ago."

Now all the other scientists had stopped their work to listen to the conversation.

"What kind of a being is she?" one said, his tone filled with awe.

"One more powerful than we could imagine, but not one capable of your magnificent temporal calculations in her present condition. If we remove that impediment, can you provide the numbers for the gate?"

"I can encode it right now," one of the computer operating scientists replied, putting actions to words.

Sajen nodded approval at his co-worker and quietly summoned the invisible bookcase, returning his tome to its correct place before dismissing the bookcase once more.

"I would so love to speak to her."

It depends on what he wants to ask, but if I'm allowed not to answer where the answer could be... ahh, difficult to explain to beings such as yourself, I'm happy to try,' Alex told Berik.

"I have Alex listening in right now," Berik said. All the scientists, barring the one who was uploading the calculations to be converted into the language needed by the gate's software, instantly stopped what they were doing and crowded around. "What do you wish to ask her? She can hear you. Remember she speaks English."

Sajen paused for a moment, doing some adjustments, then nodded to himself and looked at Berik. "Alex, I'm ninety-seven. Thanks to advances we've made in a number of areas, I have another forty or fifty years of useful life before I die. You have lived for billions of years. Has this changed your perspective on the universe?"

'Wow! I wasn't expecting that sort of question!' Alex admitted, dumbfounded.

Berik chuckled. "I think you've stumped her for a moment, Sajen."

"I apologise. I didn't mean to offend or –"

'No, no! I'm not offended. Please reassure him!'

Berik did so while Alex tried to formulate a reply, then the Siphians waited very patiently.

'Berik, you can't relay this. Ahh, can you let me out and give him the glasses or telepathically connect us so I can talk to him directly?'

'You're now connected,' he told her simply.

'Um, hi. Sajen, yes?' The scientist nodded eagerly. *'Nice to meet you. OK, normally we live our lives inside other species, so our experiences are as long or as short as the beings we inhabit. This is*

the first time I've been forced to experience the universe in one long hit, as it were.'

'I understand.' Sajen's voice was as loud as Berik's and Alex was once again struck by the Siphians' advances.

'That means, of course, that I've not really thought of it before, however,' she quickly added when she saw Sajen's face fall, *'now that you've raised the point, I realise that you do get a very different perspective. What seemed devastating while a part of it as a mortal being becomes one of numerous blips in the timeline. Wars, famines, plagues, natural disasters... they're all just parts of a greater whole, the story of a given species or planet. Empires rise and fall everywhere, and the same patterns emerge over and over, regardless of species or location. I suppose that all of us, mortal or immortal, are the product of the things that happen to us as individuals. Our past inevitably shapes how we deal with later events. Sometimes, those past events can cause us to react very poorly because we perceive a threat where there is none, but if we're not aware of the history, we don't see a threat when it's there. I think an intelligent species, like an individual, is at its best when it remembers the events of the past and learns from them so it can apply them to its present situation, but while a person can be traumatised by what happens in their lives, a species can step back, look more coldly at the data, and extrapolate vital information without sharing in the trauma. Well, theoretically. Unfortunately, time and again I've seen the trauma being relived and affecting solutions. Oh, I'm not putting this very well, am I?'*

'No, no. I understand exactly what you're saying,' Sajen assured her. *'The past is a useful tool which can work to our advantage, provided we focus on what we can learn from it rather than our feelings. But to do that properly requires excellent record-keeping.'*

'Exactly. Which would mean that properly recorded history, with no favouritism or cherry picking of any kind; records filled only with cold, hard facts, good and bad being given equal value – that kind of history is one of, if not the *most important of disciplines, while being the hardest for emotional beings to deal with. History is a story, and we can get caught up in the characters. The universe has a story, too, but there are no characters, just things. Even so, we label them good*

297

and bad. A planet with plants and animals that is thriving is deemed good, one inimical to all life is bad, but it's neither. Things simply are. I've been inside black holes and stars and I promise you that they're not thinking at all. They're simply doing what physics tells them to do. Intelligent beings can alter their behaviour, but I suppose they're as constrained by biology and physics as anything else. Still, the greater the intelligence, the more opportunity to overcome those predictors and step out on your own – which your species appears to be doing in spades! I have to say, Siphians are the most intelligent and impressive of species I've ever encountered, and that's no small compliment given how much I've seen.' She meant it, too. The Siphians had huge potential for evil, yet they had chosen to adhere to very strict moral principles, eschewing power in favour of knowledge.

Sajen wiped his eyes, but he was beaming. 'Thank you. Thank you so much!'

'I second that,' Berik added quietly.

'Seeing so much of history,' Alex continued, 'has shown me that patterns repeat, endlessly, throughout time and across species, and the species that can spot the patterns, predict them, and adjust to reap the benefits and nullify the negatives will always triumph. Your species has chosen that path. You could take over the universe if you wanted to, yet you focus on controlling your own minds and learning as much as you can. You, too, would be seen as benevolent gods by less advanced species."

'Oh no. Far too much paperwork!' Berik snorted. 'Not that paperwork isn't of value, of course, but governmental paperwork? Waste of time!'

Daniel who was, of course, privy to the conversation, roared with laughter.

'I take it you have trouble finding leaders?' Alex mused.

'Oh yes. I am, by nature, a botanist and chemist, but someone has to do it and, by doing it well, I help everyone else to meet their targets. No one of us could know everything, but by working together in an open atmosphere, we can share the load and deliver. Leadership may also be handed off to someone better suited to a particular task, which provides me with the occasional, and very welcome, break. I think everyone's favourite day of the month is when we all get to sit down and listen to the advances others have made. Not that we don't share regularly on a daily basis,' he qualified, 'and the crystals allow me to connect discussions between disciplines where their respective knowledge might help to solve a problem. I think all of us want to remain students, but some of us take turns being the professors.'

'Don't you get clashes of egos when scientists disagree?' Alex asked.

'Scientists will always disagree. Science is never settled and, I rather hope, never will be. If it were, we'd have nothing more to do! We will generally accept something if it works, but if something better comes along as an explanation, and it gives the right results when honestly applied to previous experiments, we drop the old one and take on the new. Our focus is on understanding, not personal recognition. We all share in successes and, while originally the meetings were split into streams so that scientists could focus on their own area of expertise, over the last millennium or so the disciplines have begun to overlap, so we attend whichever area is of most interest. We've all got the mathematics, and that's the common language within science.'

'Don't you have arts studies?'

'Of course, but you needed us to solve a problem that is entirely science-based. If you want, I could take you to our philosophy department and they could discuss the ethical issues?'

'No!' Alex cried. 'I'm fully apprised of my problem. I don't need them muddying the waters.' Alex was also worried that these clever characters might persuade her to hang around, which wouldn't please the other Eternals or Daniel. Since she couldn't share with the Siphians the true situation – that they were merely part of a program and ceased to exist when they died unless occupied by an Eternal – the results of the philosophical investigations wouldn't and, indeed, couldn't come up with the right answer. And, if she did share that, no doubt the next question would be that, if the Siphians were computer programs, how could she be certain that *she* wasn't a program, which was just silly! Still...

When this is over, we need to come back as one of these guys in the philosophy department,' she told Daniel. *'Imagine what we could learn about the universe!'*

'Might be worth a shot,' he allowed, *'but they're still limited and mortal. As you just said, being immortal gives you a very different perspective on things. Mind you, if any group could have insights, it's these characters.'*

"The program is complete," the still working scientist declared. "Synching our time streams... There. I've sent it to the gate workers."

"How far into the future will this send Alex?" Berik asked.

"Well, she wanted to be certain there was no life left in the universe, so we went to the max – ten to the power of one hundred or ten duotrigintillion years into the future. At that point, even black holes will have broken down. There'll be no energy in the entire universe and zero possibility of life."

'I am so glad I came across you guys,' Alex sighed, the thought of endless universe crossovers to reach that point was becoming overwhelming. Once again it occurred to her that Almega's estimate had been woefully shy of what was needed.

"Back to the gate lab, then," Berik declared. "Thank you for your help." He turned, focused, swiped his hand down and walked through the gap to the gate lab where the scientists were already inputting the program.

'Are you absolutely certain you want to go through with this?' Berik asked. *'You cannot come back. There is no gate at the other side and no power for it even if there were. It's just blackness and silence.'*

'We've been looking at their maths,' Daniel said. *'If anything goes wrong, Almega can produce a gate in the program.'*

'Yeah, but I can't pass through it!' Alex snarled.

'They've got a way to get you through this one, you can use it to come back if necessary.'

'I won't lie,' she told Berik. 'I'm scared out of my mind. The thought of being lost in nothingness for eternity doesn't appeal at all but, in theory, that should allow me to dissipate and return to my proper form.'

'But it might not,' Berik said gently.

'I'll be out of your... ahh, fur. I'm sure Tedrus will be pleased about that. Last thing you need is something like me hanging around.'

'I would get used to it.' Tedrus's voice came through loud and clear and, a few seconds later, the guard walked through the wall. 'You do not have to do this if you don't want to, and I'm certain we could give you an existence full of excitement and interest.'

Alex peered at him through Berik's eyes. 'You've changed your tune!'

'Berik has been keeping me apprised of what's been happening. You have proven yourself trustworthy. You have not violated his trust even though, as you proved to me, you could have done so at any moment. When something as powerful as you decides to conform to restrictions placed on it by lesser beings, does not complain, and is courteous, I believe we have a duty to do the same in return. Besides,' he added, with a self-deprecating shrug. 'It's not like we could have stopped you. I'd rather you stayed because you were accepting of our offer than because we had no choice in the matter.'

'Thank you. This is probably going to sound silly to you, but I feel proud I earned the trust of someone such as yourself.'

'You should,' Berik murmured. 'It's the first time I've seen Tedrus say he trusts anyone, and that includes me!'

'All right. How am I going to pass through the gate?' Alex asked Berik.

'Ahh. A neat little trick of ours. Last used it millennia ago, but it should work.' He pointed.

'You. Are. Kidding me!'

Chapter 8

Alex was still trying to work out what in the universe (never mind on Earth or even this planet, whatever it was called!) the Siphians were doing.

'That's... That's a Siphian! Did someone die?' she asked Berik, mentally pointing at the body that had been brought in on an antigravity platform.

'Not at all,' he assured her. *'We have machines that can replicate anything. We usually only use these ones to create our food – machine parts can contain toxins and are created in a different machine – but they can create whatever we program them to make. In this instance, the body of a Siphian. We did it once before, during the time of Arren and Crique, so we knew it could be done.'*

'Why did they make fake Siphians?!'

'To feed to the invaders and dose the queen with a fertility blocker. It's a rather complicated story. Suffice it to say, this body is unused and being made available to you. It has systems to keep blood flowing so it will not rot, and it will repair itself, just as we do.'

Alex was stunned. *'Why?'* she gasped.

'To give you options. With this body you could stay here, live a full life and interact with your surroundings as one of us. If, at any time, you still wish to leave, you may do so using the body to activate the gate. We can leave the gate here where only that body, with its particular DNA signature, has access, so none of the rest of us are in danger of being hurt by accident. You would be a welcome addition to whatever department you felt drawn to, or you could live outside the labs if you felt it too dangerous to join us. You could learn more about the Vayuk, since the body has the same telepathic capacity as we do, attend talks and lectures, study or do whatever you wish. You would be welcome, whatever you choose.'

If Alex had been standing, she'd have hit the floor, hard! The magnitude of the offer was so beyond generous that she was stunned into silence.

'Whatever you choose, you'll need to use the body, so you might as well climb aboard,' Berik suggested.

She stepped outside him and floated over to the body on the platform, taking in the details. It was a female, although she'd have been equally happy with a male, and its markings were different to those of any Siphian she'd yet seen. The underside of the body was half cream, half brown, with a line between the two. The ears were black but the muzzle and whiskers were brown, as was the back of the body.

"We made it distinct from us because you are distinct," Berik explained. "You deserve something special."

"And it allows them to spot you a mile off," Daniel muttered.

"I honestly don't think that entered their heads," Alex said, almost in tears. "Possibly Tedrus thought that way. For the others, I think this is a genuine effort to make me feel special."

"You *are* special!" Daniel assured her.

That did it. The incredible generosity of the Siphians, Daniel's endorsement of her, being so close to the end after so many adventures one after the other… it was all too much. She burst into tears.

"What did I say wrong?" Daniel asked, utterly bewildered.

"These are happy tears," she managed to gasp. She waved her hand at him, signalling that she should be given a moment to pull herself together. She closed her eyes, took a few deep breaths and straightened. "After everything I've been through, I'm emotionally exhausted if not physically so. Look at what these guys did for me! I'm a stranger, a being more powerful than they could imagine, but they've put their lives on hold to solve my problem and now they're offering me a life to live with them if I want to take it." She looked at the body once more. "And it is so tempting!"

"Alex, you can't!" Daniel cried.

"Look at this! A life with the most advanced species in the universe. Even if I just spent a year here, maybe two, I could still walk through the gate at the end and you and Almega could jump forward in time and pick me up when I leave."

"No! You can't because it's not fair to you or the Siphians."

She jerked her head at him, confused. "What?!"

"Think about it," he said, reasonably. "The longer you stay here, the more you'll want and need to stay here – seeing their triumphs, making friends, perhaps finding someone to spend your life with. The Siphians are an amazing species, and you would never be bored. Even if you did manage it, the Vayuk are here to put things back into perspective. But then you'll remember that everything has to be erased when you leave because they know too much, so then you won't want to leave because that would deprive them of so many good things – yes, there'll be some bad times, but they'll be occasional blips. With this lot, there'll always be more successes. You'll care about them too much to take that away from them. Meanwhile, the other Eternals can't do anything, Fortan is still trapped in his cage – OK, that I don't mind so much, but it isn't actually right – and, in the end, you'll still have to leave, but now you'll be a pariah amongst the Eternals."

Alex slumped and turned to Berik, Tedrus and the others who were patiently waiting for her to animate the body and tell them her decision.

"You're right," she sighed. "I want to stay with them – I want it so much I can taste it – but I can't." She turned back to the body. "I really hope this hopping to the end of the universe works because that body won't survive arrival at the other end. There's no receiving gate to reintegrate the matter. That means that even if Almega can create a gate, I can't pass through it to come back."

"Maybe something will have lasted?" Daniel said.

"End of the universe, remember? Nothing but cold, empty silence. Almega will just have to turn it off and hope I somehow survive the shutdown."

She got inside the body, quickly found everything needed to work it, and made it sit up. Berik nodded and went over to check Alex was all right.

"You seemed to be having some trouble," he observed.

"Not trouble, exactly. Your offer and generosity overwhelmed me, and I really had to think for a bit." She stood up and walked around, leaving the scientists in awe, while Tedrus merely grunted his approval.

"And your decision?" Berik asked.

"I want to stay, really I do. You are such an amazing society and I think I could learn to love it here..."

"But?"

She sighed. "But it's not where I truly belong. I am grateful beyond words for everything you've done, but I must walk through, whatever happens at the other end. You cannot have me living amongst you to the end of your world, making new bodies for me every time I wear one out. It's not fair on either of us. I wouldn't really be much of a contributor in my present state and, in the end, I'd have to watch you all die and I couldn't bear it." She went over to Berik and gave him a hug, which he returned, although he was saddened by her decision. "But I know, beyond a shadow of a doubt, that I and probably my friend will be back. We might be being born even now, and will live our lives as proper Siphians, contributing to your work and living a full life." She turned to Tedrus who folded his arms. She held out a paw and he looked at it for a moment, then accepted her offer and returned the shake. "Thank you for trusting me and for helping me. I will never forget it, and I'm sure I won't be the only one of my species who will visit."

The other scientists queued up and she laughingly gave each of them a hug or shook their paws. Marique and the glasses crew also arrived to say goodbye, as well as Sajen and the other temporal mechanics. At last, she was standing in front of the gate. With a final look at the Siphians and a wave, she walked through.

***

It was dark. It was darker than she imagined possible. The bottom of a mine shaft at night would have been bright in comparison. As an Eternal, she could pick up the sounds of the universe – the deafening roar of stars, the communication signals that flowed from inhabited planets to roll through space, the bursts from pulsars, and the terrifying crunching and screaming of planets as black holes sucked in entire galaxies. She could also see the tiniest photon as it flew from point to point. Now, there was nothing. She could stretch her senses to the farthest distances and there was no light, no sound, no life.

It was terrifying.

'Please let this work!' she mentally begged. *'Omskep, c'mon now. Recognise that I don't belong and pull me out of here!'*

Nothing.

Time dragged. She held position so that once Almega homed in on her, there'd be no problems, yet still she remained. There wasn't even any sign of Daniel, and she began to fear she had gone so far that no one could find her. The internal pressure built. With her eyes closed or open, it made no difference. No stars, no light of any kind, no other living thing and what non-living things still remained were dust, at best, and mostly just particles, torn apart deep in the hearts of all-consuming black holes, and even *their* insatiable appetites had been quenched and silenced.

She was nearing the point of screaming into the silence when she felt a tug. She clamped down on the cry and focused. The tug was tentative at first, as if someone was nervously checking to see if she was safe to be near. It grew stronger and then, suddenly, she was pulled out.

She shot up on the couch and heard Almega's voice.

"It's all right. You're back and you're safe. Just give it a moment."

She lay back, breathing deeply. "That was truly the most frightening thing I've ever experienced," she said at last, opening her eyes. Daniel was sitting on the other side of her and, she now realised, holding her hand.

"Sorry it took us a bit. There's a lot of empty space to scan and we had to nudge Omskep to look around for you. As soon as it found you, we came back here so you'd have friendly faces when you woke up."

"I need a long talk with Omskep!" Alex fumed. "Leaving me stuck in there when it *knew* what I was and where I belonged. Dealing with those Parchti monsters and the holographic humans and the cannibals...!"

"But the dragons and the Siphians were fun, right?" Daniel smiled, squeezing her hand.

"That's a point! Hadn't you better...?"

"Just going to do it now. I was merely waiting to make sure that you were all right," Almega assured her. "Now I know that's the case, I'll reset the universe containing the Siphians. They'll never know you were ever there, because, so far as they'll be concerned, you weren't."

"And everything will be available to us?"

"Within the limitations I already outlined, yes. And please don't ask me why, as I have no idea." He vanished.

Alex sat up on the couch and swung her legs over to rest them on the floor.

"You're sure you're all right?" Daniel asked, solicitously.

"I'll be fine." She paused and reconsidered. "Well, I'll be fine eventually." She turned to him and pressed her forehead to his, sighing at the contact. "Thank you for being there for me. Without you, I can't imagine what would have happened."

"We'd have found a way," he assured her, pulling back but squeezing her hand and holding it. "Plus, I got to experience those trips too. Rather a lot in one hit, though. I could use a break."

"Me too! I could also use some tea and cake. I know I don't have a stomach or a need for it, but after all this time I've certainly got a craving!"

She rose from the couch and together they went to the living room, Daniel calmly summoning mugs of tea and a selection of Alex's favourites which she seized upon with delight.

"Mmmm. That tastes so good!" she got out through a mouthful, cupping her hand beneath her chin to catch any crumbs.

Daniel sat back with his own mug of tea, watching her until she'd satisfied her craving and settled into the couch with her own mug, a musical sigh of satisfaction escaping her lips.

"Thank you," she smiled. "I'm starting to feel like an Eternal again." He cocked his head at her. Only an Eternal could have done what she'd been doing. Indeed, that she had done it at all was the ultimate proof of her Eternal nature. "Oh, you know what I mean."

"You feel civilised again?" he suggested.

"Yes! That bit at the end..." She shook her head. "That was the scariest of them all. I never realised silence could be deafening and blackness blinding. There was too much of it."

"I'm truly sorry I couldn't be there with you. Almega was bending over backwards to track you down and the process was using everything he had because space was stretched out so far. You'd think tracking the one living point of energy would be simple, but in so vast an oasis of emptiness it's surprisingly easy to miss. Like trying to find a single cell in the Sahara. Then, once he'd found you and locked on, we both came back here to welcome you home."

"It probably felt longer than it was," she nodded, sipping her tea. "There's nothing to give you a sense of time and I was starting to panic, which makes it seem even longer. I'm just glad to be back."

"I'm sure the others will feel the same — not least because, once Almega's reset everything, they can go back to training — now with more options."

"As if we didn't already have plenty!" she laughed. "Galaxy after galaxy and every one of them with some weird and wonderful life form. Still, it's always nice to have even more. I guess we're greedy."

"I am looking forward to revisiting the Siphians," he agreed. He took in Alex's expression. "And the dragons, too," he conceded.

"Odd about those restrictions."

"Probably due to the way Fortan switched them on. Trust that oaf to mess it up."

"And what will happen to him, now?" she asked.

"I think that will depend on if he ever admits he was in the wrong. You may be pleased to hear that even Hentric and Gracti are angry with him. Hentric laid into him after your run in with the Parchti and their slave labour; Gracti after the cannibals."

"I'm surprised they cared that much." She buried her nose in her mug.

"It was the thought that it could have been them going through it," he admitted.

"That makes more sense!" She put her mug down and, with a wave of her hand, it vanished. "Once you've finished, I'd like to take a stroll to see how Almega's doing with Omskep."

"And give Omskep a talking to?" he said, downing the last of his drink. He tossed it over his shoulder and the mug vanished in mid-air.

"Show off! And yes. That machine and I need words!"

"You know what Omskep's like. If it's not in the mood, it won't explain itself."

"Hmm."

Daniel got the impression that if there was a way to torture a computer, Alex had every intention of doing so until Omskep spilled its guts.

"The others will be keen to get back in. If you delay them because you've damaged Omskep, this time you won't be able to blame Fortan."

"I won't damage it – that would hurt us as much as anyone else – but I want to make it clear that if it *ever* treats any Eternal like that again, there'll be trouble!"

"I'm sure that, even as we speak, Almega is programming something into it that can be used as a life-raft should anything like this ever happen again. In addition, if I know Almega, he's installing security so that, when he's out with an Eternal, neither Fortan nor anyone else he doesn't trust implicitly will be allowed inside the building."

"Shall we go and see?"

With a grunt, Daniel rose and the two of them headed to the Omskep building.

***

They walked rather than simply relocating, giving Alex the chance to savour the countryside that Daniel had created around his cottage. Trees, flowers, butterflies and insects, birds (she could even hear a woodpecker) and animals were everywhere, and Alex revelled in it. Her time in nothingness had been brief, but more than enough to make her delight in so much life.

"It's no more real than the house," Daniel reminded her gently.

"Yes, but at the end I couldn't even do this. If I could have, it wouldn't have been so bad. Combine nothing with no power, and this is a paradise by comparison. It may be fake," and she summoned a couple of dogs that Daniel recognised as two she'd owned centuries ago, "but it's full of energy, and energy means life. Different forms of energy that we can manipulate into whatever we want, yes, but when you get right down to it, energy is the key. Without energy there's nothing, and nothing is possible. I never, *ever* want to feel that helpless again!"

He wrapped an arm around her, hugging her to his side to reassure her that he would do everything in his power to ensure it never happened again. She returned the hug. "I know. There's nothing you or anyone could have done about it, except Fortan, of course."

"Oh, I don't know," he grinned as they exited the forest and walked towards the location of the Omskep building. "Looks to me as if Almega's found a way."

Dozens of Eternals were milling around what was now an empty space. Amongst them, Alex and Daniel spotted Paxto, Bregar, Zorpan, Accron, Fortan, Gracti and Hentric all arguing with each other, while Fortan was being shouted at from all sides.

The two Eternals looked at each other, nodded, and shifted their sight, scanning up and down the electromagnetic spectrum until they found the gate.

"I take it Almega's not told them about the Siphians?" Alex smiled.

"I'd say not. One way of keeping the likes of Fortan away from Omskep."

"Well, it's not like we actually have to go into the building to do our trainings. All we have to do is alert Almega that we're interested in doing one, and he comes to us."

They were at the edge of the trees and hadn't been spotted by the other Eternals, who were walking around the space that used to contain the Omskep building. Alex backed up and Daniel, realising her intent, joined her.

"Think we should ask, first?" he wondered.

"I think that would be polite, don't you?" She hugged, stroked and then quietly dismissed the dogs since they would be a nuisance inside Omskep, while Daniel contacted Almega and checked whether they were welcome to visit. With certain caveats, which concerned keeping their presence and method of entry secret from the other Eternals, Almega told them that they were very welcome and yes, if they were in the correct energy form, they would be able to use the gate. With that in mind, the two Eternals shifted their energy to the wavelength Almega specified, which had the benefit of making them invisible and intangible to their fellows. They then walked down into the melee. Fortan was trying to hold his place, claiming that this was Alex, Daniel, and Almega's fault, but the Eternals shouted him down.

"*You* were the idiot who messed with Omskep, not them!" Zorpan yelled. "They were doing what we all do, but you had to screw it up. Now, thanks to you, none of us can get in, and Alex is still lost!"

They don't know I'm back,' Alex observed.

'I imagine Almega is picking his moment to reveal that. C'mon, let's get inside and see what's going on.'

They passed through the angry mob to the gate and, after a brief pause to admire its elegant simplicity, walked through. On the other side, they shifted back to their normal energy range.

Here was the building and Omskep in its usual position, Almega standing nearby and watching the fraying tempers outside on a monitor.

"Will this be permanent or temporary?" Alex asked with a smile, advancing to give Almega a grateful hug.

"You already thanked me," Almega said as they pulled apart. "What was that for?"

"You left before I had the chance. So?" She waved her hand to indicate the present situation.

"As long as Fortan continues to play the fool, permanent," Almega replied with a growl. "I'm only sorry it was required in the first place. It's good to see you both in here and back as you should be once more."

Daniel jerked his head over his shoulder. "It's getting ugly out there."

"I know," Almega sighed. "I released Fortan the moment I knew you were safe and on your way out, although he didn't know that. When I came back here, the damned fool was inside Omskep, trying to take a look at the new programs. I threw him out and took a leaf out of the Siphian's book, moving the building and Omskep itself slightly out of temporal synch with the rest of Oestragar."

Daniel frowned. "I thought there was no time in Oestragar?"

"I feel like we've had this conversation," Almega replied frowning. He shook off the feeling and continued. "There is no entropy, which is the usual measurement of the so-called arrow of time. However, in order for us to have this conversation, and to maintain the illusion of past, present and future, there is something akin to time. If there weren't, what happens in the next aeons and everything that has ever happened would all coexist in this present moment... which I think I would find rather confusing."

"You and me both!" Alex laughed.

"Anyway, we're out of synch and, consequently, invisible. Knowing you would want to visit and happy to receive you, I placed the gate. That, as you discovered, is merely in a different part of the electromagnetic spectrum. Had you not asked permission, however, you would have found it the same as those on the Siphian home world when you first attempted to use them."

"In other words, even if the Eternals out there figure it out and see the gate, they still won't be able to get inside the building without your express permission?" Daniel clarified.

"Exactly."

Daniel hummed his approval. With Fortan's truculence proving intransigent, it seemed the only solution.

"You know they'll say that you're taking privileges to which you're not entitled?" Alex said gently.

"I know! It's why I haven't gone out there, but I can't risk Fortan messing it up again. Next time, we might not be able to get a trapped Eternal out of there, and then he'll be responsible for murder!" He shook his head. "I shouldn't have lost my temper with him and locked him up in the energy ball, but he was putting others at risk, and I needed to concentrate if I was to get you out again."

"Then that's what you have to tell them," Daniel said. "We'll go out with you. We can show them Alex is all right but make it clear it was a close-run thing."

"It was?!" she said, turning to stare at the other two. Daniel rubbed the back of his neck, embarrassed by his slip, while Almega was focused on his control board. "How close, exactly?" she asked carefully.

"Ahh, Almega had to poke Omskep several times and finally effectively threaten it until it finally agreed to look for you. That was why you were stuck there for a while. It seemed interested to see how you would cope with nothingness."

"Badly!" she snarled, turning to the computer. "Very, *very* badly! It was terrifying on a level I don't think I'll ever forget. This is probably the only time in my life where the notion of erasure sounds like a very good idea!"

Daniel and Almega both looked surprised. While other Eternals routinely took erasure to wipe out negative experiences from their training sessions, Alex and Daniel were unique in that they had consistently refused the offer, despite their avatars living through (and sometimes not living through, which was part of the problem) some truly horrible events. That Alex was seriously considering it spoke volumes as to how unpleasant and psychologically damaging the experience had been.

Daniel realised Alex was close to tears and quickly hurried to support her. "Hey, hey!" he said soothingly. "You're back and you're safe."

"You can't imagine how bad it was," she blurted out through choked sobs. "It didn't matter what I did, there

314

was literally nothing – not even you! The longer it lasted, the more I thought I'd been lost, and I'd never escape. I couldn't die and I couldn't do anything. No power or agency of any kind and facing eternity like that."

"If it had gone on any longer, I promise I would have been there, but Almega was too busy trying to get you out to take the time to put me in."

"I sincerely apologise, Alex. I truly did not appreciate how traumatising it would be for you," Almega said, looking suitably contrite.

She sniffed loudly and pulled back from Daniel, composing herself. Being an Eternal, it was easy to clean everything up without even the aid of a handkerchief.

"Sorry," she said, shaking her head. "That was stupid of me. I knew where I was going but I didn't realise just how bad it would be. I guess I should have thought a bit more or got the Siphians to prepare me properly before I stepped through, but I wanted to get home and I was afraid that, if I stayed a minute longer with them, I'd never want to leave."

"Being told about it, even shown it, and living it are two very different things," Daniel said, giving her another warm hug. "I don't think any amount of information could prepare you for that reality."

"The biggest problem was that I don't know how long I was in there. It felt like hours!"

"Less than twenty minutes, in human terms," Almega told her.

"He really was working feverishly to get you out of there," Daniel agreed. "I've never seen Almega work so fast."

"I only wish Omskep hadn't been so stubborn," Almega said. "If it hadn't been so curious, I could have got you out in half the time."

"Why did Omskep want to know how I felt about it? I don't understand. It's a computer!"

"But a very intelligent one," Almega replied. "No Eternal has suffered this before, and that would make the experience worthy of study." Alex looked sharply at him. "But not for too long. I managed to persuade it, that's the main thing."

She straightened, took a deep breath and nodded. She turned to the computer. "Don't you EVER do that to me or anyone else again! If you do, I swear I will find a way to destroy you!"

"Alex…" Almega began.

"No! Mortal beings have a get out clause. They can simply die. We can't. That's torture and if Omskep thinks that torture is acceptable, it can't be trusted with any of us. Better to shut the door and abandon it."

"It won't do it again," Almega assured her. "I'll make certain of that."

After giving Omskep a long glare, Alex turned her back on the computer. "With that settled, now we have to persuade that crowd out there that denying access to Omskep is safer for all of them, thanks to Fortan."

"That, or Fortan has to be permanently restricted," Daniel said.

"Obviously, he won't agree to that," Alex snorted. "A few Eternals might even back him on the grounds that, in time, any of them could be similarly controlled. You know how adamant they are that they must be free to do whatever they want."

"Which I wholeheartedly agree with," Almega nodded, "but I cannot risk anyone else being trapped because one of our number refuses to play by the rules. We must remove the access, or we must remove the troublemaker."

"We can't be killed," Daniel pointed out.

"No, but as I've already proved, I can contain him."

"For the rest of time?" Alex asked. "Won't that be a strain on your energy?"

"I've plenty and yes, I could do it. This," and here he gestured to the present state of the building, "is a lot easier, though, and will stop any others who even think of following his example."

"Even so, they won't like it," Daniel said, shaking his head.

"But it's only the equivalent of a locked door," Alex said. "All Almega is asking is that they knock before wandering in. Considering how easily a bad actor could hurt us inside a training, it's a miracle we've never needed it before."

Almega nodded. "It's a good argument. It's to protect them all and, while they might complain they'd never do such a thing, if they've no intention of doing anything in here, why would they need access in the first place?"

"On principle," Daniel replied. "That will be the sticking point. On principle our homes, our minds and this building should be available, it's just that most of us respect other spaces. Fortan has no respect for anyone or anything."

"Which makes him a very bad Eternal!" Alex cried. "Don't you see? That's our argument! The one thing Fortan is always claiming is that he's better than any of us. He's just proved beyond doubt that he's absolutely the worst. If he can mess around with Omskep and put our existence at risk, why not violate our minds and our private spaces?"

Daniel nodded, a grim smile growing on his face. "We get to lock him out of here and shame him in ways he can't deny. I can hear him now: 'I'd never do that!' 'But you did, and this is the consequence. You can't be trusted because you don't follow the rules of etiquette practised for millennia by all Eternals. You're a terrible excuse for an Eternal, and now we all have to pay for your disgrace!' It's perfect!"

"I probably won't put it quite like that," Almega chuckled, although he couldn't help but agree with Daniel's assessment, "but the principle is sound."

"We'd better get back to the forest and come in from there," Alex said. "They know that I was trapped inside and, if I've only just been released, I wouldn't be here, I'd be back at the house."

"I'll wait for you to return, then see if I can calm that lot down," Almega nodded.

"They're also going to want to know how come you have the ability to trap others," Daniel said.

"I know. All I can offer by way of explanation is that I've always had the ability – which they won't like at all – I simply never needed it until now. If Fortan hadn't broken the rules, they would never have known about it."

"Better idea?" Alex offered.

"Hmm?"

"Tell them that Omskep gave you the talent once it realised Fortan had lost me in the program, and now the talent has been removed."

"But that's not true!" Almega protested.

"No, but it'll be easier for them to take than the idea that there's an Eternal with more power than any of them."

"It's not that you have it," Daniel added, "it's that before this happened, they didn't *know* that you had it. This way, if Fortan or any of the others tries something like this again, they know that Omskep will do whatever it needs to in order to protect itself, including giving power to an Eternal."

Almega thought about it, then shook his head. "No. That will make them scared of Omskep. We can't have that. It's their one escape and, without that, we'll have trouble breaking out all over the place. The job I've been doing since the beginning grants me certain privileges, amongst them is the ability to protect the thing we all depend on. That is why I have the job. If Fortan had not broken the rules, I would still have had the power and no one, not even you, would have known. Omskep must be protected."

"You're claiming it can't protect itself?" Daniel said, raising an eyebrow.

"Oh, it can," Almega assured him. "I've been checking through the record of his botched job. If Omskep wasn't capable of adjusting Fortan's idea of programming, it would have been wrecked. While it didn't – or couldn't – stop him, it made the result better for all of us and safer for you," and here he turned to Alex. "If it hadn't, you would never have escaped."

She looked at Omskep. "Thank you for that," she said. "Next time, though, please lock him out completely!"

She could almost feel Omskep's reassurance that this would never happen again.

"All right, back to the forest. We're in your corner, Almega. If you need any help, you don't even have to ask. You know we'll be there," Daniel said as he and Alex shifted their spectrum, checked all was clear (they could see out if not in) and exited the building. Once outside, they quickly relocated to the treeline, keen to get away from the increasingly angry and frightened crowd.

"It's getting a bit ugly," Alex commented, shifting herself back into the visible spectrum.

Daniel quickly followed. "Yeah. I think we'd better get down there before it gets completely out of hand."

"Why?" she asked, sitting down on a tree stump. The energy sparking in the crowd was extremely unpleasant, and she was in no hurry to feel it again. Privately, she contacted Almega and asked him to hold fire until she recovered herself, explaining her reasons. He agreed. "It's not like they can hurt each other. This has been brewing ever since Fortan made his mistake and everyone was banned from trainings until you and Almega got me out. It might be good for them to let off some steam."

They watched, noticing how Fortan was somehow managing to persuade the other Eternals that this wasn't his fault, leaving them confused and increasingly worried. If this wasn't a direct result of his interference, did that mean something else had happened and now they'd lost Omskep and Almega forever? Had Omskep developed a fault?

Still, they watched.

"It's silly if you think about it," Daniel observed. "Here in Oestragar we can be whatever we want to be, do whatever we want to do, and we cannot be sick or injured. We could experience every possible life we wanted without Omskep, and be the hero in all of them."

"True," she replied, "but it's boring, isn't it? We know we're never in any danger and there are no surprises. We can create whole worlds, but *we* created them. That means we know their limitations and plots. We could give the characters within those worlds freedom, but we'd still be god, never in any real danger, never having to struggle or do anything that makes life worth living."

"We're never in any danger in a training, either. Our avatars, yes, but us? We'll always be fine."

"I suppose they're like fairground rides," Alex returned thoughtfully. "You can get aboard and be scared in a safe way. I think it's the thought that it's *not* safe and that we *can* be hurt or trapped forever that's got them scared."

"And the thought that, without the option of trainings, existence is quickly going to become extremely tedious," he agreed. "Especially for those who always took the easy option and don't have a wealth of stories to build from."

"Like Gracti! Plus, there's something to be said for delayed gratification," she mused, leaning back on her hands to gaze up at the faux, perfect (it was always perfect) sky of Oestragar. "If life's too easy, it's boring. I mean, yes, for some of our avatars they could use it being more boring. Some of them seem to spend their entire lives fighting just to keep their head above water."

"Or below it, if they're aquatic!" Daniel grinned.

She adjusted her position to playfully swat him before resuming her relaxed pose. "Yes, but there's a balance to be struck. If life is nothing but ease or nothing but struggle, no one wants to be a part of it. For avatars, it's usually a struggle. For us, it's too much ease. So much so that we're becoming risk averse. Now they're torn between being scared they'll have no temporary thrills inside the trainings, and scared the training is genuinely dangerous since I have, they think, been lost."

"And I'll lay odds Fortan is arguing that since he's revealed this 'flaw' in the system, he should be rewarded rather than castigated," Daniel grumbled.

"Can't have that," Alex said, getting to her feet. "Let's get down there and point out that the only problem is Fortan himself."

"With pleasure!"

They walked down to the crowd of arguing Eternals. Fortan was looking rather pleased with himself, nodding to one Eternal before turning and seeing Daniel and, to his shock, Alex. His smile fell.

"YOU are a despicable excuse for an Eternal!" Alex shouted, bearing down on him.

"You're home and safe!" Fortan cried, aware the crowd had silenced and was watching. "I'm so glad to see you back."

"No thanks to you! If you hadn't gone in there and messed around when Almega wasn't there, I wouldn't have been forced to go through all that!"

"Yes, but clearly there's a problem with the system," he wheedled, pointing to the empty space.

"Almega put it out of your reach because, when he came to welcome me back and make sure I was all right, you snuck in AGAIN and threatened the trainings of everyone here!"

Now the crowd turned on Fortan.

"You did *what*?!" cried Paxto.

"I thought, maybe, I could help get Alex out," Fortan argued.

"Bull! You went in to check out the new worlds and see if you could get in on your own. Almega has recordings because, inside the Omskep building, everything is recorded."

"It is?"

"Yes, you idiot! Don't you ever listen to Almega?"

Paxto turned to Alex. "Almega and Omskep are all right, then?"

"Of course!" Daniel replied. "But if they were to stay all right, Almega had no choice but to move Omskep so that only those who asked and were granted permission could access it. If he left it here, we all know Fortan would find a way in when Almega wasn't there so that he could play around and wreck it for all of us."

The crowd's humour was now mixed. Relief that their fears regarding Omskep and Almega were unfounded, fury with Fortan for putting them all at risk a second time. Almega chose that moment to appear. He put a good distance between himself and the location of the Omskep building before speaking.

"Daniel is correct," he said, loud enough to silence the crowd's angry murmurs. They hurried to him to hear what he had to say, surrounding him in a tight circle. "I have moved Omskep to keep it safe for all of us because one Eternal couldn't stop interfering in something he doesn't understand." He glared at Fortan.

"You!" Fortan cried, scrabbling for purchase. "You have more power than any of us! You kept me trapped for days in an energy bubble!"

Now the crowd turned to Almega, looking for an explanation.

"It comes as a surprise to you that, after aeons working with Omskep, I figured out how to protect it? That the one of us who ended up with that job, for whatever reason, was the one who had the ability to learn those skills and do so in such a way that they protect Omskep and the rest of us? That is, until you managed to go barging in and make a mess of it. We nearly lost Alex thanks to you." He turned to the other Eternals. "There is no reason for any

322

Eternal to be inside the Omskep building when I am not there. Had Fortan not violated my trust a second time, the Omskep building would still be here. Unfortunately, he's proved there is such a thing as a completely untrustworthy Eternal. I can keep him locked up for the rest of time, or I can keep Omskep safely out of his reach. I'm happy to do either. If someone wishes to come in, they're more than welcome provided that they ask first. It's the same rule we have for our homes. You invite me to your homes to start you on a training and you expect me to be there when you return. In between, no one goes anywhere near your private spaces. Omskep has its own building as its private space but, since it's an intelligent computer, it doesn't have the ability to post guards and, like it or not, it is vulnerable. Fortan just proved that. That's what I'm for. Omskep is our servant, delivering the lives we want to live, and I'm Omskep's servant. Far from being the most powerful, I'm the least powerful, only allowed to use my strength when others – any of you or Omskep," he added, pointing first to the Eternals and then the empty space that was the proper location of the building, "are in danger. Now, if you all want me to step down, I'm happy to do that. If there's someone else that you would trust to put you into trainings and fix any problems when they arise – as they did with Alex thanks to Fortan – then, please." He bowed and the Omskep building shimmered back into place. There was a collective gasp from the Eternals while Daniel and Alex smothered their grins at Almega's spectacular party-trick. Materialising ordinary things was a matter of course for the Eternals, but Omskep was different. Omskep was the one solid thing in the whole of Oestragar. "You may go inside and see for yourself that not only is Omskep fixed and ready to run trainings again, but we now have some more options that weren't there before. For that, Fortan can take the credit." Fortan preened. "However, had he waited for me to figure out how to do it, we wouldn't have ended up with an Eternal lost in the empty blackness at the end of the program. No sound, no light, no energy, nothing!"

The others looked worryingly at Alex who gave a half smile. "I'm home. That's what matters."

With Almega's encouragement, the Eternals went inside and satisfied themselves that Omskep was in perfect working order. Almega had also added information on the new universes now available, and their limitations.

"Why are there any limitations?" Fortan cried. "Did you not do your job properly?!"

"I suspect the problem is a result of the very messy and amateur way that they were imported. Had it been done properly, we might have had access to it all. As it is, we're limited."

Several of the Eternals gave Fortan filthy looks, but the new universes did open up a wealth of new possibilities and they eagerly pored over their options.

"The data has been sent to your in-home systems, allowing you to look through the options at your leisure. These are sub-routines and not the main program, however."

"What does that mean?" Hentric asked.

"It means I can only run one at a time alongside the main program and no," he said, forestalling Fortan's next query, "I cannot disable the main program. For one thing, it still has billions upon billions of planets and lifeforms unexplored, so that would be a waste. For another, while every check I've done and Alex's experiences within them prove that they are safe and fully actualised, I don't want to remove a program that we know works to replace it with one that might prove to have a problem only revealed by use. If we do that, we might not be able to reinstall the original program."

The mumblings of the Eternals indicated that they were equally uncomfortable with the idea. Several were wary of checking out the new options at all and went to Alex to talk about her experiences. She explained that both she and Daniel wanted to fix three of the histories – the horror being meted out on the Djaroubi, figure out what was happening with the holographic humans and make that world liveable again, and help the Vynar deal with their oversized carnivorous plants. Since the Eternals had been kept abreast of Alex's experiences, and knew the problems those trips entailed, all were happy to leave the corrections to Daniel and Alex, promising to steer well clear of those particular species until they had been made rather more welcoming.

"I have already put blocks on those particular training sessions," Almega informed them. "No one, not even Fortan, will be allowed anywhere near them until the problems are resolved."

He ushered the Eternals out of the Omskep building and, once all were beyond the door, the building vanished.

"How are you doing that?" Bregar, an Eternal who had remained quiet until now, asked. He walked over to where the wall had been and reached out, but there was nothing there. He advanced, slowly at first, then with increasing confidence. "I can't even feel a hint of energy, yet I know it's here. How?"

"Another trick of Omskep's. Anyone who wants my job will, of course, be taught it all. Might take a few millennia, but you'll get there in the end."

Many of the Eternals shook their heads. They knew the job was necessary, but not being Almega meant that they were not at the beck and call of everyone else. Being by nature free spirits, that counted for a lot. Fortan, of course, stepped forward, but was dragged back by several.

"You've done enough damage," Zorpan told him sternly. "If you hadn't made a complete mess of things, we might have the entirety of those other universes, but no, you had to rush in instead of waiting!"

Alex noticed a slight tic from Almega at that comment. Apparently, while Fortan was the ostensive reason being paraded for the truncated universes, Almega knew he wasn't the real cause. Alex cocked her head at Almega who pretended not to see her. He knew that she wouldn't say anything that might give the game away.

When no one else stepped forward, Almega gave an exaggerated sigh. "I take it that this means all of you, with the obvious exclusion of Fortan, are happy with the new arrangement?"

"The building will be here if you are?" Bregar clarified.

"Yes. If I'm inside, the building will be present."

"Heck of a closed sign!" Hentric grinned.

Alex shook her head. Trust the resident joker to make fun of a security necessity.

"And we'll still be able to call on you to start trainings?" Gracti asked.

"Of course. That's what I'm here for."

"In other words, the only thing that's changed is that, from now on, neither Fortan nor anyone else can get into the building when you're not there," Paxto summarised.

"In sum," Almega agreed.

"I don't have a problem with that," Paxto declared. "If the only way to stop idiots from trying to trap us in purgatory is to effectively lock the door, I think that's a good idea."

"Hang on!" Fortan cried. "You're happy that there is an Eternal who can lock you out of a building to which we're all supposed to have access? An Eternal who has powers none of us possess?"

"If it means we're protected from being put through what Oslac... sorry, Alex went through? You bet I'm happy about it. I only wish Almega hadn't been so tolerant as to allow you that access in the first place. And, by the way, consider yourself banned from my place, too!"

"And mine!" Zorpan added.

Several others added their voices until Fortan had been banned from every other building in Oestragar.

"You can't do that!" Fortan exploded. "I'm an Eternal, with the same rights as everyone else."

326

"No," Bregar snarled. "You're an Eternal, yes, but you lost your rights the instant you thought the rules of civilised behaviour didn't apply to you. You're not better than us, and none of us have the right to violate anyone else's space. You violated Almega's space and, worse, you damaged the one thing we all rely on. That puts you beneath contempt!" When Fortan again tried to argue, Bregar bore down on him, the energy sparking around his form. "I don't have Almega's power, and you'd better be grateful for that! If I had, I'd tear you into atoms!"

"How dare you speak to me like that?!" Fortan snarled, his own energy sparking to match Bregar's. Several other Eternals were also showing the signs of heightened emotions.

"We can keep this up indefinitely and you know it," Bregar roared, now furious. "You've had a lucky escape this time. You've managed to upset everyone and unite us against you. That's quite an achievement. Are you sure you want to continue? I'm game if you are."

The others added their own menacing affirmations.

"Fortan," Almega said, projecting his voice over the crowd. "I'd quit while I'm ahead if I were you. If you behave yourself, there may come a time when I'll be able to release the lock. Until then, for the sake of everyone, Omskep is off limits to you. I will still come to your place and put you into trainings as you request, but that's it. You can come home on your own."

Fortan started at Almega. "What?! But what if something goes wrong?"

"Until you interfered, nothing ever did, and Omskep will alert me if there's any risk of a problem. When I do turn up, all you do is berate me for some thing or other that wasn't perfect, and then tell me how to fix it, even though Omskep's main program cannot be changed by me, you or anyone."

"Oslac and Eridar are changing the worlds they've been visiting!"

"Alex and Daniel," Almega said sternly, using their preferred names, "are in the secondary universes. We have more control over those. Even so, once these examples of supreme unpleasantness have been resolved, I suspect we will be leaving the rest and, after that, the worlds will be *properly*," and he emphasized the word, lowering his brows at Fortan, "installed so that everyone can *safely* interact with them. If you want a perfect version of whatever training you have experienced, there's nothing stopping you from recreating it here in Oestragar. Just put yourself far enough away from everyone else that you don't bother them." When Fortan continue to stare at him, Almega sighed. "Oestragar is infinite, as you well know, and you have the power to create whatever you want in it. However, if you intend to recreate a nuclear war with you as the victor, I'm sure the rest of us would be happier if your missiles didn't drop through our roofs. Not that they would hurt us, but clearing up afterwards is a pain. Create the world far enough away that neither the noise nor misdirected weapons bother anyone, and there won't be a problem."

With a huff, Fortan turned on his heel and marched off, the crowd of Eternals parting to give him clear passage. Once he'd passed the last Eternal, he turned.

"You'll regret this, all of you!"

Almega had been about to invite Alex and Daniel into the Omskep building to discuss what he'd discovered. Now, he sighed.

"All right, that's enough," he muttered. Instantly, Fortan was wrapped in energy and whisked away before the astonished Eternals who had, of course, heard of his earlier incarceration – Fortan wouldn't stop going on about the injustice of it – but had not seen it being employed. They turned to Almega. "I'm sorry, but I cannot run the risk that he'll deliberately target Omskep. It's the one thing in Oestragar we cannot replace."

"And he's got a mean streak that would allow him to do it," Daniel agreed.

"He does seem to have a scorched Earth mindset," Alex murmured.

The crowd nodded but a number of them looked at Almega in a mixture of awe and discomfort.

***

On the next plane up, in Anqueria, Fortan looked at the other Eternals.

"I'm truly sorry, but you know what he's like in there. There's nothing I can do about it!"

"He's out of control, Fortan," Zorpan gently pointed out. "You've got to get inside him and straighten him out before he wrecks that Oestragar completely."

"How?" Fortan asked, as appalled by the avatar's behaviour as everyone else.

"He's empty, which means you can spend some time inside him without any problems."

"Yes, but the moment I leave, he'll go back to his usual, unpleasant self!"

Anqueria's Almega, who had drawn their attention to the problem, stepped up.

"Oslac and Eridar or, as they prefer, Alex and Daniel are down there, and we can't risk them being hurt. I suggest we take a leaf out of their book and do a little reprogramming."

"Can we do that?" Fortan wondered.

"Oh, yes," Almega nodded. "Being here in Anqueria, we have a little more control than our avatars in Oestragar, provided it's done in such a way that neither Alex nor Daniel are aware of it. However," and he turned to Fortan, "I do need your permission."

"Please! By all means! That avatar is a menace and an embarrassment!"

"Very well. We can't make him too pleasant as he's the grit that keeps making the pearls within that world, but now he's threatening the oyster..." He turned to interface with Omskep.

"If you stretched that metaphor any further, I swear we'd hear it snap!" Bregar muttered. The others, except Fortan, grinned. Fortan, however, was very worried. While he wasn't inside the Fortan avatar in Oestragar, it was part of his character that had formed that creature and he was mortified to discover that he had so much capacity for petulance.

"Don't worry about it," Gracti assured him, wrapping a long, tentacle-like arm around him. Her last training had been as something in the family of Octopoda, and she was still enjoying the advantages of multiple, prehensile appendages. "We all have something negative within ourselves. Look at my idiot avatar down there. She's a total air head and certainly not something I would invite over to dinner!"

"I wouldn't mind if he was just stupid, but he's mean and stupid! I swear, that's not me!"

"It's you without the other things that make you such a stalwart member of Anqueria," Hentric said. "Don't worry. None of us come out too well in that Oestragar. Look at mine! A practical joker who doesn't care who he upsets!"

"Everyone except Alex and Daniel," Zorpan sighed.

"Yes, but the two we know from here are inside those avatars. What they'd be like without those controlling factors we've no idea," Paxto reminded him.

"Fair point."

"All right," Almega said, turning to the group. "I've put him to sleep for the time being so that he can't cause any more trouble. I'll re-write that avatar's program a bit. A little less arrogance, petulance and spite, and a little more humility and responsibility. Not too much or everyone will know something's wrong, but my avatar will hold him in the energy field for a while, giving an excuse for why he's finally apologising."

"Thank you!" Fortan nodded eagerly.

"It'll be all right," Gracti assured him as the Eternals left Almega to perform his magic. "And we don't blame you for your avatar."

"Absolutely not," Hentric agreed, and the others quickly added their endorsement.

A short while later, Almega informed them that he'd fixed Fortan's avatar. Watching events within that Oestragar they saw that, upon release, the avatar went to Almega and grumpily apologised. Finally, Anqueria's Fortan started to feel the tension leave him.

"Is he going to behave himself now?" he asked Almega.

"He's always going to be a bit of a stubborn idiot," Almega informed him. "However, he has a little more sense of guilt and responsibility towards others. He was remarkably lacking in those qualities. I'll keep an eye on him, but I don't think he'll ever go so far again."

Fortan breathed a sigh of relief. "Thank you!"

***

"I'm amazed Fortan finally came to his senses!" Daniel told Alex in Oestragar. They'd stayed home because Alex was still understandably wary of going into another training, especially while Fortan was a threat.

"I'm still not convinced," Alex replied, nursing her mug of tea. "Knowing him, it's just another ploy to put us off our guard so that he can strike while we're in the trainings."

"I don't think so. I spoke to Almega. Fortan actually allowed him to check his thoughts to prove he was genuine. There was no subterfuge. He's genuinely sorry."

Alex paused in her drinking. "Seriously? Fortan allowed that?!"

"So long trapped in another of Almega's energy nets seems to have finally woken him up. Endless visits by other Eternals making it clear to him that he would only be accepted back into the group if he stopped being a threat to everyone might also have helped."

"Peer pressure can be a potent force," she nodded, burying herself once again in her mug. "Still not convinced, though," she added, coming up for air.

"We do need to get down and fix those worlds," he reminded her. "Almega's banned every other Eternal until we do our bit."

"Hmm. I'm curious as to what he found out about the truncated worlds. Thanks to Fortan, we never had that conversation."

The bell was rung on the outside of Daniel's cottage. With a frown, he got up to answer it. It was Almega.

"Speak of the devil," he grinned. "Come in!"

"I'm the devil now?" Almega said, accepting the invitation and following Daniel into the front room.

"Only figuratively speaking. We were just talking about you." He motioned to a seat and Almega settled down. A mug appeared on the table in front of him, and he nodded his thanks. "To what do we owe the pleasure?" Daniel continued, retaking his own chair.

"Not for everyone else, of course," Almega began, "but I thought you might be interested to hear what my investigations into the other worlds threw up."

Now Alex, who had been a little lacklustre, sat up straight. "I was just wondering about that. Were you listening in?"

"Coincidence, I assure you," he replied. "Unlike some Eternals, I don't violate anyone's personal space unless asked." She smiled her thanks and urged him to continue. "It wasn't Fortan that stopped access to the previous eras within those worlds," he began, taking a sip of his mug. "It was Omskep."

"Omskep? But why?" Daniel asked, learning forward.

"I'm not quite certain. It seems there are events there that we can't interfere with and characters we cannot inhabit." He turned to look at Alex. "The lives of Darthyn and Eyowenwi being one of them."

"Nuts! I really wanted to do that!"

"I know. That's why I tried digging around, but Omskep was having none of it. I did manage to persuade him to allow a visit to the Siphians on their original home planet of Eidar, but, again, Omskep allowed it grudgingly and only so far back. The block becomes thicker the closer I get to the time of a Siphian leader called Ticcit. I'm not convinced he's the cause since the block becomes impenetrable about a hundred years after his time, but I can't even look at the events that happened during his leadership. I only know he existed because he was written up in the records. Same with Darthyn and Eyowenwi. The block locks into place and, before that, I'm not even allowed to look." He shook his head. "If you hadn't seen the film on Mithgryr, or if humans and dragons weren't such voracious archivists of events, we wouldn't know it had ever happened."

"I wanted to see how accurate the film was!" Alex moaned. "Mind you, assuming the humans were well informed, and based on the claim that they didn't want to upset the dragons, I suppose it must have been pretty close. Anything less would enrage the descendants."

"Oh, indeed. To the dragons, mis-recording of historical fact is practically heretical, and they'd see the film as a form of historical record. From what I could tell investigating the time you visited, the dragons weren't entirely happy with it. It suffered from the usual problems where some characters were amalgamated, some events omitted or mentioned rather than shown, the ordering of events was changed to improve the narrative, that kind of thing. However, with a little explanation from the humans, even they seemed satisfied, provided it wasn't used as an alternative to reading the real history by the dragons. That tells me it was, on the whole, accurate."

"Quite the adventure those characters had. I'm furious Omskep won't let us live it!" Alex grumbled.

Daniel nodded his agreement. "Why is Omskep being so picky?" he asked Almega.

"Honestly? I have no idea. Usually, it only blocks events or avatars when one of the Eternals has already played a significant part in those events, but since you didn't even know the worlds existed until Fortan's stunt, that's not possible."

"Might it be that, at some point in the future, the barrier will be removed, and we will live those lives? In that case, we couldn't insert ourselves until the right moment because we'd be doubling up," Alex suggested.

"That's my best guess," Almega nodded, "although it would require Omskep to have a knowledge of the future of Oestragar, which is impossible. The future of the universes within which you do your trainings, yes, but here?" He shook his head. "However, if it detected the presence of one or more of us in there, the same protocols would hold. The problem is, it can't tell me when the barrier might be lifted because it doesn't know when you, or whoever..." He noted Alex's face. There was absolutely no way she'd allow any other Eternal that trip. "Yes, all right, when you..." Daniel raised an eyebrow, "...two will visit. I'm afraid you may well be in for a long wait. On the upside, I've found that there is a point before those events that you *can* visit. It's before the humans arrive on Mithgryr, on a continent called Crada, and the dragons on that continent are in another residence." He paused, then snapped his fingers. "Varn, that's it. The home of the dragons on Crada is called a varn. Anyway, before they dug their caves in the extinct volcano, they lived in rather palatial accommodations inside a massive underground cave."

"Why did they move?" Daniel asked.

"Earthquake. Quite a number died as bits of the roof caved in and, after that, I think the dragons preferred to stay somewhere from which they could escape more easily."

"Makes sense. They wouldn't have understood what was happening," Alex nodded. "Not that I want to be caught in an earthquake, but seeing what the dragon society was like before humans got involved, and then revisiting after human intervention might be a lot of fun."

"I thought you might say that, so I reserved a couple of spots for you two either side of the block for when you're ready."

"Almega, you're an angel!" Alex smiled.

"You might change that back to devil in a moment," he snorted. "The other universes do need to be fixed, and sooner rather than later, so that I can release them to the other Eternals."

"Fortan kicking off?" Daniel asked.

"Funnily enough, no. Right now, he's keeping a very low profile and seems keen to prove that he is genuinely sorry, although," he added when he heard Daniel's snort of disbelief, "I'll believe it when I see it and it lasts more than a few missed trips. It's Hentric and Paxto who are most keen to go exploring. Accron's also started to show a lot of interest. I've told them they'll have to wait, but they are rather eager."

"The problem with those trips is that two of them are going to be horrible!" Alex sighed. "I'm in no hurry to be turned into a brain inside a robotic vat!"

"Not sure what to make of the holographic humans, either," Daniel agreed. "Who wants to live as a hard hologram for hundreds of years? And what could such a thing do to fix the problem anyway?"

"Ahh, I may have an idea regarding that one," Almega said.

"Oh?" Daniel said, urging Almega to explain.

"The characters you saw are not your way in. Rather, the world they connected with will be your target."

"Bit late in the day, isn't it?" Alex said. "Shouldn't we be stopping them from turning into hard holograms in the first place?"

"I'm afraid that problem starts hundreds of years before, and no one realises the consequences until it's too late."

"What causes it?" Daniel asked.

"In large part, lack of proper regulation due to corporate funding and, consequently, effective takeovers of supposedly independent regulatory bodies."

"No one was guarding the guards," Alex nodded.

"Exactly. A cabal of elites thought that they knew best for everyone and wanted to cut through the checks and balances that they saw as barriers to their grand plan. To them, the solutions were obvious, and the fact things put in place for safety were slowing them down was frustrating. Thus, they made sure they had controlling interests in the regulatory bodies and those higher up, allowing them to apply the necessary pressure. Since they weren't actual all-knowing deities, mistakes were made but now, instead of affecting a small number, they affected everyone. Sadly, as you saw, they still hadn't learned. Corporations were still running the system when you visited, despite the disaster they'd created, and any claim to beneficence was thrown out in favour of profits. With the humans now being holograms that could be adjusted on a whim, and the system to do that completely within the control of the elite, there was no need to pretend any more. The things that caused the genetic damage were genuinely beneficial, solving a problem that killed millions every year, but the tests were far from thorough and were rushed through because of the severity of the problem. Then it was employed everywhere. They did realise, many years afterwards, that there was an issue, but by then it was already too late. I could put you back in that time and you could scream the dangers from the rooftops, but no one would listen. Indeed, during my studies I saw that many did give very loud warnings, but they were shut down. With the media also in the pay of the corporations, it was easy to label those giving the warnings as ignorant troublemakers, conspiracy theorists and the like and, since most beings are not specialists in things like bio-chemical genetic manipulation and don't imagine their leaders could be so corrupt or so stupid, they accepted the claims."

"Didn't some scientists kick off?" Alex asked.

"Those in the vanguard who suspected or even knew the truth were in the pay of the corporations, so they weren't about to wreck their pensions or risk their homes by violating non-disclosure agreements. Those outside didn't know the full extent of the dangers and, by the time whistle-blowers alerted them, it was already too late."

"OK, so how can we help from the other world?"

"By being the ones who accept the call, creating what's needed to give the holo-human world a way to see the opportunity and, I'm afraid, working with the two rebels to shut down the holo-humans."

"You mean kill them," Daniel said flatly. "Billions and billions of them."

"They've been dead for a long time, Daniel, they just haven't stopped moving. The program edits that the corporations use to remove the merest hint of insurrection mean that they've become puppets, nothing more."

Alex turned to Daniel. "Perhaps we could stop those edits? Allow the holo-humans to recognise the mess they're in. I know that, if it was me, I'd rather die as me than as a shadow of myself."

"Hmm," Daniel growled, but he could see her point. "Sounds like a standard training to me."

"Not quite," Almega explained, "and we can only do this because it's not the main program." He put his mug down and leaned forward on his knees. "You need to know what's happening and what will happen while you're in the training." He raised his hand when Alex went to argue. "You can't go in as you with all your memories intact, obviously. While you're babies it would drive you crazy and, after that, your actions would draw too much attention. You'd end up arrested or the subjects of experiments."

Alex shuddered. It was a truth that those who could truly see what was coming and warned others about it were treated the same as those who only fancied that they could. Without knowledge of what was to come, it was impossible to tell the difference, as the evidence of truly dangerous conspiracy theorists sometimes looked the same as that of serious researchers fitting apparently disparate parts together.

"Exactly. Unpleasant and useless for our purposes. Rather than that," he continued, "I suggest you do a little research into the things they'll need to do to make this a reality —"

"Hang on!" Daniel said. "We saw that they did it. Why do we have to change anything?"

"Not changing, more 'nudging to a better version'," Almega replied. When Daniel gave him a look that said, 'seriously? Since when did we do that?' Almega sighed. "I took a look at how that world continues. With the human replacements it works, but it's hard. There are inventions and discoveries on the holo-human world that they need, but they don't understand, and they don't have the knowledge to understand. In some cases, they don't have the knowledge of the knowledge!"

"Hang on. Oleana said the other world was more advanced than the holo-human one," Alex blurted.

"In many ways, yes, but the holo-human world had inventions that worked better in their particular version of Earth which the normal humans couldn't fully comprehend. They got quite a bit — scientists were included amongst the initial settlers — but some was completely beyond them." He cast around, trying to find a way to explain. "Some events happened in the past of the holo-human world that had significant effects on the future. The equivalent of Galileo being lauded and encouraged instead of locked away, or Archimedes not being murdered by the Roman soldier and living many years as a free man, allowed to invent whatever he wanted."

"Those would have been big changes," Alex nodded.

"Exactly. Because of those and dozens of others, they leapt well ahead of their parallel, technologically, but in very specific areas."

"Obviously morality wasn't one of them," Daniel said.

Almega waggled his hand. "In many ways they were pretty good. The genetic mistake that killed them was done out of a wish to do good, and given away freely, for a change." He stared into the middle distance. "Ironically, that rare example of philanthropy would destroy them." He shook his head. "Anyway, the upshot is that, for centuries, the new inhabitants struggle to figure out how to use and then repair equipment, and they lose a lot before they ever figure out its value. Where it's familiar or they have a need for it, they mostly do all right, but the holo-human world had technologies the real humans didn't even know they needed. Air-filtration, climate adjustments, different energy sources and storage methods, amongst others. The real humans didn't bring their own machines because they knew the holo-human world had stuff and they assumed they'd be able to use it because, as you pointed out, Oleana had been saying how much more advanced they were. She'd assumed they knew things they didn't actually know."

"Uh huh," Alex nodded. "So? I mean, OK, they're back to a more basic way of life, but that's not necessarily a bad thing."

"No, it's not," Almega agreed, "but they could have a genuine Utopia."

"How?" Daniel frowned.

"By not switching off all the holo-humans the instant they get through. Most, yes, but a small number representing all the knowledge they need to make the most of their new world remain to pass on that knowledge."

"Wait, wait," Daniel said, raising his hand. "They're inside wristbands. Just switch them back on."

Almega shook his head. "The only way to switch them off so that the last holdouts can't reactivate them and turn them into a destructive army is a massive EMP burst or, rather, lots of massive EMP bursts across the planet, set to go off at the same moment."

"Which destroys all the electronics," Alex nodded. "You've killed the machines *and* you've killed the people who could fix the machines."

"Exactly."

"And now they're staring at a perfect world that's lost a lot of the things that make it perfect. That's going to be maddening!"

"It is. I mean, they manage, but I went forward further than I did originally. They make a huge effort for a few generations, but when it becomes clear that they can't figure it out..."

"No, hold on," Daniel cried, raising a hand in denial. "They can read! Just learn it. From scratch if they have to, but the books –"

"Were all on electronic devices," Almega explained. "A lot of the libraries had died anyway on that world, but once they became holo-humans, there was no point in hard copy, so the rest were destroyed."

"And private ownership?" Daniel prodded, still looking for a way out.

"A small number, but they weren't using the best materials to make the paper long before they went one hundred percent digital. More basic stuff was cheaper to manufacture, and to reduce environmental damage, and up the demand for replacement sales, they made them biodegradable at a much faster rate. By the time some were found, they simply crumbled to dust when they tried to open them."

"And the new owners don't have the knowledge to build the scanners to collect the data without opening them," Alex breathed. "Or they have the knowledge but can't recreate them because they don't understand the tools and equipment needed to make them."

"Exactly. A thousand years after your visit, it effectively ends up closer to a feudal society. Most are working on the land to feed them, a small number learn enough to try to advance but, after a few generations, the ones with power get more and more and they restrict what the academics can do for fear that they find ways to push the lords out. They turn it into a sort of religious cult that warns that, if they resurrect the machines, they'll go the same way as those who were there before. The usual 'end of the world' stuff used on nearly every planet at one time or another. Now they've millions of wonderful things rotting around them, adding to their sense of failure, so they destroy them because they're never going to know enough to use them."

The three sat in depressed silence for a while.

"If we make some changes, does it improve things?" Daniel asked.

"A great deal. I mean yes, inevitably, they manage to mess things up, and the society goes through the usual trials and tribulations of most advanced civilisations..."

"Except the Siphians, it seems," Alex smiled.

"I think that being telepathic helps there. You're going to know just how much you're hurting people and will probably feel it. That would be enough to put anyone off!" Daniel said.

"Quite. Anyway, the replacement humans have their problems, but they do a lot better than before and they end up with a thriving world that's clean, with plenty of space, lots of technology to give them a solid grounding for the future and, before you know it, they're into space and exploring." Almega anticipated Alex's next question. "Yes, they're very careful not to upset other worlds. They learned their lesson from their old world, the record of which is carefully preserved so that they can learn from history."

"All right, how are we going to do this?" Daniel asked.

"Right. I suggest subliminal messages. Ideas and warnings in dreams, and I can even plant things in their environment that look like happy accidents but trigger what we want – spilt coffee stains that link back to dreams and remind them in their waking hours of what they need to know, that kind of thing." He took a breath. "All of which means you're going to have to learn a lot before you make that trip, and I'm going to have to watch very carefully."

"Good thing we can download it," Daniel said. "Plus, a few million years of practice as so many different characters with different experiences will help. What Alex doesn't know about computing you could probably fit into a thimble the size of an atom."

"Not quite," she smiled, nodding her thanks for the compliment, "but I'm pretty good."

Almega rolled his eyes at the understatement. "I'll probably have to put things on hold from time to time while I'm dealing with the other Eternals…" He looked at Alex and Daniel, "unless you think one of the other Eternals can be trusted?" Both shook their heads.

"Sorry, Almega," Alex said, "but I don't think we can trust any of them to keep watch and, even if they did, watching and knowing how to alert us to potential missteps are two very different things."

"On the upside, when I do freeze you, you won't be aware of it. That will help."

"Good to know," Daniel grunted.

"I'll tweak the program a bit so that your avatars are unusually smart and receptive to the nudges I send. Your studies can be mere dreams when you're children but become a driving force as you get older." Alex and Daniel both nodded their agreement. "Moving on. The Djaroubi fix is already set up thanks to your efforts while you were there. I don't think we need to mess with your characters any further but, unlike normal trainings, you'll be free to do whatever you want. The future isn't laid out because you've changed the premises, so what kind of a world we get will be entirely down to how you handle it. Right now, everything is in flux. With that in mind, I would suggest lots of revision before you go in and I can do the same as with the previous world and allow you to subconsciously remember some of it."

"Not much to remember, is there?" Daniel said. "Get to the Parchti homeworld, build a resistance amongst the other robots –"

"Wait," Alex said, raising her hand. "The bulk of the robot Djaroubi don't know and can't remember who and what they really are thanks to the surgeries the Parchti performed on their brains, remember? One of our characters needs to be brilliant at engineering and computing…" She glanced up at Daniel, who was grinning at her. "Yes, all right. I'll do the computer training, you do the engineering training. That way we can give the others independent memories the Parchti can't erase. That means all we need is a nudge when we're brains in boxes doing trainings before we leave the Djaroubi planet." She shook her head. "I am so not looking forward to that one."

"I think the idea is horrible," Daniel agreed, "but once we've accepted what we are, we'll be in a position to do a great deal of good with minimal damage to ourselves. It's not all bad."

"One good EMP blast and we're toast," she replied flatly.

"Then blocking that will be something your engineer will have to solve, won't it?"

"It does have to be done, sadly," Almega said. "Until you resolve the new ending, it's completely open and no one can visit that universe because the Parchti are travellers and affect many parts of it. How you solve this will determine how large swathes of that universe turn out. Sorry!"

"Ugh!" Alex shivered. Feel free to give it to someone else!"

"Look at the other Eternals," Almega said, raising an eyebrow. "Do you honestly trust any of them to tidy that thread up without making a mess of it?"

"Definitely not Fortan, Gracti or Hentric," Alex admitted.

"I'm not even certain Accron, Zorpan or Bregar could do a good job with that," Daniel said. "I guess, since we started it, we'll have to finish it and make absolutely certain it's done properly. Give the Djaroubi their lives back, maybe even get them some benefits." Alex looked at him. "I've a thought I'm pondering," he replied, mysteriously. "Plus, we need to make sure the Parchti are a positive force in the universe once we've dug out the monster behind all this."

"Which leaves us with the Vynarians," Almega said, quickly stepping in. They could go through the details on their own.

"Exploring a world filled with giant, carnivorous plants," Alex nodded, happily shifting to what she perceived as a pleasanter topic. "Provided we don't get eaten the second we leave the compound, I'm quite looking forward to that one. There'll be a lot of new things to deal with, and all of them huge compared to our avatars."

"I can find you an avatar who gets to explore and survives," Almega assured her. Daniel cleared his throat. "Yes, and you, too. If I can't, I'll see if I can tweak them a bit, but I doubt I'll need to do much. Nothing to change there that requires either of you two be any more involved, though. All you need to do is see it through and make sure that they discover the options across the rest of the planet. Again, I suspect you can prompt them in the right direction. If they don't, the Vynarian's time in the locale

344

will be quite brief. They'll keep the plants at bay for a few hundred years, but after that the plants will win."

"Exploring an entire planet is going to take a while," Daniel pointed out. "The Vynarians are an advanced species. Wouldn't it make more sense for them to simply relocate their spaceship?"

"They're also a very stubborn species, which is a good thing usually, but here it works against them. At first, they won't move on principle; then they can't because there's not enough power left to get the ship off the ground."

"They've got fusion reactors and they were planning on using solar so that they didn't have to drain the ship's resources. What happened?"

"Seeds. They didn't notice – who notices tiny seeds unless you're allergic to them? – and they managed to get inside the ship via a combination of bad luck for the Vynarians and a following breeze. The shields were left down longer than usual while an awkward bit of equipment was being relocated, and the breeze blew the seeds into the ship. While the ship's insides appeared clean, wherever there are living things there's organic dust, and the plants on that planet don't need much to get started. They can also wait in seed form until everything is perfect. Eventually they manage to get to a storage area, being carried in on the shoes of an unsuspecting member of the crew. At that point, they're off. Hiding out of sight, they grow, push their way through air ducts and panels, and begin to infiltrate systems, including those needed to cool power systems. When things suddenly go critical, the Vynarians manage to stop the ship from creating a small sun on the planet and destroying it, but the ship itself is rendered useless."

"The plants managed all that without brains?"

"Luck, pure and simple. Lots of tiny things all striking together and leading to disaster," Almega replied.

"Sounds like Titanic," Alex said. "When something that devastating happens, you want it to be because of an earthquake or a meteor strike or something else spectacular, but often it's just lots and lots of small things building up over time until it takes something relatively insignificant to push everything over the edge."

"For want of a nail," Daniel murmured.

"Um hmm. Anyway, your adventure, I think – although I'll be double-checking, naturally – will be about seventy years before that. If you can make certain that your avatars head north-west when they head out across the ocean, rather than any other direction, they'll find that more liveable continent you saw. After that, it's just a question of persuading the settlers to relocate."

"Shouldn't be too hard," Daniel mused. "They saw the whole planet from space, so they know what's available."

"Yes, but the other directions are equally, if not more enticing, especially to a Vynarian."

"Oh?" Alex said, waving to indicate Almega should carry on.

"I think, rather than spoil the adventure, I'll leave it at that. Let's just say that after you've moved the ship, there'll be some very exciting discoveries."

"Really? It's sounding better and better," she grinned.

"Three trips, three worlds to fix," Almega said, folding his hands in his lap. "Any idea which one you're going to do first?"

"As much as the idea fills me with dread, probably the Djaroubi," Alex said after some thought. "Best to get it out of the way." She winced. She really wasn't looking forward to that one. "We're never going to get out of those robots, though, are we?"

Almega shook his head. "I'm afraid not. Once they relocate the brains, they're stuck in there for the duration."

"Is there any danger our avatars might remember our being the source of the changes that allow the preservation of their memories?" she asked.

"No," he assured her. "You're good in your avatars, you're not omniscient."

346

"Any danger of meeting and recognising the Parchti I used?"

"Even if you did, he doesn't remember it and you wouldn't know him."

Alex nodded but still looked uncomfortable. The entire idea made her sick to her stomach.

Daniel turned to her. "If you want to leave that one for a bit and come back when you feel you can face it, we can do that," he said, glancing at Almega for confirmation. Almega winced. There was another species in that universe that Hentric was keen to take a crack at. Daniel frowned and gave a slight motion to Alex who was clearly quite upset with the idea.

"Yes. It can wait if you're not up to it," he said. Privately he decided that if Hentric was that keen, he could volunteer to fix the Djaroubi-Parchti problems himself or shut up.

"I know it's what we ought to do, and the thought of the Djaroubi suffering that nightmare one minute longer than is necessary is repugnant," Alex began.

"I've put the new worlds in freeze mode until you've done your runs. Nothing more will happen within them until then," Almega assured her.

"Let's take our time, think about it and see if we can plan our approach a bit," Daniel suggested. "If we can plant subliminal clues with the holo-humans' world, I see no reason why we can't help ourselves dealing with this one, too."

"Daniel's right," Almega said. "These worlds aren't fixed, and the paths can be changed. Once you've finished, of course, the worlds will be finalised and the avatars' lives set in stone, so I'd make the most of the freedom. It's not something we usually get."

"If we don't want our avatars to start thinking they're going crazy, I don't think we can plant too many remarkably prescient dreams in our subconscious," Daniel said, thoughtfully. "We need to work out exactly what we're going to do, and when, and keep them to the bare minimum. That'll need more careful research." He turned to Almega. "If we screw this up, can the world be reset so we can try again?"

Alex's head, which had been bowed as she thought about the Djaroubi, shot up. "You want to do them more than once?!"

"I want the *option* of trying again if we make a mistake, which is not the same thing. Heck, if they can be reset, perhaps one of the others would care to give it a go first and see how they fare. That would get us off the hook and be a win either way. If they succeed, it's done, and everyone can start to play. If they don't, they'll now know how hard it is and, perhaps, quit pressuring us. I don't think anyone does their best when someone's forever at their back telling them to hurry up – particularly when the job is delicate."

"That's not a bad idea," Almega grinned. "And yes, if necessary, they can be put back where they were, the same way I did with the Siphians. Would knowing you've got that option make it easier?"

"Perhaps a little," Alex allowed, although the idea of going through the Djaroubi horror story more than once was more off-putting than enticing. "We'll need to plan whichever one we do, so if the other Eternals aren't happy about that, tell them they're more than welcome to take our places and fix them for themselves."

"I hope they offer," Almega chuckled, rising. "I can't see any of them being as efficient as you two, but it should be entertaining watching them try. Not to mention they might find some problems we never even considered while they're doing it. That might make your own path much easier."

"If you reset it, we can still use the same avatars, right?" Daniel asked.

"Reset means everything's available to everyone," Almega assured him. "I'm going back to Omskep. Gracti has another perfect life she wants to live in the primary world, which is easy to initiate. You take as long as you need." He started the leave, then paused. "Oh, I forgot. I gather you wanted this." He produced a photograph, around A3 size, of Alex atop Darthak – the sneaky trick she did when they visited the world of the dragons.

Alex seized it. "Oh, thank you!" She turned to Daniel. "First trip once we've fixed the others, right?"

"I've already found you some avatars," Almega assured her, relieving Daniel of the embarrassment he would suffer when he had to admit he'd forgotten. Daniel gave the Guardian a grateful nod.

Alex admired the photograph for a moment, laying it carefully beside her on the settee. There was a happy smile on her face.

"Knowing I've got this to look forward to once everything else is done makes me feel better about the trips ahead," she admitted. "I'm still not looking forward to them, mind, but they'll be worth it. Can you also book us in with the Siphians? A couple of scientist-adventurers who have long lives and make lots of new discoveries?"

"Done and done," Almega assured her. "I'll see you when you're ready."

With a wave, he walked out, leaving Alex and Daniel discussing pros and cons and which world to fix first.

The End

Entrapment in Oestragar
Book I of Oslac's Odyssey

When Dr Alex Oslac is tasked with archiving the Herabridge school history to celebrate its 500th anniversary, she encounters a past master of the school who died in World War 1. From that moment she is haunted by dreams of past lives in his company throughout history. Worse, when she looks up the details of those dreams, she finds them all to be true. Is she going mad, or is there something else going on? Something so huge she couldn't possibly get her head around it... Until after she dies.

The Anquerian Alternative
Book II of Oslac's Odyssey

Alex Oslac and Daniel Lancaster have even bigger problems than they imagined, and the canvas is much larger. In Anqueria, where fictional worlds are made real, anything is possible. Dragons, robots, ghosts... Still, at least they're home now.

Aren't they?

Ystrian Dreams
Book III of Oslac's Odyssey

Without Almega to help them, in an entirely new world and with powers greater than ever before, Alex (Oslac) and Daniel (Eridar) face the future. They have a few remaining problems to solve, a universe to create containing a uniquely gifted species, and one final mystery to address, but as Oslac's powers leave her, she fears mortality is not just for those at the lowest level.

The Dragons of Mithgryr
Book IV of Oslac's Odyssey

The adventures of Daniel and Alex continue, but this time we are with them in one of their trainings. Gorthan is still in charge of Crada (*The Anquerian Alternative*) and Darthyn is one of his most respected dragons. Together with the humans who now live on Mithgryr, it's time to explore the rest of their world.

All is not well on Crada, however. Some dragons don't care for the humans and want them gone, by any means possible. All they need to succeed is for Darthyn not to return from his trip.

Siphian Syzygy
Book V of Oslac's Odyssey

The Siphians are a telepathic rodent species who solve problems for the universe (first introduced in *The Anquerian Alternative*), but when the problem is on their own doorstep, things get a lot more complicated. When one of their own is captured by an insect queen who sees them as dinner, the Collective pulls out all the stops to remove the invader.

Meanwhile, lurking in the forest, the giant Sikets weave their webs and watch with interest. Whoever wins, someone's on the menu.

Rise of the Deyarim
Book VI of Oslac's Odyssey

On Saros, the last Ygaran outpost before the massive energy field known as The Deyar blocks the way, Zhirini is caught in the shelters under her bombed city. A senior grade medic who was accidentally left behind when the Anarxgy forces broke through the defence perimeter, she thinks she's going to have to struggle on alone until she is caught and killed. That is until enterprising Defence Coordinator and rogue genius Beyok stumbles across her. He's not willing to give in so easily. He's got an idea. They're going to steal an Anarxgy ship and escape to Ygaran space. Problem is, the Anarxgy are on their tail and The Deyar is in their way.

Powershift
Book VII of Oslac's Odyssey

On the mining planet of Omneminer, where corporate power is everything and pollution has driven all but the poorest humans and aliens to live inside or underground, Karia Kanarvan has just been promoted to Detective Inspector. Called out to a routine industrial accident, a chance encounter reveals that more is going on than meets the eye, leading to a web of intrigue that goes right to the top.

Karia has a secret that she must maintain at all costs, which makes the attentions of investigative journalist David Hatcher somewhat concerning. Even more so when she discovers that he is the son of Philip Gurdan, head of one of the five corporations that runs Omneminer.

Our heroes are off on a new adventure in a world where being honest can get you killed.

Thank you…

… for buying and reading *Eternity Beckons*.

If you liked it, please take a minute or two to give it a short review where you bought it.

Reviews really make a difference to a writer like me. They help to promote my books and that helps me put out even more.

If you want to find out more, go to:

https://oslacs-odyssey.co.uk/ or look me up on Facebook under Oslac's Odyssey (linked from the above).

Printed in Great Britain
by Amazon

23297911R00205